Lamp to My Feet

Frances Smith

Book 3 of the Ordinary Man trilogy
Based on a true story

Gazelle
PRESS
Mobile, Alabama

AUTHOR'S NOTE:

This book could not have been written without the testimony upon which it is based. Mark Smith, my wonderful husband, provided the stories told here and also important insights on theological and biblical matters. This, like *Cleft of the Rock* and *Thorn in the Flesh*, is his story.

To learn more, request a speaking engagement or book signing, or download printable discussion questions for study groups, please visit francessmith.com

ISBN 978-1-58169-713-1
For worldwide distribution.
Printed in the United States of America.

Gazelle Press
P.O. Box 191540
Mobile, AL 36619
800-367-8203

DEDICATION

To Mark, without whose true-life testimony there would have been no books, and I wouldn't have had the courage to write anyway. Rest in peace, my love. I can't wait until that reunion in heaven. I'm doing my best to do you honor until then.

To our five wonderful, amazing children. You are each gifted in your own way, and I couldn't be more proud and honored to be your mother. You, and the work God has given me, are now my reason for living.

ACKNOWLEDGMENTS

Eight years ago, I was a corporate writer. My whole life, I'd been a writer but had never written for God. One day, I knew, God would want me to write something for Him, and He'd make it clear when that day came. Not long after I met Mark Smith, I knew the day had come.

One huge message comes through his testimony and mine—God uses ordinary people to accomplish extraordinary things, if we just get out of His way and let Him work.

With *Lamp to My Feet*, the Ordinary Man trilogy is complete, and it couldn't have been written without a great deal of help and support.

Thanks to Leo Sain, Wayne McKinney, Veronica O'Hearn and Shannon Potter, my work family at the East Tennessee Technology Park for two years.

Thanks to my Sevier Heights Baptist Church family in Knoxville, Tennessee. Dr. Hollie Miller (Brother Hollie)—Mark and I love you and appreciate you so much. You're an amazing man, a teaching and caring pastor who taught both of us so much. Special thanks also to Don Wilson, who saw us both through some very tough times.

To Tom Baker, whose friendship I cherish so much. We supported each other through the writing and production of *Cleft of the Rock* and *One Dog's Faith*, and I don't see that ending anytime soon. Thanks Tom.

To my Bible study group at Sevier Heights, led by Ann Jarrard: This was my first experience with a small women's group. The love and support and prayers from you ladies were heart-warming and real, and I love you all.

To our church family at Pleasant Grove Baptist Church—what can I say? I've never had a church family like Pleasant Grove, a place where I knew I was loved, where I could feel the love of Christ as soon as I walked in the door. Greg Long, you are the ultimate shepherd pastor. Happy Helpers class—thank you for welcoming us and loving us. Wisdom Seekers class—thank you for loving us and ministering to us in the good times and the bad. Robert Galyon, Greg Wilson, and Jimmy Long—you're like Mark's brothers.

To my Devotion in Motion prayer group at Pleasant Grove—I love you ladies like sisters. Martha Galyon, DiAnne Wilson, Angie Kirby, Linda Burnette, and Mary Gene Roberts—one of the most special experiences of my life was meeting with you and loving you and praying with you. Thank you.

A special thanks and shout out to Angie Kirby. You are a warrior woman of God who walked with me through an enormous battle. Hand in hand, eyes on God, we kept our hands off the wheel and watched Him work. And didn't He do some amazing things? I love you, girl.

A big, humble thanks to my work family and clients at Extended Family Services. Tabby Hannah and Wendy Carson—you have the biggest, best hearts I've ever seen. Working there brought me to wonderful people who touched my heart and will always be part of me. Thanks also to Moe Click, who hired me in the beginning.

To my work family at Cracker Barrel Old Country Store 494 in Alcoa, especially Sue Davidson: You guys were my family. You sustained me and got me through when everyone else had gone home and back to their lives. Kris Beltz, Wendy Coppedge, Mindy McLemore, Sandie Powers, Anne Rosevear—I love you all. And to my new home, store 124 in Anderson, thanks to you guys for taking me in and loving me.

To Sharon Smith, Lisa Lambert, George and Mellie Davis, Gavin and Jessica Mayo, and Franklin and Sarah Graves—thank you for treating me like family, even now.

To my wonderful mother, sister, sons, daughter, nieces, and nephews—I love you all immeasurably. To my dad in heaven—I love you, Daddy. To my dad on earth, Cecil—I love you just as much.

Thanks to my test readers—Chris Brayton, Scott Spitler, Myrtle Walker, and Peggy Gambrell. It's hard to write in a vacuum, which is what I did with *Lamp to My Feet*. Thanks to you guys for keeping it real and keeping me on track.

To Scott Spitler and Doug Taylor—you are brothers to Mark and to me, and you know why. It's more than I could ever write. Thank you.

PREFACE

The Lord promises in Psalms that His Word will be a "lamp to our feet and a light to our path," but what does that really mean?

People who have read the first two installments in the Ordinary Man trilogy have consistently been amazed at how much Mark accomplished in a short amount of time. First in Alaska, then in East Tennessee, his every endeavor seemed blessed. And it was.

Lamp to My Feet picks up about four years after *Thorn in the Flesh* leaves off. Mark's feeble humanity crashes down on him when he makes some serious mistakes, the results of decisions that were most definitely not the Lord's will. And so he has to find his way back.

At the same time, we are introduced to a new, parallel story line when Fran Chapman begins a journey of her own, one that will ultimately lead her life to connect with Mark's. Her life has been full of love from her mother but also marked indelibly by the pain of having a terminally ill father. His life and personality have been stolen by Parkinson's, a disease that was only beginning to be studied when he was first diagnosed in 1969.

The path isn't an easy one, but Mark and Fran both learn vividly about the Psalmist's promise. God never says He will illuminate the entire future. He never promises to show us even a few steps ahead. But He does promise that He will show us the next step, if we but ask and trust Him.

Lamp to My Feet is based upon stories that are told as Mark and my mother told them to me, and as I remember them from my own life. Wherever possible I've tried to recreate hard facts, but where that's not possible, I've bridged the gap with imagination. Since memory can be faulty, please consider this a work of fiction.

The spirit, purpose, and message of our story stand firm. God can use any person, in any situation, for His glory.

I hope you enjoy, and are blessed by, *Lamp to My Feet.*

PROLOGUE

Mark Smith drove up the Florida coast in his Jeep, trailing his little boat behind him. His hair blew in the wind. Even though it was January, it was warm in South Florida. Everything he owned was with him, covered by tarps, strapped down securely with his best Boy Scout knots. It wasn't much, but it was all he had after just a short time in his first official ministry job.

He stared through his dark sunglasses at the interstate, stretching out flatly in front of him, mile after mile. The sun shone brightly down, as if unaware that his life was in shambles. Again. And he couldn't help but think—how did these things keep happening to him?

Nearly four years ago, he'd left the University of Tennessee with bright hope and promise. He was headed to the Southern Theological Seminary in Louisville, Kentucky, with three amazing years behind him. God had used him in wondrous ways in Alaska, then in Knoxville and the Great Smoky Mountains. God had been patient with Mark when he'd made wrong choices, and Mark paid dearly for those choices. His back ached fiercely even then, as the Jeep jounced over the interstate. But Paul tells us in Romans that all things work together for good for those who love Him, who are called according to His purpose. Never did Mark doubt that he was ultimately on the right path. God's path.

Looking back, Mark could clearly see where he'd taken a wrong turn. It was in October 1982, when he'd gone home to Knoxville, Tennessee, to visit family and attend the closing ceremonies of the World's Fair. He'd run into Nancy Mahoney, who had been working with the Fair. They'd been unofficially engaged before Mark left and had considered marrying then but had decided that the timing wasn't right. Mark had departed for seminary with all the doors wide open, not knowing when or if God wanted them to marry.

Watching her graceful ability, caring, and poise as she went about her work at the World's Fair, he couldn't remember why they'd backed off each other. She felt the same, and so they decided not to put it off any longer. They set a date and married in December 1982, and she moved into Mark's student housing at seminary. Remembering now, he realized that neither of them had really asked the Lord what He thought about the situation. They'd just done what seemed to make sense at the time. They figured they'd be good partners in the Lord's work, and He could use them as a team.

After Mark's first year in seminary, he found two jobs. One was as a manager of a storage facility, which came with a tiny, free, one-room apartment. The other job was as youth minister of Charlestown Baptist Church, which was just across the river in Indiana. It was there that he met some wonderful people, including Matt Monroe and his wife, Patty. They and some others were among very few people that he counted as friends now.

Mark kept those two jobs and maintained a full course load at seminary until he graduated. His schedule was frenetic, but he managed to graduate with honors and several ministry opportunities.

When an offer came from a church in Boca Raton, Florida, he grabbed it. Nancy was from Florida, and who wouldn't want to live in South Florida? Mark wanted to make his wife happy, and this seemed perfect. Again, he didn't remember spending much time asking the Lord His opinion about the matter. It just seemed obvious.

Nancy's discontentment, which should have been obvious from the beginning, escalated almost as soon as Mark started his job. Just weeks after he started work, Nancy left and went home to her mother.

The church where he worked, a staunch Southern Baptist church, was alarmed when they heard that their new youth minister was having marital difficulties. Scriptures clearly state that men in leadership positions must have their own houses in order, and Mark believed wholeheartedly in this interpretation. So, it came as no surprise when the church warned him that unless he reconciled with his wife, his job was in jeopardy.

Mark had no idea why Nancy left until her brother, Chuck, took time off from the big church where he served as youth minister to come see him. He sat in the living room, looked Mark regretfully in the eyes and told him that Nancy had been through some things when she was younger that no one had ever told Mark about. Chuck apologized that no one had told Mark until now and offered to help arrange counseling so their marriage could be saved. And he said that Nancy was willing to try to work things out.

Mark's temper came rushing out like a torrent. He couldn't believe that everything he'd worked for all these years was now in jeopardy, and it all had been avoidable if someone had just been honest with him. In the heat of his temper, he was not willing to consider counseling and had no interest in saving his marriage. And so the church rightfully asked him to leave, which effectively ended his anticipated career in the ministry, and with it, everything he'd worked and studied for. The divorce was quick and painfully final, and it was time to turn the page to whatever was next.

Even now, driving up the Interstate, Mark wasn't sure how it had come to this. He'd thought he was being so careful to follow the Lord's will for his life, but obviously he'd taken a wrong turn. Two, in fact. The first when he'd married Nancy without asking God about it, and the second when he was unwilling to try again. He knew from Scriptures that when couples are both Christians, divorce is not an option. They're supposed to seek godly counsel, pray for their marriage and each other, and do whatever it takes to work things out. He hadn't done his part, and now he would pay for those two mistakes for the rest of his life.

He was already suffering because he'd lost the close walk with God that he'd enjoyed since he'd been called to Alaska. The feeling was horrible, a kind of blind darkness. He couldn't hear God's voice or feel His guiding hand. He had two college degrees but no career path. Worse, he was off God's path and had no idea how to get back on it.

Logically, Mark knew he had to do something. The house where he and Nancy had lived was a friendly lease from a church member, and with no work he couldn't make the monthly payments. Out of money, out of a job, he had only his car and the canoe he'd gotten as a high school graduation present. His circumstances were forcing him into action, even though he didn't know where he would go or what he would do.

The first, most important thing was to find God again. And to do that, he went where he'd always gone. To his Creator in His creation. Back to nature.

PART 1:

SEARCHING

Your Word is a lamp to my feet

and a light to my path.

I have sworn and I will confirm it,

that I will keep Your righteous ordinances.

PSALM 119:105-106

1

With an enraged, twelve-foot gator pulling his small canoe through a canal near Alligator Alley, Mark Smith had little time to mull over the bad decision he'd just made.

Toward the end of his senior year in high school, Mark's dad, Richard, had brought him to a fishing camp at Lake Okeechobee, which is a huge, freshwater lake near the southern tip of Florida. His typing teacher didn't think much of his decision to leave school for a week to go fishing, but he and his dad made memories that Mark still treasured.

The lake was not far from his temporary home in Boca Raton, so it was a logical choice. Off he went, his canoe strapped to the top of his Jeep. Although the lake is the seventh largest freshwater lake in the United States, covering 730 square miles, it is surprisingly shallow. Its average depth is only about nine feet. Serious bass fishermen can always be found at Okeechobee, but they have to be exceptionally careful because of the shallow depths. In most places around the edges of the lake, the depth is only about two feet, and bass boats sit deeper in the water than that. Only when they're at full acceleration, with just the keel and propeller touching the water, can they safely traverse the lake. They zip across it, going from one prime bass fishing spot to another and sending out substantial wakes behind them.

Since southern Florida is home to big gators, and Mark was in a small canoe, he knew to avoid the areas frequented by bass boats. The last thing he wanted was to capsize here, which meant that he stayed mainly in the tributaries around the lake, not in the main lake itself.

He fished in the daytime and camped at night. He caught his meals and cooked over campfires, often spending time with the Lord in serious spiritual introspection. He read his Bible over his campfire at night and over his breakfast in the morning. He talked to God as he floated around Lake Okeechobee. After a few days, his spirit slowly began to heal, and he was able to take stock of where he was and what he needed to do now.

Undeniably, any chance Mark had to hold a staff ministry position was over. But there were ways to serve the Lord and share his faith, other than working at a church. Hadn't he learned that the past three years? Some of the most serious Christians he knew were ordinary people, people who didn't have any theological training but did have a personal relationship with the Lord that went far beyond education or advanced degrees. And their witness was greater than many ministers.

The only question was where he would go, and deep in his heart, he knew the answer. He didn't want to go back to the Knoxville area, because the community was relatively small, and too many people knew him from way back. Louisville, Kentucky, felt right. He'd just spent three years there and had no doubt that he could find work quickly, even with a bad back. He also had a church home, with friends who loved him and would welcome him back. He could rebuild his life there.

That night, he made the decision to go home; and the next day, he would begin packing up his belongings. By the end of the week, he would be on his way to Kentucky.

For his last day in South Florida, Mark opted to take his canoe to the Everglades. Who needed an airboat? He could glide around in his canoe and see just as much. And, he'd heard that a species called peacock bass were a lot of fun to catch.

Fishing in the canal running between the Everglades and the road called Alligator Alley required some adjustment. Used to looking for an underwater structure that fish love to hang around, Mark just tossed his line into the weeds along the water's edge. Sometimes it worked; sometimes it didn't.

He finally got the hang of it, and he let his thoughts drift as he hooked and tossed back bass after bass. There was no reason to keep them, because there would be no campfire tonight. Peacock bass were as entertaining as he'd heard, fighting like smallmouths on steroids. They were a lot bigger and glistened in the sunlight with their peacock colors.

Mark cast out his line, and then he saw a big, lazy gator, gliding through the water between Mark and his lure. Only his snout was visible, but it was unmistakable. It was a gator and a big one.

Mark's heartbeat quickened, and he had a brief *What if?* thought before he began to reel in his lure at a speed calculated to coincide with the gator's glide path. He guessed right because his sturdy hook sank deep into the gator's side.

The *what if* quickly became *uh-oh* as the gator took off, dragging Mark and his canoe down the canal. Mark tried desperately to give him some slack so he could get the hook loose, but the gator was moving too fast. He couldn't cut the line because he couldn't get to his knife. He wasn't about to throw his best rod in the water, and he wasn't going to give it up.

The line whirred off the reel rapidly, and then Mark could only hang on as the gator took him off the canal and into the Everglades themselves—in places he'd had no intention of going because it was just, well, stupid. The gator dived deep and resurfaced, twirling and writhing. And through it all the sturdy line—which had been carefully chosen for its strength—held up. Surprisingly, the knots did too.

Suddenly the canoe glided to a stop. Mark had a quick feeling of relief, followed by a moment of sheer terror as the gator reversed course and came straight at him. With the line now slack, he was finally able to cut it and let the beast loose. The gator passed beside him, close enough that his tail gently sideswiped the boat. He was nearly as long as the canoe, which was twelve feet. Then he was gone, with Mark's hook in his side and about a hundred feet of line trailing behind him.

Mark stared after him, stunned, with his heart racing, humbled that God had spared him yet again from a foolhardy decision. What had he been thinking, to try to hook a big gator deliberately? And why would God spare him?

The answer was so obvious that he barely had to ask Him. God wasn't finished with him yet. At some point, he would discover what His plan was for him. For now, his job was to get on with his life, his hand firmly in God's. He would get back on life's path and find whatever he was supposed to do next. He would listen for His voice every moment. And somehow, everything would be just fine.

2

If not now, when? Mark wasn't interested in women right then, and probably not in the foreseeable future, but there was one girl who was still stuck in his head and heart. Now might be his only chance to find her. He was on his way back to Kentucky, where he felt comfortable and welcome. Although he had no job and no place to live, he wasn't worried. He'd never had trouble finding work and could camp out if needed until he found housing.

The boat trailing behind Mark was a recent purchase. He had discovered that he could buy a small boat for about the same price as he could rent a U-Haul. It served the purpose quite nicely, and now he was the proud owner of an aluminum boat with a motor.

Somewhere around Melbourne, Florida, where he should have been cutting west to head to Kentucky, he abruptly changed course. Instead of heading inland, he stayed on Interstate 95 until he was just south of Walterboro, South Carolina, then headed east on Highway 17. The road wound around Charleston, then snuggled up to the South Carolina coast.

He passed through Georgetown, then Murrells Inlet, then Surfside Beach, and finally he arrived at Myrtle Beach.

He cut over to Ocean Boulevard, then pulled into a public parking lot that would accommodate both his Jeep and boat. He sat for a few minutes and watched the ocean, so timeless and eternal. The mountains in East Tennessee had always seemed like an unspoken testimony to the grandeur of God, but he'd never spent much time at the ocean. It ebbed and flowed its ancient message, and Mark was reminded of the Scripture passage that says nature is a constant reminder that God is real.

As he sat there, Mark closed his eyes and gave his situation to the Lord. "God," he prayed, "I'm not sure why I'm here, except that I have to take this chance to find her. If it's Your will, Lord, lead my steps and my heart. Amen."

He got out of his Jeep, locked up, and slowly made his way to the beach and headed north. He'd parked a good distance south of his destination, but that was okay since he was in no hurry. The breeze whipped sand around his feet, and he shivered. South Florida had been warm, but on the northern coast of South Carolina, the temperature was at least twenty degrees cooler. He zipped his jacket, pulled up the hood, and tucked his hands into his pockets.

The place didn't look all that different, except that it was January, and there were only a few stragglers on the beach. Northerners, no doubt. They probably thought this was warm.

Myrtle Beach had been a life-changing place for Mark. Six years ago, in 1980, he rode a mechanical bull there and sustained the injury that would be a life-long thorn in his flesh. In 1982, his life had changed again in one dizzying instant while walking this beach with his best friend, Doug Taylor.

The boys had come down for a few days before beginning their senior year in college—Doug at Georgia Tech, Mark at the University of Tennessee. They meandered up the beach, enjoying the last few hours before they had to head back when Mark looked across the sand, and everything changed. A slim girl slept on her stomach in the sun, blonde curls clipped atop her head and a worsening second-degree sunburn on the backs of her legs. Her friend sat beside her, absorbed in a book.

Now, as Mark trudged up that same beach, he gazed across the sand to the exact spot where that girl had sat. And he could see everything as it had happened that day, in crystal-clear 3D.

He and Doug silently approached the girl and her friend, so as not to startle them. When the girl woke, she opened her eyes; in that split second before the pain of the intense sunburn hit, her eyes locked on Mark's, and his whole world tilted. Her vivid blue eyes, framed by long, blonde lashes, lasered straight into his heart and soul. In just that instant, before the pain hit, he saw all the things he was feeling reflected in her eyes.

Being a couple of Eagle Scouts, the boys happened to have bottles of green aloe goo in their backpacks, and they spent several minutes with the two girls while Mark spread soothing gel on the blonde girl's legs. They found out that the girls were best friends and were headed home the next day. It was a five-hour ride, and they both dreaded the ordeal with a bad sunburn. The boys told the girls funny stories and soon had them howling with laughter.

When they were finished, there seemed nothing more to say. Mark and the girl locked eyes once again, and again he felt that click and soul-to-soul recognition. But his tongue tangled itself in knots—not usually an issue for him—and he simply handed her the bottle of aloe and said, "You keep this. It'll help. Have a safe trip tomorrow."

And then they turned around and walked away. He didn't get her name, her phone number, or her college. By the time he shook the cobwebs loose from his brain and they dashed back, the girls were gone.

Thinking back on it now, Mark had to admit that in all the time he'd spent with Nancy, all the times they'd been together, she had never made him feel the way this unknown girl did in one chance meeting.

As Mark sat in the very spot where the girl of his dreams had come and gone, he went to his Father for help. "Father," he prayed, "I know I've made a big mess of everything. You told me in the beginning that I should hold off on marrying Nancy. I did hold off, but not long enough, and I didn't ask Your counsel when I met up with her again. Then when I got married, Lord, that should have been it. I should have done whatever was necessary to make it work. Your Word says so. I'm sorry, so sorry that I let You down and now I can't serve You the way I've always wanted to."

Tears rolled down his cheeks and quickly dried in the ocean breeze. He opened his eyes and looked up into the darkening sky. "Please show me where to go from here. I still want to serve You, however You want. I wanted to be a minister, but I know there are other ways to serve. Show me where You want me. And if it's Your will, help me find that girl. In Jesus' name I pray, amen."

Mark closed his eyes but kept his face upturned to the sky. The breeze caressed his face like loving fingers. Then he heard a still voice in his heart, soothing the jagged edges. *Do not be anxious, My son. Remember, I have loved you with an everlasting love. Now lean on Me, not on your own understanding. In all your ways acknowledge Me, and I will make your paths straight.*

Tears flowing freely now, Mark stayed there for a long time, even after the sun was completely gone, basking in the unbelievable knowledge that his life still had value to his Creator. His plans had fallen apart, but maybe they'd never been God's plans at all. As he'd done numerous times before, he handed all his problems over to Him, knowing He was in charge.

*   *   *

Mark had prayed for the Lord to lead him to the girl of his dreams, so he decided he would start out and see where He led. He was in no real hurry to get to Louisville. No one on earth knew where he was, and he knew how to live cheap. He did want to start rebuilding his life as soon as possible, but he was on no one's deadline but his own.

The next morning he sat in his tent at a public campground, chomped on a granola bar, and surveyed the makeshift tracking system in front of him. He'd started with a big map of North Carolina, South Carolina, and Georgia, and he'd stuck a pin at Myrtle Beach and tied a string to the pin. The girl's friend, Joy, had said they had a five-hour trip in front of them. Figuring that they probably weren't speed demons, that meant about sixty miles per hour, which is about three hundred miles. Mark's string represented three hundred miles. Their school had to be in that radius.

It was good that he was on the coast because that cut out anything to the east. Even with that, though, the string covered the whole state of South Carolina and a big chunk of North Carolina and Georgia as well. Until looking at this map, he'd had no idea how many schools there were, large and small, in the South.

Mark knew that Joy and her friend weren't still in school, but it might give him a starting point. The girls were about to be juniors at the time, and he had a pretty good description of them. If he could just narrow down the schools, this might be a doable task.

Figuring on their stopping for bathroom breaks, food, gas, and possible shopping, Mark decided the actual radius was probably between one hundred fifty and two hundred miles. Nothing closer than that. The circle became a thin half-doughnut.

He went with his gut and chopped off North Carolina, then Georgia. Those girls had dyed-in-the-wool, small-town South Carolina accents, and they sounded more like people who lived inland than those on the coast. He made more cuts by eliminating any school with an enrollment of more than five thousand. He couldn't see them at Clemson or the University of South Carolina. It was probably a religious-affiliated school. More cuts.

That left about twenty schools that seemed to be real possibilities. Poring painstakingly over the map, he made a list of schools and stared at it. Limestone College, Spartanburg Methodist, and Converse College, all in Spartanburg. Furman and North Greenville, both in Greenville. The College of Charleston. Erskine. Columbia College. Coker College. Lander, Presbyterian College, Claflin, and Newberry. He added a few more and felt like he was on the right track. The schools on this list were in small or medium-sized towns all over South Carolina, from the upstate to the midlands. He looked at it some more and decided that these girls weren't the type to be at a coastal, party school. He marked out the College of Charleston. Then he narrowed his eyes and smiled when he realized that this list contained two all-female schools. For no reason he could define, that felt right.

He circled the schools that had made his final cut and underlined Columbia College and Converse. This wasn't something he could do by driving around in his little Jeep. It would require legwork, yes, but he would be driving a lot of miles when he could find out just as much on the phone.

He stared at the map, and after he thought about it some more, a plan began to gel. He needed to get to Louisville and start putting his life together. Find a job and a place to live. Then he could do some detective work and come back to South Carolina when he had a better idea of where to look.

If this were the Lord's will, He would lead.

3

Fran Chapman belted herself into the hang glider harness and squinted into the sunlight. She'd always wanted to hang-glide. A bucket list thing. There she was, on top of the massive sand dunes at Jockey's Ridge State Park in Kill Devil Hills, North Carolina, about to launch herself out into the open air. These weren't just any sand dunes, she reminded herself. Sand dunes sounded sissy. These were one hundred feet tall, the highest on the East Coast.

She mentally wrote the lead to her story, incorporating those words—highest sand dunes on the East Coast. The newspaper she worked for in Aiken, South Carolina, offered its reporters the opportunity to take short trips and write about them. The paper footed the bill and in return got some excellent, first-hand accounts of adventures within driving distance of Aiken.

Next, she was going to get to go to Louisville for the Kentucky Derby and do feature stories for the newspaper's annual horse edition. Aiken was very much a horse town, with big-time training facilities and horse enthusiasts. The paper was sending most of its staff to the Derby this year to follow the horses who'd been trained in Aiken. But that was a month away, and this was now. She took a last deep breath and tightened her helmet, careful not to catch her wayward blonde curls in the chin strap. The instructor behind her shouted last directions into her ear, and off she went.

She sailed for about ten feet, then slid on her belly all the way to the bottom of the massive dune. Ugh. She did her best to brush off the wet sand and trudged back to the top of the dune to try again. After five flights, she spent a brief amount of time soaring and lots of time getting dirty in the mud. But hey, she could say she'd been hang gliding. And her mother, who worried about everything, could stop worrying about this because it was over.

As she took off her harness, she looked around to see if she could spot Jeremy Gideon, her boyfriend and travel partner for this adventure. She had no idea where he was. They'd been in different groups because she weighed one hundred ten pounds, and he weighed one-sixty. She looked nearby, then up and up until she finally spotted him—soaring high above the state park. She could hear him whooping. His instructor ran along far below him.

After a long flight, Jeremy gradually reduced his height and then gracefully touched down near Fran. His green eyes were alive with excitement. "That was so much fun! Let's go again!"

"I can't go again. I've already had my five flights." She felt sandy and gritty and just wanted a shower. "How many more flights do you have?"

"That was just my first one. I've got four more. How did you already have five flights?"

"Because I spent all my time sliding on my belly in mud flats." She gestured to her sandy, wet clothes. Jeremy's eyes lit with disbelief and mirth, but he acted like a gentleman and didn't laugh. They'd been dating for a year, so of course, he knew she was not exactly an athletic person. She'd been a cheerleader in high school, back in the days when cheerleading didn't require athleticism. He, on the other hand, was a natural athlete, a collegiate soccer player. He could excel at any sport he wished, and he couldn't quite comprehend klutzy people.

Suddenly she saw herself as he was seeing her—with wet, dirty clothes and blonde frizz flying out from her helmet. Her blue eyes provided the only spot of color on her, from head to toe. It really was funny, she had to admit. When she began to smile, his laughter took over, and they bent over together, howling in hilarity. She finally straightened, breathless, and wiped tears of mirth from her eyes, along with a layer of sand.

"I need a shower," she said. "You go ahead and have fun. I'll head back and get cleaned up for supper."

His green eyes still twinkled, and he started to kiss her on the cheek but obviously thought better of it. "See you later."

Fran made the short walk back to the beachfront inn in no time. The Outer Banks of North Carolina were beautiful, and she loved the ocean breeze. She entered her room and shed her sandy clothes, heading gratefully into a steaming shower. And she thought about Jeremy.

They had met a year ago when she and her married best friend, Becca, were visiting Fran's mother in Laurens, South Carolina. Becca remembered that Jeremy, who was her best friend in high school, was finishing up his undergraduate degree at Lander University in nearby Greenwood, and she wanted to say hi to him. The three of them ended up spending the evening together.

The next day, Jeremy staged himself in his spiffy blue Camaro Z28 on their route back to Aiken so that he could "just happen" to run into them. He was on his way to Aiken himself, he said, to see his parents. For the next two weeks, he sent Fran cards and flowers at work, which effectively ended her casual dating relationship with a fellow reporter. They began seeing each other on weekends. When Jeremy graduated from Lander, he found a temporary job at the Savannah River Site, a nuclear reservation near Aiken, where his dad also worked as a physician, and they saw each other more often.

Looking back, Fran realized, Jeremy had pursued her with an intensity she'd only dreamed about. She felt special. She loved his family, and they seemed to love her. And for the first time since looking into a pair of deep blue eyes in Myrtle Beach four years ago, she found herself thinking about a future with someone.

Stop it, she told herself. *You don't even know his name. You don't know anything about him. It's time to stop thinking about him.*

But for just a moment, she allowed herself the luxury of stepping back in time.

4

Fran's time at Myrtle Beach with her best friend was a reprieve during the toughest time of her life. After seventeen years of withering away from Parkinson's disease, her father, Pete Chapman, had completely lost the last vestiges of the vibrant man he once was. He was still alive, but the bright, funny, capable man who was Fran's father had disappeared long before. Her mother, Julia, could trace his first symptoms back to a time when Fran was two years old. One day she noticed that he didn't swing his left arm when he walked. Six years later, in 1969, he was finally diagnosed.

Until that point, Julia Chapman was a stay-at-home mom and wife, dedicated to her husband and her girls. With thick auburn hair and sparkling green eyes, she was stunningly beautiful. She blossomed early, becoming the first girl in her grade to wear a bra. At age twelve, that was not necessarily a good thing. When Julia transferred to a new high school as a senior, she was elected cheerleader on the first day of school without anyone even knowing her name. She didn't even know what she was being picked for.

Julia and Pete had met when Julia was just thirteen. Pete was eight years her senior. His real name was Wister Wilson Chapman Jr., but everybody called him Pete, just like his dad. He'd come to visit Julia's older sister, Frankie, and their cousin, Becky. Even then, he'd said quite seriously that he was just waiting for Julia to grow up. When she was seventeen, midway through her senior year, he proposed to her, married her, and took her to Wilmington, North Carolina, where he worked in the shipyard during World War II, as he was denied military service due to asthma. After the war, they moved back home to upstate South Carolina.

In the days before they had children, Pete and Julia had no car and flew everywhere in a small airplane. Pete's parents built a short runway along the river so Pete would have a place to land his plane when he came home. When they found out they were expecting their first child, he quit cursing (he told his wife somberly that his child would never hear him curse), sold the plane, and committed himself to a safer lifestyle.

Fran's older sister, Chris, was born when Julia was twenty-two, after a pregnancy fraught with horrible sickness. It was a ten-month pregnancy, and Julia actually weighed less just before the birth than she did before she got pregnant. When Chris was twelve and Julia was thirty-four, Fran came along.

Chris grew up thinking her dad could do anything. She did everything with him, working on cars together and even building a boat from scratch. She would come into the house at night with her tiny hands blistered from where she started the screws into the boat.

Pete became a life insurance salesman, and he was good at it. He cared about his clients and made a good living for his family. They had a home in Hickory Tavern, South Carolina, and also a trailer on Lake Greenwood where they spent summers. Julia hosted circle meetings for her church, played bridge, and went to Eastern Star events with her husband. She kept a comfortable home and sang alto in the church choir. She created the church bulletin every week, typing it on an old typewriter and running it off on a mimeograph machine in the laundry room. Chris played the piano and the organ, and Pete sang tenor and taught Sunday school. Fran, lacking any musical talent whatsoever, sat in the pew with her best friend's family and proofread the bulletin, noting any typographical errors. Sometimes she even carefully tore out each misspelled word to show her mother later.

The family loved sports. They were avid Clemson fans, and Chris was an all-star basketball guard at Hickory Tavern High and head majorette for the band, complete with twirling batons of fire. The family never missed a game, bundling Fran up in warm clothes and white furry earmuffs. Julia made a tiny majorette mascot outfit, and five-year-old Fran proudly marched with the Hickory Tavern band in the Christmas parade. Chris had to carry her most of the way because the route was uphill and long.

Chris was a good girl, but she did like to have fun. She got her driver's license when she was fourteen years old, and her cousin Bill let her drive his Triumph convertible for a day. Julia got a phone call from the principal at Hickory Tavern.

"Mrs. Chapman, do you know where your daughter is?"

"Yes, she's at school," she said bewildered.

"No, she's riding up and down the road in the front of the school in a red sports car with the top down, honking the horn."

When Julia asked Chris about it later, she said, "What good would it be to have Bill's car, if people didn't see me?"

Another time, she and her friends wandered into the school during off hours because the doors were unlocked. They helped themselves to food in the cafeteria and ended up spray painting the roof with Classes of '67, '68, and '69. They were busted because a member of the group wrote the seven backwards, and the principal instantly knew who it was. Another day, they raided play practice at the school, throwing cherry bombs and running away in hilarity.

Chris dated the boy across the road, Julius LaRoche, for two years. When he went off to Clemson, she tried to convince her parents to let her go to college there. Her dad refused because at that time, Clemson had only just begun accepting females, and Pete didn't like the ratio of boys to girls. Besides, he felt education was wasted on girls.

When she was eighteen, Chris met and fell in love with a man named Danny Kirby, a bass player in a struggling rock band. When she was twenty, she came to her mother on a Monday and said, "I'm getting married Friday, and I only need you to do two things."

"What's that, sweetheart?"

"I want to get married here at home, and I want you to make my dress."

Julia pulled it off. Chris was married in the family living room under a white arbor, in a beautiful white lace dress. Fran stood at her side, a miniature maid of honor in a pale green dress with pearl buttons.

Soon after her eighth birthday, Fran walked down the aisle at church during a spring revival and gave her life to Jesus.

It was a good life. There were challenges, but everyone has them. The family had their church and each other. Then, in the span of time it took the doctors to say "Parkinson's disease," everything changed. Pete was immediately declared disabled, and Julia found herself forty-two years old with no high school diploma, no work experience, and the responsibility of caring for a sick husband and raising a little girl by herself.

Julia and Pete talked in the hospital room that night after the doctor delivered the news. Pete was very smart, smart enough to know what was going to happen to him. He sat quietly for a long time and sighed. He pulled her down beside him on the hospital bed and looked straight into her tear-filled eyes. "Julia, we need to talk."

"Pete, it's just one person's opinion. We'll get others."

He ran his thumb under her eyes, brushing away the tears. "You know better than that. This is the answer, the result of years of questions and tests. We may not like it, but it's the answer. Now we have to deal with it."

"They can treat you."

"They'll do their best, but we can't assume anything. We'll pray for a miracle, and we may just get one, but you never know. God may be planning to use my sickness for His glory."

"But ..."

"Julia. Be strong and let's talk."

She drew a shaky breath. "Okay."

"The most important thing is Fran."

"Fran?"

"Absolutely, Fran. Chris is already grown and married. Fran is just a little girl, and she won't understand any of this. Her entire life is going to be different now."

"What do you want me to do?"

"Whatever is best for her. The time is coming when I'm not

going to be myself. You think of her first in every decision you make. If I'm not safe to drive a car, you take the keys away. When the time comes that I shouldn't live at home, put me somewhere else. Base every decision you make on what's best for her, and I'm telling you now that I'm in agreement. Whatever it is. Understand?"

"Oh, Pete."

"Tell me that you understand."

"I understand."

"We'll keep praying, and God will use this for His glory. One way or another. You just be strong like you always are. I love you."

On the way home from the hospital that night, still numb and in shock, Julia pulled into the parking lot of a big church with a steeple glowing white against the night sky and looked up at the heavens. Crying softly, at the end of herself, she went to her Father.

"God, I know I'm bad about trying to handle things on my own, but this is too big for me," she whispered. "Pete told me to be strong, but I'm not. I don't know what to do. I have a little girl at home and now a husband who's facing a long sickness, and we have no idea what's going to happen. I can't handle this. I'm giving it to You. Please let me know what I need to do."

She stayed there for a long time, letting the peace soak into her soul, then went home and started the long process of simply doing whatever came next. The big picture was too big, so she just did the next thing. And the next and the next.

Over the coming years, Julia unknowingly modeled for her daughter how a servant of Christ is supposed to act. Fran could remember times when her mother put the last bit of money she had in the offering plate at church, knowing God would provide. Men paid her attention, but Julia did not care and usually did not even notice. She was too focused on caring for her daughter and her husband. When Chris had children, she cared for them so Chris could work.

Fran smiled softly to herself, remembering. Her mother was her best friend, the most amazing person she'd ever known. For so many years it had been just the two of them against the world, united in a battle no one else could possibly understand. She loved her mother fiercely, proudly, protectively, and with no small amount of fear. What in the world would she do if something happened to her? She had no idea how she would be able to bear it.

In a display of strength and faith that Fran would always admire, Julia went to college and earned her degree with honors. She found a job working third shift at Laurens Community Residence, which was a kind of halfway house in what was then known as the State Department of Mental Retardation. The mission was to help mentally challenged women learn to live on their own. When Julia filled out her application, she listed her age as ten years younger than she actually was, feeling no one would hire a woman in her mid-forties with no experience. Under her care and guidance, the women learned life skills and held down simple jobs. When they were ready, they were placed in apartments.

Julia brought life, love, and laughter to her work, and over the years, she became one of the foremost authorities in the state of South Carolina on working with mentally handicapped adults. When asked her secret, she said simply that she treated them like they didn't have any handicaps.

"When I first started working with these women, I would take them out to eat or shop and try to look normal," she would say. "It didn't take long before I quit worrying about that and let people think what they wanted."

After years of working third shift, Julia was chosen as the new manager of the Residence when her boss retired. She did everything with her girls and took Fran along with her. Fran was there the evening the Residence staff put on a talent show, and Julia and the other counselors dressed up as "Sister Dredge" and sang "We Are Family." She was there the day Julia was playing softball with the girls and ended up breaking her kneecap trying to run from first base to second. And she was there for numerous trips and outings. The women at the Residence became Fran's extended family and taught her valuable life lessons that she would not have learned otherwise.

In later years when Fran asked her mother how she did it, Julia would shrug and say, "What choice did I have? You were depending on me."

Fran had problems of her own, problems that may have stemmed from watching her father turn into a different person. He was the only father Fran had ever known, but of course, she knew he was different. In her mind she knew that he had Parkinson's, but she didn't really understand what that meant. She had a vivid imagination, and she began to imagine all sorts of reasons why he was different, things she never shared with anyone. When she was in sixth grade, her grades dramatically dropped. Julia moved her to a private school, a Presbyterian orphanage that accepted day students. The school was twenty-two miles away, so Julia drove nearly ninety miles every day, taking Fran to and from school.

As the years went by, Pete grew worse and worse. His gait became a shuffling stumble, his hands shook uncontrollably, and he couldn't formulate sentences. Julia kept him at home until he developed Sundown Syndrome. At night he shuffled around the house and hallucinated, seeing people at the windows and in the trees outside. Julia began sleeping in the same room with Fran and locking their bedroom door. The family doctor told her frankly that it was time, for their safety and sanity, to move Pete to a nursing home. Julia remembered what Pete had said that long-ago day in the hospital room and agreed.

In many ways it was easier for Julia once Pete was in the nursing home. She knew she and Fran were safer, and Pete was taken care of, so she found it easier to be patient with him when she knew it would be over soon. She visited with him nearly every day, getting his dirty laundry and taking it home with her. Once a week, on Sundays, she and Fran would go to the nursing home and sign him out. They would take him to visit his mother and spend the afternoon at home.

At the end of the day, they would take him back, and he would cry. The strong, capable man Julia had known since she was thirteen would weep silently, tears streaming down his cheeks as she left him and walked down the hall. She knew full well that he wanted it this way, but still, it was hard to see him cry.

21

Fran also found it easier to be patient with her dad when she knew it was just for one day. She could better remember the few good times she'd had with him before he got so sick. Pete would physically pull Fran through the water on two skis so she could learn to stay balanced in the water until the boat could pull her up. They fished together on the dock at the lake, and he taught her that not every snake is a bad snake. While plowing the field on the tractor one day, he came upon a baby rabbit and brought it to her to see, then returned it to where he found it. Another day he brought her a baby grass snake, which went splendidly until the snake got loose in the house. He would take her out in the woods at Christmas time and cut down a cedar tree, and they would drag it home and put it up in the living room. When she was ten years old, and he was still able to walk faster than a shuffling stumble, he pushed her on her bike down the long driveway until she was able to ride without training wheels.

Every meal, without fail, he would thank God for the food. It was the same every time. In a monotone, rhythmic way he would say, "Lord, make us thankful for these and all other blessings, for we beg for Christ's sake, amen." He never forgot to say grace. And he never blamed God for his disease or got angry in any way.

Fran made her way through high school as best she could. In stark contrast to her beautiful and popular sister, she was a very late bloomer and struggled to make friends. She was five-foot-seven and weighted eighty-nine pounds. People thought she was anorexic. She had a mane of frizzy blonde curls, which she fought to straighten and finally cut short, and very crooked teeth. She refused to get braces because she hated pain. She wanted desperately to fit in. Misfits loved her, but the popular crowd sneered at her.

By then, Chris and Danny had two children of their own, Jason and Dana. Danny had the opportunity to attend music school in Boston, so they moved north. Chris got a job in advertising at Stride Rite.

Fran made the cheerleading squad because the administration felt sorry for her and decided to accept everyone who tried out, but only after her mother had gone to the principal. Julia had complained bitterly because Fran was devastated that she was the only one cut during tryouts. She was an adequate cheerleader but still didn't fit in. She was embarrassed about her dad because she didn't know how to explain why he walked and talked the way he did. When she graduated from high school, she didn't want him to attend because of what her "friends" would think.

When she was a sophomore in high school, a representative from Columbia College, a private all-female school in Columbia, South Carolina, came to visit her school. As a result, Fran immediately knew where she wanted to go to college. Julia had no idea how she would pay the tuition for private school, but it didn't matter. She sent in the deposit and trusted God to provide.

Fran later remembered her time at Columbia College as something like a caterpillar going into a cocoon. When she entered the English program, she immediately found a family. The faculty and her fellow students loved her and accepted her, and she finally found a place where she fit in. No one there thought it was strange that she proofread everything she saw, or that she spent hours with her nose buried in books. This was a strange and new feeling. Before, her mother was the only person in her life that she'd ever felt loved her unconditionally. She even grew brave enough to take one of her friends home with her. That girl was Joy Matthews, who would become her best friend.

Fran grew her hair long, quit fighting her curls, and finally consented to get braces on her teeth. By the end of her freshman year, she'd put on twenty much-needed pounds. By the end of her sophomore year, she had a tutoring job in the writing lab and earned scholarships that covered all her tuition, room, and board.

She'd still never in her life had a real date. The boys in high school thought of her as a goofy kid sister, and there were no boys at Columbia College unless you wanted to drive across town to the University of South Carolina, which Fran decidedly did not. She was perfectly happy confining herself to the walls of Columbia College and concentrating on her studies. Boys could wait. Besides, how could she explain her father to a boy? She just did not want to go there.

Before their junior year, Fran and Joy decided to head to Myrtle Beach for a long weekend. They planned to spend a couple of days with Julia after that, and head back to school. It was a perfect end to the summer.

Now, four years later, as Fran towel-dried her hair at the inn in North Carolina, she remembered that last day at the beach. She'd had no idea it would change everything.

5

Fran had grown up spending summers on the lake and the beach, and she had never worried about sunburn. Rather than using sunscreen, she used suntan oil and simply dealt with the minor burns that came. They were usually on her face and shoulders and weren't very painful. She burned and peeled and burned again until she got a base tan. No big deal. Now she had a good base tan from a summer of lifeguarding, so she wasn't at all worried on her and Joy's last day at Myrtle Beach.

They loaded a cooler with drinks and ice and packed big beach bags with towels, sunglasses, visors, and snacks. They gathered lounge chairs and an umbrella, and made their way from their motel room down to the sand. Just above the high tide mark, they set up for the day.

"I'm so glad we got to do this," Joy said as they put their things down.

"Me, too. I really needed the break. Junior year is going to be a bear." Fran used the base of the umbrella to dig out a hole in the sand.

"You ready for Shakespeare?" Joy asked as she helped position the umbrella to provide shade just where they wanted it.

"I guess. I'm a little nervous about it. Dr. Mishoe is tough."

"Yeah, he's tough, but when we get done, we'll know those plays backward and forwards."

"It's Dr. Mott and her grammar course that I'm more nervous about. Who knows how to diagram sentences anymore? Not me."

"Are we really going to have to do that?" Joy opened her chair and spread a towel on it, smoothing it carefully.

"That's what I hear. I'm looking forward to Mr. Broome's writing classes, though."

"He's so funny."

"He's my favorite," Fran said.

Joy gave her a sidelong glance and grinned. "Everybody knows that."

Fran blushed. It was no secret that she had a massive crush on Mike Broome, one of their writing professors. "Well, he's fun, and he makes me laugh."

"I know, I know. We all love him."

They chatted about upcoming classes and when they were finally settled in their chairs, about the elephant in the room.

"You haven't talked much about your dad," Joy said as she finished applying sunscreen to her face and slipped on her sunglasses.

Fran didn't answer at first. She looked across the sand and out at the ocean. Kids with boogie boards rode waves to the shore, whooping with glee while others built sandcastles close by. Seagulls glided just above the water, hoping for a meal, and planes flew high above the beach, advertising local restaurants. Just a typical summer at Myrtle Beach. No one would have thought her heart was breaking.

"He's just so bad," she finally said. "He can hardly walk or talk at all. And the worst part is that the doctors say he's still locked in there somewhere. His mind is just fine. He can understand what's happening; he just can't control his body. And his organs could last another twenty years. I can't imagine how frustrating and depressing that must be for him, knowing that."

"That's tough," Joy said softly. "It's so much worse than something like cancer because it lasts so long."

"It's vicious," Fran agreed. "I can't imagine anything worse than diseases of the brain."

"Is your mom still taking him home every Sunday?"

"Like clockwork."

"She's so amazing."

They fell silent, took out their books, and basked in companionable silence. Fran grew sleepy and decided to turn over and roast her backside. Just to be safe, she positioned herself under the umbrella and then laid her lounge chair flat. She nestled into the chair, reached behind her back, and untied her bikini top.

After what seemed like just a few minutes, she felt Joy gently tying her top into place. She stirred, still groggy.

"Wake up," Joy said. "The sun moved."

Fran shifted and started to sit up, then came eye-to-eye with a young man with dark brown curls and deep blue eyes. His eyes locked onto hers, and her world stopped. It seemed as if even the seagulls stopped their cawing, like the very ocean waves hushed. She actually felt a click in her soul at the absolute rightness of it. But she didn't have time to process it before the pain hit.

"Don't move," the young man said. "I have something that can help you."

"I can't be sunburned," she wailed. "I never sunburn. I'm a lifeguard." She could only imagine the pain she was in for tomorrow when she and Joy had to drive five hours to her mother's house.

"You're Scotch-Irish, right?" the boy asked.

"Yes, how'd you know that?"

"You and I have the same skin. Just be still for a minute. I was a lifeguard too, and I'm an Eagle Scout. I know a second-degree burn when I see one."

Second degree? She lay still and the pain raged. She kicked herself from one end of the beach to the other, realizing that her top half was safely under the umbrella, but evidently the sun had moved quite a bit. Her legs were now entirely under the intense beach sun. How stupid could she be?

She heard the young man rummaging in his pack, then she felt a cooling sensation as something was squirted onto her right leg. This was followed by an unbelievable feeling. His hands, oh, his hands. She all but whimpered, and this time not from the pain. His hands were firm, sure and capable, and he knew just how hard to rub without causing her undue pain. On top of that, he took great care not to take liberties, so she was completely comfortable. In all her life she'd never imagined that anyone's hands could feel so good. She never wanted him to stop.

At the same time, she envisioned the trip ahead of her tomorrow and groaned. "Oh, this is going to be bad. We're supposed to head home tomorrow. How can I ride in a car for five hours like this?"

"It's going to hurt," he told her frankly as he smoothed on the aloe goo.

She lay there, with nothing to look at but the ground, and noticed that his bare right foot was wrapped with duct tape. She angled her eyes higher and saw a tanned, muscular calf. To keep her mind off the pain, and the sensations his hands were stirring up, she asked, "What's with the duct tape?"

He sighed and squirted more goo, then began to work on her left leg. "It's a long story."

"I think we've got a minute," she said.

So the young man Fran had privately nicknamed Blue Eyes and his friend—whose name evidently was Doug—alternately told them what had happened the previous week.

They had biked to a cabin out in the middle of nowhere—why, Fran had no earthly idea—for a couple of days away before school started back. When they got there, Doug went to gather firewood, and Blue Eyes caught some fish for supper.

"So I dragged this big dead tree into the yard," Doug said. "All it needed was to be cut up for firewood."

"And I'm not a good cook, but I'm better than him," Blue Eyes added. "I know how to make fish packets over a campfire. So I put these two huge …"

"Well, big but not huge…"

"…trout into foil packets and seasoned them with salt and pepper, all ready to toss into the fire. We were both working on cutting up the tree."

"Then genius here decided he was going to put two other tree trunks side by side and stand on them while he whacked away with a hatchet at the dead one between his feet."

Joy and Fran both could see where the story was going. Fran

was still face down, listening, but Joy's eyes grew big, and she covered her mouth.

"No."

"Yes. The next thing I knew, he'd quit chopping. When I turned to look, his shoe was already filled up with blood."

The hatchet had gone through Blue Eyes' shoe just below his ankle bone and taken out a huge chunk of meat, which then hung wetly by a thin piece of skin.

Doug grinned. "So what would you do?"

"I'd get myself to the hospital," Joy said.

"Smart guy here decided we had to eat, so we should just clean his foot, put it back together, and cook the fish. He thought maybe it would stop bleeding and be okay."

Fran rolled her eyes where she lay and heard Joy's unsympathetic snort.

They had built up the fire, tossed the fish packets in, then gone down to the river and cleaned out the wound. It sounded just as horrible as it probably was.

"It gets worse," Doug announced.

"How?"

"Just as we were finishing our food, the bottom fell out. Thunder, lightning, flash flooding. It was pitch dark, and all of a sudden, there was no road. Just mud. Then it started to hail."

The girls started to giggle.

"It wasn't that bad," Blue Eyes protested.

"Yes, it was. Trust me. You were delusional at that point. It's all very fresh in my memory."

"What did you do?" Joy asked.

"What could I do? Saved his sorry behind. Dragged my bike up to the road and rode until I could find someone in that godforsaken area that would answer the door, wouldn't shoot me, and had a phone."

"He left me alone for two hours," Blue Eyes interjected.

"While I was chased by dogs, almost shot, and you don't even want to know what else. Finally at the sixth house …"

"Six?"

"Six. Someone finally let me use a phone, and I called his parents. About the time I made it back to the cabin, wet as a rat, his parents came screeching down the road in their station wagon."

"My dad carried me out on his back," Blue Eyes said. "My mom carried my bike."

"And we got to a hospital, and they put him back together. It's only by the grace of God that he didn't cut his foot off and bleed to death."

"It's the truth," Blue Eyes said.

Joy and Fran stifled their giggles, tears streaming down their faces from suppressed mirth. It shouldn't have been funny, but the way the boys told the story was hilarious.

"And then what?" Joy finally caught her breath.

"He rested for a few days, and we came to the beach. My sister needed her car, and we promised."

Joy eyed the injured foot. "And you duct-taped it together? Why?"

"Duct tape is good for everything," Blue Eyes said matter-of-factly. "And I figured the stitches were holding and the salt water would do it good."

The girls finally lost it and howled.

When they calmed down, Fran finally sat up. Blue Eyes and Doug exchanged a weird look, and Blue Eyes turned and busied himself putting the top back on the aloe.

Doug stepped between Fran and Blue Eyes and spoke up again. "So, you're headed home tomorrow."

"Yep," Joy said. "Going back to college next week. We're going to be juniors."

"We're about to start our last year," Doug said. "We're headed back tomorrow too."

"Thanks for stopping when you did," Joy said. "I was so absorbed in my book, I don't know when I would have noticed she was getting burned."

Blue Eyes finally turned back around and handed Fran the bottle of aloe. "Take this with you and keep putting it on. It'll help."

Their eyes met again, and again Fran felt it. That piercing blue gaze, coupled with the way she could still feel his hands on her—it felt like her insides were melting. "Thank you," she said because she didn't know what else to say. "If you hadn't stopped to help, I'd have been in much worse shape. I appreciate it."

"No problem. Y'all have a safe trip back tomorrow."

"You too."

And just like that, they were gone. They strode around the first high-rise and out of sight.

Joy glanced at Fran and grinned. Her friend had a vacant stare that she'd never seen before. Joy snapped her fingers and waved her hand in front of Fran's face. "Hey. Earth to Fran."

"What?" Fran shook her head. "What?"

"What's going on?"

"Did you see his eyes?"

"Yeah, he was cute," Joy said innocently. "All blue eyes and curly brown hair. I liked Doug too. They were funny, the way they could finish each other's sentences."

"But, Joy…" Fran struggled to make her understand.

"What?"

"Something just happened to me."

"Yeah, and you said you've never even been on a date. You've probably never had a guy touch you before either, am I right?"

"No…"

"Much less rub aloe on your legs."

Fran felt the need to defend herself. "Well, have you?"

"No, but that's beside the point."

"And just what is the point?"

"That I think it's probably a perfectly normal reaction when a guy touches you and helps you, the way he did. You're just grateful."

Fran snorted again. "Hogwash. I know when something happens to me, and something did."

"What do you think happened?"

31

Fran's gaze went dreamy. "It was like I could see forever in his eyes."

"Oh good grief, Fran, you don't even know the guy. You don't even know his name."

"It doesn't matter," she said stubbornly. "The way I felt is the way it's supposed to feel."

"You know what, you've read too many romance novels, and you've had enough sun. Let's get you inside and into a cool tub."

So they packed up and headed inside.

*   *   *

The next day, on the interminable, pain-filled trip home, Fran tried again.

"Joy, I need you to understand."

"What?"

"I think that guy was special."

Joy looked at Fran and didn't say anything for a long minute. Her gaze softened. "Okay, maybe he was. Maybe he was really the guy for you. But how are you ever going to know? We don't know his name or where he goes to school or anything. We wouldn't know where to start looking for them."

"That's what upsets me."

"And there's absolutely nothing you can do about it. We have nothing to go on. No way to find him or Doug."

"So what do you suggest?"

"Try to put it out of your mind for now. Pray that if he is the one, God will bring you back together. But you have to trust God and go on with your life because you really don't know."

Fran didn't say any more about it, but she did pray. That day and the next, and for four long years, she prayed that if Blue Eyes were the one, God would lead them back together.

6

The next two years at Columbia College zipped by. The course load became more and more difficult. Dr. Mishoe's Shakespeare class lived up to its reputation as one of the most difficult the English Department had to offer. Fran and Joy both got A's in the class after studying until their eyes hurt. Fellow English majors and close friends Donna Watson, Deborah Brooks, and Pat Duffie were also in on the torture. Deborah and Joy always ended up getting the top grades, and Donna was close behind, with disgusting consistency. It was a good thing Fran loved them all.

Then followed English Grammar with Dr. Mott, Linguistics with Dr. Nelson, Romantics with Dr. Mott, British literature with Dr. Savory, and the list went on. Add in the writing courses with Mr. Broome, Dr. Gallo, and published romantic author Barbara Ferry Johnson, and Fran's days were full.

In October of her junior year, she seriously began to question the absence of a newspaper on campus. During her freshman and sophomore years, the *Post Script* had come out once in a blue moon, but it was not consistent and wasn't even really a newspaper. According to the mission on its masthead, it was supposed to come out every two weeks. Michael Broome, Fran's favorite professor, was the advisor, so Fran went to see him.

She stuck her head into his cluttered office, where he sat grading papers through his horn-rimmed glasses. He taught all forms of writing and had unquestionably made Fran a better writer.

She tapped on the doorjamb. "Mr. Broome?"

"Yes?" He looked up at her. She still had a mad crush on him. He had a lightning wit with a hilarious sense of sarcasm. He didn't mind giving and taking abuse, and Fran and her fellow English majors loved to dish it out. He'd once asked Joy where was "that pack" she ran with, and now that group of girls—Fran's best friends in the world—was known as The Pack. They made his life miserable, and all the parties involved loved it.

"You got a minute?" Fran asked.

"Sure. Come on in, Miss Chapman. What's on your mind?"

She sat down in the chair across from his desk. "I was wondering about the *Post Script*."

"What about it?"

"Like, why it doesn't come out like it's supposed to."

"Well, there's probably no good reason for that except that people are busy, and the current editor is working on graduating in December. Every young woman on this campus has a full load, as I'm sure you can identify with. It takes a lot of work to put out a newspaper."

"So there's no reason why it couldn't come out every two weeks like the masthead says? No monetary issue or anything?"

"Well, of course, there's always money."

"So what would need to be done to make it a real newspaper, one that students could depend on to come out on time, every two weeks?"

He looked at her more closely. "You're serious, Miss Chapman? You want to take this on?"

"I think I do, yes."

"Well then, you'd need a committed editor-in-chief, which it looks like we have." He held up his fingers and began ticking off his points. "There is a small budget, but you'd need a business manager to go out and get some ads, so we'd have enough money to publish. An assistant editor, because this is going to be more work than you realize. A news editor, a features editor, a sports editor, and a photographer." He started on his second hand when he reached sports editor. "And of course you'd need reporters—people who will buy in to helping write for you."

"Who prints it?"

"Carolina Printing, right across town. You'd need to get on their press schedule."

"If I can get all of that in place before the next semester starts, would you back me as advisor?"

"Absolutely. I think it's going to be exciting to watch this come together."

*   *   *

For the next two months, all of Fran's free time went into finding a staff, holding meetings, and brainstorming ideas for the first issue. Joy had already committed to be editor of the *Criterion*, the college literary magazine, so she couldn't hold a regular staff position but committed to write for the newspaper whenever she could. Fran likewise agreed to write for the *Criterion* as well as serve as a section editor for the *Columbian*, the college yearbook.

Fran went to the art department and announced a contest for a new banner for the *Post Script*. A wonderful artist named Amber Kirkpatrick submitted the winning design. She was also a photographer and agreed to be the chief photographer for the newspaper. A business student named Sheree Bridges signed on to be the business manager and almost instantly brought in two advertisers. The rest of the staff fell into place just as neatly. Assignments were made, and they were ready for their first issue.

Copy began to come in about a day before the deadline and continually trickled in until midnight. There were no computers back then, so everything was submitted in hard copy. Fran and her assistant editor, Emily Bradley, worked late into the night to edit the stories and get everything ready to take to the printer the next day. They had a vague idea of how many column inches a page of double-spaced typewritten copy would take up, but this was their first issue, and they didn't really know for sure. They cropped and sized every picture with red grease pencils.

Fran eventually sent Emily back to her room and finished up about dawn. Her roommate, Mitzie Eubank, who was also the dorm president, poked her head from under her covers and blinked blearily at her about six a.m.

"Have you been up all night?" she asked.

"Yep." Fran still worked steadily, finishing up a story on the Koala basketball program. Her eyes stung, but she could see the finish line ahead.

"Wow. That's nuts."

"It's the first issue. It will get better." She hoped. But even if not, she was in this for the long haul. And this newspaper would come out every two weeks without fail. Whatever she had to do.

When she got everything to the printer, and it was typeset, she discovered that she had far overestimated how much copy it would take to fill a four-page tabloid. She had way too much, so most of her time at the printer was spent cutting copy.

As the first issue came cranking off the presses, Fran held it and felt a new satisfaction she'd never felt before. She and her staff had worked so hard, and here it was—something she could hold in her hands. The ink was still wet, and she found that thrilling.

Then she turned to the masthead and saw her name in the top spot. She scanned down the list and noted with a smile all the girls who had committed their time and talents to this newspaper—each one so special and so essential. She and her staff had committed to three semesters—nineteen issues of the *Post Script*—six per semester and one special summer edition. She had no doubt they would nail it.

Fran's job now was to give the paper a final proofread, so they could shut down the presses if there were any horrible errors.

She thumbed through it, giving it a quick, surface read. The lead story was a profile on Julie Yarborough, daughter of race car driver Cale Yarborough. It had been fun talking to Julie and writing up the interview, and there it was in black and white—By Fran Chapman.

The last story she read before she gave it a thumbs-up was a column by some girl called Annie O Ms. The writer ate way too much over her month-long Christmas break and tried to find ways to take the weight off before school started back. She tried running in her neighborhood, with hilarious results. Fran smiled as she went over it one more time. The last three paragraphs read:

The first morning, enthusiasm intact, I ran down the driveway and up the street. Oh, I felt great—for about two blocks. Then the Thompsons' boxer discovered me. I've known that dog since he was a pup, but he acted like he'd never seen me before. It wouldn't have been so bad, but his barking started a chain reaction with all the other dogs in the neighborhood. All the way home I was chased by one boxer, two terriers, a German shepherd, and the most vicious Pekingese I've ever seen.

I managed to lose about ten pounds, and believe me, it wasn't easy. Running gives me a tremendous appetite, and with the rest of the family chowing down on all that delicious food, I don't understand how I lost an ounce.

I'm still trying, so if you see a large yellow object moving around on campus, or running along Columbia College drive, have a little compassion. That's not a 150-pound canary. That's me!

This writer was Fran's secret weapon. Her identity would remain top secret, and her words would hit home with every reader. There would be all kinds of speculation as to who she could possibly be, but no one would ever guess.

Because the writer was Fran's mother, Julia Chapman.

7

In Fran's last semester at Columbia College, her father began taking a turn for the worse. This had been cyclical throughout Pete's disease. At times, the drugs they gave him would cease working, so doctors would admit him to the hospital, clean out his system, and start over. The time while he was in the hospital was always difficult, but when his medicines restarted, things would go back to being the same. The prognosis never changed. His organs could last another twenty years, they said.

In January of Fran's senior year, the doctors admitted Pete to a hospital in Columbia, only about ten minutes from her school. Julia had to work, so Fran spent as much time as she could checking up on her dad. Julia came on the weekends.

When he was like this, there really wasn't much to do. He lay in his bed, hooked up to the machines that kept him stable until they were ready to restart the medications. There was no conversation. Doctors said Pete could possibly hear them if they talked to him, but one-way communication quickly grew old.

January wore into February, and medicines were restarted. Julia and Fran began to watch for him to come around, to be his old self—or as close as he would ever get to it. But this time there were other problems. Doctors still weren't pessimistic, though, since Pete's body was relatively healthy. It was his brain that was diseased.

For the rest of her life, Fran would question her actions on that night in February. Shouldn't she have known something was different? Shouldn't she somehow have known she should be there? But she didn't, and she would always live with it.

At two o'clock in the morning, the phone rang in Fran's dorm room. Mitzie answered. She was dorm president, so late-night phone calls were usually for her.

"Hello?"

Silence. Fran listened sleepily, already beginning to doze back off. Then Mitzie brought her the phone.

"It's for me?"

"Yes. It's your mom."

She looked at Mitzie with alarm, then took the phone. "Hello? Mama?"

"Baby, it's your daddy."

"Is he okay? I'll go over there right now."

One muffled sob, but then the steel-spined strength that Julia had shown all of Fran's life. "No, baby, he's gone."

The words didn't sink in. *Gone? How could he be gone?* Fran had been there the day before, and he'd looked the same.

"What happened?"

"They think it was a blood clot."

"A blood clot?" It didn't seem possible. Pete had been fighting Parkinson's disease for nineteen years, and now he'd been taken by a blood clot?

"That's what they say. I'm about to leave to come get you. You stay strong, okay? I'll be there."

"Mama, I'm so sorry."

"Why are you sorry, honey? This wasn't your fault."

"But I should have been there with him. I should have known. He shouldn't have died alone." Fran dissolved in uncontrollable weeping. Somehow, Joy's arms were around her now, hugging her hard. Mitzie had known who Fran would want, and Joy was there. Joy took the phone from her.

"It's Joy, Mrs. Chapman. I've got her. Don't worry, I'm right here with her until you get here. You just get here safe. We'll watch out for her and are all praying for you both."

For the next two hours, Fran's Columbia College sisters gathered around her, held her, and prayed. They prayed for comfort, for strength and peace, and for healing for Fran and her family. They took turns, lifting Fran and her family to the throne room of heaven until Julia arrived.

Julia helped Fran pack, and they went together to the hospital. They were allowed to look at Pete one last time before he was taken to the mortuary. He didn't look any different, except that now he was still. In all of Fran's memory, he hadn't been still; he'd always had that uncontrollable Parkinson's tremor. But now he was. Completely still. That, more than anything, made it sink in.

Fran's eyes filled with fresh tears as she gazed at her daddy. Regret, more crushing than anything she'd ever known, filled her heart and mind. Every time she'd snapped at him because he couldn't get a sentence out, or been impatient with his slow, shuffling steps, or been too embarrassed to bring friends home—every single time now pierced her heart like so many arrows. She'd had so many chances to be patient and kind, and now it was too late. Forever too late. Tidal waves of grief, guilt, and regret washed over her. She couldn't catch her breath before another wave hit her. She'd never imagined such pain.

"Daddy, I'm so sorry," she sobbed. "God, please tell my daddy I love him. I don't know if he knows or not. Please tell him!"

"Baby, of course he knows." Julia cuddled her close, her tears mingling with Fran's as they clung to each other in anguish.

"How does he know? I don't remember the last time I told him."

Julia gathered herself and took Fran's shoulders in her hands. "He knows. Remember that Sunday right before Christmas, when you were home? You took him to visit the Tumblins before you took him back to the nursing home?"

"I didn't want to. It made me mad that he wanted me to."

"But you did. It made his whole day. It made him feel normal to visit with friends."

Fran was silent, taking that in, tears still sliding down her cheeks. "And we brought him to see my school last fall, and he got to walk around. It was hard but I'm so glad now."

"Me, too. Those were just two things you did for your daddy. Of course, he knew you loved him."

The next few days were a blur of funeral preparations. Chris, heartbroken, flew in from Boston with her family.

Fran spent her time in the den, looking out the glass doors across the fields, praying. She knew, without a doubt, that Pete was happy and whole in heaven. Her daddy had loved Jesus and had modeled that love her entire life. Now, she begged God to let her talk to her daddy, then poured out her heart. She told Pete exactly how she felt, and everything she wished she'd said to him while he was alive. While there was time.

God, why didn't I know I was out of time? I should have been with him.

She knew God was listening, and she knew He was hurting for her. She could almost feel His loving arms around her. The answer came as more of a feeling in her heart than words.

Lean on Me. I am your strength, your ever-present help in times of trouble. You will get through this with My help, and you will learn from it.

With God's help, Fran and her family got through the funeral. They buried Pete in a nice casket and put a pink headstone over his gravesite. Throngs of people came, and Fran was crushed all over again when she realized how many people Pete had touched in his life and how much she'd missed by not spending more time with him. His mother, nearly ninety-five years old, bore up like the Southern lady she was. Tears streamed down her weathered, wrinkled cheeks, but she stayed strong.

The final blow came a few days later when Julia was sifting through Pete's closet, looking for the life insurance papers she knew had to be there. She found the envelope she was looking for, but it was bigger and thicker than she'd thought it would be. She moved to the bed and gently emptied the contents onto the quilt.

"Oh, Pete," she whispered.

Inside were mementos of special times through the years. A keychain from their brief time owning a gas station in Laurens. The

41

road had washed out, and they went broke, leading to Pete's career as a life insurance salesman. A repair bill for the motorcycle Pete used to ride with his brother-in-law until he crashed into the back of a pickup truck while looking at girls on the street. The program from Chris's high school graduation and, more recently, from Julia's college graduation. A dried rose from the corsage Fran had worn in the Little Miss Hickory Tavern pageant. Little things, little memories from throughout the thirty-eight years they'd been married.

Eyes filling with fresh tears, Julia took it all in. Then she saw one more envelope, sealed and carefully placed with the life insurance policy she had been looking for. On the back of it, in Pete's scrawling handwriting, was written simply: Julia.

She took a deep breath, slid her finger under the flap, and carefully withdrew a single, yellowed sheet of paper.

Dear Julia,

If you're reading this, it means I've gone home to be with Jesus.

As I write this, it's 1969 and we've just come home from the hospital. They've finally diagnosed me with Parkinson's disease. I want to write these things to you while I still can, while I'm still thinking straight. It's important to me that you know.

You know how much I love you. I've loved you since you were thirteen years old. I was always serious when I said I was just waiting for you to grow up. I love you and our girls more than life itself.

My biggest regret is that I won't really be there to help you raise Fran, but you're the best mother in the world, and I know you'll do an amazing job being both mother and father to her. Like I told you, Fran has to come first. I wish I could have been there for her big moments, but I love her more than that. You do what you have to do to get yourself and her through this.

The life insurance money should help. It's the final way I can help take care of you and her.

Be strong, baby. God will help you. Lean on Him, just like you've always done. He won't ever let you down.

I'll love you always.

Pete

Julia pulled out the policy and gasped. The insurance settlement was so much more than she'd imagined. She'd only hoped for enough to pay the funeral expenses, but Pete had indeed taken care of her. The old, rattletrap car she'd made do with could now be replaced. She could get some decent furniture to replace the old, threadbare pieces she'd been living with because she couldn't do any better. All the debts could be paid off.

She smiled through her tears at God's perfect timing. If this had come any sooner, it would have all been spent on school expenses for Fran. But because they didn't have money in the bank, Fran had qualified for a significant amount of money in grants and scholarships. Now, this money could go for things they really needed.

Then she looked back at the paragraph about Fran, about how Pete would like to have been there for her big moments. If she shared this letter with Fran, it would crush her. She hadn't wanted her dad to be there for her high school graduation, and now she was just weeks away from graduating college. If she'd already beaten herself up so much already, how much worse would this make it?

But how could she not share it? This, Pete's last coherent message to them both?

God, please help her. She sent up the brief prayer before she went to find her daughter.

* * *

Seeing her father's words did crush Fran, but somehow they helped her too. She was able to hear her daddy's real voice, something she hadn't heard since she was a very little girl and thought she'd never hear again. It soothed something in her soul, even though her heart would always ache.

She graduated with honors from Columbia College that May, knowing that if Pete had lived she would have made sure he was there. She imagined him watching her from heaven, and she knew he'd be proud.

In August she was offered a job as a reporter at the *Aiken Standard*, a daily newspaper in Aiken, South Carolina. A friend from Columbia College worked there as a sports writer and needed a roommate. One of Fran's great-aunts lived in Aiken, so it was a chance for her to get to know a whole new branch of her family.

The lessons from the *Post Script* stood her in good stead. The only new thing was immediate, daily deadlines, but that didn't bother her. She did her best work under pressure. Over the next two years, she learned how to be a real journalist and discovered she was very good at it.

She loved her job, but the money wasn't very good—just one hundred eighty dollars a week to start out. There were times when Fran and Julia met at a town halfway between Aiken and Laurens to swap checks. Fran would deposit Julia's, and the next day Julia would deposit Fran's. In this way, they helped each other make it from paycheck to paycheck.

Fran began going out with a fellow reporter. They both liked to dance, and Larry taught her the proper way to shag—the South Carolina state dance. He introduced her to Becca Duncan, who would become Fran's best friend. Fran enjoyed her and Larry's casual relationship and her life in general. There were no fireworks, but then she wasn't necessarily looking for fireworks. She was just getting her feet wet in the dating world.

Then, one night in 1985, while visiting her mother with Becca, she crossed paths with Jeremy Gideon.

8

It was late when Mark eased his Jeep and boat into the driveway at the Monroes' house in Charlestown, Indiana, a community just across the river from Louisville. When he served as youth minister at their church during his seminary years, Matt and Patty Monroe had become good friends, the kind he knew he could depend on. Even though they had no idea that his life had fallen apart, and he was about to land on their doorstep, he had no doubt that they would welcome him and be there for him.

He sat in the driveway and looked at the dark house. And remembered.

*　*　*

The youth minister job at the church in Charlestown wasn't unlike the one at Pleasant Grove. It was all about connecting with the kids and finding the best ways to relate to each one. Mark worked hard to come up with lessons and meeting locations that would intrigue them and keep them coming back. As with Pleasant Grove, this youth group grew tremendously during the two years he was there, and he was blessed to see some of these kids come to Christ.

Patty Monroe worked in the church office, and Matt was on the board of deacons. Patty was an excellent cook, and the relationship began when she began to invite Mark over and feed him. Nancy had her own work and life, and the Monroes and Mark's other friends in Charlestown were his. He and Matt became good friends, spending time together in the woods and on the lake.

He learned that Matt was a relatively recent Christian. When he and Patty married, neither of them followed Christ. Patty heeded the

Lord's call first, and she dedicated herself to being a godly wife. Before long, her husband wanted what she had and followed her example. They had one child, a daughter named Lisa Michelle. Mark had never met her.

Sitting in their driveway, Mark remembered the last time he and Matt had been on the water together before he moved to Boca Raton. They'd set out early that day, hoping to catch the bass during their morning feeding.

"You sure about this, Mark?" Matt asked as they drove toward the lake.

Mark deftly guided the truck and boat through traffic and grinned. "It's a no-brainer, Matt. It's Boca Raton, for crying out loud. Nancy gets to be closer to her mother, and I get a great job. I didn't have to think about it long."

"What other choices did you have?"

"Quite a few. But when this one came up, that was it. No more discussion."

They drove in silence for a few minutes, then Matt spoke again. "It's just a long way from home. Completely unlike anything you've ever known. Won't you miss your mountains?"

Matt knew Mark well enough to know that he needed peaceful mountain places like he needed to breathe. Mark looked at him sideways before he answered.

"Maybe. Probably. But God's grandeur is everywhere. I don't think I'll have to look far to find it."

"Just know that you always have a home here."

"I know that, Matt. Thanks."

They had spent the rest of the day just relaxing and enjoying each other's company.

* * *

A thought struck Mark as he sat in Matt's driveway and stared at the dark house. That day was the last time he had truly relaxed and enjoyed life. Since then, it had been all stress and shock, heartache, and healing.

Not even his parents or sisters knew what had happened in his life in the past few weeks. His dad had lost his pastoral position in Athens due to marital issues, and now it had happened to Mark too. He felt shamed by the thought. He had no idea how or when he would tell them. Matt and Patty would be the first to know. But he wasn't about to dump that on them at midnight.

Mark leaned his seat all the way back, burrowed deep into his warmest sleeping bag, stretched his aching back, and sighed. Here in the Monroes' familiar driveway, he felt a measure of peace for the first time in a long time. He wouldn't live with the Monroes, of course, but this would be a home base. Here were people who would welcome him and love him. He hadn't had that in what seemed like years.

With these comforting thoughts, he fell into an exhausted sleep.

* * *

"She what?" Patty Monroe stared at Mark, aghast.

He sat in the Monroes' warm and welcoming kitchen, a steaming plate of crisp bacon, buttered grits, and over-easy eggs in front of him. A piping hot mug of strong, black coffee sat at his elbow. Patty knew just how Mark liked everything, right down to the warm plate. When you put eggs on a cold plate, they get cold way too fast, and Mark liked his breakfast plates hot.

They'd both been very patient, waiting until the meal was in front of him before asking what he was doing there. They sat at the kitchen table on either side of him, still wearing their pajamas and robes. They'd been surprised to see him but welcomed him as he'd known they would.

Mark hadn't been hungry in weeks. He was too depressed. Now he was suddenly ravenous. Between bites he told them the whole story, taking all the responsibility for his failed marriage. After all, Nancy had been willing to go to counseling. Mark's own pride and temper were ultimately the reason why he was at this point now.

When he finished, they both just stared at him. Matt recovered first.

"Well," he said and watched Mark for a moment. "Now what?"

"It is what it is." Mark drained his coffee cup. Patty refilled it. "My ministry career is done. Now I start over."

"What are you going to do?" Patty put the coffee pot back on the counter and took her seat beside him.

"I have no idea. I'll figure it out. God will provide for me. He always has."

Silence. They both just looked at him. Here he was, a trained minister with a bachelor's degree in biology and a master's degree in biblical studies, and all of it seemed pretty much useless since he couldn't work in a church.

"Not to sound mean or ugly, Mark, but what are you good at?" Patty asked.

Good question. What was he good at? He was a little bit good at a lot of things. If he had to put it into words, he supposed he was best at making things happen. In high school, he built a lawn care business from scratch; by the time he was sixteen, he was taking care of twenty-two lawns. When he was called to mission work, he took the bit in his teeth and went to Alaska for a year, doing construction work for a church and building arctic entryways for natives, in addition to working as a bookkeeper for the hospital and a jillion other things he'd done to survive. God had blessed everything he did. Finding work had never been an issue, but what was he actually good at?

The Monroes were still looking at him, waiting for an answer to Patty's question.

"I guess I'm not really sure," he said finally. "For the last couple of years, I've known what I was going to do, so it hasn't been an issue."

"Let's look at it another way," Matt said. "Why did you come back here?"

"Because I know the people and the town, and I have friends here. It's home."

"So that's where you start."

"Where?"

"With what you know."

Patty nodded. "They know you at the seminary. Go over and let them know you're back in town and looking for work. I'll check the job board at the church too, and I'll pick up a copy of the paper for you."

Mark thought about it. Right now he wasn't looking for a career, just a way to eat. Patty's suggestion sounded like good common sense. "Sounds like a plan."

He dragged his duffel bag in from his Jeep and fished out some clothes that were decent-looking, if a bit rumpled. Wordlessly Patty held out her hand, and Mark knew what that meant. When she gave those clothes back to him, they would be ironed and neat.

"Mind if I take a shower?" he asked her.

"Go," she said. Matt just smiled. He'd lived with her a lot of years and knew exactly the sort of woman she was—no-nonsense, quick-thinking, and fast-acting. Matt and Mark were best friends, but Patty was like a second mom. He was grateful for them both.

Within thirty minutes, Mark was showered and dressed in freshly pressed khakis and a long-sleeved, red polo shirt. He climbed back in his Jeep and headed to the Southern Baptist Theological Seminary, where he'd just graduated mere months earlier.

9

Mark pulled up and parked at the seminary, and just sat and looked at it for a full minute. Things hadn't changed much, and he found that to be comforting in one way and alarming in another.

The campus went on as it always had, with its dignified red brick buildings and manicured lawns. Students of all ages walked past, sticking to the sidewalks and well-trodden paths. If he looked closely at the grass in the common area, he could still see the fading tire marks.

Southern was the kind of seminary Mark had wanted, one that would make him think for himself instead of having a predetermined doctrine drilled into him. They had difficult teachers and courses, with content that could lead an unseasoned Christian off track. Top-notch teachers and speakers from every viewpoint regularly appeared on the calendar, including renowned pastors such as Billy Graham alongside atheists, Buddhists, Hindus, and Islamists.

Mark was ready for a challenge like that, craved it even. There were those, however, who weren't as prepared or equipped. And he'd seen first-hand what this approach did to some people. Rather than preparing them for a life of ministry, it turned them against Christ completely.

He'd graduated from Southern in June, on a warm night that belied the cold in his heart. One after another, he'd watched classmates lose their way in Southern's merciless, challenging system. Good kids who could have been used by the Lord were lost.

On graduation night he looked around at the relatively small number who'd made it through and thought about the ones who hadn't. With icy determination, not anger, he waited until the campus was long asleep. He watched from the shadows until the sprinklers came on in the common area and then raced around and around in his Jeep, executing perfect doughnuts and leaving deep, muddy ruts in the immaculate lawn. He didn't stop until the area was a boggy, muddy mess.

No one knew; no one came running. He guessed graduation night was a night off for everyone. Then he had washed his car, picked up his wife, and headed to south Florida. She didn't ask what had taken him so long, and he didn't tell her. This was still a secret that no one knew, and it would remain that way. This act of defiance was Mark's personal protest on behalf of those who'd fallen.

He smiled slightly and sighed. It had felt good at the time, but it hadn't made a bit of difference. Things were still the same, and what he'd done was wrong. What he was about to do now carried a wry kind of justice, even if he was the only one who knew.

He climbed out of his Jeep, smoothed his clothes, and strode straight up the stairs of the building to find his favorite, most influential professor.

Dr. Dale Moody had been Mark's professor for his entire tenure at Southern. He'd written three acclaimed books and used them as texts in his classes. He taught New Testament theology, Old Testament theology, historical theology, philosophy of religion, and systematic theology. It was the latter that led to some lively conversations late into the night after Mark had spent evenings push-mowing his lawn. Systematic theology seeks to take Christian beliefs and put them into an orderly whole. Mark had never had a problem with his beliefs being other than orderly. Some things, he believed, just won't make sense until we get to heaven. We're called to accept those things on faith, and he was okay with that.

Dr. Moody was strong in his beliefs and compelling in his arguments. Mark loved matching wits with him. In the end, they agreed to disagree, and both of them continued to believe they were right.

A generation before, Dr. Moody had also taught Mark's dad Old Testament theology during his time at Southern. He'd been a good friend to Mark's parents, even at one point changing his mom's flat tire in the pelting rain. Remembering, Mark was excited to see his old friend again.

He tapped on the door of Dr. Moody's old office and stuck his head inside expectantly, but the man who looked up from his work was a stranger.

"Yes, can I help you?"

Mark glanced at the name on the door. Sure enough, the nameplate said Wendell Crane, not Dale Moody. "I'm sorry, I was looking for Dr. Moody. This used to be his office. Do you know where I can find him?"

"And you are?"

He stepped into the office and stuck out his hand. "Mark Smith. I graduated a few months ago and just got back in town."

His eyes narrowed. "Mark Smith. Yes, I remember you."

"You do?" He wasn't sure if this was good or bad.

"I was at Dr. Moody's house one day when you were cutting his grass. You came in to refill your water bottle. You were wearing cut-off blue jeans and a University of Tennessee Baptist Student Union T-shirt."

"You've got a good memory." Privately Mark thought that was a little creepy.

He smiled without humor. "Photographic."

Mark shifted his weight. This was already turning into a long day, and his back was killing him. "Where's Dr. Moody's office now?"

"He retired about the same time you graduated. Before the next semester started."

"He's not in bad health or anything?"

"Not as far as I know. I heard he and the seminary had a difference of opinion about a couple of things. Remember how he used to hand out changes to some seminary policies in class?"

"Yeah."

"I think that came to a boiling point, and he retired."

"Oh. Wow. Is he still in town?"

"Yep. Same house. Tell him hi."

"Will do."

Mark trotted back out to his car, more eager than ever to see Dr. Moody. Retired? Really? They were going to have lots to talk about.

As he drove, he remembered the issues Wendell was talking about. Southern had its Abstract of Principles, a set of beliefs it had had since its founding, and it required its professors to agree with them. Dr. Moody didn't agree with one, in particular, the one related to apostasy, and he handed out revisions of the Abstract of Principles to his students. He and Mark had had some particularly lively conversations on this subject.

Apostasy refers to the abandonment of religious beliefs. Dr. Moody believed a person can lose his or her salvation by willfully throwing it away and insisting on living their own way instead of God's way. He'd written a book about it, called *The Word of Truth*. Mark believed that when a person is truly saved, salvation is permanent. The question lies in whether a person was ever truly saved or not.

Dr. Moody often said that a lot of people were going to be very surprised at judgment time. Mark agreed with that, but their reasoning was different. Mark believed that a great many people think they're saved because they once walked down a church aisle and made a statement of faith. But Jesus clearly teaches that the gospel message takes root and flourishes in some people, while in others, it does not. When it takes root, a person is changed, and that change is evident in his character and his works. That person loves God and wants to please Him. If it does not take root, then that person was never saved to begin with.

Christians who genuinely seek to follow Jesus have no reason to worry about their salvation. If they don't seek Him or want to serve Him, then they have every reason to worry. It's a key difference, and Dr. Moody was a debate champion with the heart of a bulldog. Mark respected him immensely for sharing his views with him and listening to his own opinions. If Wendell was right, this difference of opinion had led to Dr. Moody's retirement.

The drive was short, and within ten minutes, Mark was pulling up to Dr. Moody's modest home. It looked just like it had last time he'd been here. It was a nice neighborhood, but the house wasn't a big, elaborate home, and he didn't drive a luxury car. It wasn't his style.

Smoke came out of the chimney, evidence that he was home and enjoying a fire in the fireplace. It was about lunchtime, and he and his wife were probably sitting down to eat.

The yard was brown and sparse now in the Louisville winter, but Mark knew that when spring came, Dr. Moody would hook up his hoses and water his lawn liberally. It would be the greenest one in the neighborhood.

Mark smiled as he climbed out of the Jeep and made his way carefully up the icy walk. Dr. Moody was going to be surprised.

He rang the doorbell and only waited seconds before he heard footsteps. The door swung briskly open, and Dr. Moody's mouth fell open.

"Mark!"

"Hey, Dr. Moody."

"Come in, come in!" He immediately swung the door open and motioned Mark inside. "What in the world brings you here? Last I heard you were living the high life in South Florida!"

Mark stepped inside and gave Dr. Moody a firm, brisk handshake. "It's a long story."

"Well, I want to hear it. Come on in."

"I hear you have some news too."

"Where'd you hear a thing like that?"

"Wendell Crane."

"Who?"

"The guy who has your office now. I went looking for you and found him instead."

Dr. Moody's eyes glimmered with humor. "Bet that was a shock. What'd he say?"

"That you and the school had a difference of opinion, and you retired."

"That about sums it up."

The two men rounded the corner into the kitchen and surprised

Dr. Moody's wife, who was putting lunch on the table.

"Mildred, look who the cat dragged in," Dr. Moody announced.

"Well, my stars. Mark Smith. Thought you were gone for good."

"I thought so too."

"You'll have lunch, of course." She swiftly set another place setting. "We're having chili."

In no time the three of them were plowing into Mrs. Moody's excellent white chicken chili, topped with sour cream and accompanied by cornbread. For the second time in a few hours, Mark actually found himself hungry.

"So, do tell," Dr. Moody said. "What's the long story?"

Mark sighed. Where to start? "Well, number one, I've learned my lesson about not making decisions until the Lord tells me what He wants me to do. Bad things happen when you jump the gun."

"Good advice. What's number two?"

"When you make the wrong decision, don't compound it by doing something you know perfectly well He doesn't want you to do."

As they ate, Mark filled them in. They were near the bottom of their bowls when he finished. "So now I'm looking for what God wants me to do next."

Dr. Moody put his spoon down and regarded Mark. "What are you thinking?"

"No idea yet. Right now I'm just looking to keep body and soul together. That's why I came back to Louisville. It's what I know."

"Well, you know there's money in this town."

"That's kind of why I came to see you. I thought you might know some people who need some work done."

Dr. Moody and his wife exchanged a knowing look. "Like what?" Mildred asked.

"Yard projects, small home improvement jobs, that sort of thing."

Now they smiled at each other, then at him. "Ever installed a sprinkler system?"

10

Mark was sure his back was breaking, but he'd finished the Moodys' sprinkler system and had enough work booked to last him for six months. His clients were all seminary professors with big houses and money to burn. It was exactly the type of work he wasn't supposed to do, but he couldn't worry about that now. He had to eat.

As he worked and made money, he privately marveled at God's sense of humor. He had started out thinking that this would be a kind of penance for the havoc he'd wreaked on the seminary's common area, but it was turning out to be anything but.

His housing situation had worked itself out too. Patty Monroe had come up with a job opportunity as a waterbed salesman in downtown Charlestown, and the job came with a rent-free apartment above the storefront.

Mark had never worked in sales before, but he found he was good at it. He settled into his job and his new apartment, and also his old church in Charlestown.

He hadn't forgotten about the girl on the beach, far from it. He'd spent hours on the phone, calling alumni offices at all of the colleges on his list. He'd tried everything to track down Joy and her friend, but without a last name and more information, the search was turning up nothing. There was a Joy Matthews who graduated from Columbia College in 1983, but his description of his beach girl could have fit any of a hundred girls who were there at the same time. The school wasn't giving out Joy Matthews' contact information without a better reason than Mark had, and he was not going to lie.

He was trying to track down a copy of the Columbia College yearbook from 1983, but it was slow going. In those days before the Internet, getting information was slow and difficult.

One Saturday in May, he was taking a break from work and poring over the information he'd gathered. Almost nothing, really. The ideas that had seemed so reasonable in January were weak and pitiful now. He was out of options.

He absently flipped on the television, and images at the Kentucky Derby flickered on. Oh yeah, that was today. The world-famous horse race was being held at Churchill Downs here in Louisville. In all the years Mark had been in Louisville, he'd never had any desire to go to a Derby. But now, so he wouldn't sound like an uninformed idiot when customers came into the store, he tuned half of his brain into the telecast. The other half remained focused on the list in front of him. Had he been missing something all this time, something that was right in front of him?

Then somehow, in the sea of people on the grainy color television screen, he caught a glimpse of a familiar face—a girl in a collage of other faces. He did a double take, then a triple take. The cameraman must have liked her too because the screen suddenly became filled with her face. Then she turned and looked directly at the camera. Her face, framed with curly blonde hair, was flushed with excitement, her blue eyes sparkling. She grinned and waved at the camera.

Mark couldn't breathe. It was her. Right here, not more than a few miles away from him.

He jumped up and looked wildly about—and quickly realized that there was nothing he could do. By the time he would be able to get to the racetrack, the race would have been over for hours, and the crowd would be gone. There was no way he could find the girl, and no one would know who she was. Louisville was a big place, and trying to find her would be pointless.

He watched futilely, heart pounding, as the camera panned to another scene at the packed racetrack. Then his thoughts went back slowly, inexorably, almost in nerve-wracking slow motion, to a conversation on the showroom floor this morning. He had been working up a king waterbed sale for a couple who wanted to finish the transaction quickly so they could get to the racetrack.

"What's the hurry? The race isn't until later today, right?" Mark had no idea what people do at racetracks, other than watch horses run around in circles.

"For the parties, of course," the gentleman said. "And the pretty girls, all dressed up in their best. The prettiest girls are at Churchill Downs!"

Mark privately doubted that, seeing as how the one he deemed prettiest was somewhere in South Carolina. But he kept his thoughts to himself.

"Hey, dude, you busy all day?" the man suddenly asked him. "Our friend got sick, and we've got an extra ticket if you want to come with us and see what it's all about."

"Yeah, has to be better than sitting here and watching it on TV!" his wife chimed in.

"That's assuming I'm going to be watching it on TV," Mark said. "As much as I'd like to take you up on that, I actually do have a lot going on this afternoon. I need to stick close. But thanks."

And there it was, he thought as he watched the girl of his dreams fade away yet again. Both times he'd seen her, there'd been a chance. The first time, he was just too stupid to get her phone number. This time, he hadn't realized, he hadn't even had a tiny clue that a chance invitation earlier in the day would be the key that could have gotten him close to her if only he'd known. He had no doubt that if he'd gone to the race, he would have run into her. His heart hurt at the realization.

God often doesn't answer prayers the way we expect Him to, Mark realized yet again. We work and plan, and we expect those efforts to bear fruit because that's just the best we can do. If we step back and watch how God unfolds the big picture, we would probably get a better idea of how He works. Our minds will never be His mind, and our thoughts will never be His thoughts. However, if we could get out of our own bog long enough to listen to His voice and pay attention to what He's doing around us, we might find ourselves more enlightened. More blessed.

Now Mark felt more dejected about this girl than he had since he'd first met her. Before, he'd felt like there was hope. Now he'd had two chances, four years apart. Both completely unexpected. How in the world would he know when and if another chance was coming? And how could he keep his whole life on hold, just waiting?

He couldn't. Slowly, something tipped and crashed in his heart, very much like a building imploding on itself, and he almost shuddered with the finality of it. He didn't know when or if God would give him another chance to be with his beach girl, and so he had to let her go. Yes, he needed to keep his eyes and ears and heart open but not for her. He was nearly twenty-seven years old, and he wanted to be married. He wanted someone who loved God, who would love him and cook for him, who would give him children and be beside him until they both turned old and gray. He wanted someone that he could find attractive but also easy to talk to. Someone who would be his friend as well as his lover.

His next wife would be forever.

11

Fran Chapman and her fellow reporters were having a blast at the Kentucky Derby. They were at the pre-race party in the infield, getting interviews from some of the horse owners and trainers. TV cameras were everywhere, and once a camera seemed to focus on her. She gave it her best smile and waved, hoping her mom was watching. The smile and wave were for her.

The next hours were frantically busy, as Fran worked madly to capture the atmosphere of this incredible place. She wanted her readers to be able to see the sights, hear the sounds, and smell the smells of Derby weekend in Louisville. People back in Aiken knew some of these horses and trainers, and she was skilled at finding extra nuggets that made a story much more interesting and personal. She found those nuggets, dug them out, and polished them until they shone. The results of the race itself were only secondary. The sports editor would capture that.

Much later, she was finally back in her hotel room, exhausted but still exhilarated. What a rush! A horse named Ferdinand had won the Run for the Roses. Her ears were still ringing from the roar of more than one hundred thousand people.

The phone beside her bed rang, and she smiled at it. There was only one person it could be.

"Hello?" She gripped the phone between her shoulder and her ear and settled herself on the bed.

"Hey." Jeremy's deep voice came in her ear. Even though he'd been born and raised in the South, he spoke without an accent of any kind. Aiken was a different kind of Southern town, with lots of influence from the horse community and from the nuclear reservation that was its economic heartbeat. Jeremy's parents, James and Mary Gideon, came from the North, and Jeremy had been trained in radio in college.

"Hey," she answered.

"I saw you on TV."

"That was the craziest thing. All of a sudden, the camera was just there. I barely had time to smile and wave."

"You looked great. You working hard?"

"Nonstop. I just got back to my room."

"Just now? That's a long day."

"It was long but it was amazing."

They chatted about her experiences in Louisville and then about his grandmother, who was scheduled to arrive soon from Philadelphia and spend the summer with Jeremy's parents.

"Hey, so I've got a surprise for you next weekend. Don't make plans," Jeremy said.

"A surprise?"

"Next Sunday is a special day."

She drew a blank for a minute, then remembered. Next Sunday would be May 11, which would be exactly one year since they'd met. "I know what next Sunday is. Give me a hint about the surprise."

"Nope. No hints. Just save the day."

They said goodbye, then Fran hung up the phone and stared at it. She and Jeremy had been dating steadily for nearly a year. There had been talk of the future. Could this be it?

She set the phone on the bedside table and pondered. She had no brothers and a sick father, and had gone to an all-female college, so she had no up-close experience with men at all, on any level. She found them to be mysterious creatures, who spoke and acted differently than anything she was used to. They talked loudly, spat, cursed, and seemed to need to be the center of attention. She had never felt any kind of lasting connection with any of them—except that one time at Myrtle Beach, which Jeremy knew nothing about. Now she was beginning to feel a deeper connection with Jeremy.

Jeremy had been patient with her unexpected reactions to things he thought were normal. When some workers came to his rental house, she was horrified and shocked to find urine residue beside the toilet. She was disgusted and was ready to call the landlord and complain until Jeremy explained to her that sometimes guys just don't have very good aim. That's normal, he said.

Fran and Jeremy had bonded in one very important area—they both knew what it was like to lose someone they loved. In 1981, his brother, James Jr., had gone out one night to visit an employee in the hospital and never made it home. His little car had been found wrapped around a tree, and the investigation concluded that James had dozed off at the wheel—no alcohol, no wrongdoing, just fatigue. He left a young wife, Jennifer, and a baby girl, Annemarie. The incident strained the entire family's relationship with God. His mother, Mary, never really recovered from the shock. Fran hadn't known her before the accident, but Jeremy said she was a different person. Burying a child, he said, is the most difficult thing you can do.

Fran had quickly fallen in love with Jeremy's dad, James. He adopted her into the family and treated her like a daughter. It was the first time in her life she'd had a normal, healthy dad, and she soaked it in.

She knew, because his family had told her, that Jeremy was head over heels in love with her. They told her they'd never seen him fall like this for anyone. She wasn't sure what "in love" was supposed to feel like. She did know she felt comfortable in Jeremy's family, and she enjoyed being with him. Julia had spent lots of time with him, and she approved. Fran liked his dark good looks and his strength of character, and she enjoyed his touch and his kisses. She knew Jeremy would be a good husband and father, just like his dad. She would never have to worry about whether he would be faithful to her.

It did not occur to Fran to pray for God to reveal His will to her. She'd grown up in the Presbyterian church and had given her life to Christ as a child, but her spiritual growth had stopped there. She didn't know what discipleship was until Mark Smith explained it to her many years later. She knew she belonged to Jesus, but she did not know how to have a growing, vibrant relationship with Him. She wanted one, craved one. She had rededicated her life several times, hoping to get the inner fire she saw in others. She didn't understand, and no one had ever told her, that the next step was hers. She had to seek God in His Word and in prayer before she could find a deeper relationship with Him. So she spun her spiritual wheels, and no one knew.

Not knowing how to ask God about Jeremy, Fran reached the conclusion on her own that what she shared with him was enough to build a life on. Deeper love and intimacy would come with time and familiarity. She was nearly twenty-five years old, and it was time to get on with it. Whenever he was ready to ask, she was ready to say yes.

12

"You can open your eyes now." Fran moved her hands off her eyes and saw that they were standing in a muddy vacant lot. She looked around. "What is it?"

"It's going to be home."

She looked around, then into his eyes. "What?"

"I got a permanent job at the Savannah River Site. This is going to be my house."

Her eyes grew big and round. This was huge. Jeremy had been working a temporary job at SRS while he applied for other work. Fran had been waiting to see where he found a job before she decided where she was going to apply next. The *Aiken Standard* wasn't a place where writers usually spent a career. She was hoping her next job would be in a bigger city with a bigger newspaper. Questions bubbled in her mind like Bingo balls, and she grabbed the first one that popped up. If he'd been hired at SRS...

"Here?" she squeaked.

"This is my lot, and it's going to be my house."

"It's like five minutes from your parents."

"I know! Great, right?"

She looked around and into his shining eyes, and gradually, the significance of this moment dawned on her. For him, it was the beginning of a commitment. It was his way of showing her that he was here and staying put. He was ready to settle down. This was huge, she realized. He was looking at her with love and hope. She smiled back at him and looped her arms around his neck.

"Yes, it's great. I'm so proud of you. I know your parents are over the moon."

"Dad actually helped me with the down payment on this lot. It's a great lot because it's here on a cul-de-sac. Lots of privacy. This is the first house to be built on this street."

"When does construction start?"

"As soon as weather permits. You can see it's kind of muddy now. Here, I'll show you some pictures."

He led her back to his car and pulled out a portfolio with drawings of the new house and every room. It would be a Cape Cod style house with a living room, dining room, kitchen, two bedrooms and a bath on the first floor. The second floor, Jeremy said, would be an office, a rec room, and a second bath, and it would be finished later.

"Hopefully I can move in around this time next year," he said.

"What job did you get at SRS?" she asked.

"Producing and directing videos."

"That's so good, Jeremy. It's what you've been looking for."

"It all just kind of fell into place."

"I'm so happy for you."

He looked deep into her eyes. "I always said I'd never come back to Aiken, and I'd never work at Savannah River. I know you said you didn't want to live here permanently. But I've learned that you never say never. This is a good place to put down roots."

And with that, all of Fran's plans shifted. If Jeremy were here, of course she would be here too. She would stay at the *Aiken Standard* and go back to school and get her master's degree so she would have more professional options. Maybe she would teach English.

The most important thing was she now had no doubts as to Jeremy's intentions. They would be together. It was just a matter of when.

She rested her head on his shoulder and felt at peace.

13

Mark sat in the Monroes' familiar, homey kitchen and looked over their tax information. They had had some complicating factors this year and had filed an extension. Since he'd had lots of bookkeeping experience, he'd offered to take a look.

It was June now, and the kitchen windows were open. Mark tilted his head back and let the breeze cool his face. It had been a long morning, working on a yard project in Dr. Moody's neighborhood. He still wore his sweaty t-shirt and gym shorts. It felt good to sit for a bit and rest his back. A protein drink sat at his elbow, and he munched on a granola bar as he worked.

"You're going to spoil your lunch with that drink and granola, Mark," Patty said from near the sink, where she was putting together tuna casserole for lunch.

"Never," he said without looking up, but privately thought that wouldn't be so bad. Patty was a wizard in the kitchen, but he wasn't a fan of tuna casserole.

"I'm making Lisa's favorite. She should be home any minute. It's been too long."

"Where's she been? I forget."

"Modeling school. She thought she'd give it a try. She didn't like it, so she's coming home."

"She just graduated high school, right?"

"No, that was a couple of years back. She's twenty now." Patty put the finishing touches on the casserole and popped it into the oven. "So what's up with you, Mark?"

"Just working hard." He continued to sift through the pile of tax forms. He had file folders in a box, and as he studied each form, he placed it into the appropriate file. The pile on the table was steadily dwindling. "It's been good to get back to church. I feel comfortable at Charlestown."

"Have you thought any more about what you want to do?"

"Just something where I can be serving the kingdom. People do that all the time, wherever they work. God gives opportunities all the time if you just keep your eyes open."

Patty left the kitchen to go check on the laundry, and at that moment, the back door opened. A young, slim girl with a long blonde ponytail staggered in, dragging a massive suitcase. "Mom! I'm home!" she called. So far she hadn't seen Mark sitting at the table, and he took the opportunity to watch her before he announced his presence.

So this was Lisa. He'd heard about her for years, of course. When he was in seminary here, Lisa was in high school and was rarely home. They'd never actually run into each other until now.

She was tall, probably taller than him, which made sense since she'd been at modeling school. She wore a form-fitting t-shirt, shorts, and sneakers. She was built like a wisp, all long and lean with no curves to speak of. Her blonde ponytail was looped through a baseball cap. Her mom said she was twenty, but she could easily pass for sixteen.

Then she turned and Mark got a good look at her eyes—green, honest eyes with thick dark lashes.

"Oh, hi!" She crossed the kitchen to him and held out her hand. "I'm Lisa. Matt and Patty's daughter."

He stood and took her hand. "I'm Mark. It's so good to finally meet you."

"You're Mark? Wow, finally! It feels like you're a brother I've never met before. I think my parents adopted you years ago."

"They kind of did. They're great."

"They are."

Patty came in carrying a big basket of laundry but dropped it onto the counter when she saw her daughter.

"Honey! You're home!" She folded Lisa into a big, warm hug.

"At last." She took a deep breath and blew at her bangs. "I'm not going anywhere for a while."

"You don't have to. I've got your favorite meal in the oven."

"I smell it."

"Let's get you unloaded so you can relax."

"I can help." Mark stood and stretched.

"No, Mark, you've got a lot to do here." Patty motioned him back into his chair and gave him a motherly look that said *and besides, I know your back hurts.* "We've got it."

So he dived back into his work, watching them when they didn't know he was looking. Mother and daughter chatted easily, but even though Mark had never met Lisa before, he could see the strain in her eyes. He'd always been pretty good at reading people, and he knew she was glad to be home with her mother.

By the time they got everything out of the car, the tuna casserole was ready. The four of them sat at the kitchen table and dug in. Mark moved the food around on his plate and watched the family interact. They chatted easily and lovingly as if it hadn't been months since Lisa had been home. He realized all over again that here was unconditional love, family, and something else as well.

This is cool, he thought. *They treat her just like they've always treated me. They really did adopt me.* The feeling was warm and wonderful. He loved his parents and sisters, but he'd been gone for so long that the Monroes felt more like his family now.

Mark turned his attention to Lisa, watching her as she opened up about modeling school. She was a pretty girl and had all the physical attributes to be a good model, but she hadn't expected the business end of it, and she felt uncomfortable flaunting her body.

"It just wasn't what I thought it would be," she said. "It's not what I want to do. I have no idea what I want to do."

"Honey, you're just twenty years old. You've got your whole life to figure it out," Matt said.

"Absolutely," Patty chimed in. She got up and refilled everyone's tea glasses. "You're home now, and there's no hurry at all."

*   *   *

Over the next month, Mark found himself at the Monroes' house more and more. Yes, he was working on their taxes, but there was something more. In Lisa he saw a freshness, an innocence that he found appealing. He began to spend as much time with her as her parents and the work he went there to do. They went on long walks and shared their hearts. They were both at crucial crossroads in their lives, at the beginning of whatever came next. They both wanted to settle down, have kids, and be a good, stable family.

He was completely comfortable with her and her parents. Here, he knew he was loved and accepted.

By the end of July, Mark's mind was made up, and his soul was at peace. He presented Lisa with the best diamond he could afford, and she said yes. At the end of December 1986, in a small ceremony with Doug Taylor at his side, they were married. They honeymooned in Hawaii and began their life together.

14

Several months passed and Jeremy kept Fran guessing. Every minute she was with him, she expected him to propose. She couldn't imagine what he was waiting for. She was twenty-six years old. She could almost hear her biological clock ticking.

He was preoccupied with finishing the house. It was taking much longer than he'd anticipated, well over a year already, because of weather and the schedule of the workers. His sister, Rachel, was an expert decorator. With her oversight, he made all the choices for carpet, wallpaper, paint, light fixtures, appliances, and even small decorative knick-knacks. Month by month, the house came together. It had rich red brick around its skirt and front, and blue siding on its back three sides. James and Mary were also always there, excited that their only surviving son would be living so close. Fran was excited too, but her excitement was different. She could barely breathe for the anticipation.

Maybe when the house was finished, she thought, *he would ask.*

Have patience, said the small voice in her head.

I know, I know. Still, she was on pins and needles.

One day at Augusta Mall, they went into a jewelry store, and Jeremy asked her what kind of ring she wanted. She liked a marquis diamond, and the one she wanted was a half-carat, under a thousand dollars, yellow gold. She tried it on, and they admired it together. Fran held her breath, waiting. The moment came and went. Jeremy smiled at her, and the saleslady put the ring back into the case.

The calendar flipped from November to December 1987. The date was finally set for Jeremy to move into his house. Fran eagerly sped through her day at work and flung herself into her car. She pushed every speed limit as she flew across town to see what was going on. When she pulled up into his yard, cars were everywhere, lined up in the street. Workers filed in and out, carrying things. Jeremy and Rachel strode from room to room, giving instructions. Fran eased her way inside. Jeremy spotted her, and his face lit up.

"Hey, you." He held his arm out, and she snuggled against his side.

"Hey! How's it going?"

"It's going. There're still a few more punch list things, but they'll all get done over the next week. Nothing to keep me from moving in."

"Wow."

"Yeah."

Rachel strode up to them, dusting off her hands. "Jeremy, they need you in the kitchen." She turned to Fran, smiling. "So what do you think?"

"I just walked in the door. What I've seen looks great."

"I think it's all coming together."

Fran took her time, roaming around the house and dodging workers. Everything really did look nice. Jeremy had been dedicated to this task, and Rachel was a gifted decorator. The whole house was done in blue and rose decorative accents, with neutral carpets and paint. Shiny brass light fixtures and matching hardware. An elegant chandelier in the dining room hung over a formal dining set. Charleston prints were on the walls. Boxes still stood everywhere, but that would be a work in progress.

For the next few days, Fran helped Jeremy unpack, and he supervised the last few punch list items. Then he signed off on the house and proclaimed it done. On Sunday afternoon, December 10, they unpacked the last box, flopped on the sofa, and grinned at each other.

"This calls for a celebration," Jeremy announced.

"What did you have in mind?"

"I think you should go home and put on a pretty dress and let's go have a nice dinner. I'll pick you up in an hour."

Fran did as he said, trying not to read anything into it. He was just excited and wanted to celebrate. Completely understandable. But she took great care with her look, pulling her hair up around her face and letting it hang in ringlets down her back. Just a little makeup and a little heel. She and Jeremy were nearly the same height, and she didn't want to appear taller. She was ready when he pulled up in his Camaro.

"Don't you look pretty!" He climbed out of the car and came around to open the door for her.

"Thank you. It's a night to celebrate."

They drove across the river to Augusta, Georgia, and to a nice restaurant at Augusta Mall where they both ordered thick steaks. While they waited for their food, Jeremy told Fran funny stories from work.

"So Friday, we were working on getting the company president to tape an employee message. We have, like, twenty-five thousand employees, so we can't just have a meeting."

"Right."

"And we're in the middle of a big construction project and needed to give everybody an update."

"Okay, go on."

"I don't know what happened, because our president is usually really good. But he sat in the chair in the studio and just froze. He got this deer-in-the-headlights look and couldn't do it."

Fran sipped her Pepsi. "What did you do?"

"Took a break. The president and I went outside and stretched our legs. Then a guy walked by on the sidewalk, and I had the president tell this guy what was going on with the project, and I videotaped it while he talked, like a man on the street thing. It was perfect."

"That was pretty smart."

"You do what you gotta do. Some people think best on their feet."

They finished dinner and strolled out of the restaurant into the mall. Jeremy took Fran's hand as they walked and talked. Before long, their wandering took them upstairs and to the jewelry store where Fran had picked out the ring she wanted.

"Let's go in and look at that ring again." Jeremy nudged her inside.

The saleslady remembered them and immediately pulled out the ring. "Would you like to try it on again?"

Fran looked at Jeremy. "Go ahead, try it on," he said.

She slid the ring on her finger. It was perfect, just what she wanted. She was afraid to breathe.

"Do you like it?" Jeremy asked.

"It's perfect," she said honestly.

"We'll take it," he told the saleslady.

Fran watched, eyes huge and mouth open, while he paid for the ring and the saleslady slid the box into a small bag. Bag dangling from his fingers, he took her hand and led her outside. They were on the upper level of the mall, and they went to the railing and looked down. The mall was decorated beautifully for Christmas. A choir was singing "Do You Hear What I Hear?" on the lower level. The beautiful, timeless words rang throughout the mall.

Jeremy, still holding Fran's fingers in one hand and the bag in the other, turned to her. "So, do you want to go get some dessert?"

She fumbled. "Sure."

"Do you want to marry me?"

"What?"

He grinned into her eyes, and suddenly she knew he'd been playing her for months. It had been a plan all along. "I love you. I want to spend my life with you. Will you marry me?" He pulled the box out of the bag, opened it, and started to slide the ring on her finger.

"That's the wrong hand," she whispered, and gave him her left hand. He closed his eyes, grimaced at himself, and slid it on.

Tears spilled over onto her cheeks as she watched him and laughed. "Yes, I'll marry you."

They walked back out to the car, steps lighter than air. It was already nine o'clock, but they were bursting with their news. Jeremy drove to the cemetery just outside Aiken and to a spot near the top of a hill. The moon shone down brightly on a bench set among the headstones. Fran had been there before, so she knew it had an engraving that read, "James Andrew Gideon Jr."

"Give me a minute?" he asked her.

"Of course."

She sat and watched, windows up, as Jeremy made his way to the bench and sank down. He stayed there for a long time, talking to his brother, shoulders shaking in sobs. When he came back to the car, his eyes were red-rimmed, and his face was wet. "He would have been my best man," he said simply. "I had to tell him first. He would have loved you."

"I wish I'd gotten the chance to meet him."

He took a deep breath. "What do you want to do now?"

"You up for a little road trip?"

"Are we going to Hickory Tavern?"

"I have to tell my mother this in person."

"Let's go."

It was a ninety-minute drive to Julia's house, and they held hands and filled the time with wedding talk. Fran had been thinking about this for so long that she knew exactly what she wanted. They'd get married at her church in First Presbyterian Church in Aiken. She would have two honor attendants, Joy and Chris, plus four additional bridesmaids and a flower girl. Jeremy would have an equal number of groomsmen, and his dad would be his best man.

"Where do you want to go on our honeymoon?" he asked.

"Oh, I don't know. Somewhere warm."

"We'll talk to a travel agent and figure it out," he said.

It was eleven o'clock when they pulled unannounced into Julia's driveway, but Fran saw the bedroom lights on and knew her mother was still up. It wouldn't have mattered if the house had been dark, but it was nice that they wouldn't be dragging her out of bed.

They rang the bell so Julia would know they were there, and Fran let herself in with her key. Her big cat, Freckles, wound himself around her feet like a black-and-white ribbon. "Hey, boy." She bent and picked him up. He purred and rubbed his cheek against hers.

Julia came into the room as Fran set Freckles back down on the floor. Ever astute, her eyes locked immediately onto Fran's left hand, but she said nothing.

Fran and Jeremy sat in the den, and they all made small talk for about ten minutes. Fran kept her left hand in plain sight, waiting for Julia to say something, while Julia worked hard to keep her eyes off it and keep the conversation going.

Finally, Jeremy was the one who caved. "Well, I guess you know we didn't drive all this way to make small talk, right?"

"Yes, I figured."

He took a deep breath and glanced at Fran. "Tonight, I asked Fran to be my wife, and she said yes."

"Well, it's about time." Julia stood and folded them both in an embrace. "Let me see."

Fran held out her hand, and Julia admired the ring. "Nice job, Jeremy."

"She picked it out."

"It's beautiful."

"I want you to know that I'm going to take good care of Fran."

"Oh, I don't have any doubts about that. I couldn't be happier about it. I just wish Pete could have been here to walk her down the aisle. He would have loved you. Welcome to the family, Jeremy."

15

The date was set for June 11, 1988, which meant six months of hectic wedding preparations and honeymoon planning. They'd chosen Bermuda, and all the details were coming together.

Fran soaked it all in, wanting to remember every detail of the months leading up to her wedding. There were dress fittings to be done, tuxes to be chosen, invitations to be ordered and sent, choices for flowers and colors and bridesmaid dresses, premarital counseling, and a million other details. Hundreds of invitations were sent out, and about four hundred people responded that they would attend. Jeremy's parents wanted to provide an extravagant reception at their country club, and Julia agreed.

Fran was so thankful and grateful that her mother could be a part of everything. Jeremy's parents knew everyone in Aiken, and everyone wanted to throw them a party. There was at least one per month. Last year, Chris had moved from Boston to Atlanta, and she came to as many as she could. Julia came to them all.

Most of the parties were for couples, but one was a brunch for ladies, where attendees would make birdseed packets to give out at the reception. Birdseed, not rice, would be thrown at the happy couple as they made their getaway.

Julia, Fran, and Chris shared an odd sense of humor that could be unfortunate at times. They tended to laugh hysterically when other people had mishaps. The Gideons did not share their sense of humor, so Fran often found herself laughing while Jeremy didn't see what was funny. When Fran and her mother and sister got together, it was worse. Whenever anyone tripped or fell or stubbed their toe, they dissolved in fits of giggling. Jeremy just shook his head.

The three of them attended the birdseed packet luncheon together, and it was obvious from the start that there would be issues. The house was decorated beautifully, and platters of food were everywhere. The work stations and most of the food and drinks were set up on a screened porch at the back of the house. There was a sliding glass door, with one step down to the porch.

The ladies were already heavily into the champagne punch when Fran, Julia, and Chris arrived. The party hostess was leading the way to the porch, and one of the ladies misstepped. "Whoops!" she said, bobbling her mimosa glass and barely avoiding going splat onto the refreshment table. The other ladies murmured in concern and helped her regain her balance. Fran couldn't look at her mother and sister. They were already struggling to contain themselves.

The three of them made it safely through the birdseed shower. They had packed up all the gifts and birdseed packets and were loading the car when the same lady wobbled out the front door. She misstepped again and flailed her arms, but this time did not regain her balance. With the other ladies grabbing at her, she spiraled out the front door and into the shrubbery beside the house. While the other ladies solicitously picked her up and plucked branches out of her hair, the Chapman trio fled. They barely made it to their car and around the corner before they were howling hysterically.

"Did you see her face?"

"She took out that first bush, I think."

"They were all so concerned about her. They didn't think it was funny at all."

They pulled over, out of sight of the house, and dissolved into another fit of mirth. When they calmed down and wiped their eyes, they looked fondly at each other.

"I'm so glad you're both here," Fran told her mother and sister sincerely.

Julia hugged her. "Where else would we be?"

16

On the morning of June 11, 1988, Fran had a serious case of butterflies. She didn't understand what was wrong with her. This was
what she'd been wanting for over three years, and it was finally
here. But the butterflies were so bad, she couldn't hold anything
down. She felt nauseous and lightheaded.

She was at the salon with her bridesmaids, getting her hair done,
when her soon-to-be father-in-law came to see her as she sat in the
chair being worked on. This was the man who'd acted as her father
since the day Jeremy brought her home. She loved him like a dad.
She looked at him in misery, feeling as pale as she knew she must
look.

"You okay?" he asked.

"I feel terrible."

"You're just nervous," he said soothingly. "Wedding day jit-
ters."

"I'm scared to death. All those people. What if something goes
wrong?"

"What could go wrong?"

"What if I trip coming down the aisle?" She looked at him with
genuinely terrified eyes. "That could happen. In front of four hundred people!"

"What if it does? Will you still end up married?"

"I guess."

"Isn't that the most important thing? Isn't everything else just a
story that you can tell later?"

The conversation soothed her nerves. She went to the church
and got dressed with her bridesmaids. The photographer roamed

around, taking pictures at every stage. Fran could not look at her mother because she knew she would cry if she did. They had been through so much together.

She did not trip coming down the aisle but took her time, appreciating her bridesmaids. Joy and Chris were her honor attendants. Dana, her niece, acted as junior bridesmaid. Her bridesmaids were a friend from the newspaper, her cousin Leslie, Rachel, and Jeremy's sister-in-law, Jennifer. His niece, Annemarie, was flower girl. They all wore full-length, periwinkle blue dresses and flowered combs in their hair. Chris' husband, Danny, would escort Fran down the aisle. When asked who gave the bride in marriage, he would say, "Her mother does."

The men were in black tie. Groomsmen were Fran's nephew, Jason; Jeremy's brother-in-law, Travis; and three of Jeremy's friends. His dad was best man. Rachel's sons, John and Peter, were ring bearers.

And there Jeremy stood, beside his dad, dark and handsome, his green eyes locked on hers as she made her way slowly down the aisle. Without hesitation, Fran took her place beside him, placed her hand in his, and became his wife.

PART 2:
LIVING

Be anxious for nothing, but in everything
by prayer and supplication with thanksgiving
let your requests be made known to God.
And the peace of God,
which surpasses all comprehension,
will guard your hearts
and your minds in Christ Jesus.

PHILIPPIANS 4:6-7

17

"In the next few years, every big church, like every other operation in the world, will run on computers," Mark concluded his presentation to the administrator at a megachurch in California. "Giving, bookkeeping, human resources—every part of the operation will be computerized. And it can't be just any software, because churches have very specific needs. The question is, when will you be ready to computerize? The question isn't *if,* it's *when.*"

Before he left the church that day, he had pocketed an account worth tens of thousands of dollars for his company. He finished packing up his presentation supplies and headed toward his hotel room. His back hurt more with every step he took with the heavy satchel. He had to get low.

It was the middle of 1988. Mark had spent the first few months of his marriage to Lisa working for a small church software company in Louisville. He found the job posting on a bulletin board at Southern Theological Seminary. At the beginning, he literally didn't know how to turn a computer on. But he knew how to sell, and he could learn anything he put his mind to.

He did well, but it didn't take very long before he knew which company controlled the church software business. It was the one he most often lost accounts to. He contacted the president of that company in Texas and scored an interview because his resume mentioned the fact that he was an Eagle Scout. Within days, Mark and Lisa were moving to Memphis, and Mark's career in church software sales took off.

The move was tough on Lisa. Mark said in later years that there were fingernail tracks all along the interstate between Charlestown and Memphis, so reluctant was she to leave her parents. And Mark's schedule was brutal. He was on the road, coast to coast, five days a week. Lisa was left at home in a strange town, without friends or family, while he worked. She found a job at the United Way in Memphis and attempted to make a new life for herself while he was gone.

His career boomed, mainly because he approached this job like he'd approached nearly everything else in life. Before every presentation, he led the participants in prayer. He only wanted whatever was best for every church he met with, and he sincerely didn't want to make any sale that the Lord didn't want him to make. If it wasn't the right time for that church to computerize, so be it. If God used him to help them, they would be more effective in their ministry. If they didn't buy his product, it was simply not the right time for them. But they usually did.

As he drove to his hotel room, he reflected. He was grateful for his job, his stable marriage, and a future in a field where he felt he was serving the Lord. Truly, he was touching more people than if he'd stayed in the ministry. It really was awesome how God worked.

Mark pulled into his hotel parking lot, got out of the car, and stretched stiffly. His responsibilities were physical and tough for someone with a bad back. He had to lift, twist, and lug heavy briefcases and portfolios. There were times, more often than not, when he felt burning, stabbing pains in his lower back so severe that he wasn't sure how long he could take it. When sciatica kicked in, he couldn't move at all.

Not for the first time, he fiercely regretted the day he'd gotten on that mechanical bull in Myrtle Beach. He remembered the words of the neurosurgeon in Knoxville saying that some day, the partially severed disc in his back would split completely, and then his back could be surgically repaired. He prayed for that day to come, but knew it could be years. Or never. Until then, he had to manage the best he could on pain medications and rest.

Rest? He had a young wife to provide for, and hopefully, one day soon, there would be children if he could ever be home long enough for Lisa to get pregnant. He couldn't see any rest in his near future.

Mark eased himself into his hotel room, stretched out on his bed, and sighed.

"In everything give thanks, for this is God's will for you in Christ Jesus." From nowhere, the Scripture verse from 1 Thessalonians echoed in his heart. That was pretty clear, and it was one of the few places in Scripture that tells unequivocally what God's will is. In everything give thanks. Not just the good things, but everything.

Even his back pain.

He'd studied that Scripture hundreds of times, but now it spoke to him out of nowhere. He was supposed to thank God for his back pain. He knew it helped keep him humble, like Paul and his thorn in the flesh.

So he sank into a kneeling position beside the bed and obeyed. "Lord, I know all things work to the good for those who love You, and that includes back pain. I know doors may be opened in the future that wouldn't have been opened otherwise. I know the pain keeps me humble, and You will use it for Your glory. Thank You that You have all of this under control. Please help me get a good night's sleep and give me a safe trip home tomorrow. And watch over Lisa, Father. She's having a tough time alone. In Jesus' name I pray, amen."

He eased himself back up onto the bed. Then he checked his watch, calculated the time difference, picked up the phone, and called home. Lisa answered on the second ring.

"Hi, sweetheart!" he said. "I've got some good news for you..."

18

"So can anyone tell me when ambition can be a bad thing?" Fran Gideon stopped at the front of her senior English class at South Aiken High School and asked the question to see if they were listening. She had just told them in detail how Shakespeare's Macbeth let ambition get the better of him after the witches' prophecy.

She thought she was doing a pretty good job. Bless Dr. Mishoe—his notes from that long-ago Shakespeare class at Columbia College were still holding true.

She was still technically a student teacher, finishing up the last week before Christmas vacation in 1989. Student teaching was the last step before she would earn her master's degree in English education—she would graduate at the end of the year—and she had been told she was about to get a job offer. She just didn't know when or exactly what it would be.

Fran waited for an answer, and finally it came from one of the six hulking young men who made her life a misery in this class.

"When you listen to a witch, that's what you get," he blurted.

The others snickered and eyed her.

Handling such attitudes was where Fran found teaching high school to be very difficult, and privately she was beginning to wonder if she was cut out for it. It didn't help that she still looked so young. She was now twenty-nine, but she looked about as old as these strapping young men. When the class began to get out of control, she had trouble reining it back in. And when they saw she was flustered, she was toast. It had become like a game to them.

She did have classes she loved, with students who were interested in learning about literature and being a better writer, but the bad experiences were outweighing the good, and it wasn't even close. And this horrible class was at the end of the day, so it was the one she thought about and gnashed her teeth over all evening long.

She had a couple of other possibilities. She could stay with the newspaper, which she loved, but the pay was still terrible. After six years, even with consistent raises, she was still barely making fifteen thousand dollars a year. As a long-term job, it wasn't really a viable option.

She'd also applied to the Public Affairs department at the Savannah River Site, the behemoth nuclear reservation outside Aiken where Jeremy worked. They were hiring people by the hundreds because of huge, new construction projects and also an all-out push to restart three Cold War-era nuclear production reactors. The hiring effort was so substantial that Jeremy had been transferred to a new job in Human Resources, with his only responsibility to handle the new employee orientation program. She'd had an interview two weeks ago but hadn't heard anything.

So right now, Fran didn't know what her next step was. She packed up the papers she had to grade that evening, along with the lesson plans she had to write for tomorrow, and headed home.

As she drove, she asked God His advice about the whole situation. He had stayed her rock even though she still didn't really understand how to have a relationship with Him. She knew she really needed to attend church regularly. It just seemed that when Sundays came, she only wanted to turn over and go back to sleep. When children came along, she told herself, she would make sure they attended church every week.

God, I need Your help to know what to do. Please open the door that You want me to walk through. Please make it clear. The first job offer I get, I will know that's the one You want me to take. Okay, God?

She got home before Jeremy, finished her lesson plans, and had supper nearly ready when she heard his car in the driveway. She was an old-fashioned Southern cook, like her mother and grandmothers before her—just simple, basic fried food. Her granny was over one hundred years old and still healthy as a horse, even though she had eaten this kind of meal every day of her life. Tonight it was fried cubed steak, green beans, rice and gravy. Fran was stirring the gravy when Jeremy came up behind her, slipped his arms around her waist and peered over her shoulder. He sniffed at her ear.

"Smells good."

She giggled. "Me, or the steak?"

"Both."

"It's almost ready."

"I'll wash up."

She filled their plates and set everything down at their small kitchen table, and they were sharing details about their workday when the phone rang. Fran got up to get more tea and snagged the phone on her way by.

"Hello?"

"May I speak to Fran Gideon, please?" A pleasant male voice came in her ear.

"This is she."

"This is Terry Givens, employee communications manager at the Savannah River Site."

"Yes, Terry, how are you tonight?" Terry was the one who had interviewed her two weeks before. She flashed a look in Jeremy's direction. His gaze sharpened.

"I'm fine, thanks. I'm sorry to call you so late, but I wanted to let you know that we'd like you to join our team here at SRS, to handle communications for our reactor restart efforts. I'm prepared to make you an offer of twenty-six."

She went blank. At the *Aiken Standard,* she made just over fifteen thousand a year. The starting salary as an English teacher with a master's degree would be twenty-three thousand. "Is that twenty-six thousand a year?"

He chuckled. "No, it's twenty-six hundred a month."

She did the math and gave Jeremy an astonished look; at the same time, she remembered her prayer just a couple hours earlier. This had to be the answer!

Without hesitating, she said, "Thank you, Terry—I'd be happy to accept your offer. I can't wait to join you."

"That's great! Can you start right after the first of the year? Say January 2?"

"That would be fine, and thank you again!"

"You have a great holiday, and we'll see you in January."

She hung up, mouth still open, and flung herself at her amazed husband. "I'm going to work at SRS!"

They were still talking excitedly and putting food away when the phone rang again fifteen minutes later. Smiling, she answered it. "Hello?"

"Is Fran Gideon in, please?"

"This is she."

"This is Diana Brunson in Personnel at Aiken County Schools. I know you've been wondering and I wanted to tell you as quickly as I knew. As it turns out, you actually have a choice of two teaching positions, and they're both at South Aiken High School. I just need to know which one you want, so I can fill the other one. One is the classes you've been teaching."

"What's the other one?"

"Pamela Darby's classes. She's just informed us that she's taking a position at another school next semester."

Fran sank into a dining room chair, amazed and grateful that she'd asked God for guidance earlier. Pamela Darby taught all high-level classes. She had few if any buffoons like the ones Fran had dealt with today. This would have been a tough decision, and now there wasn't a decision to be made. She'd already accepted the SRS offer.

"Ms. Brunson, I'm sorry, but just fifteen minutes ago I accepted an offer from the communications department at the Savannah River Site. I start on January 2."

A pause. "Well, that's too bad. I wish I could have called a little earlier. I had a flat tire after work, or I would have. I wish you all the best in your new job. You have a good evening now."

"You too."

The line went dead. Still holding the phone, she looked up at Jeremy.

"What's going on?"

"They just offered me not one, but two teaching positions at South Aiken."

He smiled big. "SRS timed it just right, didn't they? I really think you'll be happier there. And definitely making more money."

"I asked God to make it clear, and He did. I told Him I would take the first offer, and she would have called first except that she had a flat tire." She shook her head, still amazed. "That's crazy."

Jeremy pulled her close and kissed her. "It's wonderful. Let's celebrate."

19

"Tell me again why you picked Maryville?" Lisa asked the question as she carefully packed up breakables in the kitchen in Memphis. "They said you could be based anywhere you wanted."

Mark worked on packing a box of study books from seminary and considered her question carefully, knowing she was still upset at yet another move. It hadn't been that long—just four years—since they'd relocated to Memphis, and she was still young—only twenty-four. It had been a lot to ask. She had rebuilt her life from nothing, and now he was asking her to do it again.

It had all happened very fast. His success in church software sales had led to an opportunity with a large church supply company based in West Virginia. He would be responsible for existing major church accounts all over the United States, and they felt he could help them grow their business substantially by landing huge, megachurch accounts. Signing him was so important to them that they had offered him the chance to base anywhere he wanted. He had the autonomy to set his own schedule and work out of a home office. It was simply too good to pass up.

God had used him mightily in the church software business, and Mark knew he'd made a difference to the churches he'd worked with. Just as he knew God could and would use him on this bigger stage. It was time to move on.

He and Lisa had talked it over, and he well knew her feelings. But he felt strongly that this would be an important decision, one that would impact their lives permanently. He wanted to be in a place where they could put down roots, make lifelong friends, and eventually raise a family. He wanted a beautiful place where he felt comfortable and could be at home, a place where God's grandeur would always be at his doorstep. When he looked at all the options, one place stood out—Maryville, Tennessee, where his family had moved when he was in ninth grade, and where he had lived until he went off to college. It was a small town, near Knoxville, at the base of the Great Smoky Mountains and its hundreds of fascinating trails, near multiple lakes for boating and fishing.

Finally, he'd be in his mountains again, where he could breathe. Lisa was not an outdoor girl and didn't quite get why this was important to him, but he'd asked that she trust him. He knew she would grow to love Maryville.

Also, he admitted to himself, part of his reasoning was that Knoxville was home to excellent medical facilities for back treatments and the surgery he still hoped was coming at some point. His back pain continued to worsen. The prospect of a home office was more than enticing.

Lisa was still looking at him, waiting for an answer.

"We've been through all of this," he finally said. "Maryville is a good place to raise a family. The schools are awesome, and the neighborhoods are friendly and safe. I've been in a lot of places, and Maryville is like no other place I've ever been."

"Your parents are there."

"They are, yes."

"And your sisters."

"Yes, Lisa is in Knoxville with her husband and little girls, but Mellie is away at school."

"Two Lisas," she said wryly. "That will be interesting."

"Mom calls you Lisa M to keep it straight." This was an attempt to keep it lighthearted, but it fell flat. Lisa bit her lip and turned away. She finished packing a box, then sealed it with tape and labeled it precisely with a Sharpie. She shoved it into place in a stack of other boxes and started on another.

Finally, she turned to face him, and a sheen of tears filled her eyes. "It's not fair," she said. "I just started to like my job and make some friends here. Why do you get to make all the decisions, and I just have to go along?"

"We did talk about it," he reminded her. "Remember?"

"You talked; I listened. It wasn't a discussion. You already had your mind made up."

He moved to her, folded her in his arms, and rocked her back and forth. She was still next to nothing in his arms, just a wisp of a girl. A woman, he reminded himself. A woman and his wife. "Honey, please trust me. This will be a good move. I promise. I've prayed about it, and I know it's right."

She sighed, sniffled, and rested her head on his shoulder. "I wish I could be strong like you and have faith like yours. I keep hoping I'll learn."

"It's a process." He tipped her chin up and looked into her eyes. She still had the same sweetness about her that he'd found appealing from the beginning. "We'll find a church where that will happen. You'll find godly women that you can be close to and talk to, and that will make all the difference."

"I wish I had a baby or two."

"We'll work on that too."

Finally, late that night, they were ready for the moving truck, and the next day Mark and Lisa Smith embarked on a new chapter of their lives in the place where so much had started for him—Maryville, Tennessee.

20

Fran Gideon perched on the toilet in her bathroom, the little stick in her hand. She kept her eyes determinedly closed, counting down the seconds. She wanted to have no doubt when she finally looked at it. She wanted this too badly to get up any false hope. Five, four, three, two, one… She opened one eye and peered at the stick and quickly opened the other eye.

It was positive. She was pregnant! She let out a squeal.

"What?" Jeremy's voice came from the bedroom.

Fran erupted from the bathroom, still squealing, and flung herself at him so hard they both fell back on the bed.

"Look!" She handed him the stick.

He looked at it, then back at her. "What's it mean?"

"It means that sometime in January, we're going to have a baby."

He looked back at it. Although he'd felt the same, he hadn't wanted to get his hopes up. But now, here it was. His eyes softened and filled with wonder as they lifted to hers. "A baby?"

She giggled. "A baby. Can you believe it?"

The timing of this was intriguing. They had sold Jeremy's house and were living in an apartment while their new house was being built. Fran was busy all the time when she wasn't at work, helping oversee construction. She knew nothing about building, but she knew how she wanted her house to be. The house would be finished at the end of the year, so she would be waddling around, eight months pregnant, as they were moving in. This child would know that house as home.

Her new job was going well. She'd only been there a few

months when they moved her from the reactor restart communications department into the larger Public Relations department, putting her into a group where all the public relations writing was done. She was responsible for fact sheets, pamphlets, presentations, video scripts, speeches, booklets, and anything else that needed to be written.

This pregnancy was going to make that interesting, as well. She worked in a security area and didn't yet have her security clearance. She was going to have to be escorted every time she had to go to the bathroom until her clearance came in. The escorts would love that.

Fran gasped. "I have to call my mother."

"Don't you want to wait until after we've seen the doctor to tell anybody?"

"I can't keep this from Mama, Jeremy. She'd know the instant she looked at me or even heard my voice. I've never been able to keep anything from her."

"Okay, we'll keep it to just family right now, then."

"Until we see the doctor."

Both families were over the moon about the new baby, and they were able to get in to see Dr. Graham Barton, Fran's gynecologist, by the end of the week. Fran had been going to see him since she'd lived in Aiken. He was the only doctor she'd ever had. He practiced at University Hospital, right across the road from the Medical College of Georgia. Augusta had a bounty of top-notch medical expertise, and Dr. Barton was one of the most brilliant OB-GYNs in town.

He strolled into the examining room where Jeremy and Fran waited. Fran sat on the table in her paper gown, while Jeremy stood near the window.

"Well, what's going on?" He gave her a light hug and shook Jeremy's hand, then went to the sink to wash his hands.

"I'm pregnant!" she beamed.

"You are? Since when?"

"I took a test a few days ago."

"Well, let's take a look and see what we see."

He helped her ease back on the table, then liberally smeared a transducer with slippery jelly and turned it on. He moved the transducer this way and that across her belly, tracking its progress across the sonogram screen. At first there was only gurgling, but then suddenly he zeroed in on something else—a thump-thump sound that could only be a heartbeat. Fran's eyes got big and met her husband's. They both looked hard at the screen, barely breathing.

On the screen was a small blob, with a pulsating beat in the middle.

"Is that the heartbeat?" Jeremy's voice sounded choked, and Fran saw that there were tears in his eyes. She was crying too, looking at the screen. That little blob was their baby!

"That's the heartbeat." Dr. Barton listened attentively. "Sounds strong, too." He zoomed in on the blob. "Can't see much yet. It's too early. Everything looks good, though. I'd say you're about eight weeks along, and I'd put your due date at January 29."

He wiped his transducer off, switched off the machine, and helped Fran sit up. "Congratulations, you're parents!"

"What do we do now?" asked Jeremy, ever the pragmatic, protective one.

"We get her on some prenatal vitamins and schedule appointments every four weeks. She should make a point to eat right and get exercise."

"When will we able to tell whether it's a boy or a girl?"

"Probably in September, at nineteen weeks. That will be our next sonogram. We'll be able to tell a lot then." He grinned, and his light blue eyes sparkled. "You'll be amazed."

21

For the next few months, Fran and Jeremy doubled their attention on the new house so that there would be no doubt that it would be ready before January. They had an excellent Christian builder named Jack Sutter, who had a reputation for top quality and honest work. Jeremy prowled the new construction, jumping up and down on the floors, to make sure of it. James and Mary were regular visitors.

Fran had thought she would be sick, but she was exactly the opposite. She'd never felt better. She was full of energy, life, and wonder. She breezed through the first trimester and wondered what the big deal was. What morning sickness?

She bought a copy of *What to Expect When You're Expecting,* and it was immediately dog-eared. She devoured every word and picture. She weighed herself every day and wished for the day when she would begin to show. She bought maternity clothes well before she needed them. She planned to decorate the nursery in Disney and already had bought bedding and a mobile. They would use the crib Jeremy had slept in as a baby.

She was at work, just a week before her nineteen-week sonogram appointment when she first felt a flutter. She was working hard on an emergency information calendar that would go out to the public at the end of the year when she suddenly felt something totally new, like butterflies tickling her insides.

She stopped cold, still staring at the computer screen but not seeing it anymore. "Oh," she said and put her hand over her stomach. The flutters grew stronger. "Oh!"

Her boss's boss, a wonderful cancer survivor named Linda

96

Walter, who had no children of her own and treated her employees like sons and daughters, was passing by in the hallway outside and heard Fran's gasp. "What?" she said in alarm and was at Fran's side in a flash. "What's wrong? Is it the baby?"

Fran's stunned gaze went from the computer to Linda's face. "Yes, it's the baby, but nothing's wrong. I just felt it move!"

The new parents could hardly wait for the sonogram to confirm what they already felt in their hearts. For some reason, both were sure this baby was a boy. Their feeling turned out to be true. There was no mistaking it; even Fran could see it on the fuzzy sonogram screen. The sonographer took measurements and made calculations, and Dr. Barton confirmed that Fran and Jeremy's son, now officially named Brody James Gideon, was healthy and thriving. The due date was holding steady at January 29.

*　　*　　*

Four weeks later, Fran arrived for her regular checkup at Dr. Barton's office. Looking back years later, she still could see no reason why she should have been concerned, or any way she or Jeremy could have known that this day would be different. But a blindside was in the works that would rock their world.

She was now twenty-three weeks pregnant but still barely showing. There was a spring in her step and a light in her eyes. Things were going so well. The flutters were getting stronger, and she could hardly wait to hear her son's heartbeat again. Jeremy hadn't come with her today because of a deadline at work, but this was a routine appointment. She and Brody would get another clean bill of health, and she'd be home in time to fix supper.

Dr. Barton didn't keep her waiting. "How're we doing?" he asked brightly as he came into the room and gave her a one-armed hug.

"We're doing great!"

He consulted his charts. "Your weight gain is perfect. Not too much and not too little. You're one of the healthiest moms I've seen in a long time."

"I feel wonderful."

"Well, let's take a listen to our boy."

She lay back and lowered the waistband of her stretchy pants so he could get to her stomach, then waited breathlessly as he positioned his transducer. She loved this moment. There was something miraculous about her baby's fast, healthy heartbeat. The doctor moved the transducer this way and that. The baby moved restlessly; they could hear him whooshing around, but Dr. Barton couldn't get in the perfect position to listen to the heartbeat.

"It's nothing to worry about; I can hear him moving," he finally said. "Let's just take a quick look, though."

No sonogram was scheduled today, so this was an extra treat. The sonogram nurse came in wheeling the machine and lubed up Fran's belly. Dr. Barton watched the screen carefully as little Brody came into view. Sure enough, there he was. They could now see his little fingers, toes, mouth, and nose. He sucked his thumb as they watched.

Then something changed in the room. It was like all the air was being sucked out. Both Dr. Barton and the sonogram nurse quit smiling. Fran lay still, afraid to move or even breathe, alternately watching the screen and her doctor's face. The light had gone from his eyes, and his face was stone still. He and the nurse watched for a long time without talking, making notes and clicking on different points on the screen. They jostled Brody and made him move. He complied, rolling and flipping as they watched. Still, the doctor and nurse looked grim.

"What's wrong?" she whispered, beginning to panic. Dr. Barton reassuringly laid one hand on hers and kept watching the screen, but didn't speak. "Please, Dr. Barton, what's wrong? Is my baby all right?" She was sobbing quietly now, tears streaming unchecked down her cheeks. Terror coursed through her veins. *What could possibly be wrong? Everything was perfect just four weeks ago. How could things change so fast?*

Dr. Barton finally spoke. "Look here. See?" He pointed to Brody's heart.

"I see. It's beating fine, right?"

"It's beating, yes, but it's a lot slower than it was four weeks ago. Then, it was beating at one hundred fifty beats a minute. Now, it's just fifty beats a minute. No matter what we do, or how we stimulate him, it doesn't speed up."

"What does that mean? He's all right, isn't he?"

"He's all right at the moment, but I'm going to get you in to see Dr. Guy Loudon at the Medical College of Georgia. He moved to MCG less than a month ago, just for these kinds of cases."

"What kinds of cases?"

He looked at her with his soothing blue eyes. "Fetal pediatric cardiology. A heartbeat this slow isn't normal. We have to figure out why." He helped her sit up and held her while she dissolved into hysterical, uncontrollable tears. The nurse looked on helplessly, tears in her own eyes, as she packed up the machine and left the room. "Is Jeremy with you today?"

"N-n-n-no, he had something at work. This was supposed to be a routine appointment!"

"I'll call him for you."

They went into his office, and she sat in his chair while he called Jeremy's office and got him on the phone. Dr. Barton explained what was going on, but Fran was too distracted and upset to hear much. Then the doctor handed her the phone. "Can you talk to him?"

"Hello?" she could barely speak for the sobs.

"Sweetheart, you hang on now. It's going to be okay."

"How do you know?"

"It just will. Do you want me to come get you? It's rush hour so it will be a while before I can get there."

"No, I can get home. I don't want to wait, and I don't want to leave a car here. I'll take it slow and easy."

"You be careful. We'll deal with this. You just get home safe."

She handed Dr. Barton the phone and he hung up. "Is he coming?"

"No, he offered to come get me, but I can get home okay."

He made another phone call, talked for a few minutes in a low tone, and handed her a slip of paper. "Tomorrow morning at nine, you have an appointment with Dr. Loudon. He'll help us get to the bottom of this, and we'll see where we go from there. I want you to come see me after you see him and tell me what's going on. Got it?"

"Got it." She managed a watery smile and thanked him. He'd gotten her through the last hour, and now she had to get herself home.

"See you tomorrow. I'm praying for you and Brody."

All the way home, as Fran concentrated on driving slowly and safely, she talked to God. Her prayer was a simple, heartfelt cry for help, an anguished plea from the depths of her soul.

Please God, please God, please God. Let this be nothing. Let my baby be okay. Help him. Hold him in Your hands. Protect him. Help me get home. Please God, please God, please God.

22

When Fran got home, Jeremy was pacing the floor. His mom, dad, and sister were all there. Mary and Rachel met Fran at the door, crying and wrapping her in hugs. They led her to a chair, and Jeremy knelt in front of her and gathered her in his arms. James, ever the doctor, sat next to her and quietly asked her questions, but she had no answers other than what Dr. Barton had already said.

"We just don't know," she said, barely able to talk. "All we know is that all of a sudden, sometime in the last four weeks, his heart rate dropped from one hundred fifty beats a minute to fifty. We don't why, or how they're going to fix it. We have an appointment with a fetal cardiology specialist tomorrow morning."

"How did the doctor spot it?" James wanted to know.

She grabbed a breath and hiccupped. "He couldn't get in a good position to hear the heartbeat. He could hear the baby moving, so he wasn't really worried, but he did a sonogram just to make sure everything was okay. Then he saw it."

"You weren't scheduled for a sonogram today, were you?" Jeremy asked.

"No. It was unplanned."

"So if Dr. Barton hadn't taken the initiative to do this sonogram, we still wouldn't know. We'd still be going along thinking everything is fine."

She thought about it. "You're right."

James smiled faintly. "That doctor being extra vigilant may have just saved this baby's life. Let's see what the specialist says tomorrow. Don't you worry, honey. We'll deal with whatever comes."

*　　*　　*

There was no sleep that night, and they were in Dr. Loudon's office before nine o'clock the next morning. He turned out to be a big, sweet bear of a man, with brown eyes and a beard. It was a good thing he was nice because he put Fran and Jeremy through torture on that first visit.

First was a grueling, two-hour, color fetal echocardiogram. In intricate detail, a medical team studied how blood was entering and departing from Brody's heart, taking measurements and making notes as they went. Fran's belly grew so tender near the end that she bit her lip and cried out at the pressure of the transducer. Then there were other tests, too many to count.

After noon, Dr. Loudon sat with Fran and Jeremy in his office and delivered the news.

"I'm sorry this morning was so rough, but we had to figure out what we're dealing with," he said. "We got a good baseline, and I think we know where to go from here."

"So what we are looking at?" Jeremy asked, looking calm. Fran knew he was anything but.

"There are a couple of issues." He pulled up a portion of the echocardiogram on a monitor in his office and hit play. He used a laser to point to what he was talking about. "First, Brody has third-degree atrioventricular block. Put simply, it's like an electrical short between the two sides of his heart, and they aren't communicating with each other. AV blocks can be first degree, second degree, or third degree. Brody's is third degree, which means he has complete heart block. His atrium is beating at one hundred fifty, but his ventricle is beating at fifty. See?"

Fran and Jeremy looked closely and could see what he was describing. "What's the second issue?" Fran asked.

Dr. Loudon pointed to an area near the center of Brody's heart, where the colors of the blood were mingling. "He also has a ventricular septal defect, which amounts to a hole between the two chambers of his ventricle. Because of the hole, the oxygenated blood is getting pumped back to his lungs instead of out to his body, which makes his heart work even harder." He paused. "This hole is a significant size. Sometimes VSDs close on their own. This one is much too large for that."

They sat silently, absorbing this and waiting for Dr. Loudon to continue.

"The problem," he said, "is that while neither issue is good, these two issues together are really bad for Brody's heart. The AV block is already making his heart work harder than it should, and the VSD makes it work even harder."

Fran lost what control she had and sobbed. Jeremy held up one finger for Dr. Loudon, and he nodded sympathetically. Jeremy took Fran in his arms and soothed her until she calmed enough to go on.

"I'm sorry," she finally said. "This is a lot."

"What do we do?" Jeremy asked.

"We take it a step at a time," Dr. Loudon said simply. "We need to get this baby as far along as we can and keep a close eye on him."

"What are we looking for?"

"Signs of oncoming heart failure. At some point, his slow heart rate will not be able to sustain his growing body, and his heart will begin to fail. We'll be able to see on echocardiogram when that's happening. At that point, whenever it is, we'll deliver him."

"How far along does he need to be?" Fran asked. Her tears were flowing again, but she couldn't help it.

"We'll start breathing easier if we can get to thirty-four weeks. The longer, the better."

"Okay, so what happens when we deliver him?" Jeremy asked.

"We get him into surgery and do a pacemaker implant. That will fix the AV block and let his heart beat normally."

"What about the hole?"

"We wait until he's bigger and surgically repair it. Like I said, holes this big do not close on their own."

"When?" Fran asked. "When would we need to do that surgery?"

"Hopefully we can hold off until he's about two years old."

"So," Jeremy said, "he's going to be okay."

"If everything goes according to plan, he can lead a normal life. Yes."

"Will this impact his life expectancy?" Jeremy asked.

"Wear and tear on his heart will probably reduce his life by a few years," Dr. Loudon said honestly, "but it won't be a significant difference."

"What are his limitations?" Fran asked. "Will he be able to run and play like other kids?"

"His heart will actually work better than theirs because it will be better regulated," Dr. Loudon said. "He can't play football because he can't take a hit to the chest. He can't operate a jackhammer or a HAM radio because of the frequency. He can't go into a power plant or have an MRI because of the magnetic field. And he'll have to be careful around big magnets because they could deactivate his pacemaker."

"How about microwave ovens?"

"Not a problem. Not anymore," the doctor said.

"Anything else?" Jeremy asked. "How do we know it's working?"

"You'll have a transmitter that will let you call in once a month and check his pacemaker performance over the phone. It will take less than five minutes. And you'll have regular checkups with Dr. Wofford, our pediatric cardiologist who specializes in arrhythmia. They'll keep a close eye on everything until he turns eighteen."

Fran asked the question they both wanted to know but were afraid to ask. "Will the same thing happen to any other kids?"

"We don't know what caused this, so we don't know. To be safe, any future children will be considered high-risk, and we'll watch them closely throughout your pregnancy."

Silence. Then Jeremy took a deep breath. "So what do we do now?"

"We watch and we wait. Make an appointment with me for next week. I'll be leading and integrating this team, and I'll be responsible for the pediatric cardiology side until he's born. You'll start with Dr. Patel and Dr. Hodges next week as well. Dr. Patel specializes in high-risk pregnancies, and Dr. Hodges will deliver the baby when the time comes. He'll have to be born by caesarian section because labor would put stress on his heart and we can't risk that. You'll see all three of us every week from here on out."

"Wait," Fran said. "I already have an obstetrician. Dr. Barton is going to deliver our baby."

"I wouldn't recommend that," Dr. Loudon said firmly.

"Why not?" Her voice sounded shrill, but she couldn't help it.

"Only MCG doctors can practice at MCG. Dr. Barton is at University."

"Can't he be born there and then brought here? It's, like, right across the street."

"If he's in crisis when he's born, those extra minutes could be critical. He needs to be born here so we can be ready for him."

"It's okay, Fran," Jeremy whispered. "Don't worry about that."

"I do worry about that!" she hissed. "Dr. Barton is my doctor! I trust him!"

"We need to think about what's best for Brody. You know MCG doctors are as good as it gets."

"He's right," said Dr. Loudon. "Now, here's my prescription. Go home, eat well, get plenty of sleep, and don't worry. This baby's life depends on it."

*   *   *

Just minutes later, Jeremy and Fran were escorted into Dr. Barton's office, and he didn't keep them waiting. They gave him the complete rundown on what Dr. Loudon had told them.

Fran was still deeply in shock and couldn't get past the fact that Dr. Barton wouldn't be delivering her baby. He was the only doctor she'd ever had. She trusted him. If it weren't for him, they wouldn't even know about this. Her thoughts kept going in circles, and she couldn't find her way out, like a crazed rat in a maze. She knew she was being unreasonable, but she'd reached the end of her rope.

"I can't have anyone but you deliver this baby," she wailed.

Jeremy and the doctor exchanged glances. Jeremy shrugged helplessly. Dr. Barton held up his hand.

"Fran, what if I could just be there with you, in the operating room, even if I can't deliver him?"

"But you have other patients."

"I'll cancel them that day."

"How can you do that?"

"Let me worry about that, and you concentrate on yourself and this baby. I'm telling you now that I'll be right there with you when he's delivered. Between now and then, every week after you go see the other doctors, I want you to come see me. I'll make sure I'm in the loop with them as well."

Jeremy spoke up. "What did Dr. Loudon mean when he said Brody's life depends on her getting plenty of sleep and not worrying?"

"He just meant that stress on Fran is the same thing as stress on Brody. He needs to cook as long as he can, and the calmer she is, the better chance he has."

"No pressure," she said grimly.

He looked her dead in the eyes. "Do whatever you have to do. Find some calm place inside you. Meditate. Pray. Get counseling. Whatever you have to do, do it for him."

This was a tall order. She couldn't get her emotions under control, couldn't stop crying even for a second. Obviously, she had to find a way to get a grip. She shuddered, took a deep breath, and closed her eyes.

When she finally, slowly opened them, straight in front of her was a poster she'd never seen before in this office. She got up and went closer to study it. It depicted an orange kitten in a tree, stepping down into a waiting pair of hands. The caption read:

Sometimes, You Just Have To Go On Faith

23

After the emotional upheaval of Wednesday and Thursday, Fran went to work on Friday, just needing to get through the day so she could go home and be with Julia. When she was upset, she wanted her mother.

After seeing the poster in Dr. Barton's office, she knew she would find her peace in Jesus. She just didn't know how. For twenty years, she'd been saved but had thirsted for more. She heard other people talking about praying as if it were a conversation with God. Her prayers always felt one-sided. She felt guided by God but at a distance. Only one time in her life had she actually felt an answer, and that was when she was pouring herself out to Him after her daddy died. She needed to feel Him now. But how?

She sat at her computer and worked on a PowerPoint presentation that any member of the SRS senior staff could give to public audiences. It covered dozens of topics and had to be correct and concise. Her mind kept wandering until she pushed herself back, closed her eyes, and prayed.

Help me, God. I need You now. I need Your peace. Show me how to find You.

She heard someone sit down quietly in her visitor chair and opened her eyes. Donna Holton, who ran the SRS tour program, sat there. She was about ten years older than Fran but with lots more life experience. Donna was a single mom with two beautiful kids and a drive to succeed for them. She had snap and fire and spoke with a Pittsburgh accent.

"Hi," she said softly. "You okay?"

"Not really." Fran sniffled. "I was just trying to pray."

"Trying to pray?"

"It's something I've always had a problem with. I don't really know how, and I need Him right now."

Donna smiled gently. "It's not that hard."

"That's what everyone says. How come it's hard for me?"

"I think you're making it too difficult."

Fran drew a long, shuddering breath. "If you have any advice, I'd love to hear it."

"Let's take a little walk outside."

The two walked outside the building into the warm South Carolina September afternoon. Just last month, Fran's group had moved to an offsite building in south Aiken because of the unclassified nature of their work. No more getting escorts to go to the restroom. It had been a blessing. Fran turned her face gratefully up to the sun.

They walked along silently at first, just enjoying being outside. Finally, Donna spoke.

"Linda told me what's going on."

"Yeah, I talked to her this morning."

"That's rough."

"It is. And the hardest part is that the doctor told me this baby's life depends on me staying calm and not worrying."

Donna let out a bark of a laugh. "Well, that's nice."

"But it's true. It makes sense. Then I saw this poster in Dr. Barton's office …"

"The kitten?"

"How'd you know?"

"He's my doctor too. He's a good man."

"He is. Anyway, that poster was like a sign, pointing me in the right direction. So I know my peace will be in Jesus, I just don't know how to find it."

They walked in silence for a moment.

"Fran, I have a couple of pieces of advice for you," Donna finally said. "This is coming from someone who's been where you are—not with the baby, but in your search for peace and understanding."

"Please, tell me."

"Come sit with me."

They sat on a bench in a parklike area between buildings. A stream gurgled nearby, and a warm fall breeze rustled the leaves in the trees overhead.

"This is nice," Fran said.

"This is His creation. I feel Him best in places like this. I want you to go somewhere you can be alone. It doesn't have to be a place like this, but it has to be somewhere you can be undistracted. No telephone, no chores, no husband, just you and the Lord.

"Then I want you to ask Jesus to come and sit with you. If you're in the car, ask Him to come sit in your passenger seat. If you're in a place like this, ask Him to come sit on the bench next to you. Picture Him there and believe He's there because He will be. Once you've got that picture in your mind, then just talk to Him."

"How?"

"Like you're talking to me now. He loves you so much, and He wants to be there for you. He's the best friend you'll ever have. The Bible says, 'Seek Me, and you will find Me, when you search for Me with all your heart.' It's true."

Fran smiled through fresh tears. This was the best prayer advice she'd ever heard. "Thanks, Donna. I'll do that."

Donna hugged her. "I felt led to come to you today. I think God wanted me to share this with you. He knows you need Him, and He wants you to find Him."

*   *   *

Fran already had her car packed so she could leave straight from work to head home to her mother. Jeremy had been very understanding, knowing she needed to get away. He planned to spend the weekend working with the builder on details of the new house. They had only three more months until they needed to be moved in and settled.

Aiken and Laurens are only about seventy-five miles apart. The road goes along highway 25 through Edgefield, and then through the country to Greenwood. Fran had driven the route so often, she had it timed down to the minute. She could sometimes do it in ninety minutes, but that was in the middle of the night with no traffic. It usually took her an hour and thirty-five minutes.

At one point, between Edgefield and Greenwood, the road straightens out, and there's nothing in any direction—except one single flashing light over a crossroads. The speed limit drops to forty-five, but no one pays any attention. People are on autopilot, just getting where they're going.

The flashing light was about at the halfway point between Fran's house and her mother's. They had used it as a meeting place many times, a convenient spot for both of them. Now Fran eased to a stop, well off the road near the familiar flashing light. She turned the car off, took a deep breath, and focused her mind and heart. Cars whooshed by every few minutes, but mostly it was peaceful and quiet.

"Jesus, would You come and sit with me, please? I need to talk to You." She spoke the words aloud, eyes closed, concentrating.

Sometimes, you just have to go on faith.

Picture Him there and believe He's there because He will be.

Suddenly, like a dawning, Fran had no doubt. She was on holy ground, because Jesus was here, sitting next to her, waiting for her to pour out her heart to Him. She knew it. Her car fairly radiated with His presence.

"Jesus, I need you so much." Her words came out in a tumble. "I'm so scared for my baby, and so worried that something I do will hurt him. He's so little and right now he's pretty sick. We have to get through about three months for him to have a chance, and it's all looking pretty huge to me right now."

She talked for a long time, pouring out her heart, and finally stopped, tears streaming down her cheeks. She could feel the holy presence next to her, and suddenly she knew what He expected. She let out a choked sob. "I can't do it, Jesus. It's too much, and You can handle it so much better than I can. You love Brody even more than I do, and I'm turning him over to You right now."

She kept her eyes closed and visualized herself writing Brody's name on a slip of paper and slipping it into a jar, then sealing it tight. Clear as day, she could see a jar labeled "The God Jar." When she put something into that jar, it belonged to Him, and she needed to worry no more about it.

"He's Yours," she whispered. "Please let me know what I need to do."

Be at peace, beloved. The holy whisper echoed in her mind and heart. *I am knitting this child together in your womb, and I don't make mistakes. I know him already. I know what he is and what he will be. He is Mine.*

She stayed there, basking in the holy presence, soaking in the absolute wonder of being able to talk to Jesus like a friend. It seemed that she could actually feel His warm, loving touch on her face. Jesus, the Creator of the universe. Oh, the awe of it. Her tears still flowed, but now they were good and cleansing.

After a long time, when the sun began to set and the air grew chilly, Fran started up her car and headed toward her mother. Her heart had a new peace, and she knew absolutely that everything would be all right.

24

Throughout October, November, and December, Fran and Jeremy kept up the weekly ritual. They went to see Dr. Loudon for a color echocardiogram, followed by a visit with Dr. Neil Patel, and often followed by Dr. Burt Hodges. On their first visit to Dr. Hodges, he did an amniocentesis, which would give details on the baby's chromosomes and might help them learn more about his condition. This was a horribly painful test, compounded by the fact that Fran had to sign a form saying she understood this test could cause her to miscarry. After all of this, every week they went to see Dr. Barton and gave him an update.

Each time Fran lay down on the table for the echocardiogram, she closed her eyes and held her breath. She knew Jesus was taking care of her baby, but she didn't know how He was going to do it. So she waited each week until the doctors proclaimed no sign of oncoming heart failure. They'd tell her to go home and come back next week. High fives would be exchanged all around.

Jeremy's family didn't understand Fran's new serenity and peace. They thought her mind had snapped under pressure. They tiptoed around the house, talking in hushed voices. Fran heard Rachel whisper one day, "Does she understand that she might lose this baby?"

Only Julia understood her. When Fran told her the story about the conversation in the car, Julia looked startled and told an almost identical story about when she first found out that Pete had Parkinson's. She hadn't asked Jesus to sit in the car with her, but her heart's cry had been almost the same as Fran's. And she'd felt the same peace ever since, where Pete was concerned.

Week after week went by, with the same news. Fran could feel Brody's strong kicks now. And finally, one night as she and Jeremy were in bed, a sweet turning point came.

Fran was trying to go to sleep and having trouble because Brody was turning flips inside her. Night seemed to be his frisky time. She ran her hand over her belly to try to soothe him, and suddenly, for the first time, she could feel his movements under her hand. Before, she could feel him moving and kicking inside her, but no one else could feel it. Her eyes grew big as saucers.

"Jeremy," she whispered. "You've got to feel this.'

"Honey," he said sleepily, "I've tried to feel him before, but I never do."

"This is different. Just give me your hand."

She took Jeremy's hand and pressed it on the spot. For a few nerve-wracking seconds, she thought the baby was playing possum with his dad, but then came the hardest kick of all. Jeremy's eyes got big, and he gently rubbed the place where Brody was kicking him.

"That's my boy. I feel you," he crooned. He slid down in the bed so he could talk quietly to Brody and feel him at the same time. "We can't wait to see you and hold you, Brody. We love you so much."

The baby turned a flip and delivered a karate kick directly into Jeremy's hand. Jeremy chuckled. "He's a strong one."

Fran watched, tears sliding down her face. Jeremy had been her rock since this whole thing started. He'd held steady for her; but in many ways, he was on the outside looking in. He couldn't feel the things she felt. Now, to some degree, he could. He was experiencing this baby in ways he couldn't before, and Fran could actually see a stronger bond forming between them.

He slid up in bed and wrapped Fran in his arms, settling her head on his shoulder. "Thank you."

"For what?"

"For putting my hand there. I'd just about given up on being able to feel him move."

"It was just a matter of him being big enough. It's getting kind of cramped in there now."

"In my head I knew that. I guess I was just afraid. He feels so much more real now." He tipped her head back, looked into her eyes, and kissed her tenderly. "Our son."

*　　*　　*

Finally 1990 came to an end. Fran was thirty-six weeks pregnant, and the baby still had no signs of heart failure. Brody was now big enough to survive, but his medical team wanted him to stay inside as long as possible. They continued to watch baby and mother weekly, specifically watching for three things. They still had to watch his heart for signs of oncoming failure. They had to make sure his lungs were mature enough to function on their own. And they absolutely couldn't let Fran get so far along that she went into labor.

They set a tentative delivery date for January 22, knowing it could happen sooner if any of a hundred things occurred.

The weeks leading up to the delivery were a whir of activity. The house was finally finished, and Fran and Jeremy moved in. Fran was relegated to a chair, so worried was Jeremy that she would overdo. James, Mary, and Rachel descended upon the house, doing everything and allowing Fran to do nothing.

They allowed her to decorate the nursery because she was going stir crazy. She waddled about, putting everything carefully into place. She smoothed the Disney sheets on the crib, arranged the bumper pads precisely along the sides, and positioned the mobile just so. She put away the tiny clothes and diapers that Brody had received at a baby shower last week. Finally she hung two Disney prints on the walls. Soon, her son would sleep in this room!

Julia's contribution was a beautiful glider rocker for the nursery, so Fran would have a place to sit and rock Brody. "Read to him, but maybe you don't want to sing to him," she teased her daughter. Fran's complete lack of musical ability had been a joke for her entire life.

Fran sank into that glider and looked about. Brody protested at the increasingly confined quarters, jabbing her hard with his knees and elbows. She gently rubbed him and talked to him in a soothing voice.

"You're my miracle baby," she said, and began to sing a song her mother had sung to her all her life. "I love you, a bushel and a peck." She knew she was off-key, but she didn't think Brody cared.

She kept rocking and closed her eyes. "Thank You, Jesus," she prayed. "Thank You for getting us this far and taking care of us. Thank You for family and friends and all the blessings You've given us. And thank You for what You're going to do. I can feel it. It's going to be big."

Doctors continued to watch mother and baby. Thirty-seven weeks, then thirty-eight. No heart failure, no contractions. Dr. Hodges did one final amniocentesis to confirm that Brody's lungs were mature enough to function after birth. They were. He examined Fran to see if she was the slightest bit dilated or effaced. She was not.

"Everything's looking great." He helped her sit up and smiled. "Somebody's looking out for you."

Then came the evening of January 21, and Jeremy and Fran looked at each other in wonder and awe. God had gotten them through this part of the ordeal, and tomorrow they would see their baby.

25

At four o'clock in the morning on January 22, Fran and Jeremy eased into a parking place in the garage at the Medical College of Georgia. Theirs was the only car in the garage, and their footsteps echoed as they walked the short distance to the hospital. Jeremy walked; Fran waddled.

Fran's managers at work had given her a four-month leave of absence, long enough to recover from her own surgery and get her baby through his first few months. The couple knew that they would have to have in-home child care because Brody would not be able to tolerate the germs of a daycare.

"You okay?" Jeremy asked as they crossed the garage.

"I'm nervous but I'm fine," she answered. "God's got this."

He squeezed her hand and led her to the elevator, which took them up to the ninth floor. Everyone was ready for them, and things started to happen quickly.

Fran and Jeremy had been warned that this would not be a typical delivery. It would take place in a large operating room with dozens of people. Every necessary discipline would be represented at least two-fold. There would be pediatric cardiologists, arrhythmia specialists, obstetricians, pediatricians, perinatologists, nurses, surgeons, anesthesiologists, and of course, medical students. This was an unusual birth and would be used as a teaching opportunity. Brody would be one of the youngest patients—perhaps the youngest—ever to receive a pacemaker.

"It will be a zoo," Dr. Loudon had told them frankly. "Just know that I put this team together myself. Every single person in the room is important for you and your baby."

They trusted him. The important thing was to take care of Brody.

Fran prayed silently throughout all the preparations. *Blessed Jesus, please be with us today. Please guide the doctors as they do what they have to do. Guide their hands and their hearts. Keep them focused and let them be at their absolute best today. Be there in the room with us and take care of us. Thank You, Jesus.*

James, Mary, Julia, Chris, Rachel, and Jennifer arrived for support, and they would stay there for the duration. Linda Walter and Donna Holton came, as did Dr. Bill Johnston, the pastor at First Presbyterian Church in Aiken.

The team got her ready, started the epidural, and hooked her up to monitors that showed her and Brody's progress. Her eyes locked on the monitor that showed Brody's heartbeat. Still holding steady at fifty beats a minute. "You hang on, son. We're going to get you out," she whispered.

Jeremy squeezed her hand. "It's going to be okay," he told her.

"I know," she said.

Just before they took her into the operating room, the door opened and Dr. Barton walked in, dressed in scrubs.

"You ready?" He shook Jeremy's hand, and Fran reached up and gave him a one-armed hug, the best she could do with the IV line in her arm.

"I am so ready. It means so much that you're here."

"Of course, I'm here. I've cleared my whole morning. I'll see you in there."

Just after nine-thirty in the morning, the team wheeled Fran into the operating room with Jeremy right beside her. They positioned her into place and made sure all the machines were working. A curtain was raised just below her chin, so she couldn't see what was going on.

"Everybody ready?" Dr. Hodges finally asked.

"Let's go," said the anesthesiologist.

The epidural was doing its job, so Fran felt nothing but pressure when they made the incision and worked Brody from her body. She could see people watching intently but could see nothing below the sheet. At first, she heard nothing. Then, as the clock ticked to precisely ten o'clock, she heard a baby's enraged cry. Her eyes grew big and her tears overflowed.

"He's beautiful, Fran," Dr. Barton squeezed her hand. His eyes looked suspiciously moist above his mask. "And his lungs seem to be working just fine."

"Is he blue?"

"No. He's pink. With an amazing head of silver hair."

He stuck beside her while Dr. Hodges finished the operation. Jeremy followed the baby over to a table where the nurses worked on him, suctioning out his nose and cleaning him up. They weighed him, measured him, and took his handprints and footprints. He was none too pleased with the proceedings, letting out a series of loud wails. Each one sounded beautiful.

They brought him to her, wrapped in a blue blanket. He opened his eyes and looked at her, straight at her, with his big baby blue eyes. And Dr. Barton was right—he had a startling shock of silver-blond hair.

"Hi, Brody," she whispered, tears streaming unchecked from her eyes. She reached over and stroked his petal-soft cheek. "He's the most beautiful thing I've ever seen. Can I hold him?"

"We need to get him up to NICU and evaluate him," Dr. Loudon said. "You can come up later, okay?"

Her worried eyes met his. "Is he okay?"

He smiled at her. "He's so much better than we ever thought he would be, Fran. He's plump and pink and healthy."

"Does he still need surgery?"

"His heart rate is still fifty beats a minute, way too slow for a newborn, so yes, he needs the pacemaker. But he's not in crisis. We can take the time we need to evaluate him and settle him down."

Before long, Fran was ensconced in a big corner room, with her family arrayed around her.

Rachel was still awestruck. "They pushed the incubator right by us on their way to the elevator," she gushed, eyes big. "All we could see was his blond hair. And I swear there was a *glow* around that incubator."

This didn't surprise Fran in the least. She had asked Jesus to be with them and with Brody, and He was here. His presence was the only way to explain how they'd gotten through these four months, and how well Brody was doing now. And she knew He would stay with them because the ordeal was far from over.

26

Brody's surgery was scheduled for eight o'clock the next morning, and Fran and Jeremy were on their way down to the neonatal intensive care unit to spend some time with him tonight. Jeremy carefully helped her into a wheelchair and pushed her slowly and gently out of her room, along the hallway, and into the elevator. Her fresh incision throbbed fiercely. They'd put her on a lovely morphine drip, but the drugs made her sleepy, and she wanted to be awake to meet and hold her son. She'd sleep tonight.

The elevator took them one floor down, then Jeremy pushed Fran out of the elevator—she definitely felt the bump—and they were there. They pressed the buzzer at the entrance to the NICU. When a nurse answered on a speaker, they gave her their names and the door swung open. Jeremy slowly pushed Fran's wheelchair into the NICU, where a nurse directed them to Brody. "Your son is right over there, see?" She pointed. "He's all ready for you."

The NICU was incubator after incubator, each so tiny but full of life-sustaining technology. Some of these babies were smaller than the palm of Fran's hand, their fingers no bigger than matchsticks. They had tubes attached all over their bodies. Machines whirred and sighed in rhythm with the babies' breathing.

Brody, by contrast, had few attachments. He had cardiac leads on his chest but nothing else. That, of course, would change tomorrow. He was quiet and sleeping as they approached. He looked plump and healthy compared to the sick little ones around him.

"Oh, Jeremy…" Fran sighed.

A pretty nurse with snapping brown eyes and curly dark hair came up to them. "You're the Gideons?"

"Yes, we are," Jeremy answered for them. "I'm Jeremy and this is Fran."

"I'm Debbie Stazen, the nurse assigned to Brody. He's so sweet and beautiful, I'm already in love with him. Would you like to hold him?"

"Oh, yes, please," Fran said, her arms aching to hold her child. Debbie carefully lifted Brody out of the incubator and laid him in his mother's arms.

"There you go," she said. "Support his head. Perfect."

Fran held her son for the first time, marveling at his beauty. Button nose, perfect pink mouth, and of course that startling silver hair. He opened his eyes and stared seriously into hers. She lifted his little hand, and his tiny fingers immediately curled around hers. Fran was quickly lost in love, a love so intense she'd never imagined it. These past nine months, she'd thought she loved this baby, but the pregnancy months were nothing compared to the feeling as she held him for the first time. She felt as if her heart was going to burst.

"Hi, sweetheart, I'm your mommy." She swallowed a sob. Brody regarded her intently, and what looked like a smile lifted his little lips.

"Did you see that?" Jeremy asked whoever was in the area. "He smiled."

"It's gas," Debbie said gently. "But it did look like a smile. He's beautiful. Would you like to feed him?"

She gave Fran a small bottle of special formula, and Fran's hands trembled as she fed her son for the first time. Jeremy stroked Brody's hair and talked to him as he ate.

"I'm planning to nurse him," Fran said to Debbie while Brody worked the bottle.

"That's good, but your milk isn't in yet, so we'll feed him formula until then," she explained. "And even then, we'll need to know exactly how much he's eating. So you'll pump, and he'll take your milk in a bottle."

They found out that Debbie had just come to MCG a few days

earlier from Ohio. She had an efficient way about her and a shining love and strength that was special. Fran couldn't imagine a better nurse for Brody and also couldn't imagine doing a job like this. How would you handle it when you fell in love with a baby, and it didn't end well? How could you give your heart to these babies so completely, knowing it might well get broken? It took a unique talent and a special strength—and a calling that Fran knew she did not have.

The new parents took turns holding their son until Debbie said Brody had to get back into his controlled incubator. He had to be strong and ready for surgery tomorrow. "I'll be here with him all night," she said. "You get some sleep. Tomorrow's a big day."

*   *   *

Mercifully, Fran slept through Brody's surgery the next morning. She was only twenty hours removed from major surgery herself, and the trip downstairs had exhausted her. She went in and out of a drugged sleep, only vaguely aware that her entire family was around her, pacing anxiously. James and Jeremy stood together, talking in low tones. Chris, Rachel, and Mary took turns going to the door and looking down the hall to see if anyone was coming with news. Julia sat beside Fran, holding her hand, praying.

Fran opened her eyes and looked sleepily at her mother. "Mama? Is it over?"

"Not yet, sweetie," she said softly. "We'll let you know."

"Wake me up," Fran said and drifted back to sleep.

At not quite ten o'clock, an older man came into the room in scrubs. He had red, bushy eyebrows and a confident, smiling manner.

"I'm Victor Morris, Brody's surgeon," he announced. "You're his family?"

Julia squeezed Fran's hand. "Wake up, honey," she whispered. "The doctor's here."

Jeremy stepped forward. "Yes, I'm his father. How is he?"

"He did great. The pacemaker is in and working just fine. He's stable and in recovery now. You can go see him when he gets back to NICU."

James stepped up beside Jeremy. "I'm Dr. Gideon, Brody's grandfather. Can you tell me exactly what you did? Where is the pacemaker?"

"It's going to be different than you might expect," Dr. Morris said. "Adults get pacemakers under their collarbones, with leads placed intravenously into the heart. Brody is too small for that. His pacemaker is in his tummy, with one lead just under his skin, attached directly to his ventricle. His atrium doesn't need help; it's beating just fine on its own. Now his ventricle is keeping up."

"When can he go home?" Fran asked.

"We'll see how he does. Hopefully, in a few days."

"Thank you, Doctor," Jeremy said and shook his hand.

"You're welcome." The doctor left the room.

Parents and grandparents looked at each other in immense relief. James cautioned everyone. "This was just a step along a very long journey. We celebrate this, but it's not over. Brody's got a long road ahead."

"I think the worst is over, Dad," Jeremy said. "We get him over the surgery and get him home, and he can start being a normal little boy. That's what we want for him."

Julia partially agreed with both men, but she kept her opinions to herself. She held her daughter's hand and stroked it lightly, as Fran drifted back to sleep.

27

Fran couldn't stop crying. She was about to have to go home without her son. Dr. Hodges had stretched her hospital stay out as long as he could, but five days was the maximum.

Brody wasn't ready to go home yet; she understood that. When she and Jeremy had first seen him after his surgery, she was unprepared. His little tummy was a mass of bandages from his sternum down to his belly button. They had explained that they had to put an adult-sized pacemaker in him, one that would generate enough power to make his heart beat at the normal rate for a newborn. He looked small and pitiful lying in his incubator, with his massive bandages and all the machines attached to him.

She felt as if her heart were breaking in half. How could she go home without Brody? If he was here, she had to stay here too. He needed his mother. The tears came harder. The nurses said she had postpartum depression, but that didn't help. Her heart still hurt and the tears still came.

A nurse helped her into a wheelchair and began packing a cart with the things she'd accumulated in five days at MCG.

"Look at all the beautiful flowers and balloons!" the nurse gushed as she loaded them. "You and your baby are lucky to be loved so much." The nurse stuffed Fran and her two carts into the elevator. Jeremy was waiting downstairs.

He took one look at her flowing tears and sighed as the nurse helped her into the car. "Fran, honey, you know you have to go home. Brody is doing great, and we'll go see him as much as we want. He'll be home soon."

"I know, but I can't help it." She wept.

The tears continued for the next two days, even as Jeremy and Fran went to the hospital every day and stayed for hours, holding and feeding their son.

Finally, the day Brody was one week old, good news came. He was ready to go home. First, Fran had to stay with him overnight in a special room, just the two of them, to demonstrate to herself and the nurses that she could take care of him and his surgery area.

The room was lovely, decorated to look like a bedroom, but Fran was on pins and needles all night. She'd never actually had the full responsibility of a baby before. Babysitting didn't count. You could hand the kids over when the parents came home. Her niece and nephew didn't count because her mom was only a phone call away. So this was a first. Brody was hers.

He was a fussy baby, but she told herself that made sense. He had a huge piece of metal in his belly and a bunch of stitches. Of course, he was fussy. When he slept, Fran dozed in a chair beside the crib with her hand on his little back so she could feel him breathing. In 1991, babies still slept on their tummies. Was it her imagination, or was he breathing really hard?

Finally, mercifully, morning came. Brody stirred and Fran arose blearily with him. She was allowed to nurse him now, but after a week of eating from a bottle, he had no wish to work for his food. After looking forward to the experience of nursing him, she'd become resigned to the fact that she still had to pump her milk and feed him from a bottle.

She sank with him into a rocking chair and fed him his breakfast. His tiny hands clutched the bottle, and his blue eyes locked solemnly, trustingly, on hers. He was a little warrior to have come through everything he had. It was amazing that this day was actually here, after four long months of praying and waiting.

"You ready to go home, sweetie?" she crooned to him.

He finished eating, and she laid him down to change him into his going home outfit. Jeremy would be there soon. Weeks ago, she'd bought Brody a blue sleeper for this occasion and had washed it so it would be sterile. Gently, she slid his little arms out of the onesie he'd been wearing and looked carefully at his incision like she'd been taught to do. It seemed different than it had last night, puffier somehow.

Surely not, Lord. I'm just imagining things, right? He's fine! He's going home!

Be calm, daughter. Take a close look. I am with you. She heard the still voice in her heart.

She gently probed the edges of the wound around the stitches, and her heart froze. She could definitely feel something different. Coolly, with a strength that was not her own, she hit the nurse's button.

"Can I help you?"

"Yes, I think you need to take a look at Brody's incision. It looks different."

The nurse was there within minutes, followed quickly by the chief nurse and then a doctor. Within the hour, Brody was back in surgery. The puffiness Fran had noticed was fluid, which had dripped down from his heart to his incision area along the wire that was attached between his ventricle and his pacemaker.

She and Jeremy sat in the waiting room, staring into space, in shock. He had barely made it in time to see Brody whisked away.

"Tell me again what happened," he said.

"I was getting him ready to come home and noticed that his incision looked different," she said numbly. "I thought it was better to be safe, so I called a nurse. The next thing I knew, they were taking him away."

He rubbed his hands over his face, then leaned over and wrapped his arm around her, pulling her close and laying his cheek on top of her head. "It's a good thing you were watching him so closely. Think about what would have happened if you hadn't noticed. We'have taken him home and then what? You did good, honey."

She sniffled and closed her eyes. "I just wish they'd give us some news. They didn't really say much when they took him, except that they had to relieve the pressure."

Finally, Dr. Morris came in. "He's okay," he told them with a slight smile that didn't really reach his eyes. "Because you caught it when you did, we were able to drain the fluid."

Thank You, God.

"Can he still go home?" Fran asked.

"No, he's got a drainage tube, and we need to watch him for a few days. He's in recovery now, and he'll be going back up to NICU soon." He paused, then sat down next to Fran. "This could have been very serious. We are so fortunate that you caught it when you did. We need to understand why the fluid built up, to begin with, and stop it so it doesn't happen again. We'll be putting him on some additional medications to help the healing process."

"When can we see him?" Jeremy asked.

"A nurse will come get you. Mr. and Mrs. Gideon, I'm not going to tell you not to worry, but I assure you that we are going to figure this out. We are going to take care of Brody, and he will be just fine."

Minutes ticked by after the doctor left, and they sat silently.

"How did you find the fluid?" Jeremy finally asked.

Fran was silent for a moment. The truth, or not the truth? "God told me to look," she finally said. She knew how that was going to go over. Jeremy didn't talk about it, but she knew he was still not on good terms with God after his brother's death. She knew that somewhere inside Jeremy was the faith he'd grown up with, and she hoped and prayed that someday he and God would come back together.

"God told you to look?"

"Yes. I was seeing it, but I was denying it. I wanted so badly to take him home. God told me to be calm and look. And that's when I saw it and called the nurse."

He sighed and rubbed his face again. "Well, however it happened, I'm glad," he said.

28

With no other choice, Fran and Jeremy finally went home. There was no place for them to stay at MCG. It wasn't like Brody had a room with a cot beside his crib. He was in one of dozens of incubators in the NICU, with people continually scurrying by.

For the next week, the routine was exhaustingly the same. Fran was still recovering from major surgery, so she couldn't drive, and she was still pumping milk to supply Brody's needs. Jeremy would go to work in the morning, hop over to MCG to feed Brody his lunch, then go back to work. At the end of the day, he would drive home and pick Fran up, and they would go spend time with Brody and feed him his dinner.

They began to understand the history of some of the other tiny patients in the NICU. One baby was about half Brody's size, with tubes and wires on every available surface. She screamed and twitched in the throes of cocaine withdrawal.

There were preemies so small that they wouldn't be able to go home for months. There were others with significant sicknesses and organ malfunctions. Some were missing limbs. Fran and Jeremy looked at the others, then looked at their son and felt blessed.

They were having issues of their own, of course, as Brody recovered from his second heart surgery in one week. He had a drainage tube, an IV, heart leads, and about a dozen other things attached to his tiny body. Typically NICU nurses put IVs wherever they can find a vein. When arms, legs, hands, and feet become exhausted, they put IVs in babies' heads. To do that, they have to shave their hair. With Debbie Stazen leading the way, Brody's nurses determinedly and successfully fought to save his beautiful, silver hair. Brody had done his share of screaming at needle sticks, but none were in his head.

Day after day, there seemed to be no change. The routine was emotionally grueling. Fran was still suffering from postpartum depression. Her doctor had put her on Paxil, which helped some. She felt that once she had Brody at home, it would be better.

The first week in February was drawing to a close. Brody had now been in the hospital for well over two weeks. Fran sat in her bedroom at home and watched out the window, waiting for Jeremy to arrive. Their habit was to turn around immediately and head over to the hospital, getting something to eat as they went. They wanted to spend as much time with their son as they could.

She heard the whir as the garage door opened, and the engine of Jeremy's car as he pulled inside. Then his footsteps were on the stairs, and the door to the house opened and closed. "Hi honey, you ready?" he called to her.

"Coming!"

They hopped into the car and zoomed back out of the garage.

"How was he today?" Fran asked her husband as they drove.

"I thought he looked better. More alert," Jeremy said. "What do you want for dinner?"

"A cheeseburger?"

"Fine."

He whipped through the Burger King drive-through, and they munched on their sandwiches the rest of the way.

Fran kept glancing at Jeremy as she ate. He had an unusual look in his eye. She knew, absolutely, that there was something he wasn't telling her. He had that *I've got a surprise* twinkle, the same one he had the night they drove to Augusta, and he had proposed. And he seemed really happy. Could it be...no, she was afraid to get her hopes up. She knew she'd find out soon enough, so she held her tongue.

They eased into the parking garage and took the elevator up eight floors, as they had countless times before. When they were buzzed into NICU, Debbie Stazen and Dr. Chantrapa Bunyapen, the head of NICU, were there to meet them.

"How is he?" Fran asked. "Has there been any change?"

"Come see for yourself," Debbie said.

She led the way to Brody's incubator, and he seemed to be watching for them. When he saw Fran, he smiled.

"May I?" she asked Debbie.

"Of course."

Fran gently picked Brody up and rocked him from side to side. Then she noticed something different. "Where's his drainage tube?"

"We took it out this morning," said Dr. Bunyapen. "He's ready to go home if you have your car seat in the car."

Fran spun, the baby still nestled in her arms. Her eyes locked on Debbie's. "What did she say?"

Debbie's eyes glistened with tears. "She said Brody's ready to go home."

Fran flew to Debbie and hugged her as hard as she could with Brody still between them. Jeremy took the baby. "Here, let me," he said. Then Fran and Debbie clung to each other and sobbed.

"You have no idea," Fran could hardly talk through her tears. "You have no idea what you mean to us and to Brody. You've been his family. You've loved him and rocked him just like we have."

"I don't plan to be a stranger, either," Debbie said and gulped back more tears. "I hereby volunteer to babysit whenever you need someone. This little guy is mine too."

Debbie took Brody's blankets off, and then Fran noticed something else. Brody was already dressed in his blue going home outfit.

And then, in the single most terrifying moment of her life, Fran watched as Debbie carefully removed Brody's IV and every lead from his body. Those leads had been keeping track of his heart ever since he was born. Now, as Debbie removed them, the lines on the machines went flat. Debbie turned the machines off, bundled Brody in a fresh blanket, and handed him to his mother.

"No monitors at home?" Fran couldn't believe it. No crutches. No monitors to watch to ensure her baby was all right.

"Nope. You don't need them. He's fine, just like any other baby. We waited until we were sure he was completely recovered. You don't need a repeat of what happened a week and a half ago."

"I recommend you get a good pediatrician immediately, so he or she can get a baseline and follow Brody day to day," Dr. Bunyapen said. "Take him home and congratulations!"

After another round of hugs and tears, Jeremy and Fran made their way down the elevator and, for the first time, buckled their son into his car seat and headed for home.

29

Fran and Jeremy's first order of business was to find Brody a pediatrician. One of Fran's friends highly recommended Michael Caldwell, whose office was not far from their home.

The morning after Brody came home from the hospital, they called Dr. Caldwell's office and set up an appointment. They arrived on time and were given a bundle of new patient paperwork to complete. With Brody's history, it took a while, and they were still working on it when the nurse called them to the examining room.

Jeremy held Brody while Fran finished the forms. Just as she filled in the last line, they heard whistling and footsteps approaching. The door opened, and a young, tall, blond man stepped in. "Hi, I'm Michael Caldwell," he said, "and I guess you're the Gideons, and this is Brody."

"Hi, Dr. Caldwell." Jeremy and the doctor shook hands. "Yes, this is Brody."

Dr. Caldwell reached for the clipboard that Fran still held. "All done?"

"Yes, sir." She handed it over, and they both watched while he read it. He was completely professional, but they could both see when he reached the part about the pacemaker implant. His eyebrows raised a fraction, and a little of the color drained from his face.

"So…" He rubbed a hand over his mouth and searched for the right words. "You've brought me a two and a half week old baby with a pacemaker, and no paperwork? Nothing from his doctors?"

Fran produced a list of all Brody's doctors from MCG and their contact information. "These are his doctors. We were only released from the hospital yesterday. They said it was essential for us to find a good pediatrician and establish a baseline. That's why we're here."

Dr. Caldwell scanned the list. "This is very comprehensive," he said.

"And they were all at the delivery, plus about a dozen more," Jeremy said.

Dr. Caldwell whistled again. "How about you just tell me about it and about Brody."

They told him the story of the past four months. He examined Brody as they talked and asked questions, filling in details they wouldn't have thought to tell him.

"What about the stitches?" he asked as he carefully inspected Brody's incision.

"They say the stitches will self-absorb," Jeremy answered.

"Medications?" Fran handed him a list. He scanned it. "Not much, really. The diuretic makes sure the fluid doesn't come back, and the steroid keeps swelling down."

"They say that all things considered, he's a normal little boy," Jeremy said.

"Except for the incision, he seems completely normal. His weight and overall health are excellent," Dr. Caldwell said. He moved the stethoscope and listened some more.

"He's the youngest ever to get a pacemaker at MCG, maybe the youngest anywhere," Fran put in.

"I'd say that's true." He closed Brody's shirt and took his stethoscope off, then smiled. "He's my first and only pacemaker patient. I'm going to make some calls to MCG and get more information. Make a follow-up appointment for two weeks from now, and we'll recheck him."

*   *   *

Before two weeks were up, Fran and Jeremy were at the Aiken emergency room with a feverish Brody. He had frequently been fretful and colicky, which was understandable given what he'd been through, but having a fever was not acceptable. Dr. Caldwell had instructed them to rush Brody there, and he'd meet them.

The ER physician took one look at Brody's incision and admitted him. Dr. Caldwell arrived shortly afterward and agreed. Brody had an infected stitch, which they said was exacerbated because the steroid he was taking to reduce inflammation had also impaired his immune system and made him more prone to infection.

All of that made sense, but it was of little comfort to Fran as she and her husband raced through the hallways of the hospital alongside Brody's crib.

What next? An infected stitch, for crying out loud? They'd been through two heart surgeries and were now back in the hospital for an infected stitch?

They got the baby settled in his room and took a breath. "What now?" Jeremy asked Dr. Caldwell.

"We get him on some antibiotics, get on top of the infection, and get that fever down."

So the vigil began. Nobody could find a vein in Brody's hands and arms, so the IV was put into his right heel. He shrieked. Fran cringed and cried. Hours crawled by as medicines dripped continuously into his little body. Everyone anxiously watched for the redness to go away and his fever to go down. But the infection still raged.

Fran never left Brody's side. She sat and prayed and held him and rocked him as best she could in the uncomfortable straight chair. Jeremy had to work, but otherwise, he was there as well. James and Mary came and went. Julia called for frequent updates. Nobody was panicking; it was just an infected stitch, after all. Surely Brody would go home soon.

At the end of the second day, when Fran had spent a solid forty-eight hours in Brody's hospital room, Julia could stand it no longer and drove to Aiken to see for herself. She blew into Brody's room like a blonde, green-eyed tornado and took in the scene in a glance.

Brody lay in his crib, dozing but feverish and fretful. Fran was flopped in the uncomfortable chair beside him, looking like a ghost. Julia put her foot down.

"I will take care of Brody," she said. "You are going to go home and get some sleep."

"I can't leave him," Fran protested.

Julia pointed Fran to the mirror in the bathroom. "Look at yourself. You're not far removed from major surgery yourself, and you're about to be in the bed beside him. Do you think you're going to be able to take care of him when he gets home?"

Fran wilted. Julia pounced.

"Go. I will take care of my grandson, I promise you."

"He just ate," she said feebly. "I'll take a nap and come right back."

"Don't set any alarms. I've got this. I'll call you if anything happens."

At last, Julia thought as Fran left the room. *I've got Brody all to myself. Let's just see about this.* She sat down in the chair Fran had vacated and watched her fretful grandson. He wasn't crying, exactly, just restless and uncomfortable. Before long, though, he started crying in earnest.

She carefully picked him up, cradling him lovingly against her chest. The chair wouldn't let her rock him, so she stayed on her feet and gently rocked him from side to side. She walked him and talked to him. Nothing helped. His cries became screams. Julia checked his diaper and found it clean and dry. She became concerned and hit the nurse's button.

"Can I help you?"

"I think something's wrong. Brody won't stop screaming."

The nurse came in, examined the baby, and discovered that the IV in his heel had come dislodged. The needle was still in, but it was wiggling with every kick of Brody's feet. No wonder he was screaming.

"We'll need to reinsert the IV," the nurse announced.

She took all the tape off, withdrew the needle, and started over on his left heel. The first stick didn't work. Nor did the second. Minutes passed, and the nurse was still digging into Brody's tender little heel. The more she dug, the louder Brody screamed, and the angrier Julia became. Finally she could stand no more.

"Give him to me," she snarled and took Brody from the nurse. "You're not helping anything."

She cuddled him to her and crooned. The torture having ceased, Brody immediately began to quiet and soon dozed off. The nurse stood and stared.

"He needs his IV…" she stammered.

"Not right now he doesn't," Julia shot back, fire in her eyes. "You're going to let him calm down first."

The nurse fled, leaving Julia alone with her grandson. This was really the first time she'd had a chance to be alone with Brody and hold him as a grandmother does, and her eyes filled with tears. Her baby's baby. What a sweet treasure. Still on her feet, calm now, she pressed her cheek to his and rocked him from side to side.

After a few minutes, the nurse came back in, more subdued. "I talked to the doctor. He says we can give him the medicine in shots, every four hours. We don't need to put the IV back in."

"Good. Thank you," Julia said softly, not wanting to wake her sleeping grandbaby.

The nurse left, and before long, she and another nurse returned, dragging a big, padded rocking chair. "Maybe this will be more comfortable," she said. Julia knew this was a peace offering, and she accepted it gratefully.

"That will be so much better. Thank you."

When Fran and Jeremy arrived back at the hospital early the next morning, Fran was somewhat rested but still looking haggard. They found Julia cozily ensconced in the big, stuffed rocking chair, Brody sleeping peacefully in her arms.

"What in the world?" Fran asked. She laid her hand gently on Brody's forehead. He was still warm but unmistakably cooler.

Julia shrugged. "They made me mad. They were hurting him. He's resting better now."

Fran started to grin, then to laugh. "That's my mama," she said. Jeremy just shook his head and smiled.

Dr. Caldwell strode into the room, whistling as usual, and took in the scene.

"Dr. Caldwell, I don't think you've met my mother," Fran said. "This is Julia Chapman."

"So you're the one I've heard so much about." His eyes twinkled. "Good for you. Let me take a look."

He took what seemed like forever to take Brody's temperature, inspect his incision, and listen to his heart. Finally, he nodded with a smile. "He's on the upswing," he said. "We're getting it under control."

Parents and grandmother released their collective breath. Fran said, "Thank You, God."

Knowing Brody was going to be okay, Jeremy went to work.

After a few minutes, Julia eyed Fran. "You know, you've still got a long way to go before you're recovered," she said in a no-nonsense tone. "We're okay. You go back home and get some more rest."

Fran let herself be convinced, only because it was Julia—the one person on the planet she would have allowed to care for her son today.

By the end of the fourth day, finally recovered from all he'd been through, Brody was allowed to go home.

30

In June 1991, Julia stood in the shower at her second-floor town-house in Laurens, her head under the water as she scrubbed at her hair. She'd lived at the townhouse since 1988 when she'd sold the Hickory Tavern house to her next-door neighbor and downsized. The townhouse was just blocks from her job, and the smaller place suited her—no yard work, no mowing. Julia most decidedly did not miss mowing. Nor did she miss the responsibilities of being a homeowner. Renting was just fine.

She lived contentedly with Lucky, Fran's big, fluffy black-and-white cat to whom Fran had now developed an allergy. Julia was resigned to the fact that Lucky was her cat now.

She'd been alone for more than eight years since Pete died in 1983. Fran had come home for mere weeks before she got the reporter job in Aiken and moved away for good. Chris and Danny had moved to Atlanta from Boston in 1986 when Jason was sixteen and Dana fourteen. They were closer but still a couple of hours away.

Also in 1986, Julia's mother, Lizelle, had passed away at eighty-three. She'd lived in a small apartment in Laurens for the last several years of her life, with Julia providing for her and spending lots of time with her. Finally, decades of smoking had done their work on Lizelle's heart. She'd quit but far too late. When she went, she took a piece of Julia's own heart with her. Every minute of every day, Julia wished she'd had more time with her mother, but she was so grateful she'd been there for her in the last decade of her life.

In 1989, Chris and Danny had divorced after twenty years of marriage. Chris now lived alone but had begun dating a kind man named Jesse Giles. Jason and Dana were nineteen and seventeen years old. Everyone had their own lives now, and Julia was all alone at the age of fifty-four. She was still beautiful, inside and out. Men had been interested, but she had never had it in her heart to reciprocate. She was there for Chris and Fran, but they were all grown up. Her work at Laurens Community Residence had become a full-fledged career and demanded most of her time. The women there were like her daughters.

She lathered, rinsed, and repeated, then applied conditioner and rinsed again. Through the roar of the water in her ears, she thought she heard a pounding at her back door. She hurriedly turned off the shower and listened again. Someone was definitely knocking.

"Coming!" she shouted. It could only be the maintenance man, coming to check on the faulty light switch in the kitchen. She'd called days ago. She swiftly toweled her hair dry, wrapped herself in a robe, and applied lipstick. The lipstick was a lifelong habit—a lady did not leave the house without her lipstick, even if it was just to open the back door for the maintenance man.

She rushed through the apartment, almost tripping over Lucky, and breathlessly flung open the back door. No one was there. Julia stepped out onto the landing and looked down the steps.

A man, halfway down the steps, stopped and looked up at her. He wore a tool belt, a Clemson baseball hat, a t-shirt, and jeans. He looked vaguely familiar, but Julia couldn't immediately place him. What she noticed most was his eyes, warm and appreciative.

"Hello, Julia," he said.

As the man was fixing the light switch, Julia figured out why she knew him. His name was Cecil Walker, and he owned a heating and air conditioning business in town. Cecil did the maintenance work on the townhouse as a favor to the owner and had also worked on the Hickory Tavern house in the past. He had a history with Pete, from when Pete sold life insurance. Cecil had bought a policy, and years later cashed it in to get started in the heating and air business.

Julia didn't think she'd ever actually met him before today, but Cecil definitely knew her.

He finished his work, took a deep breath, and looked at her.

"Should be working fine now," he said and hesitated. "I'm sorry about Pete. He was a good man."

"Yes, he was," she said simply.

He looked down, then back up into her eyes. "Listen, I'm not going to ask you right now, because my divorce isn't final yet. But when I'm free, would you consider going to dinner with me?"

Looking into his eyes, for the first time in a very long time, Julia felt a stirring interest. She nodded slowly.

"When you're free, call me," she said.

*　　*　　*

Within weeks, Cecil was a free man, and he asked Julia out. Soon Julia took him to Aiken to meet Fran and her family. Fran greeted Cecil with suspicion and coolness. Jeremy shook his hand warmly, and Brody—the little traitor—grinned and cooed in his arms. Fran was full of doubts. Her mother had never dated before, and Fran was not interested in sharing her. Besides, no one could ever possibly be good enough for Julia. No one. Ever.

Cecil did not give up. He showed Chris and Fran patience and promised to take care of their mother forever. Slowly, he won them both over, and they began to love and trust him. No one was surprised when he proposed to Julia in the fall.

In October, Fran was Chris's matron of honor when she married Jesse. And in December, in a beautiful Christmas wedding, Fran and Chris both stood proudly with their mother as she became Julia Chapman Walker.

31

"Now, it's time for Mark Smith to present the children's sermon," said the worship pastor at East Maryville Baptist Church. "Will the children please come down?"

Mark huddled under a pew near the back of the church, hidden from the children. The people sitting next to his spot kept his secret, smiling a little but not looking in his direction. He carefully checked the microphone to be sure it was turned off and remained silent as the children's little feet passed within inches of his face. Peering through a sliver between the pews, he could see a portion of the stage, enough to know what was going on.

The kids sat down on the steps at the front of the church and looked around with wide eyes, wondering where he was. Mark had been doing children's sermons every Sunday for two years, shortly after he and Lisa moved to Maryville and started coming to church here. There was usually a good turnout, at least twenty or thirty kids under six. His sermons were always unusual and to the point, designed to get the kids' attention and teach them a morsel of spiritual truth.

He milked the moment, wanting to build suspense but not give the kids time to get fidgety. Then he turned the microphone on.

"Good morning, everybody!"

Silence, then rustling as the kids stood and peered around.

"Good morning!" he said again.

"Good morning, Mr. Smith!" Their young voices came in a chorus.

"How is everybody this morning?"

"Fine!"

He could still hear little feet moving around on the stage and steps. They went out of his line of sight, but he could tell they were looking behind the pulpit, near the piano and organ, and even over the rail to the choir area. They thought it was a game of hide-and-seek.

"Everybody settle down and listen, okay?"

More rustling as the kids returned to their places on the steps and sat.

"That's good. Thank you," Mark said into the microphone. His deep voice resonated around the sanctuary. "Can you hear me okay?"

"Yes!" they chorused.

He dropped his voice to a more conversational level. "Can you hear me now?"

"Yes!"

He dropped his voice even more, to a whisper now, and held the microphone away from his face. "How about now?"

Their voices were more uncertain. "Yes."

"You can't hear me as well, but you know I'm still here, even though you can't see me."

"Where are you?" Mark recognized the voice of Lucas Fields, one of the regulars. He and his little sister, Hannah, were front and center every week.

"Come find me." He issued the challenge and waited. "I'm nearby."

They came off the stage in a rush and fanned out around the sanctuary. Within a minute, little Hannah peered under his pew and locked eyes with him. "Got you!" she announced and dragged him out by the hand. He let her lead him back to the stage, where they all settled in their usual spots.

"Okay, what did you learn today?" he asked them.

A newcomer raised his hand. Mark passed him the microphone. "You're not very good at hiding," the little boy said and looked startled as his voice echoed around the sanctuary. Everybody laughed.

"You're probably right, but here's what I want you to remember about today. Listen up."

The kids leaned in, their eyes round and focused on Mark's.

"Even though you couldn't see me, you knew I was there, right?"

They nodded.

"When you could barely hear me, you still knew I was there."

They nodded again, their eyes intent.

"When you looked for me, you found me." He opened his Bible and turned to the book of Jeremiah. "Listen to God's promise. 'Seek Me, and you will find Me, when you search for Me with all your heart.'

"That's what God wants us to do. Have faith that He's there and look for Him. He promises that you'll find Him, and He always keeps His promises. Let's pray."

They bowed their heads and closed their eyes, and Mark said a brief prayer thanking the Lord for always being there, no matter what. As he said the words, he felt the meaning in his own life. Even through the tough times—maybe especially in the tough times—God had been right there with him, helping him through and showing him ways to minister, wherever he found himself.

He rose from the steps and took his place in the pew with his wife and let his thoughts drift back over the past couple of years.

32

The road for Mark and Lisa in Maryville had not been any smoother than it was in Memphis. Although Mark had a home office, he still found himself on the road constantly, scouting and selling new churches. He specialized in offering envelopes and could guarantee a significant increase in congregational giving when churches switched to his design. More contributions meant more ministry and more opportunities to serve. When large churches signed with him, other large churches found out and wanted to do the same. Large churches meant bigger commissions.

Mark was the most successful salesman in the company, but it meant lots of face-to-face meetings with hundreds of churches over the entire Southeast. He handled church supply sales the same way he had done church software sales—every meeting began with prayer because he sincerely did not want a church to buy his products if it wasn't what the Lord wanted.

Then, just a couple of months earlier, Mark also joined forces with his dad and his uncle in the lumber business. His job with Century Hardwoods was to find sawmills and convince them to let him take their lumber and sell it to furniture manufacturers. His territory was the same as his church territory, and he could combine trips and make thousands of extra dollars every week.

The money was essential to him because his back was getting worse and worse, and he knew there had to be a breaking point. Either God would work a miracle, or he would need surgery with a long recovery time, or he would become unable to work at all. He was driven to stash away as much money as he could, while he could. It might have to last him and his family for a long, long time.

His time at home was increasingly taken up at church. In addition to doing children's sermons, he taught a Sunday school class and now there was talk of him taking over as Sunday school director in a volunteer capacity. He would be responsible for teaching all the teachers the lesson every week and equipping them with everything they needed to minister to their small flocks.

He was still convicted that he could never serve in an official ministerial role because of his divorce, but he could volunteer. And as long as God was opening doors, he would walk through them.

While Mark had hoped Lisa would form bonds with his parents and sisters, or with the women at church, it had not happened. She had no interest in either of them having social contact with anyone outside their home. Her dreams of having children had not yet materialized either. She busied herself keeping their home, but Mark knew she wouldn't be truly happy until God saw fit to bless them with children. They'd been married for over five years and were both eager to be parents.

The offering ended, and the sermon began. The pastor was doing a series on Revelation, which had always fascinated Mark. For the next twenty minutes, he listened intently and made copious notes in a notebook and in the margins of his Bible. Beside him, Lisa sat very still and listened quietly but made no notes. She had a distant look in her eyes and a slightly green tint to her skin, and Mark made a mental note to ask her later what was wrong.

He didn't get the chance. The instant they got home, she bolted for the bathroom. He could hear miserable retching as he followed her down the hall. He found her huddled over the toilet, holding her long hair back while she retched. Wordlessly, he took out a washcloth, ran it under cold water, and wrung it out. When the heaves finally stopped, he gently picked her up from the floor and pressed the cold cloth to her forehead, then the back of her neck.

"Better?" he asked.

She moaned. "I've been feeling rotten all day. For several days, really. I haven't been able to keep anything down."

"Must be some kind of virus. If it were something you ate, it would have gone away by now."

"Maybe you shouldn't be around me. You have meetings to-morrow. You really don't want this, whatever it is."

He led her by the hand while she staggered to the bed. "Don't worry about that. If you're not better, I'll postpone my meetings and work from home."

She was too weak to protest. He tucked her into bed and sat with her while she drifted off to sleep, then sat watching her and thinking. What if…

Lord, have You answered our prayers?

While Lisa slept, Mark darted to the pharmacy and fumbled his way through the family planning section, where he spent twenty minutes comparing pregnancy tests. Some had a plus and a minus, some had two little pink lines—good grief. He just wanted one that was clear and fool-proof, because he wanted no mistakes. If he could figure some way for Lisa to take the test without knowing it, he would do it. He really didn't want to get her hopes up and then break her heart.

He considered that for a few minutes, but since it was impossible to have his wife pee on a stick without knowing about it, he gave up that notion. He finally chose two tests, purchased them, and headed back home. Lisa was still sleeping, so he sat at his desk and studied the boxes. It would have to be done first thing in the morning, he learned, because the pregnancy hormones were most highly concentrated then.

Lisa slept the afternoon away and woke more clear-eyed, but still didn't want to eat anything. Mark finally coaxed her into eating a can of chicken noodle soup with some crackers.

How to bring up the subject? Finally, he just blurted it out while she ate her soup.

"Honey, are you sure it's a virus?"

"At first I thought it was something I ate, but it's going on for too long. What else could it be?"

He looked at her for a long time. "Could you be pregnant?"

She stared back, and he could see her brain working as she did the math. "I'm a week late, but that's not unusual for me. I didn't think anything about it. I've been too miserable."

He went to his office and brought back the tests. "I went out while you were sleeping," he said and handed her the boxes. "You have to do this first thing in the morning. It can't hurt."

She stared at the boxes, then back at him. Tears welled up in her eyes. "Yes, it can hurt," she whispered. "It will break my heart if it's negative. I want a baby so bad."

"And how will you feel if you are?"

"I can't even imagine. We've waited so long."

"Let's just have a nice, quiet evening and watch *America's Funniest Home Videos*. We'll think about it in the morning."

*　　*　　*

Morning came and with it, more miserable retching. Between rounds of huddling over the toilet, Mark got Lisa to pee on the stick. They both waited tensely, counting down the seconds. Before their very eyes, two clear pink lines formed on the stick. They stared at it and at each other.

With trembling hands, she covered her face and sobbed. "A baby," she whispered. "Finally."

He held her, tears forming in his own eyes. "A baby." *Thank You, God.*

The months went by, and the sickness continued. Lisa did not gain any weight. Halfway through, a sonogram told them clearly that the baby was a boy. Even going into her sixth month, she still didn't look pregnant. Her doctor continued to monitor her and said the baby must be getting all the nutrients he needed because he was doing fine. Lisa, however, was continually miserable.

By now, Matt and Patty Monroe were in town to stay. As soon as they found out they were going to be grandparents, they told Mark to find them a house and bought it sight unseen. With Patty there to take care of Lisa, Mark could continue to work. Mark's mother came and went, but Lisa wanted only Patty.

Finally, when Lisa entered her seventh month, she stopped being sick and became the radiant, expectant mother she'd always envisioned. Suddenly, with new energy, she prepared for the new baby and decorated a beautiful nursery. The ladies at East Maryville threw her a shower, and both grandmothers were in proud attendance as Lisa played baby games and opened dozens of baby blue outfits, diapers, and booties.

In November 1992, right on time, Lisa went into labor. Twenty hours later, Richard Morgan Smith came wailing into the world, plump and perfect.

From the moment he arrived, Lisa changed. This was all she'd ever wanted—to be a wife and mother. She continued being the sweet person she'd always been, but overnight she went from being an impatient, unhappy girl to being a contented woman. As Mark had always expected, this baby completed her. Now the next phase of their life could begin.

33

Fran and Jeremy Gideon dragged load after load into the house from their minivan. It was true, babies traveled with everything they owned. Swings, strollers, bouncers, clothes, toys—it was really ridiculous. They'd lugged all that stuff on vacation in Florida, to the extent that they barely had room for themselves and one suitcase apiece.

Jeremy's aunt had a condo near Cocoa Beach, and she'd offered it to the Gideons' small family so they could take a proper vacation without worrying about paying for a hotel. It worked out great, allowing them days at the beach, time exploring Cape Canaveral and the Kennedy Space Center, and also a couple of days at the parks in Orlando. And, of course, shopping. Brody would be starting 2K this fall. He would be at school for two mornings per week, and he needed to be stylish.

They'd been making a concentrated effort in the past year to get their second child started but nothing yet. They'd wanted their kids to be about two years apart but were now resigned to the fact that Brody would be at least three years older than his brother or sister. When they went to Florida, they threw all the ovulation thermometers and charts in a drawer and said they were just going to enjoy their vacation.

Who knew? Maybe she was pregnant right now! If so, she'd be having a child who loved roller coasters and water slides, because that was how they'd spent their time that week.

It was now August 1993. Brody was two and a half years old, and he was as healthy and normal as everyone had predicted. There were days when Fran actually forgot he had a pacemaker in his tummy until she went to change his diaper and saw the bulge, or when they called once a month to check his pacemaker. Then it hit her again—he was a special child.

He was a miracle child, actually. When he went for his six-month checkup, the plan was to assess the condition of his large ventricular-septal defect and determine when to plan the surgery. But after a thorough exam, the doctors could find no VSD or any sign that one had ever been there.

"It was there, right?" Fran asked Dr. Loudon when he, baffled, delivered the news. "For sure?"

"It was absolutely there," he said. "And like I told you at the time, holes that size do not close on their own. I can't explain this."

"You don't have to," she said in wonder. "I know exactly what happened. He's my miracle baby." Everyone looked at Brody, who seemed unfazed by it all. He sat in his carrier, looking at everybody as if to say, "Yeah, God worked a miracle on me. Why are you surprised?"

Overwhelmed and thankful, Fran picked him up and spoke softly into his ear. "God did this for you, sweet thing, and He's got special plans for you. I can't want to see what you do with your life."

Brody had in-home daycare with a wonderful, energetic woman named Phyllis Butler. They had put an ad in the paper and chose her after several arduous interviews. Fran had gone back to work when Brody was four months old. It was necessary for her to stay home that long but not one second longer. She was going stir crazy and needed to get back to work. She knew Brody was in good hands with Phyllis.

As NICU nurse Debbie Stazen had promised, she was their regular babysitter whenever Fran and Jeremy went out for the evening. When Brody received infant baptism at First Presbyterian Church, Debbie sat with the family. When he had his first birthday party, she was there with a man she introduced as her fiancé, Greg Matthei. Several months later, Debbie and Greg were married. Eighteen-month-old Brody was a special honor attendant.

Debbie's job with MCG had expanded to include being a member of the neonatal transport team. A pilot would fly her and a respiratory therapist from Augusta in a specially equipped small plane to pick up a desperately sick baby and bring it back to MCG. The flight saved many hours in the treatment of a little one who would have died otherwise. Lately, that had been all Debbie could talk about. She loved this new aspect of her job, knowing that she was making a real, measurable difference.

The two couples had become good friends. Not only did they have the strong bond they'd developed when Brody was in the hospital, but they'd had meaningful life experiences together since. They'd grown as close as family. Fran and Debbie loved each other like sisters. Brody called her Aunt Debbie.

This day in August was hot, muggy hot, and Fran sweated as she lugged in suitcase after suitcase from the van. She was exhausted. They'd only been in Florida for a week, but they'd packed a lot in, and it seemed like longer. Brody toddled around, running up and down the steps, happy to be home.

She was bringing the diaper bag into the kitchen to unload some things into the refrigerator when the phone rang. She snagged it as she went by and leaned back against the counter to answer it.

"Hello?" she said breathlessly.

"Hello, is this Fran?"

"It is, who's this?"

"This is Kim, in NICU at MCG." Fran knew Kim, but she didn't sound like herself. Her voice sounded nasal, like she had a bad cold or had been crying.

"Hi, Kim. What's up? Is anything wrong?"

Kim let out a deep sigh that turned into a sob. "I don't know how to say this. I guess you haven't turned the TV on in the past half-hour."

"No, we just walked in the door from Florida. What's happened?" Fran could literally feel the blood draining from her face. Jeremy stopped what he was doing to listen, as something was obviously wrong.

"Debbie and the respiratory therapist, Art Hardy, flew to Adel, Georgia, this morning to pick up a baby. That's down toward the Florida line near Valdosta. They did the pickup and were on their way back." Kim paused and Fran could hear her sobbing. "When they got close to the Augusta airport, they hit a thunderstorm, and the plane crashed."

"What? Did you say the plane crashed?"

"Just before it reached the airport. It crashed in the woods in the swampy area near the airport."

"Is Debbie okay?"

Kim paused and sobbed again. "Everybody on the plane is gone, Fran."

Fran slid to the floor. She couldn't feel her legs. She stared at her husband in shock, too stunned to cry. Debbie? Dead? That was impossible. She was too full of life; she had too much to give. Too much work to do here. Why would God take her now? And that little baby? No, it made no sense.

Jeremy lifted her to her feet, wrapped her in his arms, and took the phone from her. He put it on speaker so Fran could still hear. "Kim, this is Jeremy, and I've got you on speaker. Is there anything else you can tell us?"

"That's all we know." Kim was sobbing harder now. "The plane is still burning. We just know they're all gone. Debbie, Art, the pilot, and the baby. We're all in such shock. Debbie and Art—they did what they did because they loved these babies. They...I can't even put it into words. We're an absolute wreck. Everybody's here, even people who aren't on shift. It's like we have to be together."

"Do you mind if we come over too?"

"Please. Be careful."

Fran and Jeremy packed Brody back into the car and sped over to MCG. A haze of smoke settled heavily over the airport area. They could see it from the hill as they descended across the state line from South Carolina into Georgia. The smoke made the news somehow more real. That was where the plane had crashed, where Debbie had died doing what she loved. Fran knew she'd do it again in a heartbeat. Her heart hurt, but she knew Debbie would have willingly given up her life for any of those babies.

Fran's heart stumbled, then stopped for a second as she remembered Greg. Debbie also had a fifteen-year-old daughter, Whitney. What an absolute nightmare for them. Debbie and Greg had only just found each other, and now Whitney had lost her mother. With a lurch in her heart, Fran remembered that Whitney had just gotten her learner's permit, and Debbie was teaching her to drive.

Oh, dear Jesus, please be with them, Fran prayed. *Wrap Your loving arms around them and get them through this. It's going to be roughest on them.*

They pulled into the parking garage at MCG, but there was not a space to be found. Finally, after circling several times, they squeezed into an illegal spot at the end of a row. undoubtedly, today the police would have other things to concentrate on than illegal parking. They gathered their son and raced upstairs.

The scene as Fran and Jeremy stepped off the elevator was unlike any they'd ever seen here before. They'd been here numerous times, and it was always busy. Doctors and nurses zipped busily about as they simultaneously cared for their small patients and their haggard parents. Older people volunteered to spend their time here rocking the little ones so that even babies who didn't get any visitors would still receive some loving.

All of that was still going on today, but with an air of sadness so thick it was tangible. And there were triple the usual number of people here. As Kim said, they just had to be here. They walked around dazed, eyes red and dulled with shock and disbelief, needing to give and receive comfort. There was little talk; this was too deep for words. People hugged, cried, and prayed quietly as they held each other tight.

When the Gideons stepped into the NICU, Dr. Bunyapen met them and pulled them wordlessly into a group hug. They stood, locked in each other's arms and swaying slightly, for a long time.

Finally, Jeremy stepped back and wiped his eyes. "Do we know anything else?"

"There will be a memorial service on Friday downstairs in the auditorium," she said sadly. "I can't even imagine. Debbie and Art..."

"Is there any more news on why the plane crashed?" he asked.

"Just that it had something to do with the thunderstorm," she said. "Greg has been asking those same questions."

"How's Whitney?"

"She's a wreck."

"I can't even imagine losing my mother. And for it to happen suddenly, like that..." Fran trailed off and shook her head. "I can't even imagine."

The Gideons wandered around the NICU for the next hour, comforting and being comforted. They hadn't known Art Hardy, but they learned more about him that day. He had done all kinds of ground transports, but this had been his first air transport. Respiratory therapists had two-week call periods. Art had been scheduled for the second half of the month, but he learned that a co-worker's wife was about to go into labor at any moment, so he volunteered to switch calls with him. That respiratory therapist was there that day, shattered, knowing that Art had taken his place on that plane. The new baby was now to be named Arthur, after Art Hardy.

Fran and Jeremy went home that day with heavy hearts. She spent hours over the next few days writing a tribute to Debbie to be included in the package that would be presented to Greg at the memorial service. She only hoped it would help.

*   *   *

At the memorial service later that week, it was standing room only. Greg and Whitney sat in the front row with Art Hardy's parents and pregnant wife. Greg sat stone still, his eyes fixed on the floor. Whitney looked pale and in shock. Staff members and friends at MCG spoke heart-wrenchingly about their lost co-workers and friends.

At the end, Dr. Bill Kanto, chief of neonatology, took the

podium without notes. He looked as if he were carrying a twenty-foot beam on his shoulders. With difficulty, he straightened and looked out at the audience. With tears in his voice, he told about an experience in his rose garden at home that morning.

"The sun was coming up. I heard a squirrel run through the trees. A bird called. It was answered by another. It was a peaceful and beautiful morning. I looked to the east where the sun was rising. My eyes filled with tears. I tasted the salt of the tears as they ran down my face. I was unhappy. I still could not understand what had happened." He paused, got himself under shaky control, and continued. "And I lifted my eyes, and in my own way I prayed, and I said, 'Big Fella, if You ever take me up there to heaven, You're going to have to explain this one to me because I just don't understand what happened, and what You've done.'"

Crying, hurting with the loss of her friend, Fran could visualize the scene as he described it. Early morning in God's creation, with the sun rising to begin a new day. His mercies are new each morning, as the verse in Lamentations says. But even with her heart breaking, she leaned on God as she always had. She wondered as she always did when there was tragedy—how do people survive hard times without faith? Without hope? Dr. Kanto was questioning God, as everyone does from time to time. The questioning can be crippling if you don't arrive at the right answers. She'd had a few of those questions herself when she first heard the news.

A Scripture verse flashed across Fran's mind, one she hadn't thought about in years. She'd had a wonderful youth director at Friendship Presbyterian Church in Hickory Tavern, and it was because of Margie Wallace that Fran had a foundation of Scripture verses in her head. This one, from the gospel of John, spoke to her now. Jesus was speaking to His disciples the night before He was arrested and crucified.

"I have told you these things, so that in Me you may have peace. In this world you will have trouble. But take heart! I have overcome the world."

Fran sobbed again and wished a pastor was there to tell

everyone that God was there, crying along with them, because they were all hurting and He loved them. He didn't cause that plane to crash, but He was going to make something good out of it. And Debbie's and Art's legacies would live on. She hurt for Greg and Whitney and Art's family, and she prayed for God to reach out to them and comfort them and bring them peace.

The service ended, and gradually everyone dispersed. Within the next few days, a tree was planted near the front entrance of the Children's Medical Center at the Medical College of Georgia. Today that tree still stands, tall and strong, with a plaque at its base so Art and Debbie will never be forgotten.

This tree is dedicated in loving memory of
Art Hardy, respiratory therapist
and
Debbie Matthei, registered nurse
Died August 7, 1993

"To those who knew and loved them,
their memory will never grow old."

Art and Debbie were members
of the Neonatal Transport Team
who died during the air transport of a sick infant.
Art and Debbie made the ultimate sacrifice
while doing a job they believed in and loved.

34

Just a few short weeks later, Fran found out that she had indeed gotten pregnant in Florida. As Dr. Loudon had warned her, this pregnancy was considered at-risk because of what had happened with Brody, so they had to go through the same tests and same procedures and the same doctors—with the notable exception that Dr. Barton would be delivering this baby. Fran held her breath as week twenty-three came and went. They found out that it was another boy, and his heart continued to be healthy and strong.

This child's name would be Andrew Wilson Gideon. Andrew was an old family name on Jeremy's side, and Wilson was Pete's middle name. They would call their son Andy. Other than constant doctor visits, the pregnancy was uneventful, and Dr. Barton said Fran could potentially have a normal delivery, even though she'd already had one C-section.

Three weeks before her due date, Fran couldn't sleep. It was curious because she usually slept like a stone. Jeremy snored peacefully in bed, so Fran got up and wandered around the house. She looked in on Brody and then ended up in the other upstairs bedroom, the one that would be the nursery but was not yet set up because Andy's birth was still three weeks away. She stretched out, stared at the ceiling, and thought about everything.

Fran grieved over how much Debbie would have loved this new baby. Greg visited often. Whitney had gone to live with her dad, and Fran had not heard from her again.

When the results came back from the National Transportation Safety Board, the cause of the crash was determined to be "the pilot's failure to adequately evaluate inflight weather conditions, which resulted in a loss of control when the plane encountered a thunderstorm."

So that was that. There was no mechanical failure, no one to blame. The lives of four people had ended, just like that, because of a freak storm.

Thinking about everything, Fran finally drifted off to sleep and woke a couple of hours later, needing to go to the bathroom. When she got up, a surge of liquid gushed out between her legs. She gasped in horror, at first terrified that she was hemorrhaging. But there was no pain, and she could tell when she turned on the light that the liquid was not blood. It was clear.

She waddled downstairs and shook Jeremy.

"Jeremy, my water broke. Wake up!"

"What?" he mumbled sleepily.

"My water broke!"

"Well, clean it up!" he said and turned over.

She kept shaking him. "Jeremy! We have to go to the hospital!"

"Because you dropped a glass of water, and it broke? Clean it up and go back to sleep."

"No!" She shook him again. "My water! It broke!"

His mind finally cleared. "You mean your *water*?"

"Yes!"

They called Mary to come take care of Brody, hastily threw together a bag for Fran, and flew out the door. Fran expected at any moment to go into labor but did not. That changed quickly when she got to the hospital. Without the amniotic sac, the baby had to come out—one way or the other. Dr. Barton immediately put her on a Pitocin drip, which put her instantly into hard labor.

By noon there was no progress. No dilation. Nothing but one hard contraction after another. By then, James and Julia had arrived. Dr. Barton came in to check her progress.

"Anything?" Jeremy asked.

"Not even a little bit dilated," he said and stepped to the sink to wash his hands. He was silent for a moment, then he stepped up to Fran's side and looked at her with the warm, caring blue eyes she'd trusted for ten years. "Listen to me. You could do this. But I'm not putting you or Andy through it. I'm taking him."

She didn't hesitate for an instant. "Go ahead."

She was whisked away into an operating room and given an epidural. At one o'clock on the dot, Andrew Wilson Gideon was born, less than six pounds but perfect, lungs working beautifully as he let the world know he was not pleased to be out of his warm, peaceful surroundings.

The nurse wrapped Andy up and placed him into his mother's arms while Dr. Barton finished the procedure and stitched Fran up.

"Look, isn't he beautiful?" She ran her finger down his cheek, and he hushed for a moment, looking into his mother's eyes. "Yes, it's me, sweetie. Your mom. I'm the one who will always love you, no matter what."

After a few minutes, she relinquished the baby to his father, who then handed him off to the nurses so they could get him cleaned up and settled.

Mary brought Brody, now over three years old, to see his mother and new baby brother. He was instantly enthralled with this new addition. He wore a pin that said "Big Brother" and proudly held Andy for pictures. Within two days, they were home; and after six weeks, Fran was back at work.

35

Fran was now thirty-two years old and still struggled with one significant crimp in her soul—her regret and guilt over how she'd treated her dad when he was alive. No one could make her see that she'd only been a teenager at the time, and Pete had loved her and understood her no matter what. She knew that God forgave her, but she could not forgive herself. Even after eleven years, she still lived with paralyzing regret and guilt.

No matter how she rationalized it, she kept beating herself up. Her mind kept coming back to the fact that even after how she'd acted, she'd had one final chance to be there for Pete in the end, but he had died alone.

She confided in one of her leaders at work, Linda Walter, who listened attentively and said, "It's time to sign you up for The Wall," and promptly did just that.

Linda was a huge believer in The Excellence Series, consisting of three courses—The Pursuit of Excellence, The Wall, and The Advancement of Excellence. The series was presented by Context International, and Fran had already traveled to Baltimore to take the first course. She'd known she would be scheduled for the second course but didn't know when.

Why now, when Andy was so small? Then, looking at the literature, Fran understood. The course description could have been written for her.

How many times in your life have you found yourself stuck on the road to achieving a goal you want? Sometimes what keeps you stuck is a fear, real or imagined. Sometimes it is a perception of what others may think. It may be a self-limiting judgment: too young, too old, too tired, not enough time or money. We call those stuck places "walls." And they often seem as impenetrable as the real thing in brick and mortar.

Building on The Pursuit of Excellence, the work you do in The Wall unveils the experiences, fears, judgments, or other reasons you've let yourself hold back—and helps you discover tangible tools for working your way through those obstacles.

In July 1994, Fran was on a plane to Baltimore. She and eighteen others were briefly and cheerfully greeted and packed onto a bus, where the leader said simply, "Welcome to your Wall." Then they were taken to a camp in the hills near the city, with simple dormitory-style rooms and a comfortable conference center. Fran had no idea where they were, and it really didn't matter. She was there for a reason.

They arrived on a Thursday. The course was twenty-four hours a day, considering that you would be spending nights doing homework with your roommate, and was scheduled through the end of the day Sunday. There were no smartphones in 1994 and no reason for anyone to have a cell phone of any kind because there was no reception here anyway. Participants had to turn in their watches because time did not matter.

Their leader, Larry Stone, started the weekend by having each of the participants state what, specifically, they were there for. Some had issues with their kids, some with their bosses, some with their spouses. Some had confidence problems that were keeping them from advancing in their careers, so their issues were with themselves.

When Fran's turn came, she said honestly, "I'm here because I can't forgive myself, and now it's too late."

"What is it that you can't forgive yourself for, and why is too late?" Larry probed.

Fran searched for words. The pain was still so real, so fresh, just like it was that horrible night in 1983. "I had twenty years to be kind and patient to my father. He had Parkinson's and died all alone in the hospital when I was twenty-one. Now he's gone, and it's too late to be good to him."

This was all they needed to get started. For the next three days, they all worked on their specific issues. The participants began each day with a run in the hills—which Fran particularly hated because she had never run in her life and still could not figure out why anyone would want to. They worked together and separately, sometimes going off in pairs and sometimes going into the woods to reflect. They had specific assignments, all targeted at digging deep to address the issues that plagued each of them.

Through it all, Fran continued to feel just like she'd felt for eleven years, as if she were spinning her wheels but getting nowhere. Since Pete died, she'd spent hours talking with friends and family, and there was simply nothing new she or anyone else could say or do to help her get past this.

She could see how The Wall was terrific for some people. She watched as one person after another had breakthroughs, conquering issues they'd had for years. She was happy for them, but when Sunday afternoon came, she still felt no closer to resolving her own pain, guilt, and regret. Her wall was still there, and she had no idea how she would ever get over it, through it, around it, or under it. She was beginning to feel that this was something she was just going to have to live with, like a punishment.

Before the last group meeting on Sunday afternoon, Fran sought Larry out and told him where her heart was. He sat her down.

"What, exactly, is it that you feel so guilty for?" he asked her.

She tried to explain herself. "I was so impatient with him. He couldn't get a sentence out, and I would get impatient with him and walk away. He couldn't walk, and I would get mad and walk off and leave him. He couldn't remember anything, and I said awful things to him. He couldn't help it. He was sick. But I couldn't see that and didn't care."

"How old were you?"

"I was fifteen when we put him in a nursing home, and twenty-one when he died."

162

"Did he love you?"

This was what hurt the worst. Fran knew, absolutely, that Pete had loved her and Chris more than anything or anyone except God and her mother. "Yes," she whispered. "He loved me."

Larry let that sit for a minute. "What did you learn?"

Tears streamed now. "I learned that I will never again, as long as I live, treat anyone I love in such a way that I will have to be sorry. It hurts too much when they're gone, and it's too late."

He paused for another few seconds. Then he looked deep into her tear-filled eyes and said gently, "And don't you think your dad would think it was worth it for you to learn this kind of life lesson from him?"

Fran stared at him and could literally feel the walls around her heart crumbling. Yes. The answer was yes. Absolutely, Pete would think it was worth it to go through everything he'd gone through to have her learn something as important as this. He wasn't able to do the things for her that he'd wanted to do, but God had used him to teach her a life lesson that she wouldn't have learned any other way.

Now, when she made the choice to be kind instead of cruel, tolerant instead of impatient, she would think of her dad with love and gratitude.

Larry was still looking at her with tenderness and understanding, waiting for an answer. Her brimming eyes told him all he needed to know.

"Yes," she whispered. "Oh, yes."

36

With a happy wife and a beautiful son waiting for him at home, Mark attacked his work with a new vengeance and sense of purpose. The clients he met with saw a completely new Mark and did not quite know what to make of him. He had a new light in his eyes and a bounce in his step—even a little swagger that hadn't been there before.

It was happiness, pure and simple. He and Lisa had been doing fine before, but there was an underlying sadness, an air of being incomplete that Mark had not fully recognized until Rick came home, and their silent, empty house came to life.

Now, Mark was reluctant to go on the road and keep making a living. He just wanted to stay home and watch his son grow. But go on the road he did, where he doubled and tripled his previous successes.

He could not sleep at all because of the pain in his back, so he used the nighttime hours to drive, then had meetings all day every day. Every three or four days, the exhaustion would consume him, and he would go to bed for twenty-four hours. He made it a point to be home on Wednesdays, Saturdays, and Sundays. On Wednesday evenings, he spent two hours at church, teaching all the adult Sunday school teachers the curriculum for that week. They would watch him teach it, ask questions about it, and then be given all the materials they needed to teach it themselves.

Saturdays Mark spent at home, enjoying his family and preparing for the next day's children's sermon. He had endless new sermon material now, watching his exuberant toddler drink in life. Rick was a precocious two years old, asking questions about everything. He was absolutely a daddy's boy, living for the days when Mark was at home and shadowing his every step. Every week, the children's sermon was about something Rick said or did. Mark was inspired and skilled at translating these small, everyday occurrences into nuggets of spiritual truth for the children of the church. Sundays were for church, family, and rest.

Mark was now thirty-four years old and hoped there would be one more child—hopefully, a daughter—in their future. He wanted to live a full life and have God use him every minute of every day. When he went on the road, he was extra vigilant and careful. One Friday he was heading home from his week's trips. His route took him along an interstate through the mountains, with concrete barriers protecting the shoulders and the median. Beside the roads, on the other side of the concrete barriers, was a steep drop-off to the valley below.

Mark saw the whole thing happen, right in front of his eyes. Two cars were speeding along side by side, with only inches to spare between them and the concrete barriers. One of the vehicles swerved slightly, and that was all it took. The other car bounced against the concrete barrier and over it. There it hung, teetering like a see-saw, with at least two people in the car—the female driver and her child, who sat in a car seat on the back passenger side. With traffic whizzing by, Mark slammed on his brakes and screeched to a stop just feet from the car.

"Get away from the car!" he shouted to the young mother, who was about to grab for the door handle to free her child. Mark was afraid that in her zeal, she would push the car over the edge with the child inside.

"My baby!" she screamed.

"I'll get him! You get to a safe distance."

Mark eased up to the car, where it still balanced precariously between safety and oblivion. The slightest wrong touch would send it over. He got a good look at the little boy, sitting wide-eyed in his car seat. He looked like he was about Rick's age. Mark smiled reassuringly at him and motioned for him to sit still, then reached carefully for the door handle. Once he had it, he held it tight and pulled. The door opened easily, and Mark still held onto it.

"Buddy, you okay?"

"I'm okay, who are you?"

"Just somebody who wants to help. Stay still for me, all right?"

Still holding the door tight with one hand, Mark reached into his pocket with the other and pulled out the big, sharp pocketknife he always carried. There was no time to try to unbuckle the seat belt holding the seat in place. A movement like that would send the car over the edge. Once again, Mark silently thanked his Scoutmaster, Prof Powers. "Be Prepared" was about to take on a whole new meaning.

He flipped open the knife and in one smooth, swift movement cut the belts holding the car seat and pulled the boy out of the car, seat and all. The slight difference in weight was enough to instantly send the car plummeting over the side, far down the hill. They could hear the explosion as it hit.

Shaking a little now, Mark gently set the car seat down and let the little boy out. His mother ran up, white-faced and semi-hysterical. She snatched up her son and held him tight, murmuring into his ear. "Oh, baby," she said. "Oh, baby."

Mark made his way on trembling legs back to his car, which was at the front of the gathering line of gawkers, and smoothly pulled back onto the road. He was on his way before anyone realized he was gone.

He had no need for thanks or interviews or any kind of recognition. The boy and the mom were both alive. Mark only wanted to be used here on this earth, and he tried to stay vigilant and watchful so he wouldn't miss an opportunity to help. Then, when God put him in those positions, he was ready.

37

Mark's work with his dad and his uncle at Century Hardwoods was turning into a ministry of its own.

When Mark made trips to meet with churches, he was always scouting for new sources of hardwood timber. When he saw a truck full of logs, he paid special attention and tried to find out where it came from. He ventured high up into the mountains, looking for little roads that might lead to sawmills. Those sawmills often produced the highest quality hardwood, and the owners would happily sell Mark the lumber. He paid them generously in cash, then took the lumber to furniture manufacturers and negotiated an even higher price.

Sometimes these trips didn't go as planned. One sunny day, Mark was following a trail of a road into the mountain wilderness when he came into a clearing and found himself looking down the barrel of a shotgun. The man bluntly told him he was on private property and needed to turn around. Wordlessly, Mark obeyed, knowing he'd stumbled onto a moonshine operation, and this was not the time to even open his mouth. He got out of there with his skin and learned from the experience.

He went home and told his dad about it. Richard thought it was funny.

"Son, you'd best be careful up there. Where you find sawmills, you're also liable to find moonshine. You've got to be able to think on your feet."

It was interesting to spend this much time with Richard in a professional setting. All of Mark's growing up life, his dad had been a pastor. Mark had never gotten to see him in this environment before, and they were developing a new relationship as coworkers and friends.

Jim, Richard's brother, was savvy in his own way. He had multiple sclerosis but was still able to function at work and carry out office tasks. He too had valuable advice for Mark.

Mark listened, thought, prayed, and learned, and after that, he knew how to act and what to say in those situations too. He carried raisins in his car, and when he walked up to a sawmill, he tucked a wad in his lip and spat as if it were tobacco. He became adept at talking with all kinds of mountain people, and even sometimes brought moonshine samples back to the lumber office. Those samples never went home with him because Lisa allowed no alcohol of any kind in her home. Richard would suspiciously ask what it was, and Mark told him honestly that it was a new moonshine that one of his clients had given him. Richard's mouth fell open, and he shook his head.

"That wasn't exactly what I meant when I said you had to be able to think on your feet," he said.

When Mark established relationships with the mountain people, he went back again and again. When sawmill owners saw him coming, they knew they could get quick, ready cash for the inventory they had on hand. Moonshiners were not nervous to see him anymore. He sucked on his raisins and spat black juice, and they felt he was one of them.

Sometimes, he had a chance to witness for Jesus. He got into a long, deep conversation with a moonshiner named Vernon Harris, high in the mountains of Virginia. Vernon didn't understand how salvation worked.

Mark walked him through the Scriptures and the gospel message, explaining that whatever we've done, no matter how bad, Jesus has already paid for it all. All we have to do is accept His gift and let Him into our lives.

Mark could see the truth dawning in Vernon's eyes and knew God was reaching out for this man's heart. There, on the rough-hewn floor of a moonshine office in Virginia, Vernon went to his knees, and Mark helped him pray the sinner's prayer. He became a Christian on the spot and said he was giving up moonshining for good.

"Good for you, man," Mark said. "God will show you what He wants you to do."

Vernon heartily shook his hand. "Thank you. You showed me the way."

"No, God showed you the way. I'm so happy I could be here to see it. All glory to Him."

Mark left that day in awe of how God works. He had a feeling that Vernon would do good things for Jesus, and sure enough, soon after his salvation, Vernon and his wife became successful bluegrass gospel singers, sharing the love of Christ through music.

And his involvement in Mark's life was not over.

38

When Brody was four years old, Fran and Jeremy took him for a regular checkup with his pacemaker doctor, Barbara Wofford. There, they got the news they'd been expecting and dreading.

Brody's pacemaker had continuously worked since he was born to keep his heart beating at the fast rate of a healthy child's. They were in uncharted territory because Brody was so young, but logically they could expect the pacemaker battery to run down sooner than an adult's pacemaker would.

Every six months, Dr. Wofford, her nurse, and her pacemaker technician hooked Brody up to a computer that, essentially, talked to his pacemaker. This time, the pacemaker told the computer that its battery was low.

It wasn't like it was a huge shock. They'd known this was coming. But the idea of putting their little boy through another surgery was hard for them both. It was so easy, day to day, to forget Brody was different in any way. He was such a normal, active little boy with an outgoing, ebullient personality.

"It's not a major surgery," Dr. Wofford assured them. "All we're going to do is go in through the original incision, slide the pacemaker out, and slide a new one in. The wires are all fine, so we'll keep them. We won't even have to touch his heart."

"Didn't you tell us that when he got bigger, you would move his pacemaker to above his heart, where adults have it?" Jeremy wanted to know.

"Yes, and that will be a major surgery when it happens, but that time is not now. He's still too small."

"How soon do you have to do this?"

"The sooner, the better. Remember, without the pacemaker, his ventricle still beats at only fifty beats per minute. The pacemaker keeps his heart from having to work too hard."

"Are you sure that's still true?" Fran asked.

"Yes, we're sure. That's one thing we do every time we check him. We turn the pacemaker off to see what his heart will do. Nothing has changed."

Jeremy sighed and exchanged glances with his wife. She nodded.

"Okay then," he said. "Let's get it scheduled."

Victor Morris had an opening two days later, and Dr. Wofford swiftly locked it in.

Julia came to stay with Andy, and Fran and Jeremy showed up at MCG before dawn on the day of surgery. Before they went upstairs, they wandered outside and looked at the tree that had been planted for Debbie and Art. It was a strong, young tree and would grow to tower over the entire medical complex.

Brody pointed to the plaque. "What's that, Mommy?" he asked.

Fran lifted him up and read it to him, choking up when she got to the end. "That's your Aunt Debbie, sweetheart," she said. "She loved helping babies. She helped you when you were very tiny."

"I don't have an Aunt Debbie, Mommy," he said, confused.

"Yes, you do, baby. She's in heaven now. You'll see her again someday. She loves you very much."

It was time to go upstairs and check in. For the first time, they were not in the neonatal area but in the pediatric area. Nurses swiftly checked Brody in and got him ready for surgery. Dr. Wofford and Dr. Morris came in to speak to them one more time.

"You ready, buddy?" Dr. Wofford took Brody's little hand and looked down at him. He looked back at her trustingly.

"Sure. I've had two heart surgeries before, you know. This is nothing new."

They all hid smiles. Yes, he had had two heart surgeries, but he was a tiny baby then. He knew all about it because he had asked lots of questions at every checkup and had learned an enormous amount about his own condition. Amazing, for a child of four.

Brody spoke to his surgeon then. "Dr. Morris, what's going to happen now?"

"Well, we're going to give you something to make you sleepy and then take you into the operating room. When you wake up, it will be all over."

"But I want to see the operating room."

The doctors exchanged glances. "You want to wait until you get into the operating room before we give you the medicine?"

"Yes. I want to see everything before I go to sleep. Would that be okay?"

Dr. Morris shrugged helplessly and smiled. "I don't see why not."

"Let's go!" he said. "I'm excited now."

So, rather than watching a sleeping Brody be wheeled down the hall to the operating room, Fran and Jeremy watched as their alert son, in his small sized hospital gown, walked hand in hand with the surgeon through the operating room doors.

They smiled and waved as long as they could see Brody, but when he disappeared and the door shut behind them, Fran collapsed, sobbing, into Jeremy's arms. "Did you see that?" she wailed. "He *walked* into the operating room!"

"He's really something, that's for sure." Jeremy held her gently and stroked her hair. "He's going to be okay, honey. This won't take long."

They found seats in the waiting room. Jeremy was unable to sit still. He paced the floor and talked to the other people. Fran tried to distract herself by reading a book, but when she thought about what was going on the operating room, the butterflies in her stomach rose in a swarm and threatened to choke her. She calmed herself by praying for her son, then tried to read some more, then the cycle started again.

It was only an hour, but it seemed like much longer. Dr. Morris came out smiling. It's always good when your surgeon smiles.

"He's fine," he said and shook his head. "That's one special little boy. He had to look at everything in the operating room and talk to all the anesthesiologists and nurses before he'd let us put him to sleep and get started. I finally had to tell him that other people were waiting in line to have surgery in that room."

Pressure off, Fran laughed. "That's Brody," she said. "Can we see him?"

"He'll be waking up soon. We'll come get you."

He shook their hands and disappeared. They sank back into their chairs, where Fran bowed her head and thanked God for the successful surgery.

39

"It's a girl."

"Are you sure?"

"Absolutely. No question." The sonogram technician increased the size of the image on the screen. "See?"

Fran had no idea what she was looking at, but she was ecstatic. She and Jeremy had decided they were not going to actively try for a third child because trying was too stressful. If one came, they would be excited; but otherwise, they would be happy with their two boys. Secretly, though, she'd always wanted a little girl she could dress in ruffles and bows and frills.

Brody was five years old now, and Andy was two. The two of them ran Phyllis Butler ragged every day. Andy went full-bore at everything he did. The first time he climbed out of his crib, he was too young to talk in sentences. Phyllis asked him how he got out. "Boom," he said.

He would be in a different room from the rest of the family, and they would hear a crash. "I'm okay!" he would shout before they had a chance to run and check on him.

Fran found out in May 1996 that she was pregnant and would be due in early January, and she was again considered to be high risk because of Brody's heart condition. She had more confidence now because of Andy's good health, and she breezed through her pregnancy in high spirits even with the constant doctor appointments. The baby's heart remained healthy, and now came the good news that it was a girl.

Fran went home with the news. Jeremy swung her around and gleefully reminded her that he would be the one to name this child.

"You what?" she said incredulously.

"Remember when you wanted to name Andy after your dad?"

"Of course."

"You made a deal with me. You said that if Andy could have your dad's middle name, I would get to name our third child."

She stared at him. He didn't have his usual *I'm kidding* twinkle. "You're going to hold me to that?"

"I absolutely am."

For the next three months, Jeremy and Brody collaborated and snickered behind Fran's back. She tried to pry information out of them, but they clammed up.

"You're going to tell me before she comes, right?" she said.

Jeremy winked at his son. "Maybe," he answered.

Dr. Barton said this birth would unquestionably be a C-section since Fran had already had two. His decision was finalized as the baby grew and settled into a frank breech position—rear end down. Fran was now thirty-five years old, and she and Jeremy decided that their family would now be complete. Dr. Barton would tie her tubes during the operation.

Pre-term labor started in November, and Fran was given medications to stop contractions and relegated to bed rest. She obediently stayed on the couch as December crawled by. The baby was scheduled to be born on January 8, but she evidently had her own schedule in mind. On January 7, the contractions could not be stopped, and Jeremy rushed his wife to the hospital.

The epidural was put in but did not have time to work. Fran felt the incision and had to be put to sleep. When Mommy is knocked out, so is baby. In a silent operating room, at 8:58 a.m., Jeremy welcomed his daughter into the world and named her Veronica May. Brody had chosen Veronica after a little girl in his kindergarten class. Jeremy simply liked the name May.

And so it was that Fran did not know her daughter's name until she awoke.

* * *

Less than two months later, on February 27, Mark and Lisa welcomed their second son. Patrick David Smith came so fast that they barely had time to get to the hospital. Delivery was quick and uneventful, and Lisa was radiant. They too determined that this would be their last child. Mark was now thirty-seven years old and quite happy with his two boys. Days later, he had a vasectomy.

40

"Fran, I don't know what to do. She's burning up with fever, and I can't get it down." Phyllis Butler cradled a very hot Veronica in her arms.

"I'll be home in ten minutes." *What next?* Fran thought as she drove. *Please, God.*

She walked in the door to find that Phyllis was right but had actually understated the situation. Veronica was so hot she was listless. "You didn't tell me everything, did you?" she asked Phyllis.

"No, I didn't. I knew you'd get here as quickly as you could. I wanted you to get home safe and not wrap yourself around a telephone pole."

Fran was already on the phone to Dr. Caldwell's office and was told to take Veronica straight to the emergency room. He'd meet them there. High fevers in small babies are not minor matters.

"You'll stay with the boys?" she asked Phyllis.

"Of course."

"Brody has a tee ball game this evening. Jeremy will be here to get him."

"Yes, yes. Get out of here!"

Fran raced her tiny daughter to the hospital, and it didn't take long to determine the problem. Urine tests showed that Veronica had a kidney infection.

"How in the world?" Fran asked when she heard the news. She was still alone at the hospital; Jeremy was Brody's tee-ball coach, so he was tied up with the game. Mary was staying with Andy, and when Jeremy and Brody got home, she would take care of both boys so Jeremy could go to the hospital.

"We're going to figure that out," Dr. Caldwell said. "We're admitting her until we get her fever down and get some answers."

They took blood and did scans and x-rays, and by evening, all that was left to do was wait for news. James went to the hospital to find out the medical facts for himself. He entered the room to check on mother and baby, then went to find Veronica's doctors.

And just as they were trying to get Veronica's IV started, and she was shrieking in protest, Julia walked in the room.

"Cecil wanted to come, but I left while he was still at work," Julia said. "I heard her screaming when I got off the elevator. What in the world is happening?"

"We're waiting for test results," Fran said. "All we know is that she has a kidney infection."

"For heaven's sake," Julia said. "If it's not one thing, it's another."

Jeremy arrived after the tee ball game, but there was no news to be had. He, James and Julia eventually left, promising to be back first thing in the morning.

Fran sat through the night in a chair beside her infant daughter. The medications seemed to be working because Veronica's skin didn't seem quite so hot, and she seemed to be resting easier. It did not make Fran feel much better. She wanted answers. How did a tiny baby get a kidney infection?

The answers came first thing in the morning when a troop of doctors led by Dr. Caldwell entered the room. They came very early, before any of Fran's family arrived. Fran scanned their faces. Their looks were grim but confident.

"What's going on?" she asked.

"It's pretty cut and dried," Dr. Caldwell said. "We took a look at her kidney function, and it's a clear case of urinary reflux."

"Urinary reflux?"

"This is her urologist, Dr. Quinn. I'll let him explain it."

A young dark-haired man with warm brown eyes reached to shake Fran's hand. "Good morning, Mrs. Gideon. Let me explain how the basic anatomy works. Our kidneys have valves leading into our ureters. Urine drains down the ureters into our bladder. In Veronica's case, one of her valves isn't working, so the urine is backing up into her kidney and causing infection. We rate urinary reflux on a scale of one to five, five being the worst. Veronica is a grade four. The good news is that we can fix it."

"And the bad news?"

"We can't do it yet. She's too small."

"So what do we do?"

"She'll take an antibiotic every day to keep infection away. We don't want to do that any longer than we have to, so we'll keep an eye on her, and we'll do the surgery the minute we think she's big enough."

"When do you think that will be?"

"Before she turns two."

Fran took a deep breath. Seven years ago she might have thought the sky was falling, but after what she'd been through with Brody, this did not sound so bad. She nodded. "When can I take her home?"

"Today," Dr. Caldwell said. "Her fever is already coming down, and we'll send you home with everything you need."

Fran called home and told them the news. Jeremy came by on his way to work to hug and kiss his wife and daughter. Julia came to keep Fran company for the duration.

"She looks better," Julia said as she settled into a chair.

"Yes, she's better. I feel good just knowing what we're dealing with. She'll have a surgery to go through, but she'll be fine."

Julia turned her knowing gaze on her daughter. "Do you realize how different you'd be handling this if you hadn't been through so much already? You'd be a basket case."

"I thought about that when the doctors were in here. I guess I have a bigger perspective now. All the sick babies at MCG affected me too. They were so much worse than Brody. I was grateful then, and I'm grateful now. My kids are fine."

By early afternoon Veronica was released to go home, with a prescription for antibiotics that she would take every day for the immediate future.

41

Sometimes prayers are answered in unexpected ways. Finally, it happened—the day Mark had been dreaming of and praying for since that summer in 1980.

Patrick was a very colicky baby, almost constantly screaming and clutching his tiny belly. When Mark would come home at night, Lisa would flee, desperate for some silence, and leave Mark with the boys.

By accident, Mark hit on one thing that quieted Patrick, but it caused unspeakable pain in his back. He positioned his screaming son so that Patrick's head was at the crook of his elbow, and his bottom was in Mark's hand. Then he bounced the baby upside down. He walked and bounced, and Patrick's sobbing gradually ceased. The instant Mark stopped the bouncing, the shrieking started again. He gritted his teeth and kept going.

Mark walked and bounced, bounced and walked, until his son fell into an exhausted, deep sleep for a couple of hours. Then the whole thing would start over again. After two months of this, everyone's nerves were frazzled.

Late one night, about three o'clock in the morning, father and son were going through this routine. Lisa was trying to sleep while Mark was downstairs, walking and bouncing through the otherwise quiet house. Suddenly, in mid-bounce, all the pain from the past seventeen years was like nothing compared to the searing, excruciating torment that spread from his lower back like lightning down his left leg. He understood in that instant what Dr. Reid had meant in 1980 when he said, "You walked in here. Come back when you're crawling."

Incapacitated and screaming, he collapsed in the living room floor, writhing but somehow still holding Patrick. Lisa came running and fell to her knees beside him. "What, Mark? What?" Carefully, she took the baby, who immediately resumed his shrieking.

"Can't ... move."

"What happened?"

He breathed hard through his teeth and tried to make sense through the agony. "I think...my disc just split through like Dr. Reid said it would."

Mark's mother, Sharon, lived only minutes away. She came instantly but suggested that she be the one to take Mark to the emergency room. "The boys need you, Lisa. You stay here, and we'll call you."

Mark was seen and evaluated quickly, and was immediately referred to the orthopedists at the University of Tennessee Medical Center on an emergency basis. Sharon took him straight to the doctor's office from the ER, and within hours after he collapsed, he was in the office of an orthopedic surgeon, Dr. Jesse Froome.

"I don't know how you've been walking around, much less working." The doctor looked at the x-rays and shook his head. "How long did you say it's been since the initial injury?"

"It was in 1980," Sharon supplied. "He rode a mechanical bull at the beach."

"Seventeen years." The doctor shook his head again. "Incredible."

"Dr. Reid said he couldn't tell for sure what happened with that initial injury because the disc hadn't split all the way through," Mark said.

"Well, now it has. It's unmistakable."

"What can you do for him?" Sharon asked.

"We're going to have to fuse L5 and S1," he said.

"Will that give him relief?"

"Once the surgery itself heals, he should see a huge amount of relief because that split disc will be gone," Dr. Froome said.

"Will it stay fixed?" Mark asked.

"The answer to that question is not cut and dried, Mr. Smith. The L5 and S1 area is where the actual injury is right now, so that's where your acute pain is, and that's what we're going to fix. But you have degenerative disc disease. You know how the spine works, right?"

"Yes, I understand," Mark said. "The discs provide cushions between the vertebrae."

"That's exactly right. Every single one of your discs is at risk for future problems. You might go for months or years with minimal pain, but one by one, your discs will get to the point where they no longer serve as cushions. You'll be bone on bone, and your nerves will become exposed. You'll have to deal with those problem areas one at a time, as they give you significant trouble."

"How long will that take?" Sharon asked.

"Years probably. He can help himself by taking care of his back, eating right, getting healthy exercise, and taking supplements to strengthen his bones."

Mark understood what the doctor was telling him, but right then, all of that seemed light years away. He just wanted to fix the current issue and get back to his life. The idea that he might actually be pain free, even if it was only for a short time, sounded like heaven.

"Let's get the surgery done," he said. "You said we need to fuse L5 and S1. Exactly what are you going to do?"

"The best approach is to go in from the front," the doctor said. "That way, we completely avoid all the nerve bundles that are on the other side of your spine. We make an incision in your lower abdomen, cutting through all the muscles and pulling aside your intestines to keep them safe."

"That sounds like a big surgery," Sharon put in.

"With a long recovery time," Mark added.

"You're both right. But the other option is to go in through your back and risk damaging all those nerves."

"I'd opt for the anterior approach," Mark said.

"Me, too. We have two choices for fusion. We can use screws and rods, or we can install a cage. The cage is new technology. It was approved by the FDA less than a year ago. We place a titanium cylinder in your disc space and use a bone graft from your hip. You'd have less discomfort after the surgery, and we see better fusion."

"Why is that?"

"The cages are porous, so they allow the bone graft to grow through the vertebrae. Most patients don't need additional screws or postoperative back braces. This part of your back is where the lumbar and sacral areas meet, and you don't have a lot of movement there. The cage should work particularly well in that spot."

"How quickly can we get it done?"

"Let's see what my schedule is."

By the time Mark and Sharon left, Mark was scheduled to have fusion surgery in two days. He was in excellent health, other than his back pain. He was not on any medications that would delay the process. All he needed was to do his preoperative lab work, and that could be done the morning of the surgery.

In the car, headed home, Sharon shook her head and smiled. "The Lord sure does work in His own way, doesn't He?"

Mark shifted, several degrees beyond uncomfortable. He couldn't wait to get this fixed. "Yes, He does, but what exactly do you mean?"

"All these years, you've been doing everything you could do, to try to get this disc to split so you could get it fixed. Who would have thought you'd break it by bouncing your baby son in your arms?"

Mark laughed, then winced. "Years from now, we can tell Patrick he broke my back."

42

In August 1997, Mark finally had his long-awaited back surgery. As the doctor had predicted, the recovery was long and painful because of the magnitude of the operation. Not only did he have a cage implanted in his lower back, but all of his guts had to be moved aside in the process. The place in his hip where they'd taken the bone graft hurt as much as his abdomen wound and his healing spine.

He was very thankful that he'd worked so hard to put money aside because he absolutely couldn't work right now. He spent time with his wife and boys and recovered.

Slowly, slowly, he began to see results. No longer did he have the constant, nagging, gnawing pain in his lower back. Follow-up scans showed that the fusion was solidifying just as it was supposed to. Tentatively, afraid to really believe it, Mark ramped up his activity and began to breathe easier. If he was careful, he could do anything he wanted.

Rick would be in Boy Scouts the next year when he started first grade. Mark was particularly excited about this because scouting had shaped his life and he wanted to be there for both of his sons on their scouting journey. Lisa had already volunteered to be their den leader as long as they were at the younger levels. Mark couldn't wait to be involved when they entered their actual Boy Scout years. Maybe he could be an assistant Scoutmaster.

The doctor's warnings about his degenerative disc disease faded away and became someday. Someday he might have more back issues, but not right now. And it felt wonderful.

*   *   *

Back in South Carolina, the Gideons were in the midst of Brody's first soccer season. He was small and not very athletic but enjoyed being on the team. The coach put him far back on the field, as far as he could get without being goalie.

On this particular cold, rainy night in October, they were scheduled for their monthly pacemaker transmission before the game. At six years old, Brody could now do his end of the test by himself. The pacemaker nurse, Joanne, would call at a predetermined time. He would hook himself up to the machine, then put the telephone receiver down onto the transmitter. The nurse's computer would talk to Brody's pacemaker, and then Fran would get on the phone, and the nurse would tell her everything was fine and would schedule the transmission for the next month. This was the way it had been since Brody was born.

His pacemaker was only two years old, so right then it was smooth sailing. Hopefully, he would be ten or twelve before they had to have it replaced again.

Fran sat and watched her son go through the process. He went through it three times, which she thought was odd. Then he abruptly handed her the phone. "She wants to talk to you," he said, and looked at her with eyes that said *whatever it is, she could have told me herself.*

"Hello?"

"Fran, it's not working," Joanne blurted.

Fran looked into the trusting blue eyes of her son, still locked intently on her own, and struggled to keep her face blank.

"What do you mean?" she asked carefully. "Your machine?"

"His pacemaker. It's not working. At all. You'll need to see the doctor immediately. I'll let her know, and she'll call you and tell you what to do."

Fran hung up the phone, unable to believe what she'd just heard. Brody still looked at her, unafraid, waiting for her to say something. "What's the matter, Mom? What did she say?"

"I'm not sure yet, sweetheart. Dr. Wofford is about to call us. Go get your dad, okay?"

Obediently he trotted down the hall and Fran heard him calling for his father. "Dad! Mom needs you!"

Jeremy's footsteps came toward the bedroom, trailed by Brody. "What is it, honey? I'm trying to get the kids fed, and we need to leave for the game."

"There's a problem with Brody's pacemaker," she said.

"What kind of problem?"

"The nurse said it's not working. Dr. Wofford is going to call us."

Just then, the phone rang. Fran snatched it up. "Hello?"

"Fran, this is Barbara Wofford."

"Hi, Dr. Wofford. What's going on?"

"I can't tell exactly, but it's obvious that for whatever reason, Brody's pacemaker is not working. Joanne did everything she could from our end to get it going again. We're going to have to go in and fix it."

The room tilted. Fran sat down heavily on the bed. "Go in?"

"Yes, operate. First thing in the morning."

Fran looked at her husband and her son, still in shock. "They want to operate first thing in the morning to fix his pacemaker."

"Tomorrow?" Jeremy asked, incredulous.

"Yes."

"Let me talk to her."

Jeremy got on the phone, and Fran gathered Brody up into her lap and snuggled him. He was listening attentively to every word his father said.

After a few minutes, Jeremy put the phone down. "She said we could come in tonight and they'd monitor him overnight, then operate in the morning. Or we could just stay home tonight and go in early. We have to remember this could have happened anytime in the last month, and he's been completely asymptomatic. His condition isn't going to change between tonight and tomorrow morning. She said it was up to us."

"What do you think?"

"I think we stay home."

That made Fran very uncomfortable. She wanted to ensure her son's safety, above all. Then she looked at Brody. He seemed completely normal, completely himself, soaking in their conversation with a maturity well beyond his six years.

"What do you want to do, Brody?"

"I want to stay home, and I want to play in my soccer game."

"That's out of the question …" Fran began, but Jeremy held up his hand in a *wait a second* motion.

"Why do you want to play in the game, son? You understand that your pacemaker isn't working, so that would make your heart work really hard."

"I understand. But since I'm going to have surgery, it will be my last game this year, and I want to play in it. I don't run much, anyway."

Jeremy was silent, and Fran realized to her horror that he was actually considering this lunacy. To put their young son out on the cold, rainy, windy soccer field with a known heart condition that was going to require surgery tomorrow morning? To her, this was a slam dunk decision. No way, no how.

Brody's voice filled the silence. "If I don't feel good, I'll sit down."

Never taking his eyes from his son's face, Jeremy slowly nodded. "Okay. If you don't feel good, you sit down."

"Thanks, Dad." Brody left the room to get dressed and finish his dinner.

Fran turned on her husband. "Have you lost your mind?"

"Brody isn't an average kid, in case you haven't noticed," he said. "He understands things and knows his body."

"He's six years old!"

"He walked into the operating room when he was four, holding his surgeon's hand, remember? He's not an average six-year-old, and I trust him. If he wants to play, knowing what's going on with his heart, I say we let him."

"We're his parents! It's up to us to make these decisions for him!"

"I agree, and I just made it."

"Can we at least see what your dad says?"

"It's not going to change my mind."

James agreed with Fran. "I know he's asymptomatic right now, but there's no way he should be out in that environment with heart surgery coming up tomorrow morning. That's my medical opinion."

But the decision stood. Brody played.

Jeremy stood on the sidelines. James sat in the bleachers, ready to run to his grandson's aid at any moment. Beside him, Fran held Veronica and watched Andy play near his father. She was too terrified to speak. What if he got sick from this? What if he collapsed from lack of blood flow? They would go from Brody being a strong, healthy surgical risk to a sick child in crisis.

Brody got through the game, cold and wet but otherwise fine.

The next morning they were in Dr. Wofford's office at eight o'clock. One x-ray told the doctor all she needed to know. She pointed to the screen.

"See? There? His wire is broken."

"How could that have happened?" Fran asked.

"He's a normal, active little boy and the wire is right under the skin. It could have been anything. So now we fix it."

"How?" Jeremy asked.

"I recommend we take this opportunity to do what we were going to do at his next pacemaker replacement anyway. We put it in its permanent position, under his clavicle and feed leads into both his atrium and ventricle."

"You said that was going to be a major surgery."

"It is, and there's more."

She explained that in addition to his AV block, Brody had something called a patent ductus arteriosus. "The ductus arteriosus is a normal part of a baby's circulatory system before birth, but it normally closes shortly after birth," she explained. "Brody's didn't close, which puts him at risk for infection. It's small and evidently hasn't been giving him any problems, but it could in the future, and I think we should go ahead and take care of it now."

Every new revelation felt like a hammer blow to Fran's heart. She felt battered and wasn't sure she could take much more. Yesterday, she'd been sailing along, with everything going great. Now they were looking at a double major surgery on their precious little boy. Tears filled her eyes, and she felt herself crumbling under the pressure.

God, help me. I don't think I can handle this.

You can do all things through Christ, who gives you strength.

She closed her eyes, took a deep breath, and let the Scripture soothe the jagged edges.

"Is that it?" she asked.

"That's it."

"When?" Jeremy asked.

"Now."

43

It felt so good to Mark to be living normally again. It had been eighteen long years, and Mark had forgotten what it felt like. As soon as he was cleared by his doctors, he resumed his previous schedule—but now it was different. He had hope—hope that this wonderful absence of pain would continue, and he could do all the things he wanted to do.

He could sleep at night, which was marvelous. And he could be the spiritual leader to his boys that he'd always envisioned.

Rick was now six years old, and Patrick was two. Lisa was Rick's Cub Scout den leader. Cub Scouts were intended for younger boys to get a firm scouting foundation, so they were ready for full-fledged Boy Scouts when they were old enough. Under Mark's unseen guidance, Lisa provided that foundation. She organized meetings and planned activities, which were often art projects and field trips. Patrick tagged along and tried to do everything the bigger boys did.

The tiny boat Mark had bought years ago in South Florida was too small for a family of four, so he upgraded. Lisa had no interest in fishing; she only wanted to sun herself and play with her children in the water. So although Mark wanted a bass boat, he compromised and found a pontoon boat. Then he customized it so he could also use it for fishing.

In every way Rick was his father's son. He was Mark's shadow, drinking in everything his dad could teach him from tying knots to fixing things in the house to reeling in a largemouth bass. When Mark arrived home from work, Rick erupted from the house like a bullet and hurled himself at his dad. They fell together in the yard, wrestling and tumbling as Lisa and Patrick watched from the front porch.

Mark bought a prayer bench and set it up in the dining room. Above it, he hung a picture of Jesus. If you looked closely, you could see that the picture was actually the entire gospel of Luke, printed very small and stylized into a likeness of the Savior.

Every night, the family gathered at the prayer bench for prayer time and worked on memory verses. Mark typed the verses onto index cards and kept them organized in a Rolodex. The cards were color-coded to represent every family member who'd memorized the verse. Patrick, at two years old, was learning to pray and soaking in Scriptures before he could even talk well.

Mark had a way of turning everything into a game. The boys knew what was coming at the end of prayer time. Rick, ever the competitor, was on high alert. The instant Mark said "Amen," he and the boys attacked each other in a tickling and wrestling contest that ended only when there was one victor. Everyone else had to say, "Uncle!"

At work, Mark was rejuvenated. He redoubled his efforts at both jobs, reeling in one large church account after another and re-vamping the office at Century Hardwoods to be more modern and computerized. He did the hiring, firing, and tax paperwork. Previously, Century had a very specific niche. They bought high-quality hardwood and sold it to manufacturers of fine furniture. Mark saw growth opportunities here. He found markets for every-thing his sawmills produced, even the lower-quality products. Their profits soared, and so did his. He kept padding his bank account, knowing from experience that the more money he could put away, the better. He tried his hand at investments, and they soared.

He faithfully tithed on every penny, often going over and above his tithe for causes that God put on his heart.

East Maryville Baptist Church asked him to do more and more, and soon he was on various search committees, running the home-bound ministry, and participating in prison ministry, in addition to teaching teachers and giving children's sermons.

It seemed that everything he did was blessed, and Mark had been through so much that he didn't take any of it for granted. He felt almost like Job, who'd had everything taken away and then had his fortunes restored. Mark did not compare himself to Job, but he thought he understood how Job felt.

This was life, finally, and he was soaking in every second.

44

On April 4, 1999, Fran was at work when she got a call from home. She eyed the caller ID with dread. What now? They had a new sitter, an older woman named Mamie. She was extremely competent and never called Fran at work.

Veronica had her kidney surgery last summer. She was doing fine and was off her antibiotics. She was a beautiful little girl, with dark ringlets and big blue eyes. She wasn't talking much because she simply didn't need to. Her brothers did all the talking for her. Brody had recovered well from his fourth heart surgery and was back to playing tee ball. Andy was running around being his full-speed self, impatient to begin his own youth sports career this fall.

Julia, having been a Clemson fan her entire life, was doing her best to ensure that her grandchildren loved the Tigers. When each of them was born, she signed them up for the Tiger Cub Club, so all of their lives they regularly received cool Tiger gifts in the mail. Since the boys were tiny, Julia had given Fran two tickets for several Clemson games each season. Fran took them each to one and would take Veronica when she got old enough. Julia took them to other games. They went early and tailgated with their great-aunt and cousins, playing football in the parking lot and sliding down a big hill on a piece of cardboard. The Gideon kids learned to be real fans, the kind who pull for their team no matter what, who never leave early no matter what the record is, what the score is, or how hard it's raining.

The Gideons were fulfilling Fran's longtime commitment to herself to bring her children up in the church. They went to South Aiken Presbyterian, the church where the boys had both gone to preschool and kindergarten, and where Veronica was registered to begin 2K in the fall. Fran had lots of friends there and was active in Presbyterian Women. The pastor, Olin McBride, was wonderful.

Today was Andy's fifth birthday, and they were in the middle of planning a big birthday party this weekend. Tonight was a family birthday celebration with Andy's favorite homemade double chocolate cake. Fran had made it last night.

Now, sitting in her office, she stared at the phone as if it were a crouching tarantula. *Please, nothing bad.* She sent the short prayer up before she picked it up.

"Hello?"

"Fran, I think you need to come home."

"What's up?"

"Veronica has a fever."

Those words sent dread through Fran's heart. A fever with Veronica wasn't like a fever with other kids. Many, many times a fever had sent them to Dr. Caldwell, where he used a catheter to collect a urine sample and make sure there was no kidney infection. Now, even though Veronica had had the surgery that was supposed to fix the problem, Fran couldn't help but worry.

Her job now was much farther away from home. She still worked for the same department in the same company, but her boss had assigned communications staffers to work directly for the vice presidents of various operational divisions across the Savannah River Site. Communicators handled all internal and external communications for their assigned division, and their offices were wherever their division was.

The Savannah River Site was a big place, more than three hundred and ten square miles. The nuclear facilities themselves were near the center. Fran was assigned to the Spent Fuel Storage Division, with offices in the backyard of one of the historic old nuclear production reactors. In its Cold War heyday, this reactor had produced plutonium for the United States' nuclear warheads. Now, with the Cold War over, its storage basins were being used for safe underwater storage of spent nuclear fuel from around the nation's nuclear complex until it could be processed in other facilities at SRS.

She found the work fascinating and loved being in the field with the workers. But today, the thirty-minute commute was torture.

She hung up the phone and called Jeremy and then Dr. Caldwell's office. His partner, Dr. Adam Myers, was in this afternoon. Fran was told to bring Veronica in immediately. "I'll be there in forty-five minutes," she said and took off.

She went home, picked up her feverish daughter, and was in the waiting room in forty minutes. She and Veronica were called immediately to an examining room, and Dr. Myers didn't keep her waiting.

"What's up?" he said when he walked in.

"I have no idea."

He examined Veronica and took a throat sample for a strep test. Then he said, "Neither of you is going to like this, but I've got to get a urine sample."

"I figured you would."

Veronica was tired of all the probing and prodding, and screamed through the entire procedure. Fran couldn't blame her. She wouldn't like it much either. Dr. Myers said he would have preliminary results in a few minutes and left.

Fran sat in the examining room and tried to calm her agitated daughter. What if it was another kidney infection? What then? They'd already fixed her kidney; Fran had no idea what would be next.

Another of Margie Wallace's Scripture passages drifted across the unsettled waves of her heart. "Be anxious for nothing, but in everything by prayer and supplication with thanksgiving let your requests be made known to God. And the peace of God which surpasses all understanding will guard your hearts and your minds in Christ Jesus."

Be anxious for nothing. She closed her eyes and prayed as she waited. *Please, let it be nothing. Please, God.* She knew that they would get through whatever this was, but she wished with all her heart for some smooth sailing. Veronica calmed and dozed. Dr. Myers finally came back in, the test results in his hand.

"Well," he said, "we know where the fever is coming from. She has strep."

Fran sagged in relief. This was the easiest possible answer right now. *Thank You, God.*

Dr. Myers wasn't finished. "But her urine test is concerning. It shows glucose spilling over into her urine, which is a classic sign of oncoming juvenile diabetes."

"Diabetes?"

"Yes. I want you to go to the ER now, and we'll do a second, more sophisticated test. If it shows the same thing, we'll need to talk about a path forward for her."

Fran was full of questions. "What…"

Dr. Myers held up his hand. "Let's get the second test first. Then we'll talk."

Numbly, Fran strapped her daughter into the car and drove to the ER. More screaming as Veronica was subjected to the indignity of another urine sample. Jeremy rushed in just as Dr. Myers returned with the results, which confirmed that their little girl did indeed have high levels of glucose in her urine.

"This is pretty conclusive," Dr. Myers said, "But I want you to come back in the morning, and we'll do a fasting test just to make sure. If it's the same, we'll need to talk about ways you can do things differently for her now to make her life easier going forward."

Sobbing, unable to believe it, Fran trudged to the car with her daughter in her arms, Jeremy by her side. They already had one child with major health issues. Now another? How much was she expected to bear? And tonight was supposed to be about Andy. It was his birthday, and she still wanted him to have a good evening. There were final preparations for Saturday's party to be done too.

The weight of it all suddenly seemed overwhelming. She tried to remember the Scripture verse from earlier, but her mind was numb.

On autopilot, she strapped her daughter in and got behind the wheel. Jeremy leaned in her window and put his hand on her shoulder. "We'll deal with this," he said. "We always do."

She drove home, and they pulled into the driveway at the same time and climbed out of their cars. Andy came running out the front door. Jeremy caught his son in his arms and kissed him on top of his head. This was one thing Fran loved about her husband—he was unabashed about showing affection to his children. "Happy birthday, sport!" he said to Andy.

"Finally, you're home!" Andy squirmed free, then shouted and danced in place. "Now we can have our party! I want some cake!"

Fran lifted Veronica out of her car seat and dragged herself into the house with a heavy heart. She tried to be upbeat for her son, but the dread draped around her shoulders like a lead blanket. She hadn't stopped asking God to spare Veronica from having to go through diabetes, but she was beginning to resign herself.

Then she walked into the kitchen and saw it. The double chocolate birthday cake she'd made last night was only two-thirds there.

"Mamie?" Fran called for her sitter.

"Yes, Mrs. Gideon?" Mamie was gathering her things and getting ready to leave for the day. She came into the kitchen.

"Do you know anything about this cake?"

Mamie took a good look at the cake and gasped. "I cut a tiny slice for Veronica this morning. She wasn't feeling good, so I thought it would be okay."

"Just one tiny piece? Did you give Andy any?"

"Of course not." Mamie looked indignant. "I knew you were having a party tonight so I made him wait."

"Did anyone else have any?"

"No. I only gave Veronica a little piece because she wasn't feeling good."

Fran looked at the cake, then at Veronica, then at Jeremy. Veronica looked guilty as only a toddler can. Jeremy's face was beginning to light with laughter as he put the pieces together.

At two years old, the little girl was now adept at climbing and getting things for herself. She liked the sliver of cake Mamie sliced for her, so she got more. Then more, then more—until she ate nearly half of the cake. Mamie never noticed. Looked closely at her now, Fran saw chocolate on the front of her shirt.

"Veronica, honey, did you eat all of this cake?" she asked.

Veronica looked at the cake and then at her mother. "Cake," she said, and reached for it.

"Well, the little scamp. I wondered why she wasn't hungry all day," Mamie said.

Fran picked up the phone, called Dr. Myers, and told him about the cake.

"Would this explain her glucose levels?" she asked.

"Absolutely," he said, not quite stifling a chuckle. "Don't bother to come to the ER tomorrow morning. She's fine."

Fran hung up the phone and eyed her daughter, who looked back at her with those innocent blue eyes. "It's a good thing you're cute," she said.

45

In 2001, just weeks after the September 11 terrorist attacks, Richard Smith was on a business trip at Hilton Head Island in South Carolina. One morning, he took a long walk on the beach and collapsed. Witnesses later stated that he grabbed his chest and simply fell in a heap. He was gone before the first person reached him.

The only identification in his pocket was the key to his hotel room. It was nondescript and provided minimal clues as to which of the dozens of beachfront hotels he was staying in. It took hours for police to track him back to his hotel and find his next of kin.

The first person they reached was his eldest child, Lisa Lambert. She called Mark, who happened to be at the Century Hardwoods office, and arranged to meet him at their mother's house so they could tell her together, face to face, that the man who'd been her husband for decades was dead.

Mellie and her husband, George Davis, lived in Texas, where he was an agricultural economics professor at Texas A&M. She immediately arranged for plane tickets home, but the task of telling Sharon fell to Mark and his older sister.

When they walked into the house, she somehow knew.

"It's Richard, isn't it?" she said as soon as she saw their faces. "I've felt it all day."

They looked at each other, then at her. "Let's sit down, Mom," Lisa said gently.

She planted her feet and stood where she was, in the middle of the kitchen. "He's dead, isn't he? That's why he hasn't called."

Mark wrapped his arms around her. She felt small and frail in his arms. "Yes, Mom. He's gone." He felt her knees tremble and lowered her into a kitchen chair, then squatted in front of her. "Get her some water, Lisa."

"I don't want any water." Her voice trembled, but she maintained control. "What happened?"

Lisa eased into a chair next to her. "It looks like a heart attack. He was walking on the beach and collapsed. Some people saw the whole thing."

"When?"

"This morning."

"And it took them this long to call us?"

"He didn't have any identification on him. They had to track him down by his hotel room key. It took them a while."

"Oh, Richard." Her breath came out in a rasping sigh, and she closed her eyes. "He was never the same since we separated thirty years ago and he lost his pastorate. By the grace of God, our marriage survived, but he was never the same."

"I know," Mark said. "I know."

The three of them huddled there for a long time, wrapped in sorrow. Sharon finally broke the silence. "We need to call Mellie."

"I called her. She and George are flying home tonight," Lisa said. "I'll stay with you until she gets here."

"So will I," Mark said.

"No. You won't." Sharon stiffened her spine. "You both have families. You need to be with them. I'll be fine until Mellie gets here. You'll both go home, and we'll all meet here tomorrow to plan the service."

"Mom, I don't think you need to be alone," Mark protested.

"Yes, I do. The phone is going to be ringing off the hook when the church finds out. I need some quiet time now."

When the two of them reluctantly left, Sharon wandered through the silent house, remembering when she and Richard built it in 1982. Mark was already at the University of Tennessee, so Mellie was the only child still left at home. They'd built this house from the ground up, choosing every piece with care, knowing that this was going to be their forever home. It was lovingly furnished with antiques that she'd found and refinished.

Every piece had a story. Memories whispered from every shadowy corner. She had no intention of selling this house. Ever. She didn't know much at this moment, but she did know that.

She eased into Richard's study. She could still see him there, sitting at his desk, working on a sermon or a lumber deal. Even though he'd lost his pastorate, he was still much in demand as an interim pastor and revival preacher. He had thick files containing every sermon he'd ever preached. He worked while she kept the house and tended the children. It had been that way since Lisa was born in 1958.

Sharon blinked, and the memory faded.

Lord, what do I do now? The tears filled her eyes and trickled down her cheeks as the shock began to set in. *What in the world do I do now?*

Be strong and courageous. The holy whisper filled her soul. *I will not fail you nor forsake you.*

I can't do it, Father. I don't have the strength.

Lean on Me.

Somehow, she knew, she would put one foot in front of the other. When she didn't have the strength, God would carry her. She would do whatever came next, and she would be there for her children and grandchildren. God would handle anything else.

Days later, people packed First Baptist Church in Maryville. They came from Richard's churches in Oak Ridge and Athens, and all the other churches where he'd served and touched people for fifty years. His wife, children, and grandchildren sat in the front pew, humbled and amazed at the impact this one ordinary man had. Although he'd lost his pastorate, God had continued to use him. Mark wondered why he was surprised. He'd learned this lesson himself, the hard way. He was still learning it.

The entire entourage followed them to the cemetery, where Richard was laid to rest on a hilltop, overlooking the mountains.

46

Sitting in his office at Century Hardwoods late one night, Mark Smith rubbed the back of his tense neck and made a decision. His family needed a break.

Not long after Richard died, his brother, Jim, had succumbed to multiple sclerosis and passed away, leaving Mark to run Century Hardwoods all by himself. The company had been his dad's bequest to him, but Mark had decided enough was enough and liquidated the business. Unfortunately, he discovered that the company's stock was worth less than nothing. It sent him into a financial tailspin that he was still recovering from. Then, months later, Sharon's sister, Sandra, died of cancer.

Lisa Smith had been gamely keeping their home afloat while her husband dealt with the stress, the details, and his grief. Their sons were now a very active nine and four years old. Rick was in fourth grade and devouring Cub Scouts, and Patrick did everything his brother did. Mark hadn't been there for them as much as he'd wanted to be, and Lisa had been a real trooper through it all. He knew she deserved more than she was getting from him.

In a flash, sitting at his computer, Mark abruptly switched course. He closed down the dull financial software and opened up a travel website. With all his traveling, he had airline miles and bonus hotel nights built up. Thankfully his back surgery was still holding up, so that wasn't an issue. If they were going to get away, he wanted to really get away.

West, he thought. *Let's go west.* As he perused the options, he felt the first stirrings of real excitement that he hadn't felt since his father died. Over the next hour, he made his choices and booked the tickets. He printed out everything and tucked it into a folder, then headed home.

As he drove, he grinned. Lisa would be ecstatic to have something to look forward during spring break. When he pulled into the driveway, the house was dark. He glanced at his dashboard clock and winced. He'd had no idea it was this late. The boys might even be asleep by now. He turned the engine off, retrieved the thick folder from the passenger seat, and climbed out of the car.

"Lisa?" he called out as he opened the kitchen door.

"Up here." Her voice came from upstairs.

She entered the kitchen as he put his things down on the counter. Everything except the folder, which he hid behind his back. He hugged her with his free arm. "Sorry I'm so late," he said and kissed her lightly.

"What's behind your back?" She tried to sneak a peek, but he evaded her.

"Later," he said.

"You're up to something," she said suspiciously. They'd been married for sixteen years now, and she knew him well.

"Later," he said again. "Are the boys in bed?"

"They are, but they're probably not asleep yet."

"I'll go up and say goodnight."

"They'd like that."

He walked lightly up the stairs and went into Rick's room first, then Patrick's. Both were barely awake, just enough to know he was there. He tousled their hair and kissed them goodnight, then went to the end of the hall to the room he and Lisa shared. She was in the bathroom, sitting at her vanity, removing her makeup. He leaned against the door, watching her, and wondered for the hundredth time why she used so much makeup. She didn't need it. She was thirty-seven now but looked at least ten years younger.

Her eyes met his in the mirror. "Were they asleep?"

"Not quite. I got to say goodnight to them."

"That's good." She smoothed night cream on her face and realized he was still looking at her. "What?"

"You just look so young and pretty without your makeup. I feel like a cradle robber."

She blushed. "You are a cradle robber."

"Let's go to bed."

She shook her head slowly, smiling slightly. She pulled the rubber band out of her hair, and it fell over her shoulders and down her back in a silky blonde waterfall. She eyed the folder still in his hand. "Not until you spill your secret."

He sighed dramatically, sat on the edge of the bed, and patted the spot beside him. "If you insist. Come sit with me."

She perched beside him and looked at him expectantly.

"What would you think about getting out of here?" he asked.

She looked puzzled. "What do you mean, getting out of here?"

"Just what I said. It's been a rough few months for all of us. Let's take the kids and go somewhere."

"Why do I get the feeling this is a done deal?"

"Because it is." He opened the folder and showed her the print-outs. "We're headed to Arizona for spring break."

She gasped. "Spring break! Mark, that's in two weeks!"

"I know. Surprise!"

"Can we afford this? With everything going on at Century Hardwoods?"

"I cashed in frequent flyer miles and hotel rewards. We'll base ourselves in Phoenix and explore. The only cost will be a rental car and food. And we can even get that back because there are churches in the area that I can go visit and maybe get a couple new contracts. Who knows, maybe we'll even make a little money."

"This means so much that you did this."

"We need it."

"Yes, we do."

"Now can we go to bed?"

She framed his face and kissed him. "Absolutely."

47

The Smith family sped along Interstate 17 in Arizona, headed north from Phoenix toward Sedona in a spiffy, muscular red Mustang convertible with the top down. Mark was driving, enjoying the feel of the wind on his face. Lisa sat beside him, hair blowing, sunglasses perched on her nose. The boys couldn't decide where to look next as they whooped and shouted in glee.

Mark was fascinated by geology, and the scenery in this area was breathtaking. They could literally see the layers of rock everywhere they looked. They pulled over and stopped wherever they wanted, and just enjoyed the journey. They were in no hurry to get anywhere.

But he did have a surprise destination in mind for his family today. When they got to the Oak Canyon exit, he veered off the interstate.

"Restroom break," he said.

"I don't see a restroom," Lisa said.

He didn't answer, just smiled and kept driving for five more minutes, then and pulled into the entrance to Slide Rock State Park. "Here's a restroom," he said innocently. He'd sneaked and packed swimming clothes and towels for everyone, along with a picnic lunch and a blanket. Sort of a surprise within a surprise. He loved seeing his family's faces when they were happy. "I thought a little pit stop would be nice. Everybody change into your swimsuits."

"Whoa, cool!" Rick shouted and hurled himself out of the car.

Within fifteen minutes, they were all changed and settled with their picnic on a flat rock near a rushing river that narrowed and made a natural water slide. As they watched and ate, the most adventurous people jumped from a cliff into the narrow, deep channel and rode the chute down the slide. Others gingerly made their way out onto the slippery rocks and eased themselves into the flow, some pinwheeling their arms wildly to keep from falling.

"Can we go, Dad? Can we?" Rick was jumping up and down.

"Be careful," Lisa said.

"You wanna go in?" Mark asked her, knowing what the answer would be. She'd never been the adventurous type. It was always Mark and Rick who were the daredevils. Patrick wanted to do everything they did, but he was still small and more tentative.

"No, the sun is so nice," she said. "I'll just sit here and take a video of you guys."

And so it was that Lisa caught the whole thing on video.

After several runs down the slide, Patrick tired and played in the shallow area near the edge of the river, near his mother, while Mark and Rick made their way up the cliff. They jumped off twice, hooting and hollering as they hit the deep, fast-running water. Rick was on his way up to do it again, but Mark made his way to where Patrick was playing in the shallows.

"Wanna go down the slide with me?" he asked his small son. Patrick nodded.

Mark had no premonition that this moment would shape the rest of his life. It was just him and Patrick, about to have a little adventure. Together they walked to the top of the natural slide, where the water ran over smooth rocks before it formed the chute. For Mark, it seemed as if the next few seconds happened in slow motion. One moment he had Patrick by the hand, leading him to the slide, and the next instant his feet were flying out from under him, and he was landing flat on his back, on the wickedly hard rocks.

He actually felt it when his back broke. All the old pain was instantly back as if he'd never had his surgery at all. He lay there, stunned and afraid to move, while Rick and Patrick howled in hysterical laughter and Lisa hooted, "I got it on video!"

Patrick, although barely four years old, was the first one to realize that something was wrong.

"Daddy? Are you okay?"

Mark groaned and rolled slightly to his side as Lisa dropped the camera and rushed to him.

"It's your back, isn't it?"

He nodded painfully. "I think I just messed up my surgery," he said. He looked at Lisa with pain-filled, apologetic eyes. "I'm sorry."

Forest Service rangers were on the spot almost immediately. An ambulance drove right out onto the rocks, stabilized Mark's back, and whisked him to the Sedona hospital. Lisa and the boys leaped into the convertible, right behind the speeding ambulance.

X-rays confirmed what Mark already knew. His surgery area had been badly compromised, particularly in the space between his back and the cage. The decaying, unstable vertebrae around the fusion had given way under the impact.

As he lay there and listened, he knew what the doctors were going to say before they said it. They could stabilize him, but he had to go back to his orthopedic doctors in Knoxville. They were going to tell him he needed another surgery to repair the damage, but this surgery would have to be done through his back, right through the fragile nerve bundles.

And all he could think about was a man he knew at home who'd just been faced with this same decision, had opted for surgery, and had ended up paralyzed from the waist down.

48

"I can't do it, Lisa," Mark told his wife a week later after Dr. Froome left the examining room at the UT Medical Center. He'd said precisely what Mark had known he would say.

"Why not?"

"Did you hear the risks? I'd rather try to manage the pain in other ways first. I do not want to risk being paralyzed."

"We've been down that road, Mark."

"It's been five years, and there are better drugs now. I want to try."

She sighed and looked at him with weary, troubled eyes. "It's your decision."

For the next year, in the darkest time of his life so far, he tried. He contacted every pain doctor within driving distance of Knoxville and finally found one in Charlotte, North Carolina, who prescribed methadone, a high-powered drug normally used to help heroin addicts through withdrawal. The prescription came with restrictions— Mark had to go to Charlotte once a month for refills and had to be under the care of a psychologist to be sure he remained mentally healthy. He also was prescribed Wellbutrin to combat depression, and Ambien to help him sleep. Most pharmacists looked at him askance and refused to fill the prescriptions. Only one, an old friend who knew his history, consented.

He recovered enough, with the help of the drugs, to resume his job. Although Lisa did not allow alcohol at home, Mark was under no such restrictions when he was on the road. A glass of wine with dinner helped him relax and made the pain recede. Two glasses helped even more. He was in his hotel and wasn't going to drive anywhere, so what was the harm? Then the alcohol began to extend to bedtime, when he took his Ambien to sleep. And that's where the real trouble began. Because Ambien is an amnesiac, and when you combine it with alcohol, you do things you wouldn't otherwise do. Things you don't even remember.

Nearly every day, Mark awoke in the morning and walked around his hotel room piecing together the events of the night before. Usually, it was simple things like finding the remains of a snack in bed with him. Sometimes he'd find evidence that he'd cooked a full-fledged meal in his kitchenette in the wee hours of the morning. Sometimes he'd check his phone and see strange outgoing calls from the night before. Who in the world had he been calling, and why? He was afraid to hit redial and find out.

Sometimes, though, what he'd done was downright scary.

One night during a road trip to Alabama, Mark evidently decided to get in his car and go to the drug store for some shaving cream. Police found him on the side of the road near his Mazda SUV, with the whole right side torn off from where he'd sideswiped a tree. He was wandering down the road, headed uncertainly toward his hotel.

They pulled up beside him. "You okay, fella?"

"I'm fine. Just had a little problem with my car."

"We saw that. You been drinking?"

"Had a glass of wine about six o'clock with dinner, but not since then. I did take a sleeping pill. I was trying to get an errand done before it hit."

Somehow, miraculously, Mark was not arrested that night but was simply given a ride back to his hotel. He called Lisa the next morning and told her his trip had been extended. Then he contacted AAA and arranged to have his car fixed before he went home. Lisa never knew about it.

Another night, he got the bright idea that prostitutes needed Jesus, and he should call one and witness to her. He found one on the internet and made the call, and she arrived at his room expecting what prostitutes usually expect. He refused to touch her, and instead started sharing the gospel with her. Her pimp showed up and demanded all of Mark's money in exchange for the time the girl had spent. Mark woke the next morning several hundred dollars poorer, with only a vague recollection of what had happened.

After these and other narrow escapes, Mark finally realized that somehow, undeservedly, God had spared him yet again from his foolhardy decisions, and he couldn't do this any longer. He went back to see Dr. Froome and scheduled another surgery, knowing it would either fix him or paralyze him.

This time, as anticipated, the doctor went in through Mark's back, picking through the delicate nerve bundles. He left the cage in place and reinforced it with screws, rods, and cadaver bones. The surgery was deemed a complete success. All that was left was a very lengthy recovery.

49

From the moment Mark Smith woke from his surgery and discovered that he still had the use of his legs, he was focused on rehabilitation. He and Matt Monroe went in together and traded in the pontoon for a used red G3 bass boat. They took Patrick and Rick out and showed them what real fishing was like.

Mark had an unexpected, exciting incentive to get better quick—Tom Taylor, the mayor of Maryville and a local leader in scouting, came to see him in the hospital and suggested he take over as Scoutmaster of Boy Scout Troop 87.

Rick would be eleven years old this November, which would make him too old for Cub Scouts. His staying in scouting was not even a question. It had been such a huge part of Mark's life, so key in instilling important character traits, that he knew he wanted both of his boys to be a part of it. He'd hoped that he could be an assistant Scoutmaster but hadn't realized being a Scoutmaster would even be an option.

Taking on Troop 87 would, Tom explained, be essentially like starting over and building the troop from scratch. That didn't scare Mark; he had Tom to help him and also the example of his old Scoutmaster, Prof Powers. Secretly, in his heart of hearts, Mark had been dreaming about this since he was a scout himself. He'd known what he would do if he were ever handed the keys to a troop.

"You just have to get yourself healthy so you can pass the physical," Tom told him.

"Not a problem," Mark said confidently. "I'll be ready by the time Rick turns eleven."

That gave him six months, and he attacked his rehabilitation with everything he had. By November, Dr. Froome had declared his new fusions mature and stable, and Mark was pain-free. His general practitioner checked all the boxes on the medical form for scouting. The only thing Mark had to do was get a pair of reading glasses.

With him taking over as Scoutmaster, Lisa would no longer be Patrick's Cub Scout den mother. Although Patrick wasn't technically old enough, he could tag along on Boy Scout events until he was old enough to join officially.

To build his new troop, Mark started with Rick's Cub Scout pack, to see how many boys wanted to go to the next level. He met with each boy's parents at their homes, one at a time, and told them what would be expected. Scouting welcomed people of all faiths, but Mark was open about his Christianity. His faith had become even more solid since the rocky times before his most recent surgery.

First, every boy would be expected to be at every meeting and participate in every campout. They would go to scout camp every year with no exceptions. And they would camp out one weekend every month, no matter what the weather was. This had been a specific Tom Taylor recommendation. "If you wait until it's warm and dry, you won't go," Tom said.

Second, scouts would be expected to advance steadily and earn badges regularly. Mark had completed all his requirements for his Eagle rank before he turned fourteen, and he knew that boys who don't reach it early often don't reach it at all. When they get into their mid-teens, they become far too distracted by other things—like girls.

Third, he told the families specifically what their sons would need, and the list was long and expensive. Mark realized this, but he also knew from first-hand experience that quality was important in outdoor equipment. There would be fundraising, but most of the burden would land squarely on the parents' shoulders. They had to realize this up front.

The final item was where Mark knew he might lose the moms. "When they're with me, they're mine," he said baldly. "Parents are welcome at meetings, and some dads can go along on campouts to help as needed, but that's it. What I say goes."

He started with a core group of a dozen boys consisting mainly of Rick's original Cub Scout pack. Their first campout was in January 2004, in single-digit temperatures, in a little hollow not far from Maryville. The boys, almost all of them eleven years old, shivered their way through the weekend, but the experience cemented their bond in a way that a more hospitable environment wouldn't have.

Another weekend, they drove through the snow up the Cherohala Skyway to get to a trailhead and discovered they couldn't make the final climb due to ice. Charles Tungett, Mark's close friend and dad of one of the scouts, came to the rescue and pulled the vehicles up the mountain to the trailhead. Several moms took one look at the road and took their sons home. One said, "You're crazy," as she left.

Tom Taylor accompanied the group on all the camping trips in those early months, and Mark, fascinated, watched his leadership style. Tom would tell ghost stories as they went along trails and sat around the campfire. Boys sat wide-eyed, edging closer to each other, screaming at the key points. Mark soaked in every word. Ultimately his own style would be a blend of the people he respected most, and Tom would be at the top of the list along with Prof Powers. Also on that list were trusted assistants, men like Spence McCachren, Mark Colquitt, Pete Carter, Jack Bray, Russell George, Kevin Kilpatrick, and others. Without them, he wouldn't have a troop, and he knew it.

It was a happy coincidence that Mark Colquitt was a surgeon, so the troop had the added safety net of having a doctor with them on most of their trips.

New kids joined at the end of the summer, and Mark instituted the practice of letting the older boys lead. He watched, satisfied, as they took their jobs seriously. When they went on campouts, the boys initiated the new members by putting Slim Jims under their tents and then watching from out of sight as skunks burrowed under the tent and sent the new boys screaming into the night.

On one camping trip, a boy didn't have the proper food or clothes, and nearly froze during the night. His tent mate gave the boy his own food and drink and kept him warm until dawn, and Mark ran the boy down the mountain on his back when the sun came up. From that point on, there was a new rule. Before every campout there was a shakedown. Boys had to bring their backpacks, loaded with all the supplies and clothing they planned to take on the trip, to be inspected. If anything wasn't right, those items had to be replaced satisfactorily, or the scout wasn't allowed to go.

Mark had a way of making everything fun. He could be stern when he had to, but the reality was that he was just a big kid himself, and he loved these boys. Troop 87 dominated at camporees, winning all the awards every year. While other troops roasted hot dogs, Mark's boys cooked savory meals in iron Dutch ovens in the embers of the fire. Other leaders watched, open-mouthed, as he and his boys did cannonballs into the lake and had water gun fights.

They began a program in which they visited nursing homes and gave every resident Christmas cards. They built wheelchair ramps for handicapped senior citizens.

In the fall of 2006, Mark and Lisa watched proudly as Rick attained his Eagle rank before his fourteenth birthday—just like his dad. Over the next three years, ten more reached that goal, and more were in the pipeline.

Mark's troop grew to include more than fifty families. It got so big that they could no longer hike the trails in the Great Smoky Mountains due to the size of the group, so they ranged far afield to find places to camp. Parents sought him out, seeking for their sons to be able to join, but some boys were suited for Troop 87, and some weren't. Mark didn't hesitate to send them to other good troops in town if he thought it best. It wasn't about the numbers.

For all the right reasons, Troop 87 became a juggernaut in the scouting world.

50

As his philosophies with the scouts were proven right, and the troop took off, Mark became more and more frustrated with Lisa's parenting style. She hovered and babied her boys. It had worked well enough when the boys were young, but now that they were older, he felt it was vital that they have opportunities to become independent. They didn't get that chance when she did everything for them. Rick, in particular, was beginning to rebel against Lisa's smothering style.

Mark could see it, even if she couldn't. Lisa was continually questioning Rick, hovering over him, pressuring him to go to college and be involved in church and make good grades—and that just wasn't how Rick was built. If he were pressured, he would dig in his heels. They even switched churches in an effort to find a place where he would be comfortable. Nothing was working, and Mark knew why. Rick was brilliant and just needed the space to figure things out for himself.

Mark tried to talk to his wife, but she continued to do it her way. The more things stayed the same, the angrier Mark became. He'd always had a temper, and now the house became a bubbling cauldron. Things looked fine on the surface, but he simmered underneath and occasionally exploded. He punched holes through walls and had to fix them the next day. He slammed his fists into countertops so hard that he bruised and sometimes fractured his knuckles. He had episodes of road rage and even was arrested and spent a night in jail while on a road trip in Nevada. And one night, he came a whisker away from striking his wife. He pushed her into the wall but stopped himself just in time. She stood her ground, staring him down, as he raised his fist and then lowered it.

Appalled at himself and feeling desperate, he left home and checked into a hotel for the night. Alone, he thought back to his own childhood years. He stared into the mirror and saw his father. Richard had his good points but also some very bad ones. The man Mark saw in the mirror was the Richard who'd terrorized his family, not the one who'd loved them.

He sank to his knees in his silent hotel room and prayed out loud. "God, this isn't the husband I want to be, and it's not the one You want me to be. I know it's not. Please, Father, show me what to do and where to go from here."

It didn't take long. Just a whisper of time, not even long enough to shed one more tear. Clearly, as if God were in the room with him, Mark knew where to look. He pulled out his Bible and turned straight to Ephesians, chapter 5. And there he found it and read it aloud.

Husbands, love your wives, just as Christ also loved the church and gave Himself up for her, so that He might sanctify her, having cleansed her by the washing of water with the word, that He might present to Himself the church in all her glory, having no spot or wrinkle or any such thing, but that she would be holy and blameless. So husbands ought also to love their wives as their own bodies. He who loves his own wife loves himself.

Mark stopped and closed his eyes. Did he really, truly, love Lisa like this? Was he unconditionally willing to give up his life for her as Christ had for His church? They'd been married for more than two decades, and he was committed to her, but did he honestly love her like God commanded him to? Obviously, no. His actions spoke for themselves. He had reason to be frustrated, but he could only control himself and pray for them both.

Beginning that night, he prayed constantly for God to help him with his temper and help him love his wife as he was commanded to love her. Over the next weeks and months, he discovered that love is a decision, not just an emotion. He turned himself around so he displayed the good traits of his dad but not the bad. His home situation didn't change, but the way he handled it did. He did what he could do and trusted God with the rest.

And, in a breathtaking display of grace, God gradually took Mark's temper away.

51

After twenty years of marriage, Fran wasn't sure how she and Jeremy had gotten to this point. They'd had their issues, but so does everyone. When had they lost each other?

Maybe it started in 2002 when James Gideon passed away from congestive heart failure. It was a hard hit to them both. Jeremy had now lost both his father and his brother, and Fran—in essence—had lost two dads.

That same year, Brody entered middle school. They made him try band class to see if he liked it. He only had to do it one year—kind of an item on a checklist. No one expected him to like it.

He didn't even get his first choice of instrument. He wanted trombone, but his arms were too short. The band director assigned him the flute—and he fell in love with it. From that point on, Brody knew what he wanted to do with his life. He played on the middle school golf team when he was in seventh grade, but his heart was already irrevocably with the band. He loved three things in life—music, Godzilla, and the Clemson Tigers.

When Brody joined the high school band in ninth grade, Fran was a band parent. She marched in parades, worked football games and the concession stands, went to competitions, and helped her son sell fruit. He was a seven-time champion fruit salesman.

Veronica tried youth sports but hated them all. When she was in first grade, she was offered the chance to cheer for the youth football league. She ended up cheering for the youth league through sixth grade, and Fran coached her for all but one of those years. Fran and her co-coach, Rhonda Roberts, treated the girls like the athletes they were. They recruited two excellent high school cheerleaders—one of whom happened to be Rhonda's daughter, Christy—to work with the girls, and the young squad excelled. They went to competitions and had real tryouts with real judges, and the expectations for them were the same as for the football team. It didn't matter if it was raining or cold—if the team was playing, the cheerleaders were cheering.

The girls were more than ready to compete for spots on the middle school squad, and they all earned spots on their respective middle school teams. Fran never missed a game in her daughter's cheer career. Privately, she had to admit she was thrilled that Veronica had followed in the footsteps of her mother and grandmother, although Veronica was a better cheerleader than Fran had ever been. She stayed tiny and was a natural flyer.

Andy found his passion when he was twelve years old. He played and excelled at baseball, basketball, and soccer, but the fire was lit when he went to an all-sports camp at the country club and discovered tennis. That summer, Andy went to camp at Clemson under hall of fame coach Chuck Kriese, and there was no looking back. At first, he said he wanted to play professional tennis, but he quickly evolved into wanting to coach. As a seventh grader, he earned a starting spot on the Aiken High School team and was instantly an on-the-court leader and motivator. Fran immediately volunteered as a team mom, helping supply the boys with meals and drinks for their practices and matches.

Andy's drive to excel extended to everything he did. He was self-motivated, self-driven, and determined to succeed. Fran was always willing to go to battle in any way for any of her kids but never had to do it with Andy. He always did his homework when he first got home from school, even back when he was two years old and had simple things to do, which he took very seriously. His papers were inevitably spot-on and never required her editing or proofreading. His classroom grades were top-notch, even as he struggled a bit with standardized testing. As soon as he was old enough, he went to see the club tennis director and arranged for a job maintaining the tennis courts before school every day. He was at work by five in the morning, came home to take a shower, and was at school by eight. After school during the offseason, he flipped burgers at Aiken's favorite greasy spoon.

Jeremy was a good tennis player, while Fran was still miserably lacking in any athletic talent whatsoever. Together, they served as captains for Andy's Junior Team Tennis team. Jeremy handled things on the court, and Fran dealt with the administrative end. Andy's teams were five-time district and state champions, and three times placed in the top three in the regional tournament in Mobile, Alabama.

Andy's favorite movie was *Facing the Giants*, and Fran encouraged him to apply those principles in every match he played. Win or lose, praise God.

Fran held offices for the Aiken High School band, the Aiken Elementary School PTA, and the Presbyterian Women. She and her best friend directed weddings for South Aiken Presbyterian Church. Her career gathered steam. She was labeled top talent, and the sky was the limit. Her children and her work were her life.

Somewhere along the way, she and Jeremy stopped being important to each other. She became distant, and he became frustrated, and neither of them knew how to find their way back. Still very much a spiritual infant, she didn't know how to pray for her husband, seek counsel from godly women, or find answers in the Scriptures. And that was where she and Mark differed in how they handled their marital situations. He knew how to seek God and recover, and she did not.

In 2008, just as Brody was beginning his college search, Fran and Jeremy separated.

52

Brody had two requirements for his college. It had to have an excellent music department, and it had to have a marching band. Tuition wasn't a problem because when each of the kids was born, James Gideon had taken advantage of the South Carolina Tuition Prepayment Program. He'd locked in the tuition rate at that point in time and had paid each of the kids' tuition in full to any South Carolina public college. If they chose to go to a private state school, that amount would be applied to their tuition. If they chose to go out of state, they'd get the money back. It was a no-lose situation and a very generous gift.

Brody's high score on his ACT was a feather in his cap in the college application process, as long as he didn't crash and burn his senior year—and Fran would make sure he did not. By the beginning of his senior year, he'd narrowed his choices to Appalachian State University, Furman University, and Clemson. He'd been to music camp at Furman every year since seventh grade. Its music program was the best, and it had a good football team and a small marching band. It was, however, the most expensive school in the state.

He didn't know much about Appalachian State except that it was in the mountains, had an excellent music program, and had just gone into the Big House and beaten Michigan.

Clemson, of course, was Clemson. He'd grown up going there for football games. Some of his best memories were from there. And the band was awesome.

Another pacemaker replacement in the fall of his senior year sidelined him a little but not much. Fran poured herself into helping him with the applications and with planning campus visits. Applying for music would mean stiff auditions. She prayed that he would give his best ever audition at the school he was meant to go to, and that he would know beyond a doubt which school was right for him.

Brody's visit to Appalachian State left him lukewarm. At Furman, he fizzled at his audition—he was good but not great.

When they went to Clemson, Fran cautioned him to think like a student, not like a fan. The precaution was unnecessary. From the minute he stepped on campus as a prospective student, he knew he was home. He toured the campus, and the student center, the dorms, and the beautiful Brooks Center for the Performing Arts. He discovered that although Clemson's music program wasn't as well-known as its engineering and its agriculture, it was state of the art. He was told that the music program accepted just thirty freshmen each year, and they wouldn't make final decisions until the spring.

Then, at his audition, while Fran prayed outside in the hall, Brody soared as never before in his life. Within a week, he got his letter accepting him into the program and awarding him a Tiger Band scholarship. With that, his course was set.

*   *   *

Fran sat at her desk at work, in a bit of shock. The Savannah River Site had a significant change recently, with a new company winning the contract. The leadership under which she had thrived was out, and a new team was in. She'd had to start over and prove herself to the new leaders, and one year into the new contract, everything was going well.

Then, with one phone call, her old boss—who had now been promoted to Director of Public Affairs at URS' corporate headquarters in Aiken—turned everything on its head.

"How would you like to come to work for us at URS?" he asked. "We need you."

After a long conversation, she had the big picture. They were creating a new position called Corporate Communications Manager.

She would have to apply for it, just like everyone else, and would have to win the job fair and square. But the position description could have been written for her specific experience and skills. They knew her. Her references consisted of top brass at the corporate level, the very ones she'd worked for at SRS. And it would come with a substantial salary boost.

She would be located in town, minutes from home and her children's schools, which was important now that she was a single parent. There was no one else in her life, and Fran doubted there ever would be. She was completely consumed with her kids and her work. She and Jeremy weren't divorced yet, but their case was working its way through the system, and that day was soon coming.

Fran had always prayed that God would make her decisions on choices obvious. Since she didn't know how to discern His will, she prayed that He would make it clear. Was this His way of providing for her and her kids? She believed in signs, and this seemed to be one.

And now, the phone call had just come in. They were officially offering her the position. After just shy of twenty years at SRS, she was going corporate.

53

When Rick turned seventeen, Lisa began exploring the possibility of doing some work outside the home. A local agency who provided non-medical in-home care for seniors seemed perfect—she could take only the clients she wanted and work only while her boys were in school.

Mark had two stipulations. He wanted her to have only female clients, and he did not want her to work in remote locations. The agency paired her with wonderful clients, and she loved her work. She ran errands, cooked meals, did light housework and whatever else they needed her to do. And she was helping people. Her clients would not have been able to stay in their own homes without the agency's help.

She had a feeling she hadn't had since Memphis, when she was working for the United Way. Mark was happy for her.

The family was now attending Sevier Heights Baptist Church in Knoxville, where Mark helped teach Sunday school, and Lisa played clarinet in the orchestra.

Mark had lots of friends, but no close friend since Doug Taylor. Doug was now married with three daughters and living in Huntsville, Alabama. He and Mark still kept in touch and considered each other brothers but hadn't been able to spend time together in many years.

At Sevier Heights, Mark instantly bonded with Scott Spitler, who worked as a pilot and lived in Maryville with his wife and four kids. Scott's older son, Michael, joined Mark's scout troop. The two men quickly became best friends, meeting a need that Mark did not even know about yet.

In early March 2010, Lisa began having trouble with her eyes—nothing serious, just a little blurring around the edges. Mark took her to the eye doctor, but he could find nothing wrong. Then, several weeks into her time with Extended Family Services, she began having nausea and headaches. At first, Mark thought she was just suffering from stress and maybe a stomach bug, but she kept getting worse. In April, the Smith family celebrated Easter with the Lambert family in Knoxville. Lisa was supposed to bring a vegetable and bread, but they arrived empty-handed because she had forgotten. The next morning, she woke and couldn't remember the names of her sons.

Alarmed, Mark made an appointment with Lisa's general practitioner. After hearing her symptoms, he said he'd like to rule out the possibility that she had a brain tumor. A sick dread formed in Mark's gut like a leaden, pulsating knot. That night, after the scout meeting, he mentioned the situation to Pete Carter, one of his trusted assistants. Patrick, now thirteen years old and in the final stretch of getting his own Eagle rank, was running around with the other boys. Mark and Pete were in the kitchen gathering the trash.

"Why don't you ask Spence about it?" Pete asked.

"Spence?"

"Spence McCachren."

"Sam's dad? Why?" Sam was one of Mark's Eagle scouts. He'd earned his rank two years ago, not long after Rick.

Pete looked at him funny. "He's one of the best cancer doctors in the area. You didn't know that?"

Mark stared at him. Spence, the guy he'd spent years with on the trail, was a cancer doctor? One of the best? This was no coincidence. "Thanks, Pete. I had no idea. I'll call him tonight."

When he got home, he closed himself in his office and did just that. Spence answered on the first ring. After they caught up for a few minutes, Spence said, "What's up, Mark? You didn't call just to chat. I can hear it in your voice. Something's wrong."

Mark sighed. "You're right. It's Lisa."

"What's going on with Lisa?"

Mark almost didn't want to continue the conversation. To talk about it would be to make it real. But it was real, and it had to be dealt with. "Believe it or not, I had no idea until tonight what you do for a living. You've always just been my friend and Sam's dad. Pete and I were talking, and he told me."

"Go on." Spence seemed to know what was coming. "How can I help?"

Since he'd become aware of Lisa's symptoms, Mark had been keeping notes and observations, so he was able to provide Spence with details on the headaches, nausea, vomiting, and mental episodes.

"How long has this been going on?" Spence asked.

"She's had trouble with her eyes for several weeks. When she didn't remember the boys' names this morning, I got scared and took her to the doctor."

"Bring her to see me tomorrow morning, first thing. We'll get to the bottom of it."

"Thanks, Spence."

54

Spence McCachren wasted no time. By Thursday afternoon, four days later, he had results. Lisa and Patty sat in the two chairs facing Spence's desk, holding hands silently. Patty's eyes were swollen, her knuckles white. Mark and Matt stood behind them, unified, while Spence delivered the devastating news.

"It's a brain tumor," he said. "A glioblastoma."

Patty let out a sob. Matt laid his hand on her shoulder and squeezed lightly.

"How big is it?" Mark asked.

"It's the size of a man's fist."

"Where?"

"In the middle of her brain."

"Can you take it out?" Matt asked. He was staying calm for his wife and daughter, but barely.

"We're going to try, but this is the most aggressive kind of brain tumor there is. It doesn't have a clear boundary—it actually grows into the brain cells with something like finger tentacles, so we're definitely not going to be able to get it all. After we operate, we'll do radiation and chemotherapy to try to shrink what's left."

There was silence while everyone absorbed this. Mark spoke first. "What's the prognosis?"

Spence paused, obviously not wanting to deliver this final blow, then sighed. "Glioblastoma is always fatal."

Patty looked like she might faint. "Always?"

"Always. The only question is how long," Spence said. "Like I said, it's very aggressive, so the quicker we can start treating her, the longer she might have."

"How long do you think?" Mark asked.

Spence paused again. "Given the size of the tumor, I'd say no more than six months, probably less. I'm so sorry."

Lisa spoke for the first time. "What can I expect?" she asked.

Spence's voice was full of compassion. "Your symptoms will increase in severity and frequency. You'll probably have seizures as the tumor grows. Depending on its progression, you may have more memory loss, things like not being able to come up with the words you want or forgetting how to do simple daily tasks. You'll lose your hair, of course, when the chemotherapy starts, and the medication may cause some personality changes."

"Will it hurt?"

"Yes," he said regretfully. "We're talking about a brain tumor and surgery. It will hurt."

Patty's chin came up. "We'll fight this. Lisa, we'll fight it. Just because no one has ever beaten this, doesn't mean you can't."

Lisa's eyes stayed on her mother's. She seemed to gather strength from the determination in Patty's eyes. "Yes," she said. "I'll fight."

"It would take a miracle like the medical world has never seen," Spence said.

"God is in the business of miracles," Matt said.

*   *   *

Spence scheduled Lisa's brain surgery for eleven o'clock the next morning. Mark sent a communication to their Sunday school class and asked for prayer. He called Lisa's manager at Extended Family Services, explained the situation, and submitted Lisa's resignation.

Lisa remained quiet and pale through it all. How do you concentrate on anything when you know there's a tumor growing in your brain and trying to steal your life? When Spence described it, she had a mental picture of an octopus, settled firmly in her brain and growing, with greedy, grasping tentacles reaching farther out every day and stealing a little more of her. It wanted not only to kill her but to steal her very self. That was terrifying, and it also made her angry. She had so many emotions, and she didn't know what to do with them. So she conserved her strength, tried to stay calm, and let Mark do all of the talking. She would need all her strength and concentration tomorrow and for the fight ahead.

The prayer chain at Sevier Heights ignited. Senior pastor Hollie Miller and one of his trusted staff, Don Wilson, were at the hospital Friday morning to offer support and pray. Rick and Patrick were both in school, and Sharon would be at their house when they got home. The boys knew that their mom was sick and was having surgery but were given no details yet. Lisa hadn't wanted to worry them unnecessarily, with Rick about to enter his senior year in high school and Patrick in the final stretch of scouting. Mark would level with them completely when he had the full story.

Mark's entire family, along with Scott Spitler and his wife, Cynthia, were there for the duration. Scott acted as communications liaison that day, shielding the family, answering all the phone calls, and keeping everyone updated. He ran interference, talking to the dozens of people who came and went, giving Mark someone to lean on, even as everyone else was leaning on Mark. Doug Taylor was coming after work and would stay for the weekend. He was keeping in constant contact today.

Four hours passed, then five, then six. Mark pictured Lisa lying on that table, part of her head shaved, doctors making their painstaking way through the tentacles of the tumor. He prayed continuously for those doctors, that they would stay focused and be at their absolute best, and that Lisa would have a good outcome and a fighting chance.

After seven hours, an exhausted Spence McCachren and another surgeon came into the waiting room. Mark, Patty, and Matt stood to meet him. Spence wearily pulled off his surgical cap and rubbed his tired neck. "Let's find a private place and sit," he said. He led them into a family room, where they all took seats. Patty and Matt held hands and never took their eyes off the doctor. Mark sat stoically and watched his friend's eyes.

"How did it go?" Mark asked.

"As I've already described, these tumors are vicious," Spence said. "It had actually spread to two areas of her brain. We got as much as we could, but there's still a lot left, buried down deep. If we'd tried to get more, it would have meant severe cognitive damage or worse."

"Now what?" Matt asked quietly.

"We let her recover from this trauma, then start immediately with aggressive chemotherapy and then radiation. Our hope is to shrink the size of the tumor and buy her time."

"Do you still think six months?" Mark asked.

"More like four," Spence said honestly. "I'd advise you to start getting her affairs in order."

"No." Patty spoke up. "My daughter is not going to die, not anytime soon. We're praying for a miracle, and we're going to get one. You'll see. "

"I'll be praying for that," Spence said kindly. "We'll start treatment and see how she responds. My nurse will come in later and give you the schedule. She's in recovery now. They'll let you know when you can see her."

"Is there anything else we can do, anything at all?" Mark asked.

He thought about it. "Try Duke. They do some amazing things in their clinical trials to prolong the lives of glioblastoma patients. See if you can get her into one. I'll make an advance call for you and give them some details."

Mark shook the doctors' hands and thanked them, and the three of them returned to the main waiting room. Mark and Scott stepped outside into the warm spring afternoon.

As soon as they rounded the corner, Scott stepped close and wrapped Mark in a hug like men share, holding him tight for a long time. When they stepped back, both men had tears in their eyes.

"Man, I'm so sorry," Scott said. "I don't know what to say."

"She's going to die," Mark said and gave him the summary from the surgeons. "I need to be there for her and somehow prepare the boys."

"Maybe you'll get your miracle."

"Or maybe we'll get one, but it won't look like we think and hope it will. God's ways can be hard for us to understand."

"What do you want me to tell the prayer chain?"

"Tell them exactly what the doctors said. We need prayers now more than ever."

55

Mellie was staying with Lisa in the hospital tonight. She'd arrived at the hospital with Lisa's cosmetic case and had helped her apply a little makeup, which was absolutely essential for Lisa.

Mark headed toward home and steeled himself for the conversation he had to have with his boys. Rick and Patrick knew their mom was sick, but this news was going to rock their world forever. Not only were they about to lose their mother, but it was going to happen fast, and they were going to have a front-row seat.

Mark would, of course, be there for Lisa and take care of her, but his top priority was to protect his sons and get them through this so they wouldn't be scarred for life. Many people had offered to be there with him tonight as he broke the news, but he'd turned everyone down. Doug Taylor was on his way, but right then Mark was on his own, and that was as it should be. He knew this needed to be just him and his boys.

As he drove home, he prayed. *God, I don't know how to begin to do this. You're going to have to do it. Please, help them understand, give them comfort, and carry us through the next hour.*

Sharon had just left, knowing that Mark was nearly home, and he wanted to be alone with Patrick and Rick. Mark walked up onto the front porch and hesitated, sending up another prayer for strength. He put one foot in front of the other and dragged himself through the front door and around the corner into the kitchen, then squared his shoulders. His sons were sitting at the kitchen bar, digging into the dinner their grandmother had made. They both looked up when he walked in.

"Hey, Dad!" Patrick greeted him. Rick regarded him sadly as if he already knew. He'd always been astute. Mark wouldn't be surprised if Rick had already put the whole thing together in his mind.

"Hey, guys. What are you eating?"

"Gran's chicken casserole," Patrick answered.

"I love your Gran's chicken casserole. I think it's the cornbread topping that makes it." He shook his head. Enough stalling. "Guys, we need to talk."

"How's Mom?" Rick asked.

"She came through the surgery fine, but the news isn't great." Mark sat heavily on one of the padded chairs at the bar.

"What's wrong with her?" Patrick asked.

"You know she's been pretty sick for a while. It's been getting worse, and we've been trying to figure out what's going on. Spence McCachren, Sam's dad, is a cancer doctor, and he was one of the ones who did the surgery today."

"Cancer?" Rick picked up on that instantly. "She has cancer?"

"She does. They confirmed everything today. She has brain cancer."

"Did they get it out?" Patrick asked anxiously.

"No, Pat. Because of the kind of cancer it is, they couldn't get it all."

"What are they going to do?" Patrick's eyes were wide. Rick was listening, just taking it in. "She's going to be okay, right?"

"They're going to do some treatments to try to shrink the cancer, but she's very sick. No, she's not going to be okay."

"Is she going to die?" Rick asked the question, but he already knew.

"Unless God gives us a miracle, yes, she's going to die."

"When?"

"It depends on how the treatments go. Maybe in less than six months. We'll take good care of her and see."

Patrick stared at his dad as if he'd grown a third eye. "Six *months*?"

Mark nodded, trying to stay strong but came undone as he watched the shock take root in Patrick's heart and explode through him. He'd always been his mother's son, shadowing her in the kitchen and running errands with her while Mark and Rick had been occupied with household projects. Losing her now, for Patrick, was inconceivable.

Mark stood up and moved between his sons' chairs and wrapped his arms around them both. Patrick's sobs shook his slight frame. At thirteen, he was all arms and legs and feet. He was going to be a tall man one day, but now he was just a gangly kid who'd been hit with the most devastating news possible.

"What are we going to do?" he wailed. "What?"

Mark held onto them tight. "We're going to stick together, take care of her, and keep praying. It's hard to imagine right now, but God will do something amazing with this. He will."

Rick, tears brimming in his own eyes, edged free of the embrace. "I need to get out for a bit. I'll be back later."

"You okay?" Mark felt stupid asking the question. Rick was not good with emotional scenes, and his relationship with God and his mother had been strained for a while. Of course, he was having trouble.

"I'm going to go over to Andrea's house." Andrea was his girlfriend for the past two years. If anyone could talk to Rick now, it was her.

"Go ahead. Be careful."

Rick didn't answer, just walked out the door. Mark heard the garage door open and close, and Rick's old Pathfinder started up and pulled away.

Mark sat back down in the chair next to Patrick and looked into his son's green eyes, so like Lisa's. "We're going to be okay."

Patrick nodded automatically. "Do the scouts know?"

"Some of the leaders do. Not everybody. It's all happened pretty quickly."

"We need to tell them. They need to help us pray."

And with that, Mark saw the resiliency at his son's core and knew that, ultimately, he'd be okay. They all would, with God's help.

*   *   *

When Doug arrived later in the evening, Patrick answered the door and let him in.

"Dad's out back," he said simply.

Doug gave Patrick a big hug and went to find his best friend. He opened the back door and peered into the dark. Mark sat silently in one of the padded lawn chairs on the screened porch. The sun had set, and the cicadas were loud in the woods behind the house. Doug eased into the chair beside him.

"Thanks for coming," Mark said softly.

"It's been a long day, huh?"

"A long few weeks. I've known something was off for a while. She just hasn't been herself. Then she woke up Tuesday morning and couldn't remember the boys' names. And here we are."

They sat in silence for a minute. This was a far cry from all the lighthearted times they'd had together since they were twelve years old. Tennis matches and bottle rockets and trail mishaps and beach trips. This was life, as real as it got. Mark was grateful his best friend was by his side. Doug's very presence made something settle down in his soul.

"Have you ever heard of CaringBridge?" Doug asked him.

"Vaguely. What is it?"

"It's a website where you can post updates and keep everyone informed on what's happening. People can give you support however you need it, prayers or meals or rides for the boys or whatever. It would keep you from having to tell the story over and over and over. You're going to wear yourself out doing that. You should check it out."

"I wouldn't want everyone knowing every detail. Some things are private."

"You can set up the privacy however you want. It's something to think about. Here, check it out." Doug pulled out his cell phone and clicked several times and handed it to Mark. "See, this is one of my friends in Huntsville."

Mark took the phone and scrolled slowly down. "This is pretty cool. And you can set the privacy however you want?"

"Yep. And include as many details as you want." He clicked a couple more buttons. "See, they specified the ways people can help, even down to what the family likes to eat. And it's really easy to set up. I can help you."

Mark nodded. "I think that would be great," he said. "You'll be here until Sunday?"

"That's the plan."

"Let's do it while you're here."

56

Mark and Doug set up a CaringBridge site the next day. Mark thought it through carefully and decided that he wanted to have subscribers by invitation only, and the two things he would most need would be prayer and food. He got the boys involved, and they helped him list the foods they liked and didn't like—he had no idea because Lisa had always handled all of that.

First thing Monday morning, Mark was on the phone with Duke University's Brain Tumor Center. Spence McCachren had paved the way, and they were expecting his call.

A plan was set. Appointments were made for them to go in two weeks when Lisa had recovered from her surgery enough to travel.

Mark's first CaringBridge post was after their first trip to Duke:

> Connecting with the right doctors at just the right time has been a great blessing. The wisdom and word of our local oncologist allowed us to move quickly and be accepted into a clinical trial quarterbacked by Duke Brain Tumor Center. Several days of testing and consultation in NC were tiring but are resulting in a treatment plan that will address Lisa's needs in a timely and thorough way. We expect a few months of chemo followed by a round of radiation. Shrink and starve the tumor, then blast it.
>
> Thank you, local church family, scouting friends, and long-distance friends for your love and support! In her good moments, Lisa recognizes a few names now. The memory portion of her brain was struck hard. We are seeing first-hand how the brain seeks to find new pathways to the information stored

when there is an interruption of this magnitude. She's enjoying the food and is stronger physically daily now.

Lisa Lambert and Scott Spitler were the local people Mark leaned on and confided in. Scott got Mark out of the house whenever he could, and they bought bicycles and started biking together. Lisa Lambert taught Mark how to do things he'd never had a reason to learn before—sorting laundry, cleaning house, making a grocery list, etc. Brother and sister regained the closeness they'd had when they were much younger. Lisa Lambert went over every Monday after work and cleaned the house. Finally, the two Lisas spent time together and became friends, which had always been Mark's wish.

Mellie, who now lived in Blacksburg, Virginia, with her husband and small daughter, was Mark's go-to person for cooking. He hadn't really had to cook anything since Nome. Under his sisters' tutelage, he discovered anew that he hated cooking and housework with a vicious passion. Thankfully, every day, generous volunteers came with meals and left them in a cooler on the front porch.

On May 9, Mark posted:

I thought I was a "working man" until recently. Helping non-profits obtain the best stewardship program is a big job. Helping raise two boys, being active in our church, the Scout troop, and a few other responsibilities, and my plate is full.

I am an appreciative person, but I have greatly underappreciated what Lisa did for our family and me. Now that I am making beds, picking up socks, running laundry while answering the phone and jotting items on a grocery list, filling up the dog bowl, while I think about when am I going to fit in reconciling the credit card bill, I realized in a new way what a team effort having a family is.

Women are super multi-taskers. A tribute to Lisa and all moms and wives out there! A woman with a job on top of that—I cannot even approach.

In May, Lisa had her first two five-hour chemotherapy treatments and showed her fighting spirit. Mark could see a transformation in her character as she hugged nurses and other patients.

However, by early June, Lisa had lost ground mentally. Every day, Mark had to reteach her what her sons' names were and how to use a toothbrush and put on her clothes. She was on steroids that completely changed her personality and appearance. Her hair began to fall out, and Rick was the one to shave her head.

In mid-June, her doctors at Duke reevaluated the tumor and reported that it had responded to the chemotherapy and had retreated significantly. In July, it was even smaller, and doctors were declaring Lisa the new "poster child" for this course of treatment. Mark took this news positively, but he remembered that the whole point was to prolong Lisa's life, not save it.

Matt and Patty were beaming and saying God had granted them a miracle, but Mark continued keeping it real for his boys and not giving them false hope. Glioblastoma, he knew, is one hundred percent fatal. It was just a matter of time. He believed completely that God can perform any miracle He wants, whenever He wants, but he knew in his heart that this miracle wasn't going to be the one everyone was praying for. His prayers were different—whatever happened, he wanted God to be glorified.

Lisa continued to fight but was absent emotionally. She could not carry on a conversation. Her personality was gone, and with it, the essence of Lisa that had been a part of Mark's life for nearly twenty-five years. During those months, Mark did his mourning and became a full-time caregiver. He fed Lisa, bathed her, carried her up and down the steps, and lifted her in and out of her chair. His back surgery seemed to hold up for the most part, although his back sometimes hurt fiercely at the end of the day.

Worse, he began to have pain in his abdomen and understood that he was giving himself a hernia. It did not matter. He had to soldier on. Taking care of her was his job, and that was what he would do.

As he cared for his wife, he developed a new appreciation for her. Even as she went through the horror of cancer, she showed love for everyone around her, not just her husband and sons. She was now allowing people to get close to her as she never had before, and truly relating to them even in the midst of her suffering. She couldn't carry on a conversation, but she could love people. And she did. This was a new Lisa, and Mark recognized this as one of God's miracles.

Just a week after the positive report at Duke, Lisa had a major seizure and lost all memory of her diagnosis, surgery, and treatment. Mark spent two hours explaining what had happened, and she took it very hard.

On August 2, Mark posted again, this time about a fundraiser led by Vernon Harris—the moonshiner-turned-gospel-singer from Virginia.

> We were completely overwhelmed this weekend by the show of support from folks at Broadway Baptist, East Maryville, Pleasant Grove, and Sevier Heights. Vernon Harris instigated and spearheaded a gospel music fundraiser that featured local groups and raised over $7000 (!!) to go toward Lisa's medical expenses. We are so grateful and blessed to have this kind of support.
>
> Our pastor and youth minister came by today with the check. It is no coincidence that we hit our $6000 out-of-pocket maximum this week. When you add in our travel expenses to Duke, it comes out to almost exactly the right amount. God is right on time with manna for His children, isn't He?

Three days later, doctors reported that the tumor was still retreating on one side but advancing on the other. Radiation treatments were scheduled, and Lisa was fitted for a stabilizing mask. She was bolted to a table and daily treatments began, even as chemotherapy continued. She responded with violent illness but gradually rebounded and had her forty-fifth birthday in October. At the end of October, she had her last radiation treatment.

On October 30, Mark posted:

While we work on survival, God is teaching us how precious is each moment and each encounter. I am worried about getting the gas and milk, and Lisa asks the clerk at the market how their day is going. She loves their hairdo or asks what color is their lipstick. They respond to her, and she says, "Anything good comes from the Lord." They nod, and so do I.

In November, Rick turned eighteen, and Lisa's care was transferred back to Dr. McCachren in Knoxville, with ongoing chemotherapy still planned for at least eight months.

Lisa had already survived seven months after her diagnosis—more than a month longer than anyone thought she would. A self-described spiritual infant for her entire life, now she was a spiritual warrior and an inspiration for everyone who knew her—thanks mainly to Mark's journaling on CaringBridge.

And she was still fighting.

57

Back in South Carolina, Brody Gabriel was in his second year at Clemson, so Fran was down to two kids in the house. Andy was a junior, and Veronica was in eighth grade. The Gabriels' divorce was final in July 2010. The house she and Jeremy had built was hers as part of the divorce. She'd immediately listed it for sale, wanting something smaller.

Fran's boss called her into his office and told her about a contract URS was bidding on with one of its partners for cleanup work in Oak Ridge, Tennessee. Leo Sain, one of her mentors from SRS, was being featured as president on the bid.

"How would you feel about us listing you as Public Affairs manager?" he asked her. "You know everyone on the team. They're planning to award the contract next spring."

She didn't even hesitate. "I can't move right now," she said. "I need five more years here to get my kids out of school. Then I'll go wherever you want."

He looked at her, clearly not convinced. "This job was always intended to be a stepping stone for you. Oak Ridge would be a perfect next step."

"I can't leave now," she repeated firmly.

Meanwhile, something was up with Brody. He'd been having some curious health issues, dating back to his senior year in high school. He'd fainted from heat during a parade at Disney World's Epcot Center, and it was getting worse. This year in Tiger Band he'd been unable to stay in the stands for the entire game because of the heat.

It all came to a head during an away game at Auburn in

September 2010. Fran came home from a weekend trip the next day to find Brody in her living room.

"I need to go to the doctor," he said.

They were in Dr. Caldwell's office the next day. He took one look at Brody and said, "It's his thyroid. See how his eyes are bulging, and the thickness around his neck?"

Fran looked and did see. The changes weren't apparent if you were with Brody as much as she was, but Dr. Caldwell spotted his condition instantly.

He sent Brody to a specialist, who diagnosed him with acute Graves Disease and first tried medication for several weeks, but the treatment was unsuccessful in bringing his raging thyroid levels under control. The next option was to kill his thyroid with radiation, which wasn't a possibility because of Brody's pacemaker. The third and final option was surgery, which Brody underwent in November 2010. He was in the hospital for several days but was determined to be with Tiger Band at Clemson's game at Florida State in Tallahassee on November 13.

He went back to school in time but called his mother in the middle of the week.

"The band bus and hotel are already full," he said. "They didn't think I was going to be able to come, so they didn't include me. I need to get to Tallahassee Friday."

"I'll take you," she said. This was fine with her; she knew Brody was determined to go, and she'd be more comfortable having him with her for this game anyway. Andy and Veronica would be with Jeremy this weekend. While they were talking, she jumped onto StubHub, bought tickets to the game, and booked a hotel. It was a done deal by the time they hung up the phone.

Fran called her sister.

"Wanna go to the Florida State game this weekend?" she asked.

"Are you serious?"

"Very." She explained what had happened.

"Yes, I want to go!" Chris squealed.

"We'll pick you up on Friday."

Brody got through that game and that semester, but his grades suffered because of his illness. He still hadn't recovered by the spring, and Fran was able to get him a medical withdrawal for one semester.

Andy was finishing his junior season of high school tennis, and Veronica had been selected for next year's high school cheerleading squad during tryouts in March.

With everything going on, Fran was glad she had turned down the Oak Ridge contract. If she'd said yes, she would be with the bid team, working night and day to write and perfect the company's proposal. Obviously, just as she had thought, her children needed her.

58

In early 2011, Lisa's back began to hurt. The news from the Duke team at the end of December was good—scans showed that the original tumor was cold and dead. But the damage had already been done. Before it died, the tumor had spread its nasty tentacles down Lisa's spine and established multiple smaller tumors there. They lurked and spread, causing debilitating pain in her back.

The Smiths, mercifully, did not yet know this. They were still dealing with regular chemotherapy too. They had MRIs on her discs to try to find the source of her back pain. They tried injections, which did not help much.

In February, in his last official act as Scoutmaster for Troop 87, Mark signed Patrick's Eagle application. Then he stepped down and handed the reins of the troop over to Kevin Kilpatrick. Over his seven years as Scoutmaster, counting the young men still in the pipeline, Mark was responsible for forty young men achieving their Eagle ranks, and countless others who were part of his troop had been touched.

Now, though, he had to dedicate his attention to his work and his sick wife. She had now been through nearly constant chemotherapy for ten months and was down to one hundred pounds. In February, Patrick turned fourteen.

April 11 marked one year since the Smiths' cancer journey had begun. On April 19, Mark posted:

> We are going through a rough patch. The last few days have gotten more difficult, which is unusual. After the chemo, Lisa seemed to have fewer side effects as time went on. Not so

the last couple times.

It is not scientific, maybe, but I have felt (and have expressed to the doctors) that her body has had all the chemo it can take for now after a full year of treatments. We plan to have a serious talk with our doctors in the next few days and next week at Duke. Lisa got IV replacements and an injection at the hospital yesterday. She is under 100 pounds, very weak and fragile. Let's pray for a better ending today…it has not started well.

It was great to have my friend Doug come up from Alabama and support us this past weekend. He is family to us. Thanks to all of you for your love and support.

In mid-May, Rick graduated from high school, and his mother was able to be there. On May 23, Patrick received his Eagle rank, with his mother on the front row. He pinned the Eagle Mom pin on her shirt with tears in his eyes.

A few days later, the other shoe dropped. Mark got the news he'd been dreading for over a year. On June 1, he sat at his computer with a heavy heart and contemplated the empty screen. He didn't want to write this, but the people who'd carried him and his family through the past fourteen months deserved to know. Letter by painstaking letter, he wrote the post.

The scans done all last week are conclusive. All doctors conferred and agreed. Our questions are now answered. The cancer has spread throughout Lisa's spinal cord, forming numerous tumors. The condition is called Carcinomatous Meningitis. You can Google it. Not many with Lisa's original condition live so long to develop the secondary metastasis.

Folks, it is particularly nasty. She is already in considerable pain and is unable to sit up and move around for more than a minute or so. The other side effects and symptoms we are dealing with are beyond what I can share here. We had all my family in this last weekend, and Lisa's side is coming to-morrow.

Pray for us as we seek the best ways to manage her final care, ease her suffering, and spend some precious time with family.

This weekend her son held her hands and told her he did not want her to go. She said, "Honey, I wanted to stay too, but it's time for me to go ahead to heaven. I'll get a place ready for you there."

I would ask that you pray and not call. Feel free to post your comments here—we read them, and they are great inspiration and comfort to us. You have shared this journey with us over the last 13 months. It is a treasure to have you walk beside us now.

The side effects he alluded to were things he couldn't share with anyone other than Matt and Patty. Lisa refused pain medications because she wanted to be as alert as possible for as long as possible. She had always particularly feared suffocating, and that was what was happening. She struggled for every breath, every swallow, every blink of her eyes.

Matt and Patty wanted her with them for the final days of her life, and Mark agreed for his boys' sake. A hospital bed was set up in their home, and Mark spent as much time as he could with her. Every day, he took the boys to visit with their mom, and she gathered all of her strength for those few minutes. So, they were spared the horror of watching their mother die.

On June 13, he posted:

The last two days have seemed like two months to us. No amount of training, reading, talking, or coaching could have prepared us for the excruciating times we are experiencing. Pray for mercy as Lisa walks through the valley of the shadow of death. In her last lucid moments yesterday there was no fear, zero panic, and absolutely no hesitation on her part about what lies out there for her—just the work of dying, which she is doing like she did her living, with everything she has got.

Many of you are asking, "What can we do?" There is one thing you can do for me, and only one thing besides praying… hug the one you love. Hold them. Cherish what you have. Be there for them! Right now while you can.

On June 14, 2011, Lisa Smith took her last breath and went to glory.

* * *

That night, after everything was over and Lisa's body had been removed from her parents' house, Mark sat with his boys on their back porch.

Rick spoke first. "You were right, Dad. You said it would take a miracle for Mom not to die, and we didn't get one."

Mark took a shaky breath. What he had to say next was maybe the most important thing he would ever say to his sons, so he had to get it right.

"I didn't say we wouldn't get a miracle. I said the miracle might look different than what we asked for. We did get a miracle. We got more than one."

"How?" Patrick asked. "She's gone."

"Last April, they told us your mom wouldn't live six months. She lived fourteen months, and she faced her cancer with everything she had, even knowing it was going to kill her. She never gave up, and she touched people with her strength and faith and character and courage. That extra time was a gift from the Lord. That time, and her testimony—that was our miracle."

"Nana and Granddad said she was going to be healed." Patrick's voice was muffled with his sorrow.

"And I told you all along that every minute was a gift, didn't I? It hurts a lot right now, but down the road, we're all going to find that we learned something and grew because of this. I told you before, and I'll say it again—God will use this for good. He already has, and He's not done."

"I miss her," Patrick said.

"I do too. But I don't miss the Lisa who was hurting so bad and going through so much. Would you really wish for her to be back with us like she was? Think of how happy she is right now. She's with Jesus."

The Smith men sat on the porch and prayed, and over the next few days, they went about the business of saying goodbye to a wife, mother, sister, and daughter and—somehow—getting on with their lives.

59

Leo Sain had just gotten some news that might change everything. Before he called Fran Gideon into his office, he sat and thought about what he would say.

Leo was the URS executive at the helm of the company that had been awarded the contract to clean up the East Tennessee Technology Park in Oak Ridge, Tennessee. He and Fran had worked together for fifteen years, at SRS and then at the URS corporate office. He had wanted her as his public affairs manager in Oak Ridge, but she'd turned him down flat.

When Fran said no, they'd gone out and enlisted a wonderful woman named Carole Wolfe to lead their public affairs effort. The team was strong, and they'd beaten their competition handily.

The contract had been awarded on May 1, 2011, and Fran had agreed to go to Oak Ridge and help Carole with the transition. They'd worked hard for five weeks, and the transition was wrapping up. Then, just a few minutes ago, Carole had gone into Leo's office and turned everything upside down.

There was only one answer to the situation he was now in. He rose from the desk, stepped out into the hallway, and shouted, "Gideon!" in his booming voice.

Throughout their fifteen-year history, this was how he'd summoned Fran when he wanted her. He knew she'd come running, and she did. She came around the corner breathlessly, a pad and pen in her hand.

"Yes, Leo?"

"I have some news for you. Have a seat."

She sat, her eyes on his. "What is it?"

"Carole Wolfe just now left my office. She told me that she's stepping down."

"Stepping down? Why?"

"She's been diagnosed with a pretty serious melanoma. She's going to be okay, but she's got to deal with her health right now and is not going to be able to do what she would have to do to lead the Public Affairs team."

Understanding dawned in Fran's eyes. She knew what Leo was going to say, and she had her answer ready before he opened his mouth.

"We need you, Gideon," he said. "I wanted you in the beginning, and I want you now. You're the only one who can step in right now, on the spot, and do this job. We'll give you a big pay raise and a signing bonus."

"Leo, all the reasons I turned down the job last fall are still in play, except more so." Her eyes pleaded with him to understand. "My daughter has been named a high school cheerleader as an incoming freshman. My son is about to start his senior tennis season. They have a chance to win the state title, and he's the team captain. He's trying to attract the attention of colleges so he can play at the next level. I cannot uproot them now. I can't."

"All I'm asking you is this. Just don't say no off the top of your head. This is Thursday. Take the next three days. Do some research into this area and the schools here. Go home and talk to your kids. See what they think. Then come back Monday and tell me what you've decided. Can you do that?"

She looked at him and nodded slowly. "I can do that."

She walked back to her office and digested what Leo had said, and realized that both times she'd turned down this job—last fall and a few minutes ago—she hadn't asked God what He thought about it. All on her own, she'd made the decision that seemed to make sense to her.

Now, she shut her office door and prayed fervently, as she hadn't in quite some time.

God, are You trying to tell me something? This is a huge decision, and I need to know without any shadow of a doubt what You want me to do. Make it clear, God. Make it a neon sign. I need to know for sure. If you want me to go to Tennessee, I'll go because I'll know you have a reason. If You don't, I'll stay in South Carolina and stick with my plan. Just show me clearly.

Fran left work early that day and drove around, looking at the town with eyes that were open to possibilities. She went by Oak Ridge High and talked to the administration, the cheerleading coach and the tennis coach. She learned that the school had a preschool program, which Veronica would love to work at. The cheerleading coach said Veronica would be allowed to earn a spot on the squad for the fall season, and there were also competitive squads in Knoxville that she could join. Finally, the tennis coach said that Roger Federer's brother had a tennis academy nearby that was skilled at showcasing its players to attract the interest of colleges.

Fran made the five-hour trip home the next day, talking to God the entire time.

Are you telling me what I think You are, God? It's a big decision. I need this to be really clear.

She called Andy and told him she was on her way home and about what was going on. At first he was in shock, but when he heard about the tennis academy, he was instantly on board. "I'm with you, Mom. We'll talk to Veronica when you get here."

Her daughter was less enthusiastic, but when she saw her brother's excitement and heard about the opportunities at Oak Ridge High, she agreed. "I'll go," she said.

Less than an hour later, the phone rang twice. The first one was the Human Resources manager in Oak Ridge, telling her what her salary and signing bonus would be. Fran was glad she was sitting down. The second call was from her Aiken real estate agent. She'd gotten an offer on her house at the listing price.

She hung up and looked at her kids. "The house just sold," she said. She was in shock at the magnitude of the answer to her prayer. God wanted them in Tennessee. He'd made it clear. "I guess we're going to Tennessee."

On Monday, June 13, the day before Lisa Smith died, Fran called Leo and told him her decision.

PART 3:
LOVING

And we know that God
causes all things
to work together for good
to those who love God,
to those who are called
according to His purpose.

ROMANS 8:28

60

In July 2011, Mark took Patrick and one of his friends on a weekend cruise to the Bahamas, feeling that they all needed time to relax and get away. Rick was working and getting ready for school and didn't want to leave his girlfriend.

At the same time, Fran was constantly on the road between South Carolina and Tennessee. She was doing her job in Aiken, packing up her house, learning her new job in Tennessee, and locating the perfect house in Oak Ridge.

In August, Rick moved into the dorm at the University of Tennessee, leaving Mark and Patrick alone in the big house. Patrick started his freshman year in high school and joined the Maryville High School marching band. Mark spent time with Patrick, worked on his unfinished basement, biked with Scott Spitler, and tried to work his job. His hernia was not going away, and he knew he was eventually going to have to deal with it but did not want to mention to Patrick that he was going to need surgery. So he just kept on coping as best he could.

Fran's new job began, and she and her kids lived in a hotel in Oak Ridge until they could get into their new house, which wouldn't happen until mid-September, well after school started.

Now that the dust had settled, Mark was trying to come to terms with his new reality. He had lost Lisa, the essence of her, a year before she actually died. She'd become unable to converse with him, to participate in their lives, or to be a real wife to him in any way. He'd done his mourning back then. Now, he was getting a clear sense that it was okay to live again. He just wasn't sure what that would look like.

He was perfectly willing to pour the next four years of his life into Patrick. He'd finish the basement, take his son fishing, and get back into work. Maybe they'd buy a convertible and take some road trips. Currently, that was his loose plan.

Now that he was all Patrick had, Mark was taking his health very seriously. He went to the gym every morning at five o'clock, and his body began to change and become more toned. The hernia stubbornly remained and grew steadily worse, but the weight dropped off.

One night in September, he and Patrick were having dinner at Sullivan's restaurant in Maryville. Mark absolutely loathed cooking. Patrick had a natural feel for it and handled some meals for the two of them, but eating out was a regular thing.

This particular night, Patrick wiped his mouth, put his fork down, and leaned across the table. "Dad," he said, "I'm okay with being your date, but you're going to have to get back out there."

Mark was stunned. "What do you mean, get back out there?"

"Meet people. Date. You're a good-looking guy, and you're too young to be alone."

"Patrick, I haven't talked to a woman in twenty-five years. I have no idea where to start."

"You'll figure it out. Just get out there. I'm only going to be home four more years. It's not good for you to be alone."

A Scripture from Genesis flashed into Mark's mind, because Patrick had just unwittingly quoted it almost word for word. "The Lord God said, 'It is not good for the man to be alone. I will make a helper suitable for him.'"

Could it be that there was someone else out there for him? He had just turned fifty-two years old, and being alone for the rest of his life was a depressing prospect.

That night, sitting at his desk, he thought about it. He had an idea of what the perfect woman would be like. Preferably she would be unmarried and have no kids, but he knew that would probably be asking a bit much. It would be okay if she had kids, as long as they were older. A daughter would be nice. He'd always wanted one. The perfect woman would love to cook and keep house. She would enjoy the same outdoor activities that he did and be his fishing, golfing, and hiking buddy. She would be adventuresome and sweet, spontaneous and openly affectionate, the perfect intimate partner and godly mate. Mark had sorely missed intimacy the past year and a half.

What would she look like? The image of that long-ago girl on the beach popped into his head. Not so much her, but the idea of her. It would be great if the woman could look like that, but he didn't want to be too picky. Looks weren't everything.

He could start out with church singles groups and hiking groups, but what about going online? He didn't expect to find a mate on the web, but it might be a good way to get his feet wet. He was serious when he told Patrick he hadn't talked to a woman in twenty-five years. Not like this. He needed practice.

He went onto Match.com and carefully, painstakingly, created a profile. Where it asked about his religion, he listed Baptist, then noted that religion and faith were completely different things, and his faith was real. He was willing to travel a short distance to meet people, so he wrote that the woman needed to live within a hundred-mile radius of Knoxville.

Then, in a burst of inspiration, he wrote about himself, his vision of a relationship, and the woman he was looking for.

I feel like a 40-year-old man most (!) days. My wife was 45 when she passed away this year. It was a huge loss, but we have no regrets or hang-ups. Zero baggage—just 25 years with a beautiful person.

I do love living in the shadows of these Smoky Mountains. Hikes, picnics, and spontaneous adventures are only a few miles from the house. I feel things deeply—beauty brings tears to my eyes faster than sadness. I communicate with words, touch, hands, and expression. This computer media only captures a tiny part of that.

I am not complicated but multi-faceted. Hopelessly optimistic and trusting—not that good at discerning motives and hidden meanings. Not fond of sarcasm and totally speechless in the face of consistent negativity or pessimism. Very open-minded on how to handle a situation but stubborn on principle. Introverted in large groups and ebullient one-on-one. I love companionship and intimacy but do not feel lonely when alone. A good book over TV any day—or a handyman project is even better!

I believe any healthy relationship has to first be anchored in a total commitment to each other (come what may). Consistent, honest, patient communication makes living together better (most) every day. Just like raising beautiful flowers: Good roots, rich soil, and regular care = vibrant colors.

Would you be comfortable wearing very little makeup and flip-flops one day, then willing to put on spikes and a little black dress for steak and symphony the next? Down the road, how about a short backcountry hike to see some vistas, take pictures, cook on our open fire, look up at the stars, then snuggle in our tent?

He thought about adding more about the trials of the past year but decided to leave it alone. More information could come face to face, if he actually found any matches.

As his profile picture, he posted a photo of himself and Patrick in their dress shirts and ties, taken immediately after Lisa's funeral. He added one of himself on the trail with a backpack on his back, one of himself at Lisa's grave, one in his Scoutmaster shirt with the boys in his troop, and one with Tater, the family dog.

He hit "publish," then took a deep breath. God would lead him.

61

By the end of September, Fran and her kids were in their new house and were drowning in boxes. They loved their neighborhood. Deer roamed the streets and could almost always be found in their back yard, which backed up to federal land. It was a great house, with three bedrooms on the main floor and an entire basement with a living room, bedroom, and bathroom. Andy had turned the entire area into his man cave.

Andy had immediately started clinics at Smoky Mountain Tennis Academy and was already getting noticed by college scouts. He didn't like Oak Ridge High much, but the tennis academy was the reason he'd come here, and it was paying off. Fran was scheduling college visits for him in the coming weeks at multiple schools in the Carolinas, Virginia, and Alabama.

Veronica hadn't made it onto the Oak Ridge High cheerleading squad because she didn't have a back handspring, but she was cheering with a competitive team at Premier Athletics in Knoxville. She could learn her required tumbling skills and try again in the spring if she wanted to. The Sharks practiced weekly and were scheduled for competitions throughout the Southeast over the coming year. It was a completely different kind of cheerleading—they were appalled that there were no pom-poms in competitive cheerleading—but she was having fun with it.

She absolutely loved the preschool program at Oak Ridge High, as Fran had known she would. She'd always been good with little kids. She was burrowing in, making new friends, and starting her life over again, and Fran was proud of her.

Brody was in his third year at Clemson, counting the one he'd lost due to health issues. Fran and the kids continued to make trips back to South Carolina for every home game, which in 2011 included four in a row in September. They stayed with Julia and spent time with her and Cecil. At the moment the Tigers were undefeated, coming off big wins over Auburn and Florida State the previous two Saturdays.

The kids and work were taking up all of Fran's time, as usual. As the new company leading this contract, they were working hard to put their programs in place. Communication was critical, and that was Fran's job. Her team was the company's mouthpiece to employees, the community, the media, political leaders, and their Department of Energy customer. As she'd been for fifteen years, she was Leo's right hand. Her plate was full.

In some distant part of her mind, she wondered about God's purpose for bringing her there. She knew there was a reason. Could a man be part of it? She worked with men all day, every day, but no one had caught her eye. *I've only been here a few weeks,* she reminded herself. Patience was a virtue, but it had never been one of hers. She figured God would show her in due time why He had brought her here. Right then, she was far too busy to worry about it.

*   *   *

Mark Smith and his best friend, Scott Spitler, rode their bikes toward Look Rock on Montvale Road in Maryville. It was a beautiful October morning in East Tennessee. Patrick was at school, and Mark had some free time this morning. Scott worked as a pilot for NetJets, where he spent a week flying and a week at home. This was his week off.

Getting into biking had been a lesson for Mark. Scott had been right there with him, starting at the same time and on the same level. They were discovering together that exercising new muscles is a shock to the body. Everything hurts, and then it gets sore. A little recovery time, then you see growing strength and endurance. Kind of like life—hang in there until it gets better, and the struggle can make you stronger.

Mark mused on all of this as he and Scott rode higher, and the strain on their legs grew. Gasping, they stopped at a little church to take a break.

Sweating, they flopped onto the ground in the shade of a tree and guzzled water. Finally, they caught their breath enough to talk.

"How's the family?" Mark asked.

"Good. Mary Beth is at Maryville College, living in the cottage behind the house. Christy is at Maryville High, a year ahead of Patrick. She's interested in visiting the engineering school at Alabama. Michael's doing great in scouting, absolutely loves it. And Scotty will be joining this year."

"And Cynthia?"

"Liking her job as a teaching assistant at the junior high school. It gives her a chance to get out, be involved in the school, and use her English and education degrees."

Mark stared at the mountains in the distance. They fell silent for a moment, then Scott asked, "How's the dating scene?"

"Terrible," Mark said. "Absolutely nothing with the singles groups, and the online thing has been a disaster. I've met a few people, but I'm not encouraged. If that's what I can expect, I'll just finish the basement and stay single until Patrick goes off to college."

"Come on, it can't be that bad."

"I guess I expected more." Mark eyed his friend. "One of the women I met actually had a brain tumor."

"You have got to be kidding me."

"I am not. And I contacted a couple of friends from high school and college to see if by chance they were single. One is now a witch."

"That's not very nice, Mark."

"No, I mean literally. She's into witchcraft."

"Oh."

"I hung up very quickly."

They sat companionably and then the humor of the situation hit them both. A witch? Seriously? They started laughing together.

As he laughed, Mark shifted uncomfortably and stuck his hand down the front of his tight biking shorts.

"Man, what are you doing?" Scott asked.

"I have this hernia from when I was taking care of Lisa, you know."

"Yeah, I remember."

"Well, I put an electrical plate over it and taped it down with duct tape to keep it from slipping out. It keeps popping out, and I'm pushing it back in."

Scott stared, eyes popping. "You duct-taped your hernia?"

"Yes."

"With an electrical plate?"

"Yes." Mark had a *so what?* look on his face. "Duct tape is good for everything."

"Dude, you need to get that taken care of!"

"I know, but I can't spring that on Patrick right now. I can't tell him I need surgery after what he just went through. I'm trying to go as long as I can." He shifted again and adjusted his electrical plate. "I'll call Dr. Colquitt soon. He'll fix me up."

"Make it very soon."

62

By mid-October, Mark had enough. His free trial membership in Match.com was going to expire at the end of the month, and he wasn't going to renew it. He still checked his daily matches, just in case, but he'd all but given up. His "dates" had all been disasters. The woman of his dreams didn't seem to be out there, at least not right now. The thought was depressing.

Getting back to God's creation always comforted him and stilled his anxious soul. So he took a weekend for himself, reinforced the protection on his hernia, and went hiking with a group. Susan Bryant Roberts, his old friend from the University of Tennessee, always an avid hiker, and her husband were part of the group. Patrick was spending this weekend with a friend in the mountains, and Mark looked forward to being with Susan and the other hikers and just relaxing.

That weekend the group trekked to White Rocks Park, a beautiful area in Cumberland Gap, straddling the border between Kentucky and Virginia border. Mark had been there with his scout troop before and knew it well. The group left Friday morning and got there in time to make camp before sunset. They all sat around a campfire that night, three couples and Mark. He couldn't help noticing these things.

His musings were not about Lisa, about wishing she was there with him. Even if she'd still been alive, she would have chosen to be home tonight because she hated stuff like this. Mark had put Lisa to rest. He knew he'd stayed committed to her for twenty-four years and had taken good care of her in those last horrible months. Now she was much better off than he was, safe in the arms of Jesus. But he was ready to find the woman who would share things like this with him. He craved that woman, and he didn't even know who she was.

The group put out the fire and turned in early. Mark waited until everyone was safely asleep before taking his Ambien and snuggling into his sleeping bag. Even though his back surgery from eight years ago was still mostly holding—so far—his body had gotten used to the Ambien, and he could not sleep without it. Not a wink. When he was around other people, he took great care to wait until everyone was asleep before taking it, because he knew he would not remember anything and that could be embarrassing.

Early, before dawn, he was up. The cliffs of White Rocks were only about a tenth of a mile away, along a steep, rocky trail. He slipped his coffee press, jet boil, a granola bar, and a butt cushion into his light backpack, and set off.

Alone on the rocks, he sipped strong coffee, listened to the birds wake up, and watched the sun rise. Ribbons of color stretched from the rising sun across the sky. The sun's beams illuminated the majestic, rugged outcrops of White Rocks. The sky was blue, brilliantly blue, and so clear that Mark could see four states—Tennessee, Virginia, Kentucky, and North Carolina.

This, *this* was what he'd needed—just to sit here and be. It was amazing to him that anyone could sit here and look at this, and not know—just *know*—that they have an awesome Creator.

Mark looked down, down into the shadows of the canyon below. For a heartbeat, he considered just letting go. No one knew he was out here, and it would be easy to slide to the edge and into the void. Life right now looked pretty lonely. It seemed that although God had used him mightily in the past thirty years, now he'd been put out to pasture. What was he living for? If it weren't for Patrick, he might be tempted to embrace that empty space, knowing that after just a second or two, he would be with Jesus.

Then he heard soft footsteps coming up the trail and knew he wasn't alone anymore. He glanced behind him and saw Susan making her way out onto the rock. She eased down beside him and looked out at the view.

"Wow, look at that," she said, then looked at him. "You're up early."

"I wanted to see the sunrise."

"It's stunning," she agreed.

"I was here when it was still dark. I love it when everything wakes up. Want some coffee?" He nudged his coffee press toward her.

"Sure. Thanks." She poured herself a cup and took a swallow, and her eyes got big. "That's some strong coffee."

"No point in drinking it any other way."

They sat for a few minutes in silence, taking in the grandeur.

"How are you, Mark? I mean, really?"

He didn't even consider giving her the pat answers he gave nearly everybody else. This was Susan, and she knew him too well. He could still see her in his mind, helping at the Baptist Student Union the day a demon-possessed boy was in their midst. Susan had been the one to rescue the girl who'd had a knife to her throat. Sweet, spunky Susan.

"I'm lonely," he said. "This is really the first time in my life I've lived alone, and I'm not even actually alone yet because Patrick lives with me. He's gone a lot and it's just me and Tater. The house seems so big, and I just wander around in it. It took me a while, but I've packed up all her things and put them in bins in the basement."

"Have you considered dating again? It seems to me like you're ready."

"I agree with that. I really lost Lisa a long, long time ago. She wasn't herself, and she couldn't do any of the things that wives do. It's been a year and a half since I really had a wife, you know, in the ways that are important." Delicately, he tried to express himself without coming out and saying it. "I've met some people through singles groups and online, and it hasn't gone well."

She looked off into the distance and collected her thoughts. "Mark, I really do think there's someone else for you out there. But you need to listen to God right now, in this time, in this season. Remember what Paul said to the Corinthians about being single?

"Yes, he encouraged being single, but you have to take that in the whole context of Scripture. In some cases, it's better to stay single, but generally, God created us to be married."

"I understand that. My point is that right here, right now, you need to be patient and embrace being single until God sends you the right woman. There may be things you're supposed to do now."

"Like what?"

Susan shrugged one slim shoulder. "What do you think?'

He thought about it. "Kevin Kilpatrick might be able to use me as an assistant Scoutmaster."

"That's good."

"And the homebound ministry at church needs some volunteers."

"Excellent. Start there. God can use you, you know. Anytime, anywhere."

Mark looped the crook of his arm around Susan's neck and kissed the top of her head. "When did you get so smart?"

"I had this really great leader in college. He taught me a lot."

"I guess we should head back. They're going to be wondering where we are."

"They'll all fixing breakfast. They sent me to get you."

"They did, did they? You drew the short straw?"

"No, I won. Let's go eat."

63

One week after Mark and Susan had their conversation at White Rocks, Fran Gideon sent her kids to Aiken to spend their fall break with their dad. The three of them had gone to the Clemson game the day before, watching their Tigers beat North Carolina and go 8-0 on the season. It was such fun to watch Brody march in the band and spend some time with him before and after the games.

After the game, Andy and Veronica made the short hop to Aiken from Julia and Cecil's house near Greenwood, and Fran headed back to Tennessee. She intended to put the next few days to good use, unpacking the rest of the boxes and putting in some long hours at work.

After three days, she was feeling the strain. She had never had issues with spending time by herself, but this was different somehow. The stress at work, the thick silence in the house, and the overall uncertainty of her life were crushing her spirit.

There had to be something she was supposed to do, some reason God had brought her here. She and her kids had a life in South Carolina, and she had uprooted the three of them to come to Tennessee because He had clearly told her to come. She'd asked for neon signs, and He'd provided them. Now, she wanted to know why.

Overcome with loneliness and exhaustion, and just needing some encouragement, she collapsed to her knees right where she was and begged God for a clue.

"Did You bring me here because of a man, God?" She stared earnestly at the ceiling. "If You did, please show him to me. Make our paths cross. And if it wasn't a man, please show me that too.

Maybe there's someone I can help, someone I can be Your light for. Please, please show me. Show me what I'm supposed to do."

She stayed there for a long time on her knees. The empty house pulsed around her. When she finally rose to her feet, she decided she'd had enough housework for the day. She'd check her emails and go to bed early.

The next few minutes would change her life. What she did next was completely uncharacteristic for her, and she would never be able to explain why she did it—other than that it was a God thing. When her email popped up, so did a link to Match.com. Usually, she would have ignored it. Tonight, she clicked on it.

Fran looked over the guidelines for the website, and it seemed safe and harmless. It was free for a trial period. All communication was done via an anonymous messaging system within the website. There were guidelines for safety and privacy. Photos were screened for appropriateness before they were accepted. She didn't have to respond to anyone if she didn't want to, and she certainly didn't have to meet anyone face to face.

She thought about it. What could it hurt?

She created a profile with minimal information, listing her age, her location, what she did for a living, and the basics of what she was looking for in a man. Faith was high on her priority list, and she said so. If God had a man for her, she prayed that it would be someone who could help her grow spiritually in ways she'd been missing all her life. She mentioned her children and the things she enjoyed doing with them. If her kids scared a man off, she didn't want him contacting her in the first place. She hated pictures of herself, so she uploaded only one. Then she hit "publish."

The next three days were hectic. After work on Friday, Fran made the four-hour drive to Chris's house near Atlanta. Andy and Veronica arrived early on Saturday morning, and they went to Clemson's game at Georgia Tech. They spent Saturday night at Chris's house and left as soon as they got up on Sunday morning, October 30, to head back to Tennessee. The kids had to unpack and do laundry before school the next day.

They got home shortly after noon, dropped their stuff, and settled in. Fran realized she hadn't checked her emails in days, so she got on her computer. Her email informed her that she had mail, and her jaw dropped. There were dozens upon dozens of notifications from Match.com.

She flipped over to the match.com website, clicked on the "Messages" icon, and scrolled down. Every day they'd sent her "featured" matches. In some cases, she had popped up on men's searches, and they'd messaged her. She looked them over and shook her head. It was pretty obvious who was for real. These guys weren't interested in the same thing she was. She read a few more and made a face. If a guy couldn't write a simple sentence without misspelling a word, she had no use for him.

She clicked away from her messages and almost left the website, but then changed her mind and dived directly into the vast Match.com sea. If he wasn't going to find her, then maybe she could find him. In the search field, she entered specifics about the kind of man she was looking for, then hit "search."

The computer churned, and soon gave her a long list of results—but it was the first man who popped up on her screen who caught her attention, a man who called himself tnmountainlover. The pictures were small, and she couldn't tell much about his looks; but when she read his profile, she was captivated. It was beautifully written. Everything he wrote about himself touched something deep in her. She could feel his pain, his longing, his very heart.

She looked back and reread his second paragraph.

I do love living in the shadows of these Smoky Mountains. Hikes, picnics, and spontaneous adventures are only a few miles from the house. I feel things deeply—beauty brings tears to my eyes faster than sadness. I communicate with words, touch, hands, and expression. This computer media only captures a tiny part of that.

Slowly, she moved her mouse to the "send message" button. Her fingers moved across her keyboard.

Everything about you appeals to me. Everything you wrote struck a chord. Read my profile and email me if you are interested.

Her mouse hovered for a moment. Then she hit "send."

64

Mark Smith saw the incoming message from Match.com and sighed. His subscription would run out the next day, and he had decided this wasn't for him. All of his meetings so far had been horrible. A woman with a brain tumor, for crying out loud? After all he'd been through? He was going to concentrate on his work and Scouts, finish his basement, and try again when Patrick graduated. Maybe then, God would have someone for him.

But he clicked on the link anyway and read the woman's short message. He clicked over to her profile and sighed again. A divorced professional woman with three children? No wonder she hadn't popped up on his daily matches. She probably had all kinds of baggage, and he wasn't interested in baggage. He'd discovered that much in the meetings he'd already had.

The woman did sound fun-loving and spontaneous, though—and there was something about her eyes, even in the small picture. He checked to see if there were other photos, but she'd only posted one. Smart, really. Single women had to be careful. What would it hurt to reach out? He could meet one more person, and then he'd be done. He only had a minute—Patrick and some of his friends were here, and he could hear the ruckus from downstairs. He hit the "Reply Now" button and wrote a short message.

Running crazy with a bunch of boys in the house tonight and can barely hear myself think! Yes, I would be interested in meeting. Maybe coffee tomorrow evening?

His reply popped up on Fran's screen within seconds, and she gasped. She thought quickly. Tomorrow was Halloween. Veronica had an event for the preschool program at Oak Ridge High, but Andy could easily take her. Fran could think of no reason why she shouldn't arrange the meeting. It was coffee in a public place, not even dinner. If it didn't work out, she'd only lost an hour or so.

Looking at her watch, not wanting to seem eager, she waited a few minutes to respond. By the end of the evening, it was all set. She was meeting the man at eight-thirty tomorrow night at RJ's Courtyard Restaurant in Alcoa, which was between Oak Ridge and Maryville. They were meeting at eight-thirty because he and his son had a Boy Scout meeting until eight. He would get someone else to take his son home. He sent her his phone number so she could call if she had trouble finding the place and told her what kind of car he was driving—a maroon Mazda SUV—so she could spot him.

He gave his name as Mark Smith and a phone number ending in 6000, both of which she found a bit suspicious. What real person had a number ending in three zeroes? And his name sounded too ordinary to be authentic. She had no idea where Alcoa was, so she plugged it into her GPS to see how long it would take her.

She had to tell her kids where she was going. They looked at her as if she'd told them she was going deep-sea diving off the Pacific Shelf tomorrow. Like she'd totally lost her mind.

"You have a date?" Veronica asked incredulously. It was a reasonable reaction. This was a first.

"Not exactly a date. More like a meeting."

"And you met him online?" Andy asked.

"Yes, just a little while ago."

"Since when do you do online dating?" he asked suspiciously.

"I signed up while you were in Aiken last week, just to see what would happen. It's nothing. It's just coffee."

"You hate coffee," Veronica said.

Fran looked at her, exasperated. "I don't have to order any. I'll get dessert and a Pepsi. Look, I just wanted you guys to know where I'm going. I'll be home probably by ten or so, sooner if I can't stand him."

And so it was set. It was a coffee date that would change both their lives.

65

Fran Gideon was severely directionally impaired, just like her mother. When she went anywhere, she always built in time to get lost. When she and Jeremy separated in 2008, Julia bought her a GPS for Christmas, knowing that Fran was taking her three kids to the Gator Bowl and wouldn't be able to find Jacksonville without help.

So, she was proud of herself when she pulled up at RJ's Courtyard in Alcoa ten minutes early. She sat in her little blue Ford Focus, directly under a street light, and looked around. There were only a few other cars in the lot this late on Halloween night, and none were maroon Mazda SUVs. She pulled out her phone and considered. Might as well see if this weird phone number was real. She punched it in and hit send.

After one ring, a deep male voice answered. "This is Mark."

"Hey, this is Fran. Just wanted to let you know I'm here. I'm sitting in the parking lot."

"I'm about five minutes away. See you soon."

Precisely five minutes later, a spiffy Mazda slid into the space next to her. Fran swung her door open and stood waiting as the man walked around his car. It was a chilly Halloween night in the Tennessee mountains, so they greeted each other quickly and exchanged a light hug, then walked briskly into the restaurant together.

Finally, when they were seated at a booth across from each other, their eyes locked. They stared at each other, even as they both tried not to. It had been nearly thirty years, and they both looked completely different—but it was all in the eyes and the electricity. It was something neither of them had felt before or since that one brief meeting in 1982.

"It's you," Mark finally said.

"I can't believe it," Fran whispered.

The waitress came up at that moment to take their drink order. "What can I get you?"

Mark shook the cobwebs loose. "Decaf," he said, and smiled pleasantly at the waitress.

"A Pepsi for me," Fran said.

"Coke okay?"

"Sure."

Mark looked curiously at her. "No coffee tonight?"

"Not tonight or any night," she said. "I don't like coffee."

"Not any kind of coffee?"

"No. I don't even like coffee flavor."

"Wow," he said. "That might be a deal breaker." And they both broke out into laughter.

With that, the ice was broken. They had nearly thirty years to cover, and they really didn't know each other at all. Chemistry was a start, but it was just that. A start.

"Let me guess—you went to Columbia College," he began.

"How'd you know?"

"Because I tracked your friend that far, but the trail went cold because I didn't know your name. And you were at the Kentucky Derby in 1986."

"Yes, with my newspaper."

"I saw you on TV. I was just a few miles away. It nearly killed me, but that was when I knew I had to let go and let God handle it."

"And He brought us together in the end."

He told her about Lisa and his boys, and she told him about her three children—the pride and joy of her life. He told her a little about the dates he'd had since he'd joined Match.com, and she told him about her recent move to Oak Ridge and, briefly, about her twenty-year marriage. As he sipped his coffee and regaled her with stories from the trail with the Boy Scouts, she remembered how he'd made her laugh on the beach that day.

"During one trip, a friend of mine, Pete Carter, and I were sharing the Scoutmaster tent. It was late, and I was eating a cookie in my bunk." He dug into his dessert and told the story between bites. "I guess I was really tired, because I dozed off right after I finished the cookie and left some crumbs on my chest. I felt something that woke me up, and there was this mouse sitting on my chest, eating the crumbs and looking me dead in the eyes."

"You're making that up." Her eyes lit with mirth at the mental picture.

"I am absolutely not making it up. I stared at the mouse, and he stared at me, and then I screamed and knocked him across the room and onto Pete's chest. Then he started screaming. It was pandemonium for a few minutes. People came running, and I had to tell all these manly men that I screamed at a mouse. I wish I could have said it was a bear or a snake, but Pete was a witness. He was laughing his head off."

She laughed until she cried, holding her sides. When she calmed down, the mental picture came back, and she laughed some more. This felt so good. She couldn't remember the last time she'd really laughed.

The conversation went back to 1982, and the events that had brought them to the beach that day. She told him about her father, and how his sickness had shaped her life. She had never lost a spouse, but she'd lost someone she loved after a long, vicious illness. She knew it wasn't the same, but she did understand pain.

He told her about his year in Alaska, and how it had begun in the cleft of the rock. He'd heeded God's call to serve Him as a missionary in Nome. He sold his car, dropped out of school, gave up his campus housing, and bought a one-way plane ticket. When he arrived, the pastor delivered the news that the funding had been canceled, and there was no job.

"I had a temper back then." Mark smiled at the memory. "I was six thousand miles from home, with everything I owned in my pockets and no way to get home. I was so mad at God. I was just trying to do what He wanted me to do, and it didn't seem fair. I screamed at Him the whole way, and I walked and walked. I had this vague idea that I was going to walk to the North Pole. The next thing I knew, I was miles outside of town and headed up the tallest peak anywhere around Nome. It was called Anvil Rock."

"What happened?" Fran asked, fascinated.

He shook his head, remembering. "I was drenched in sweat and tears from the long walk and from crying. Then a storm blew in. All I had on was a pair of jeans and a thin shirt, and I had nothing to eat. My clothes literally froze to my body in a solid sheet of ice. Remember, this was Nome, near the Arctic Circle, in October. It was well below zero, and the wind was just howling. I had nowhere to go, and I knew hypothermia was about to set in. I could feel it. I crawled up into the rock formation and passed out."

She watched him silently, eyes big, waiting for him to go on.

He finished the last bite of his dessert and wiped his mouth. "So, hours later, I woke up. The storm was still howling outside, but somehow I was warm and dry. I stayed in that cleft through the night and walked down that mountain the next morning. There was a search party at the bottom, waiting until dawn to come up and find my body. I knew there was a reason I was there and that God would use me."

"That's amazing."

"It was the most amazing thing that's ever happened to me."

They talked and laughed, lost in each other until Mark finally noticed that the restaurant was empty, and the servers were looking at their watches.

"I think we've closed the place down," he said.

"Really?" She glanced at her watch for the first time tonight and was appalled that it was ten-thirty. RJ's had closed at ten, and they hadn't even noticed. He paid the check, and the manager unlocked the front door and let them out.

They stood at Fran's car and looked at each other. Words were so inadequate. "I'll call you," he said.

"Please do," she replied.

They shared another light hug, got in their cars, and drove in opposite directions.

As she was driving home, her phone beeped and she pulled over. *You're so special. Looking forward to what's ahead.*

She smiled softly, still amazed at the evening, and tapped in her response. *Me too. I still can't believe tonight.*

It was God, without a doubt, he texted back. *This is going to be fun.*

With that, they drove back to their homes and their children, lost in thoughts of each other.

66

With campus trips for Andy, Veronica's cheerleading practices and competitions, and trips to Clemson for Brody's games, Fran's free time for November and December was completely booked. But she was an expert juggler. She and Mark arranged to meet at his house in Maryville Friday evening, November 4, after she returned from a trip to Brevard College with Andy.

She texted Mark on her way. *I've been on the courts with Andy all day and I'm a sweaty mess.*

The response came quickly. *Don't let the flies come in with you.*

She let out a snort of laughter at the mental image. Kind of like Pigpen, in the comic strip Peanuts.

She learned much later that Mark, not knowing if she was a fastidious housekeeper or not, had spent the entire day cleaning up and straightening his house for her. She met Rick and his girlfriend and took a brief tour of the house, and then the two of them spent hours talking, Fran on the sofa and Mark in a chair. The fact that they'd met once before, a long time ago, was still amazing but it meant little in the big picture. They knew it was important to get to know each other. They also respected the chemistry between them enough to know they needed to keep their distance.

Unexpectedly, Tater jumped up on the couch and curled up in Fran's lap. Mark stared. "She doesn't usually do that with people she doesn't know," he said.

As she was leaving, they shared a light hug and their eyes locked. Then he touched his lips to hers in a light kiss that was over almost before it began, but it was enough to send shocks through them both. He smiled into her eyes. "See you soon."

"See you." She floated to her car and backed out of his driveway, headed back to Oak Ridge. Before she got out of his neighborhood, her phone dinged. *Tater wants to know when she can borrow your lap again.*

She stopped at a traffic light and her fingers flew. *I had a good time tonight. I think we might have something here. Weekends are pretty busy, but how about next Wednesday night? You could come to Oak Ridge.*

Did I mention I was born in Oak Ridge? He texted back. *My dad pastored there. How about chasing some tennis balls?*

Fran read that text with trepidation. No one except her family could imagine just how horrible she was at anything athletic. Natural athletes like Mark and Jeremy couldn't understand it. But she plucked up her courage and agreed. *See you then.*

*   *   *

Wednesday, November 4, dawned rainy and cold, and Fran was thankful that she wouldn't have to embarrass herself on a tennis court. She and Mark made alternate plans to meet at the bowling alley, where she proceeded to spank him soundly twice. Yes, she bowled her lifetime best, and he said he was struggling with tendonitis in his right arm, but still. This was a win worthy of a victory dance.

They went to Big Ed's in Oak Ridge for pizza afterward, and during the meal, Fran made her decision.

"So...after we eat, do you want to come to my house and meet Andy and Veronica?"

He looked into her eyes for a long while before he answered. "I'd like that very much," he said.

When they left Big Ed's in two cars, Fran hastily called Veronica. "I'm bringing my friend over to meet you guys," she said. "Clean up the house."

"When?"

"Now. Right now."

"Holy crap. Drive slow."

She drove as slowly as she could and led him to her house, where he took a tour and spent over an hour talking to her kids and getting to know them. Mark could especially relate to Andy because of their shared love of tennis.

At one point, Mark asked both kids, "What's the worst thing you can tell me about your mom?"

Andy didn't even hesitate. "She's a klutz."

Veronica nodded. "Without a doubt."

Mark stared at them both. "Seriously? I don't believe you."

"Believe us. She's a serious klutz. She knocks things over, and bumps into things, and breaks things."

"She can trip over absolutely anything," Veronica added.

"Anything else?" Mark asked.

Andy thought about it. "She's terrified of granddaddy longlegs."

"No way. Those things can't hurt you."

"I know, but she's scared to death of them."

"We can fix that."

"No, we cannot." Fran jumped in and put her foot down. "I have no desire to fix it because then I would have to be around them and touch them…" she visibly paled, shuddered, and gave a small scream. "No. I won't do it. I'll just avoid them my whole life."

Trying not to laugh, Mark nodded. "Okay, then. If those are the worst things you can say about your mom, that's pretty good."

"Yeah, she's a good mom," Veronica said.

Mark said he needed to head back to Maryville before Patrick went to bed, and Fran walked him out to his car. The rain had stopped, and the night was chilly but clear. Stars shone brightly above. Deer grazed, unconcerned, in Fran's back yard.

They turned to face each other.

"You have great kids," Mark said.

"They're my life," Fran said simply.

"Maybe you have room for me in there somewhere?"

"I think we can make a little room," she teased.

They stared at each other for another couple of seconds, and then Mark made a confession. "I don't really know where to go from here, like, in terms of affection. I was married for almost twenty-five years, and I'm a little...I don't know...bottled up."

Her eyes softened with compassion. "Do you want some help with that, or do you want to deal with it on your own?"

"I'm open."

She looped her arms around his neck and made a quick decision. How much could happen, here in her driveway, with her children right inside the house? It seemed safe enough, with built-in boundaries. She slowly pulled his head down to hers and pressed her lips to his.

They both felt it. The insane sparks between them flash-fired into a full inferno. For several long minutes, they were unable to let each other go. When they came up for air, they dived right back in again, long and deep. Finally, breathless, he braced his forehead on hers.

"I think we have some chemistry here," he said huskily.

"And how."

"We're going to have to be careful with this."

"I agree."

Unable to help themselves, they came back together again and again, until Fran became uncomfortably aware that it had been a long time and her kids were no doubt wondering what was going on. Thankfully, there were no windows on this side of the house, but still.

She tore her lips from his and forced herself to cool down.

"I need to get back inside," she said.

"And I need to get home," he said. "I had a wonderful night. Even if you did beat me bowling."

She grinned. "I didn't just beat you. I beat you bad."

Restrained now, he gave her one last light kiss and then climbed into his truck. "See you soon."

She watched his truck until she couldn't see his taillights anymore, then let herself back into the house. *What the heck?*

It would be a while before they could see each other again, because she was leaving Friday for a cheerleading competition in Cincinnati, followed by a week-long recruiting trip in North Carolina, with Andy visiting five schools in five days. They planned to finish up in Raleigh and take in the Tigers' game against North Carolina State, then come back home the next day, November 20. By then, it would be Thanksgiving week, and Fran was planning to take her kids to Chris's house for a big family get-together.

So, she and Mark planned to get together the Saturday after Thanksgiving. That was two and a half weeks away, which seemed like eons. But maybe that was a good thing. It would give her time to catch her breath.

Today's society has made it seem okay to have sex outside of marriage, but the Bible clearly teaches the opposite. If tonight was any indication, they were going to have to be very careful.

67

Fran's phone woke her up at five o'clock the next morning, dinging with an incoming text message. Blearily she read it and smiled. Mark was texting her from the gym.

I got my diagnosis. I have FG disorder. It's a condition of the heart. It's medically untreatable, so you'll have to help me when it reoccurs.

She tapped out her response. *Two weeks seems like a really long time, doesn't it?*

It's worse than that. It's two weeks and three days.

We'll both be busy, but we'll talk every day. We'll get through it.

I miss you already. There's a Fran place on my heart.

She shook her head incredulously. *Who says things like that?* Certainly no one she'd ever known before. Her heart swelled with something she was afraid to examine too closely.

You have a good workout. We'll talk later.

The next ten days were all-consuming. Fran and Veronica were in Cincinnati until Sunday with the cheerleading competition, then they had to go home, pick up Andy, and hit the road. They had to be at Mount Olive University in eastern North Carolina—a seven-hour drive—the next day. Then they would cut a trail back west for the following four days, visiting one college every day. It was a serious time for Andy, as he began the process of deciding where he was going to play his college tennis and get his undergraduate degree.

Mark spent part of the week on the road in Atlanta, working with some of his client churches. At night, they talked and texted, and their bond grew stronger.

"I'm going to have to have this hernia fixed," he confessed to her one night.

"What hernia?" she asked.

"Remember I told you I gave myself a hernia, taking care of Lisa?"

"I remember you mentioning it, but it didn't sound like a big deal."

"It's now a big deal. I've been keeping it in place with duct tape."

"Wait, did you say duct tape? Like how you taped your foot together the day we met?"

"Yes, duct tape and an electrical plate. Like I told you then, duct tape is good for everything."

She couldn't believe her ears. "You've been holding your guts in with duct tape and an electrical plate?"

"Yes."

"For how long?"

"Several months. There was nothing I could do about it while Lisa was still alive, and I really didn't want to tell Patrick I needed surgery right after she passed. So I've been getting by."

"Well." She had no idea what to say. Some things were just beyond comment.

"Anyway," he said, "I finally went to see one of my doctor friends, and he said I have two hernias, not one. I'm going through all the pre-op stuff Monday, and the surgery will be on Tuesday. It's not a big deal, just arthroscopic. Tiny little incisions."

"Tuesday the twenty-second?"

"Yes."

She made a decision. She'd be back in Tennessee on Sunday, and suddenly it was clear. "I want to see you before your surgery. How about if I come over Sunday when I get home?"

"Sounds great to me. You'll need a shoulder rub by then. How's the recruiting going?"

"These are great schools. There's no bad choice. The biggest thing is that Andy wants a school that can get him where he wants to be professionally."

"Which is where?"

"He wants to coach tennis on a collegiate level, and he wants to have his own tennis clinic."

"That's very cool. I'll pray that God will lead."

"That's what I'm praying. Just like I prayed for Brody, I pray that Andy will know when it's the right school. So far they're all looking good. It might be that he just hasn't found the exact right one yet."

"I'll pray that he does. Take care of my you. I'll see you on Sunday."

*   *   *

Fran, Andy, and Veronica went to Clemson's game at North Carolina State on Saturday, then set out for Oak Ridge early Sunday morning. After a long, harrowing drive, she dropped the kids at home and raced to Maryville, arriving around two o'clock.

As she pulled up to the house, she noticed a dark-haired young man riding his bike in the street with some other kids. This, she would bet, was Patrick. This thought was confirmed moments after she knocked on the door, and Mark let her in. The young man came in right behind her, holding his bike helmet.

"Hey, Dad, we're going to ride over to Ben's house. Okay?"

"That's fine. Have fun. Patrick, I want you to meet Fran."

His green eyes, completely unlike his father's, shifted to her. "It's nice to finally meet you."

"Patrick was the reason I started—as he put it—getting back out there," Mark said. "He told me to."

"I was tired of being his date." His face lit up in a smile that Fran knew had to be his mother's. "I'll see you guys later."

Fran turned to Mark when the door closed. "He's so healthy."

"That was my whole focus while Lisa was sick—getting the boys through it as healthy as I could. People kept telling them their mom was going to be okay, but I kept it real. Unless we got a miracle, she was going to die."

"Well, you did a good job. They're both great."

They looked at each other and suddenly, acutely, became aware that they were alone in the house for what could be quite a while. Mark cleared his throat.

"So, I was thinking—you up for a little hike?"

She looked down at herself. She was still wearing the clothes she'd traveled in, right down to the flip-flops on her feet. "I'm not exactly dressed for it, and I have no shoes."

"I think I can help with that."

He led her down to the basement and pulled a bin labeled LISA SHOES down from one of the shelves. She noticed that there were many other bins, all meticulously labeled. Immediately, Fran realized what he was doing. "Mark, you don't have to do this."

"It's just shoes," he said. "What size do you wear?"

"Nine."

"So did Lisa." He rummaged through the bin and pulled out a pair of black sneakers with pink soles. "See, I have a whole bin of shoes here. I knew there was a reason I didn't donate them already. Now I know why."

Disbelieving, she took the shoes. They looked new. "I can't believe this but thank you."

"Put them on and let's go. I know a perfect place, and it's not far."

They piled in the car and headed out of town.

"How did you do it?" she asked.

"What?"

"Get over it so fast."

"I didn't," he said. "You have to remember that Lisa was diagnosed over a year before she died. Every day, I had to teach her all over again how to brush her teeth and put her clothes on. She didn't remember her boys' names. She couldn't carry on a conversation and certainly couldn't function as a wife and mother. That was when I lost her, and I did my mourning then."

"It still has to be hard."

"It is, sometimes. Like this week is Thanksgiving, and I remember what was going on last year. It was pretty sad. Christmas is going to be tough, but I've already made plans to spend it in

Virginia with my sister and her family, and take the boys skiing. December 28 would have been our twenty-fifth wedding anniversary."

"Lots of stuff coming up, then."

"Yeah."

"I'll try to be a bright spot for you."

He looked at her sideways, smiled, and took her hand. "You already are. You give me hope."

*   *   *

Montvale Road winds out of Maryville, then steeply up and up in switchback curves to the Foothills Parkway, which straddles the ridge all the way to the edge of the Great Smoky Mountains National Park. From vantage points along the parkway, you can see the mountains on one side and the valley on the other. The tower atop Look Rock provides the best vantage point.

Mark took Fran's hand and led her over the roots and rocks as they made their way up the short trail. A few tourists passed them, coming and going. Finally, at the top of the tower, they stood silently, taking it in. It was Fran's first time, and for Mark, it never got old.

On the Tennessee Valley side, the landscape far below was flat for about fifty miles all the way to the other side of the valley, where it began to rise again at the edge of the Cumberland Plateau. Houses, ponds, and farmland dotted the land. Maryville was clearly visible to the right, and beyond that, the lights of Knoxville's McGhee-Tyson airport and the city itself.

The mountainside was pure natural splendor. The soft, undulating blue-green of the Great Smoky Mountains stretched on and on and on. Not far away was Chilhowee Lake. Peaks gave way to other, higher peaks. A map on top of the tower identified them as Gregory's Bald, Spence Field, Thunder Head, and Rocky Top. At the far end of the range was Mt. LeConte, the highest peak in the Smokies.

At first, Mark and Fran were among a small crowd, moving

around the tower and taking in the views. Then, for just a moment, they were alone. They could hear voices headed their way up the trail, but this moment was theirs. Without any words, she turned in his arms, and they came together in a long, sweet, aching kiss.

The voices came closer, and Mark pulled away just enough for Fran to turn around and nestle into him, his arms looped around her waist, her back snuggled against him. As they silently looked out at the mountain grandeur, Mark felt it. He felt his heart moving out of his body and melding with hers. It was terrifying and exhilarating at the same time, knowing that his heart didn't belong to him anymore. It resided in the body of the amazing woman in his arms. She could treasure it or crush it—and she didn't even know. He closed his eyes, gathered her closer, and rested his chin on her head.

He couldn't tell her now. She wasn't ready, and she probably didn't think he was either. All his friends and family would definitely say it was too soon—everyone except Patrick and maybe Scott—but Mark had never been more certain of anything in his life. Now he knew what love felt like. God had brought them together. It wouldn't have happened any other way. But they'd already lived a lifetime apart, and now they had to navigate some treacherous waters and find their way to whatever came next.

*   *   *

Fran loved Look Rock. She loved spending time with Mark even more. Those moments in his arms on top of that tower were the most soul-stirring of her life. When they pulled back into his garage, Mark gestured at the bicycle rack. "Patrick's home."

They went into the house and heard shouts coming from the basement, accompanied by the unmistakable sound of ping pong balls hitting paddles at high speed.

"Wanna play?" he asked playfully. "I still have to avenge my loss at bowling the other night."

"I'm actually okay at ping pong," she said. "Bring it on."

They went downstairs and found Patrick in a high-pitched battle against Isaac, one of their neighbors. They watched the end of that match and then picked sides in the next one, with Mark partnering with Isaac and Fran playing with Patrick. Mark played with slams and spins and drop shots as if he were on a tennis court, and he and Isaac won easily. Patrick didn't look surprised.

"That was so not fair," she told him as they trooped upstairs to relax for a bit. Patrick and Isaac were gearing up for round three.

"Why wasn't it fair?"

"Who serves like that? When it hit the table, it went instantly into the wall."

"That's called spin. I'll show you how."

"You even hit it off the ceiling."

"Hey, there's nothing in the rules that says you can't do that."

They went into his bedroom, and he flipped the TV on. In one corner of the room were two recliners. He sat down in one and gestured to the floor between his feet. "I think I promised you a shoulder rub," he said. "You've had a long week."

"Turn on anything but college football." She groaned and shook her head. "I don't even want to see the highlights from yesterday. N.C. State scored twenty-seven points in the second quarter alone. It was ugly."

"I'll turn on the NFL," he said. "Peyton's out with neck surgery this year, but I like the Packers too. They're undefeated, and they're playing Tampa Bay today."

She settled between his feet as he found the football game. When his thumbs pressed into the tight muscles and knots in her shoulders, she groaned. He bent her head forward and worked up her neck and into her hair, then gradually worked his way down her shoulders, arms, and hands. He took his time, giving attention to every muscle, ligament, and sinew, all the way down to her fingertips. He spent an hour working her upper body until she was completely relaxed. Groggily she remembered the first time he'd touched her, that day on the beach. Nothing had ever felt as good as his touch, and she felt the same way now. She never wanted him to stop.

Dimly, she was aware that he was doing something other than just giving her a shoulder rub. He was pouring all his feelings, all his heart, into her. And then it happened. Suddenly, with no warning, her heart felt as if it pulsed out of her body and fell, *splat*, on the floor at his feet. She could almost see it, wetly beating between them. It was his if he but knew it.

The words almost burst out of her mouth, but she bit them back.

He's not ready, she told herself. *There's no way he's ready. Don't say it, don't say it.*

Slowly she lifted her head all the way back and looked at him upside down. His hands left her shoulders and framed her face. Helplessly, his mouth came down on hers in a passionate kiss that stopped only when they heard Patrick and Isaac clatter up the stairs and into the kitchen.

"Dad! What's for dinner?"

Mark lifted his head, never taking his eyes from hers, and called down to his son. "Sorry, Patrick, the time got away from me. Want to call for a pizza?"

"I need to go," she told him softly. "I have kids to feed too. Thanks for the shoulder rub."

"Let me know when you get home?"

"Of course. I'll talk to you tomorrow."

All the way home, she warred with herself. There was no way Mark Smith was ready to move on to the next step in his life, whether he thought he was or not. He'd told her himself that the holidays would be rough. And his family would never understand, anyway. She had to just be there for him, bide her time, and wait. And definitely not tell him she loved him, although everything in her wanted to shout it out.

68

All of those good intentions collapsed about noon the next day when Fran's phone dinged with an incoming email. Mark was at the hospital, having his pre-op work done, and he sent her the schedule for tomorrow's surgery. His sister, Lisa Lambert, and his best friend, Scott Spitler, were going to be at the hospital with him. Mark's family didn't know about her yet, so he'd asked Scott to update her on his progress.

Then she came to the last line of his message. Heart racing, she backed up and read it again. *You have to know, I am falling for you fast. It is unexpected but undeniable now.*

She could almost feel him waiting for her response. He'd put his heart out there for her, and she wouldn't leave him dangling. Her fingers raced over her keyboard. *I'm falling for you too. I almost told you yesterday, but I didn't think you were ready to hear it.*

He answered quickly. *You'll be the last thing on my mind when I go to sleep and the first thing when I wake up. Scott will call you.*

I'll be waiting, she wrote.

She waited, on pins and needles, the next day. Scott took his commitment to Mark very seriously. Every time there was an update, he called Fran with assurance that her guy was okay. That evening, as she sat watching Veronica's cheerleading practice, a text came in.

Hey, baby. I know you're busy at cheerleading practice. I know Scott's been updating you, but I wanted you to hear it from me. I'm okay and at home. Patrick's taking good care of me. Let's get together when you get back from Atlanta, okay? I love you.

Tears filled Fran's eyes, and she quickly typed out her response. *If I can wait that long. I've never fallen so hard, so fast. I didn't*

even know it was possible. I'm going to have to tell my sister. She's
going to see the silly grin on my face.

His response came almost instantly. *I like that grin. TCOMY*
and I'll see you this weekend.

She thought about it but drew a blank. *TCOMY?*

Take care of my you.

*   *   *

Fran walked into Mark's house on Friday, the day after
Thanksgiving, and looked for the invalid who was recovering from
surgery. What she found was Mark, looking whole and healthy, in
the back yard with a stranger. When the man spoke one sentence,
she knew who it was. They'd talked on the phone three times on
Tuesday.

"You're Scott," she said.

"You're Fran." He gave her a side hug. "It's nice to meet the
lady who's putting a smile on my friend's face."

"He's putting a smile on mine, too."

"And he's not held together with duct tape anymore."

She rolled her eyes. "I couldn't believe that."

"Me, neither. But that's Mark."

The man in question stood and listened, waiting for them to
finish ribbing him. "Are you about done?" he asked.

"Yeah, we're done," Scott said with a twinkle.

"Good. You're my good friend and everything, but I'm starving
for the sight of this girl."

"I can take a hint. See you later, brother."

"See you. Thanks for everything."

Scott left, and Mark folded Fran in his arms. "Ahhh, that's
better already," he said into her hair as he gently rocked her back
and forth. "Just breathing the same air makes everything better."

Over the weekend, they discovered that they could enjoy just
being together and snuggling for hours, without talking or doing
anything else. The chemistry was intense, but it could be channeled
into just getting to know each other better. He came over on

Saturday and watched football—another depressing day for Clemson—with her and the kids. On Sunday, Fran went to church with Mark and Patrick and spent the afternoon at their house. Patrick made her some apple candy.

The two of them were sitting and talking that afternoon, and Mark mentioned that he was thinking about being a counselor. He felt that his experiences might specifically equip him to help others.

"That's a great idea," she said. "Would you have to get some extra schooling to do that?"

He looked uncomfortable as it hit him again that they really had a lot to learn about each other. She only knew about his career in church supply sales. They'd never talked about his life before that.

"Actually," he said, "I'm a licensed pastor and an ordained minister."

Her mouth dropped open. "You're what?"

"I have a master's degree in Biblical Studies. I'm a seminary graduate."

She stared at him, trying to assimilate this new knowledge. "Why aren't you in the ministry?"

Another uncomfortable look. "Because I was married before Lisa, and I'm divorced. I can't be a minister. Even Patrick doesn't know that."

"Wow." She didn't know what to say.

"God uses everything, though. He's used me in the church stewardship field to touch and help people in hundreds of churches, more than I could have helped in a lifetime by serving at one church." He looked at her closely. "Does that change anything?"

"Yes, actually it does," she said. "It makes me more sure. I wanted a man with a faith at least as strong as mine, someone who could help me grow spiritually. It sure seems like you check all my boxes, doesn't it?"

He snuggled her into his arms. "Maybe I can check off even more."

"Maybe you can."

"We're going to have to do something about this, you know."

"I know."

"We have to wait until after June, after Lisa has been gone a year."

She closed her eyes. "It sounds like forever, but I understand."

Before she left that day, he gave her an iPod full of hand-picked songs, so she could listen and think of him until they could be together again. The playlist began with "Nothing Like This," by Rascal Flatts.

*　　*　　*

The email that woke Fran up Monday morning filled her eyes with tears. It was the lyrics to "Nothing Like This," followed by Mark's words.

> I am the type that sits on the porch and stares at the stars. On the beach I can watch the waves for hours. I see and feel the beauty in nature. I feel it deep down, and it washes strength and peace into my spirit. YOU, Frannie, are my new ocean, my new night sky. I look into your eyes and feel it deeper. The longer I look, the more I see and feel with you.

At work that afternoon, her phone rang. A flower deliveryman was in the lobby, looking for her. She could barely see him over the enormous bouquet of a dozen roses and five Calla lilies—one for each of their children. The card read simply: *Nothing Like This, Your Man*

*　　*　　*

They decided to have a "date night" every Wednesday, so they would know they had at least one evening together in the midst of all the chaos. This week the plan was to meet for Japanese food at a restaurant in Knoxville. The day before, Mark sent Fran the link to Lisa's CaringBridge website, so she could see for herself and understand what he'd been through. When she saw him Wednesday, he looked at her with questions in his eyes. Had this changed anything?

"It just makes me love you more," she said.

They spent the rest of the evening at Rooms to Go, looking for a chair they could cuddle in, to replace the two recliners in the master bedroom. To the chagrin of the salespeople, they snuggled in every oversized chair on the showroom floor. It was a difficult decision because they locked together like two puzzle pieces, no matter which chair they were in. Finally, after the doors were locked and the last salesperson was staring at his watch, they made a decision and arranged for delivery.

As they drove in separate directions that night, Mark sent Fran a good-night text. *Somebody custom made us for each other. We fit perfectly. You are a treasure to me.*

*　　*　　*

When Fran floated through the door at home that night, Andy was waiting for her. "Mom, I need to talk to you," he began.

"Sure. You sound serious."

"I've made a decision."

"You have? You know which college you want?"

"No, not yet, but just the fact that so many colleges want me to visit means the tennis academy has done its job."

"I agree with that."

"That was the only reason I came here, Mom. I wanted to attract the attention of college coaches, and I've done that."

She stared at him, somehow knowing what was coming, waiting to hear him say it.

"I hate Oak Ridge High. I want to go back to Aiken High to finish my senior year. I want to play with my team, and maybe win that state championship."

"You want to live with your dad."

"For one semester, yes. I want to play this season with my real team, Mom. Those are the guys I've been with the whole time. You have to understand that."

"I do understand it, but it breaks my heart anyway." She started to sob, and Andy came to her and held her tight.

295

"I love you, Mom. I'm not choosing between you and Dad. I'm choosing between Oak Ridge and Aiken. I'm choosing my old team over some people I barely know. Think of it as I'm leaving for college one semester early."

She hugged him hard as the truth set in. All her kids were special, and she loved them equally, but Andy had a unique piece of her heart. He was confident, self-motivated, self-driven, absolutely determined, funny, smart, and athletic. He would be an amazing coach one day.

And he loved his mother. Maybe not more than his brother and sister did, but he definitely showed it more. Looking at this child of hers, she had no idea what traits he'd gotten from either her or Jeremy because he was so much better in every way than either of them.

"Yeah." She wiped her tears. "You're just leaving one semester early. Don't be surprised when I cry a lot."

69

Wedding talk, even though Mark and Fran weren't officially engaged yet, picked up steam in the first week of December. They scouted scenic wedding locations and locked one in for July 14.

Mark found a simple onyx and diamond ring and slipped it on Fran's finger as a "placeholder," until he could get her the perfect diamond.

Another day he was on his computer and noticed the dates for the Tour de France, which happens in July every year in France. He tapped out a text message. *What would you think about honeymooning in Europe and ending up in Paris on July 22? It's always been on my bucket list to see the Tour de France come in on the Champs Elysees.*

July 22? she wrote back. *That's my birthday. Sounds great to me.*

Mark read that text and paled a bit. July 22 was Fran's birthday? Holy cow, his mother wasn't going to like that. What were the odds that he'd find a woman who had the same birthday as his mom?

Then, abruptly, as the holiday season went into full swing, Mark hit a wall. The boys were supposed to be here making Christmas cookies with him. It was a family tradition. But then they had other plans, so he ended up doing it by himself. Standing in the kitchen by himself, doing the task that Lisa had done with her boys every year, everything came crashing in.

In his mind, he knew he was moving on, and that God had gifted him with the woman of his dreams. He was excited for the future, truly he was. But at this moment, all he could see was a big empty house, and all he could remember was the sadness and the future that never was. Lisa should be here with them, laughing and shopping and wrapping and baking cookies. They should be choosing a tree, and bringing it home, and setting it up just so. The boys should be digging around in their box of homemade ornaments, giggling over the memories and carefully placing each ornament.

Instead, here he was, all alone.

Yes, he loved Fran and was excited for their future together. But twenty-five years of history was here, now, and it was suffocating him.

He took a long walk in the rain and emerged from his depression enough to send Fran a text message. *Having a really bad night.*

Her response came quickly. *I'll come to you after cheerleading.*

No, he wrote. *This is something I just have to work through. I told you this would happen. The promise of the two of us together is giving me hope for the future, but the present is extremely difficult.*

Fran read that text, and her heart hurt for the pain she knew he must be feeling. All she could do was pray.

Unable to face the empty bed in his room, Mark bedded down on the couch in the bonus room, drank a glass of wine, and took a double dose of Ambien. He had to escape.

*   *   *

The next day, he woke and made a decision. It was time to stop sneaking around because people thought he wasn't ready. His family and friends needed to get on board and be happy for him, but first, they needed to start getting a clue that Fran existed and that she was important to him. Most of his friends and family were on Facebook, so that's where he went.

He found Fran's Facebook wall and wrote a post.

Fran, I am not sure if this is the right place to say this, but I am going on record here. You are a terrific person…so unselfish, such a diligent worker, and a great mom. Your love and sacrifice for your kids is an example of devotion and care. You are a beautiful flower blooming in a most wonderful way! Your smile, love, and ways bless everyone around you. I am so glad to be a part of your life now.

He hit "post," then just sat and watched people react. The first person to like the post was Doug Taylor. Predictably, as Mark sat and watched the "likes" pile up, his phone rang.

"Dude, what in the world?" Doug asked. "Who is she? Her picture—it looks familiar."

Mark smiled and kept watching the screen. "Bro, it's her."

"Who?"

"Remember the girl on the beach, thirty years ago? The one I couldn't get out of my mind?"

"You mean, this woman looks like her?"

"No, Doug, it *is* her. We found each other on Match.com. I'm going to marry her on July 14. Mark the date, because I want you to be here. I'd like to bring her to Huntsville to meet you and Connie, just as soon as we can. It's way too much to tell on the phone. We need to get together."

"Just let us know when you want to come, and of course I'll be there for your wedding. I'm so happy for you, brother. She must be something else."

"Thanks, Doug. She is."

*　　*　　*

The next step for Mark was to tell his boys. Patrick felt like a participant in this journey and had a ringside seat as things unfolded, so he was unsurprised and happy for his dad. Rick, having already moved out, was more of a spectator and offered his best wishes. Andy and Veronica knew when Mark put the placeholder ring on Fran's finger. They were still a little shell-shocked but liked Mark and wanted to see their mom happy.

Brody was coming in after exams to meet everyone. Football season was over except for the Orange Bowl, and Fran had a surprise for him. Brody had made the dean's list for the first time this semester, after a catastrophic first two years at Clemson. He loved Elvis, and Fran was surprising him with a trip to Graceland. Not co-incidentally, their trip would happen at the same time Mark and his boys would be in Virginia with Mellie and her family.

On Sunday, December 18, the whole new family was together for the first time. Mark brought Rick and Patrick to Oak Ridge, and Brody drove up from Clemson, planning to stay until Christmas. They had dinner, and everyone opened a present since this would be the only time they'd be together. Having no idea what to give Brody and Andy, Mark gave them both subzero sleeping bags. They'd never been on a serious camping trip in their lives, but they smiled politely and thanked him. To Veronica, Mark gave a dainty neck-lace.

It was the first time Brody had seen his mother's Oak Ridge house. While everyone else was cleaning the kitchen, she gave him the tour. She showed him the room she'd fixed especially for him, although he was seldom home. He finally asked the question that had obviously been on his mind. He hadn't had a front-row seat like Patrick, Andy, and Veronica had, to watch the whole thing unfold. His doubts were reasonable.

"Who is this guy, Mom? Are you actually engaged to him?"

"Not officially, but yes. He wants to wait until his wife has been gone for over a year, for his sons' sakes. The wedding date is July 14, and I'd like you to do the music."

"Isn't this a little quick? Don't you want to get to know him better?"

"I know him," she said, "and I'll get to know him even better over the next seven months. God brought us together. This is what He wants."

"Mom—"

"Just trust me, okay? I know this is right."

"At least it's still seven months away," he finally said grudg-ingly.

"Will you do the music? I'll pay you, just like any other profes-sional musician."

"Yes, I'll do the music."

"Thank you, Brody." She changed the subject. "So, I have a surprise for you. I hope you don't have any plans for the next couple of days."

"No, not really."

"Good, because we're going to Graceland."

He stared at her. "Graceland? Like, Elvis's house? In Memphis?"

"The one and only. I'm so proud of you for making the dean's list. Congratulations and Merry Christmas."

*   *   *

While their kids watched television at her house, Mark and Fran stole a few minutes for themselves. They drove the short distance down the road to Fran's deserted workplace and parked in the corner of the parking lot. The East Tennessee Technology Park was a Manhattan Project nuclear production site, but it had been shut down for a very long time. The goal here was to clean up and reclaim. Nature was very willing to oblige.

They sat, locked together, and watched wildlife come and go.

"Uh oh," Mark said as a skunk wandered near his truck. "Be very quiet. He won't hurt us, but he could stink up this truck if he gets scared."

They sat, as still as a deer in headlights, until the skunk had meandered on his way. Then, her head on Mark's shoulder, Fran looked up at him. "You're going to be out of cell range, aren't you?"

"For the time we're at Snowshoe, probably."

"You won't even be able to let me know you got there okay."

"I'll try to find a way to get a message out, but I'll be okay." He looked into her worried eyes. Then, helplessly, like a magnet connecting with its perfect counterpart, he lowered his mouth to hers. They only had a few minutes to last them for the next week. What could possibly happen here, in this place?

The combustion was instantaneous. They caught fire in the front seat of his truck, exchanging long, desperate kisses, unable to pull apart for more than milliseconds. Finally, Mark's phone buzzed in his pocket and brought them to their senses. Breathing hard, he pulled it out and looked at the screen.

"It's Patrick," he said thickly. "He says it's time to go."

"Saved by the bell."

"Or, in this case, the buzz. Look at this, the windows are actually fogged up."

"I thought that was a metaphor, not a real thing. This is going to be the longest week of my life." She had the Graceland trip, and Julia and Cecil were coming down later in the week, so she should be happy. Instead, the whole prospect just felt incredibly empty as they drove the short distance back to her house. "I guess I've got it bad."

"A week will go by in no time, and we'll be back together and planning our wedding."

"You don't really believe that."

"No, I don't, but it's what we've got. Enjoy Graceland and your family, okay? And I'll enjoy the time with my sister and my guys the best I can. We'll get through it."

Later that night, as she was getting ready for bed, Fran's phone dinged. She read his message with a soft smile.

This year I have seen moments of total despair when I was not sure how to push on. Today I have a view of a new and beautiful land. Fran, the idea of a life ahead with you and yours is unspeakable joy. You are my sunshine, my night sky, my new land.

70

They both tried, they really did. They tried to put their cell phones away and concentrate on family, but it was futile—especially knowing that when Wednesday came, communication would likely be nonexistent.

Mark and his sons made it safely to Mellie and George's house in Blacksburg. Fran and Brody made it to Memphis, although she'd had no idea how long a drive it was going to be. Memphis was almost to Arkansas, nearly four hundred miles away, in a whole different time zone. With traffic, the drive took eight hours.

Tuesday they planned to spend most of the day at Graceland, then make the long drive back to Oak Ridge. Fran offered to extend their hotel reservation for one more night and drive back on Wednesday, but Brody didn't want to do that. "We'll take turns driving if you get tired," he said. "Let's go ahead and get back." It was mid-afternoon when they hit the road.

After six long hours, they were in the homestretch. They'd passed through Nashville, Crossville, and Cookeville and were munching on Steak 'n Shake from a drive-through. Fran had just sent Mark an update, telling him she should be home within a couple of hours. They whizzed along in the left lane of Interstate 40, with the cruise control set at seventy-seven miles an hour. A new Elvis CD played loudly, and they sang along.

Fran was balancing her food on her lap and had her milkshake in her left hand when her left front tire suddenly and violently exploded. The milkshake flew everywhere. Somehow, she managed to keep control of the car, avoid hitting anyone or being hit, and steer safely into the emergency lane. Brody, to his credit, kept absolutely silent until the car came to a shuddering stop.

"Nice driving," he said calmly. "You okay?"

Now that it was over, she was shaking from head to foot. "What in the world?" she said. "That was a new tire."

He looked around. "Where are we?"

"I have no idea. I wasn't paying attention to anything, just trying to get us home."

She pulled out her phone and called AAA, who of course wanted to know where she was.

"I have no idea. On I-40, somewhere between Cookeville and Oak Ridge. I can see a bridge up ahead." She got out of the car and walked far enough to be able to see the sign. "It's Falling Water River."

"What mile marker?"

"I don't see any signs." She was beginning to feel a little desperate. She was acutely aware that they were stranded on a busy interstate, trucks whizzing by, in the middle of the night. If it weren't for Brody, she'd be downright frightened. "Can't you find me with what I've given you?"

"I'm trying." Several long minutes later, the AAA representative came back on the line and said he had to have more specific information. "Here's what you need to do. Hang up and call 911. Tell them what's going on and ask them to ping you and tell you your mile marker. I'll call you back on this number."

"When?"

"Five minutes."

It worked. 911 reported their mile marker promptly, and AAA dispatched a truck. ETA, thirty minutes. While they waited, Fran texted Mark an update. She knew he'd be frantic.

*   *   *

Nearly three hundred miles east, Mark was having trouble concentrating on what his sister and brother-in-law were telling him. They were all up late, celebrating Christmas together because Mark and the boys were heading to Snowshoe tomorrow.

Until his wedding to Lisa, he and Mellie had been close, and now they were regaining their relationship. George, along with Doug and Scott, were the men Mark loved the most in the world. Olivia, their adorable little daughter, was beside herself to have her uncle and two favorite cousins in the house. She perched on Patrick's knee and chattered away.

But there was something, a big something that Mark wasn't telling them. It consumed him. And they knew something was up because he'd never been one to be glued to his phone. Now, he couldn't put it down. Maybe, once he knew Fran and Brody were home okay, he'd be able to concentrate on his family.

His phone buzzed with three consecutive incoming messages. He glanced at it. And paled.

"I'm sorry," he muttered. "I need to make a call."

"Now? What's going on?" Mellie asked, but she was talking to thin air. Mark had already walked away, phone in hand.

Fran picked up almost immediately. "Are you okay?" he asked frantically.

"Somehow, we are," she said wearily. "We're waiting for the AAA truck. God was taking care of us, Mark. There's no other explanation for it. I'm a good driver, but I'm not that good. My tire exploded at seventy-seven miles an hour on Interstate 40."

He almost cried with relief and thanks. "I'm so glad Brody is with you. Just stay in the car and wait, and keep me updated until you get home safe. I love you."

"I will. I love you, too."

Mark hung up and went back into the living room. There was no help for it now—he had to tell his family. They already knew something was up anyway, and he was going to be a mess until he knew Fran was safely home. She needed him, and he was hundreds of miles away, unable to be there for her. He could barely stand it.

George looked up when Mark sat down heavily beside him. "Everything okay?"

"Can we pray?"

"Of course."

They all joined hands and bowed their heads. "Father," Mark began, "thank You for Your providence and protection tonight, being there for Fran and Brody when they needed You. You delivered them, Father, and I am so grateful. Please be with them now. Protect them, and see them safely home. In Your Son's precious name I pray, amen."

He released their hands and looked up. Mellie's eyes were locked on his.

"Who's Fran?" she asked.

"I have something to tell you," he said. "I found someone."

For the next two hours, they sat with him, riveted, as he told the story. Olivia fell asleep in Patrick's arms. Every few minutes, Mark was interrupted by his phone buzzing, and he tapped out an answer. Step by step, he tracked Fran until he knew she had safely limped into her garage in Oak Ridge on her temporary tire. Finally, drained, he sent one final message, sat back in his chair, and closed his eyes in relief.

"So," Mellie asked softly, "when do we get to meet my new sister?

"Soon," he said. "You're the first family member outside our kids who knows. I didn't think people would think I'm ready."

"You've been through so much, and we just want you to be happy," George said. "If Fran makes you happy, we love her too."

Back in Oak Ridge, Fran was staggering into the house when Mark's last message of the night flashed on her screen. *With every breath, I love you more. How is that possible?*

71

Only one spot in Snowshoe had—sometimes—internet service. To get there, a person had to go onto the third floor, go out onto a tiny deck, and stretch high up toward the corner of the lodge. The footing was iffy, and service was fleeting and unreliable, but that spot was the only option if you wanted to get a message out.

In the mornings and the evenings, and sometimes in between, Mark went to that spot. Freezing and shivering, he poured out his heart to his sweetheart so she'd know he was still alive and loved her. Friday morning, he sat in the freezing cold and thought about her and began to write.

> I woke up rested and alert this Friday morning. After listening to Patrick snore for an hour, then all my music, I got up. I did not mind the quiet time to think about you, pray for our kids, and ponder a future life with the one woman who has ever outstripped my dreams.
>
> You are a woman with such quality, such beauty, so much life and love and charm. Your smile is worth every mile of hard work a man would have to put in on the hardest days. Your hug shuts out the most bitter thoughts and memories. When you rest those beautiful locks on my shoulder, I would cherish and protect you from any harm, any stray word, or even thought that would hurt you.

He spent the day on the slopes and sent her a message describing his antics while trying to learn to snowboard. He knew it would make her laugh.

Can't dance or snowboard. Know that now. Rick took pics of me wiping out all down the mountain. I took out two dudes, a chick and a poor kid getting a ski lesson from an instructor. But I did say that I was real sorry!

Her response was instant. *You took out people on the bunny slope?*

Hey, it was a semi-controlled descent down the mountain, AND I was almost getting it by the time I got toward the bottom! And I will have you know there was a snowboarder at the bottom that saw my final feat (he missed the rest), and he gave me the hang ten sign. I nodded like I was cool with it all. Then I fell getting on the lift.

Fran dropped the phone and howled. She could just see it all. Poor Mark. She did love a man who could make her laugh, which Mark did all the time.

The next morning, Christmas Eve, Mark sat on his deck at Snowshoe and composed one final message. Later today, he would be back in East Tennessee, and this torture would be over.

True to his word, the moment his plane touched down, Mark sent a text that he was now back on Tennessee soil. They knew they wouldn't see each other that day or even the next—which was Christmas—but just being back in proximity settled something in their spirits. Monday would be theirs. Mark hadn't yet told Fran what he had up his sleeve, but he had a feeling it would be a big hit.

*   *   *

"Hiking?" she asked incredulously. "It's the end of December. Isn't hiking supposed to be when it's warm?"

"Hiking is for any time," Mark said. "Maybe the crowds will be smaller today. I've got the perfect trail picked out. You'll love it."

"I don't have any hiking clothes."

"Not a problem. I've got you all fixed up."

He led her to his bedroom, where he had her outfit all laid out. A nylon neon yellow scouting shirt, a long-sleeved shirt, nylon pants that could be unzipped at the knee, a light jacket, gloves, ear warmers, two sets of socks, a pair of sturdy hiking shoes, and even a pair of hiking poles.

"Man," she said. "You think of everything."

"I'm a Boy Scout," he said simply. "I've got your fanny pack all fixed, too."

"Do tell."

"Dried fruit, granola, jerky, and two water bottles. It's a short hike. That should be plenty."

Fran stared and considered. She was more than willing to do this—excited, even—but the only hike she'd ever been on in her life had been at Mt. Charleston, just outside Las Vegas, in 1998. That didn't really count, because they'd had four kids with them and hadn't taken it seriously. They'd just played in the snow.

Her only other hiking experience—if you could call it that— was when she took Brody to Japan for his high school graduation present. He wanted to climb Mount Fuji because that was where Godzilla was born. They barely made it any distance at all before the safety police stopped them. In retrospect, she should have known this was out of her league when they were selling oxygen on the bus.

Now, though, she shrugged and gave in. It was important to Mark, and therefore, it was important to her. She did love nature and beautiful views—she just hoped she didn't trip on a rock and fall off the mountain.

They drove to Cades Cove, where they discovered that thousands of other people had the same idea. Cars clogged the cove and slowed to a standstill as people gawked at deer in the pastures that were spread throughout the property. Finally, Mark and Fran arrived at the trailhead for Abrams Falls. She studied the sign with a touch of dread. It was a five-mile, "moderately strenuous" hike. Well, she'd come too far to turn back now.

At first, it seemed easy. The trail was beautiful, rising and falling along ridges and waterways. Fran kept up what she thought was a good pace—until the trail got steep. Then, she gasped for air and had to stop and rest. She was so busy watching her footing that she didn't get much of a chance to look at the scenery on the way up. What if she saw a granddaddy longlegs? The entire mountain would know about it. This wasn't something she could control.

After less than an hour, they reached Abrams Falls. They heard it before they saw it—the rushing, roaring sound water makes when it crashes down a mountain. Sitting there on the rocks, enjoying the beautiful waterfall, knowing she'd made it—Fran suddenly and completely understood why people like to climb mountains.

"So," Mark said, "what do you think?"

"I can do this," she said with a touch of pride and wonder. "I really enjoyed it."

"You can do the more strenuous stuff too, as long as you pace yourself. You took that trail a little too fast. I was just watching to see how you'd handle it."

"I did?"

He nodded, eyes twinkling. "You were like a jackrabbit. I couldn't do that."

They were silent for a while, watching the river. Kids waded into the water and shrieked at the cold. Some brave souls climbed the rocks to the top of the falls. They weren't very tall, but they were obviously powerful. Water boiled violently at their base.

"This is actually the ninth most dangerous hike in the country," Mark told her.

"This? Why?"

"Because of the falls. The rocks look stable, and people think they can climb them, but then hikers slip off. In the same way, people think the water looks tame, and they can just jump in. It's a lot more dangerous than it looks with strong currents in there. That's why they put up the warning signs."

Mark was thoroughly enjoying showing Fran that she could do this. He'd purposely chosen something a little bit challenging and very beautiful, to give her confidence and joy. She'd proven that she could share and enjoy things like this with him, as he'd always dreamed. And this day wasn't over yet.

They traversed back down the trail and to the car. It was nearly five o'clock when they headed out of Cades Cove. Mark casually said, "I've got a place in mind in Knoxville for dinner. Sound okay?"

"Sure."

"My sister's meeting us there. She wants to meet you."

"Wait. Sister? Which sister?"

"The one who lives here in town. Lisa Lambert. I told Mellie about you when I was at her house."

"You did? I didn't think you were going to."

"Well, those plans kind of changed when you had your blowout, and I couldn't think about anything but you. I told them everything. I made Mellie stay quiet until I could tell Lisa, but she won't be able to hold it in for long. That's why we need to tell Lisa now."

"I look terrible."

"You look beautiful. This is the way I like you best. Not much makeup, hair kind of wild."

"That is not very encouraging."

He took her hand and stroked her thumb with his. "It will be fine. You'll like Lisa. We're meeting her at seven. There's an errand I need to run first."

"What kind of errand?"

"You'll see."

*　　*　　*

The errand turned out to be a stop at Markman's Jewelers, on Kingston Pike in Knoxville. They pulled into the parking lot, and Mark could see on Fran's face when she realized where they were.

"A jeweler?" she asked.

"The best jeweler in town," he said.

"Why?"

"I want you to pick out your stone. Just the stone."

"Oh, Mark..." her eyes filled with tears.

"No crying yet. Let's go inside."

For the next thirty minutes, the sales manager brought out stone after stone after stone. They glimmered and shone, shooting miniature rainbows under the bright display lights. The manager explained the importance of color, cut, carat, and clarity in determining the value of a diamond.

Mark watched Fran's eyes as she looked at the stones. He would know when she saw the one she wanted.

When the manager pulled out one particular oval stone, a shade larger than the others he'd shown so far, Mark could see the difference in her eyes. The stone glittered and sparkled and beckoned, and Fran's eyes positively lit up when she looked at it.

"That's the one," Mark said.

The manager checked the price tag and named a number. Fran choked. "Maybe you could show us the smaller ones again."

"No, that's the one." Mark smiled and wrapped his arm around her. "There goes the bass boat. She's worth it."

Then they looked at possible settings and mounts. The end result was going to be a designer ring, custom made by Tacori, with this stone cut to Mark's specifications. He wasn't going to show her everything today—he'd just wanted her to pick the stone. Some things had to stay a surprise. They also picked their wedding rings.

"I'll call you tomorrow with a quote for all three rings," the sales manager said. "It's going to be beautiful. Congratulations."

"She's the one who's beautiful." Mark kissed the top of her head and pulled her back to his side. "Maybe this ring will do her justice. I'll look forward to your call."

When they got back into the car, Fran looked at this man who just kept surprising her. "So, does this mean we're engaged?"

"No," he said. "We're not engaged until I officially ask you, and I won't ask you until I have the ring in my pocket. It will take weeks for them to make the ring. You'll just have to make do with the placeholder ring until then."

She looked at the pretty onyx and diamond ring on her left hand. "I do love it," she said. "But I can't wait to flash that diamond and have everybody know how special you are."

He took her hand and smiled. "That will come soon enough. There's plenty to do. We can go ahead and plan the wedding and the honeymoon, and there are lots of other decisions we have to make too."

*   *   *

Lisa Lambert was pleasant and beautiful and poised, and Fran liked her instantly. They had a nice dinner at Calhoun's, and Mark regaled her with stories from the ski slopes. They chatted about Lisa's husband and two daughters, and Fran and Lisa got to know each other a bit.

When Mark dropped the bomb that they were serious, Lisa was not surprised.

"I knew something was up when you had your hernia surgery," she said. "When Scott kept leaving to make phone calls and acting secretive. And you've seemed awfully happy for the last few weeks. Mellie and I have been talking about it."

"I am happy," Mark said. "She makes me happy."

Fran looked at Mark and whispered, "Can I tell her?"

"She can be the first," he whispered back.

"We picked out rings today," Fran blurted.

"Rings?"

"An engagement ring and two wedding rings. At Markman's."

"Oh!" Lisa closed her gaping mouth and recovered quickly. "I'm the first to know?"

"We just left Markman's. Like, right before we came here. Yes, you're the first to know."

"Please, please, can I be the one to tell Mellie?"

Fran looked at Mark, and he nodded. "Yes, you can tell her. She won't be surprised."

"Now," Lisa said, "you have to tell Mom."

A shadow fell over Mark's face at that. "You know what the worst thing is?"

"What?"

"Fran and Mom have the same birthday."

Lisa burst out laughing. "Fran, welcome to the family," she said. "We're weird, but we love each other."

72

New Year's Eve, Fran and Mark traveled to Atlanta, so Mark could meet Chris and her family. Seven days later, Veronica turned fifteen and chose to go bowling and have pigs in blankets, macaroni and cheese, and homemade double chocolate cake. Fran made Mark and Patrick howl with the story of Andy's birthday cake when Veronica was two years old. They planned to go to Julia's house on January 22 for a double birthday celebration—Julia's and Brody's—so that Julia and Mark could finally meet face to face.

Julia knew everything that was going on; Fran had never been able to keep anything from her. But Mark wanted to meet her and tell her himself that he was going to take care of her baby. First, though, a mountain stood in the way—literally and figuratively. Mark wanted to take Fran on her first serious hike on January 21.

"How serious?" she asked.

"The tallest peak in the Smokies. Mt. LeConte."

Fran wilted a bit. It was wonderful that he thought she could do these things, but she had to make him understand. "Honey, I've never really been in shape in my life. I'm flabby. I can't walk fast for a hundred yards without huffing and puffing. I'll go and I'll have fun, but please don't expect too much out of me."

"You can do it. You have good muscle tone. You're not out of shape. You just need to increase your lung capacity. Trust me."

The morning of January 21 dawned with rain, thunder, and lightning in Oak Ridge. Fran woke early to the crashing thunder with more than a little relief. There was no way they could hike in this weather. She reached for the phone to see what else Mark had in mind. He answered on the first ring.

"We can still do it," he said. "I've looked at the radar. It's way worse in Oak Ridge than it is here, and it's fine on the mountain. As long as we leave the house by ten, we'll be fine."

"Are you sure?"

"Would I put you in danger?"

No, she knew he would not. She got dressed and headed to Maryville.

They dressed in rain gear, filled hydration bags with water, packed protein-filled snacks, and headed out on the hour-long drive to the Mt. LeConte trailhead. When they pulled in, there were only two other cars in the parking lot, which was apparently unusual because this was one of the Smokies' most popular trails. Mark checked his watch. "We're getting a late start, so we need to get moving," he said. "It's a six-hour trip up and down."

"That's assuming I make it to the top," she said.

"You will."

He wrote a note and put it in the windshield, telling rangers who they were and where they were headed. "Standard procedure," he assured her.

Rain pelted them as they climbed out of the truck and put on their light backpacks. They adjusted their hiking poles to the right length and put on their gloves. Fran also added an extra shirt, coat, a scarf, a hat, and ear warmers. "You'll shed most of that soon enough," Mark predicted.

For the next three hours, they made their way steadily up the mountain, and Fran saw what Mark was talking about. Her body warmed, and she took off all her extra clothes and stuffed them in her backpack. Mark let her lead, and she found a pace that worked for her. They traversed footbridges, rocky areas that required them to hold onto cables, frozen rocky stream beds, and sandy areas with no footholds. Along the way they saw breathtaking vistas, waterfalls, and rushing mountain streams.

They stopped every few minutes to drink from their hydration packs and munch on handfuls of trail mix. "If you eat this now," Mark said, "the energy will kick in when you need it." She did everything he did and listened to every word he said.

The higher they climbed, the more she began to feel that she could actually do this. She pictured herself at the top and how wonderful that would feel. Then, all of a sudden, the trees thinned, and they were at the top of Mt. LeConte, elevation 6,593 feet. And Fran had hiked every inch of it.

This was new territory for her, both literally and figuratively. She'd accomplished some things in her life, personally and professionally. But standing on the top of that mountain, tucked safely against Mark's side, his praise and encouragement ringing in her ears, she didn't remember ever being more proud of anything. She was there because he'd believed in her, pure and simple, far more than she'd believed in herself. There was no way she would have tried this on her own. And here they were.

They sat on the porch of one of the boarded-up lodges and shared a quick lunch with a brazen little squirrel. Fran gazed out over the beautiful scene before her. "Why did you pick this hike—the highest peak in the Smokies—for my first serious hike ever?"

"Because Mt. LeConte is the gold standard, and I wanted you to see that you could do it. If you can do this, you can do anything." He glanced at his watch. "We can't stay here long, though. We have less than three hours to get back down the mountain before dark. Here, take some Advil now. You'll be glad later."

In a way, Fran discovered, getting down is even harder than going up. It's very hard on the hips and knees—thus the Advil. They all but sprinted down the icy trail and made it to the car just before six o'clock. It was almost entirely dark. They stripped off their rain gear and collapsed in the car, grinning at each other.

"Well? What did you think?" he asked, knowing the answer.

"I'm so glad you made me go," she said. "I love knowing that I can do this."

"That was the point," he said. "Now, we get ready for eight hours in the car tomorrow. I can't wait to meet your mom."

"I can't wait, either. She's going to love you. And I can't believe Brody is going to turn twenty-one tomorrow. He's been through so much. I've told you."

"He's a fine young man."

On the way back, they stopped at Sugarlands Visitor Center to freshen up. As they walked in, Mark confessed that this was the location of one of his most embarrassing moments ever.

"In a visitor center? How bad could it be?"

"Pretty bad," he said. "So, I went into the restroom, but the WO on the sign was kind of shadowed, so I went into the wrong one. It was kind of an urgent situation, and I was in a hurry. I was in a stall before I realized I'd made a mistake."

"How did you figure out you were in the wrong place?"

"Well, I heard the door open, and some high heels clicking on the floor. Then the door opens in the stall next to me, and this woman plops on the toilet, and the clothes come down around her feet. Then she lets out this awful groan, and there's splattering noises and everything. The smell, oh my goodness, I have no idea what she could have eaten to smell like that. I was gagging. And she kept making all these noises, and it just went on and on. I thought females were all dainty. I had no idea."

"No, we're not dainty at all. What did you do?"

"What could I do? I was trapped. I just stayed quiet as a mouse and pulled my feet up on my tippy toes, so if she looked over, maybe she'd think it was just a woman with big feet."

She collapsed in hysterical giggles at the picture he painted. Him, with his size twelve feet, pulling up on his tippy toes, hiding in a bathroom stall.

"What happened?" she asked when she calmed down enough to talk again.

"She finally pulled up her clothes and checked herself in the mirror and left. I waited a minute to be sure she'd really gone, then lit out of there like a cat on fire."

"Poor thing."

"It scarred me for life. Now I know what you ladies do in there, and it's not pretty."

73

Much like Fran's reaction to Julia's husband, Cecil, twenty years before, Julia regarded Mark at first with a bit of suspicion. Unquestionably, Fran was glowing with happiness. Undoubtedly, she was madly in love with this man. But who was he? It had happened so fast. Julia had far too much experience watching Fran get hurt. She was not going to let it happen again if she could help it. She had some questions for Mark.

Mark actually took the initiative in the conversation by asking to see some childhood pictures of the woman he loved. Julia led him around the house and showed him pictures of Fran from infant to present. Brilliantly, she had the foresight to run through the house before Mark arrived and remove any photos of Jeremy. The two of them went from picture to picture and had a marvelous talk going down memory lane.

They did not want Fran to be part of their conversation. When she came near, they shooed her away, so she spent time with her birthday boy. The last time she'd seen Brody was only a month ago, Christmas week in Oak Ridge. Then, he'd had long, shaggy hair and an unkempt beard. Now, he had the haircut of a military man and looked incredibly handsome. Fran had hated the long-haired phase and was glad it was over.

Mark and Julia finally emerged from their long talk, both smiling. "I've assured your mom that I love her daughter and will take good care of her," he told Fran.

"And that's all I ask," Julia said simply. She gave her daughter a soft nod and a hug.

They ate Brody's birthday meal, cut the cake, sang happy

birthday, and opened presents. Fran and Mark still had a four-hour drive back to Tennessee, so they left soon after the party. Fran took Mark by some scenes from her childhood—the church where she grew up, the house she lived in until she was eighteen, the spot where her daddy was buried, the school she graduated from in Clinton, and the lake house where she grew up spending summers. Each place spawned lots of conversation, especially the lake house, although now it was just a vacant lot. They got out of the car and walked down the hill toward the water.

"That," Fran gestured to the rotting pier, "was where we tied our boat up. Right out there," she pointed out to far end, "was where I actually learned to swim."

She led him along the bank, toward the woods at the corner. "Over here was where we used to sit and fish from the bank."

Mark's eagle eye took it in. "Yeah, I bet you caught a lot here. Rocks and brush are hidden under there."

"We did," she said. "Every time."

She led him up to where the house used to be. Actually, it had been just a very old trailer with a big porch built onto the front of it. Now there was nothing. "Here," she said, "is where I became afraid of granddaddy longlegs."

He looked at her and knew there was more to this. It had to have been very bad. He'd seen first-hand that her terror was intensely real. "What happened?"

"I must have been about five years old, because it was just me and my daddy here, and he wasn't sick yet. We were getting the place ready to move in for the summer. There was this big, black spot up high on the porch, kind of up near the top. Daddy wanted to clean off that black spot."

"This isn't going where I think it is, is it?"

"Probably. He aimed the strongest stream of his hose on that black spot, and you know what it was?"

"A nest."

"A big one. That black spot was thousands of granddaddy longlegs, all bunched up together. When he blew it apart, they all came raining down. All over little five-year-old me." Even now, forty-five years later, her voice trembled, her hands shook and tears sprang to her eyes. "If I see one, I scream, and I can't help it. If one were to actually get on me, I think my heart might stop. I don't like to tell people because they might think it would be fun to chase me with one. Little boys, especially. I don't think I'd survive it."

He held her until the trembling went away. He'd never seen a phobia this bad, and there was just one answer to it. "I know how to take it away," he said. She looked up, automatically shaking her head in fear. He put a finger across her mouth. "I'll just make sure to keep them away from you. You watch. Our house will be dll free."

"Dll?"

"So we don't even have to say its name. They won't dare come anywhere near."

*　　*　　*

Over the next week, Fran found her wedding dress and brought Veronica back to see it—and she found her maid of honor dress as well. Both of them got to ring the bell at David's Bridal—a tradition when you find your dress. Fran picked up Mark's wedding ring at Markman's, showed it to Veronica, and promptly hid it away.

The couple began to have serious conversations about living arrangements. They both had big, fully furnished houses. One child was at Oak Ridge High, and one was at Maryville High. Her work was in Oak Ridge, but the commute wasn't bad from Maryville.

Ultimately, it came down to the size of the house and roots in the community. The Oak Ridge house wouldn't be big enough to accommodate everyone if the whole family were together. The Maryville house would, especially when the basement was finished. Mark and his boys had deep roots in Maryville, whereas Fran and Veronica had just moved to Oak Ridge.

The other option would be to sell both current houses and buy a new one, but that didn't seem to make sense. As an alternative, Mark said he would completely redo his house for Fran, so it would feel like hers. And, he said, it would be finished before the wedding.

Privately, Fran wondered if Veronica would take a cue from her brother and decide to move back to Aiken. If she was going to have to change schools again anyway, why not go home? She hoped her daughter would want to stay with her and Mark, but it would be her decision. She was fifteen years old now.

Serious work began when they had to choose which pieces of furniture were going to stay with them, and which were not. The best pieces from both houses would end up in Maryville, while the rejects would be staged in the Oak Ridge house and be part of an estate sale that would, hopefully, pay for the wedding and honeymoon expenses.

The final piece that fell into place in January was for Fran to meet her future mother-in-law. They met at the Tomato Head restaurant in Maryville.

Mark had warned Fran that his mother was a former debate champion. "I don't mean to scare you," he said. "I love her. But I know her. She'll ask you lots of questions. She doesn't mean any harm, she just loves her family and wants to protect them, and in our case, I'm very sure she will think it's too quick. She won't preach at you, but she will definitely preach at me later. Let's just make this a good meeting."

With Mark's warnings in her ears, Fran was able to steer the conversation away from areas that would be troublesome. When it was over, she heaved a sigh. Of all the meetings, that was the one that had terrified her most. Now it was behind them.

74

In early February, Mark got a call from Markman's Jewelers. "Your ring is here," the salesperson said. "It will be in the safe, whenever you want to come pick it up."

"I'll be right there," he said.

Forty minutes later, Mark stood at Markman's, surrounded by the entire twelve-person sales team, each of whom was goggling at Fran's ring.

"Wow," one said, "she must be queen of the world."

"No," Mark said. "She's just *my* girl."

Grinning to himself, he tapped out a text to his lady: *Holy cow! There is nothing that remotely compares to your ring, baby.*

What? The response came instantly. *You've got it?*

Standing in Markman's right now. The sales team can't believe their eyes.

Oh, baby. When I have that ring on my hand, the whole world will know that I belong to the most wonderful guy in the world. I can't wait.

Mark paid for the ring and got in his car. As he drove, love washed over him again, so much he couldn't see the road. Tears pouring down his cheeks, he maneuvered into the emergency lane, where he let the feelings flow. How was it that God had been so good to him, had seen him through so much, and had now hand-picked this wonderful woman for him? It seemed as if God had giftwrapped Fran and dropped her straight into Mark's waiting arms.

Safely stopped in the emergency lane, eyes still clouded with tears, he texted Fran. *I teared up and pulled off the road right now. I am very deeply emotional how I feel about you, baby. I can't see to drive.*

The response was immediate. *I love you so much, sweetheart. Please be careful and take care of my man.*

Mark had a riding date with Scott, so he went straight there—with the ring in his pocket. They rode through Townsend, and Mark showed his friend the place where the wedding would take place on July 14. He pulled out the ring.

"This is what I'm going to be putting on her finger."

Scott's eyes popped. "Holy cow, man, that's a rock."

"It's the stone she wanted. Her eyes just sparkled when she saw it, and I knew it was the one. I designed the ring to complement the stone. See, the detail on the undersides and the band?"

"That must have cost you."

"I was planning to trade up and get a new bass boat, but the one I have will do. Fran will be wearing the bass boat on her hand."

"She'll love that. Don't let Cynthia see it."

Mark laughed. "There's something else I want to ask you, man."

"Name it."

"Would you be best man at my wedding?"

"Me?"

"Yes, you. You've had a ringside seat for this whole thing. You love us as a couple like no one else does. Of course, you. You're my best friend."

"I'd be honored," Scott said.

*   *   *

Fran and Veronica arrived at Mark's house after work the same day, and Fran was on pins and needles. She was pretty sure he wouldn't let her see the ring, and she was right. He did, however, call Veronica up to his office, where they spent a very long time whispering and giggling. Fran could hear that much from the bottom of the steps, which was as far as she was allowed to go.

"We're almost done," Veronica called down, then giggled and whispered some more.

Fran rolled her eyes.

When they came down, it was apparent that Mark had confided his plans to Veronica, and Veronica excelled at keeping secrets. There was a ring, and there was a plan, and Fran was in the dark.

Veronica only told Fran one thing about that conversation. "Mom, he told me he loves you very much, and he wants to marry you. I gave him my permission. Now, don't ask me anything else because I'm not going to tell you."

"You know what he's going to do, though?"

Veronica just stared at her, neither nodding nor shaking her head. Fran gave up.

It would happen when it happened. She only hoped it would be soon.

75

The morning of Valentine's Day, Mark Smith drove around town tying up some final details. Fran was at work, and the plan—although it was going to change—was for her to meet him at the Japanese restaurant at seven o'clock. He had a lot to do before then.

His phone buzzed just as he got back in his car. He glanced at it and grinned. Veronica had been such an excellent little co-conspirator the past two weeks. All the kids knew that tonight was proposal night, but Veronica knew all the details and hadn't breathed a word. She was texting him now. *Hey Mark! What'd you decide to do?*

He tapped back. *It's going to happen at the place where we met, RJ's Courtyard.*

Good luck!

Thanks, Lil Bit. This was now his pet name for Veronica since she was such a tiny little thing. *I love your mom with all my heart.*

Good. One problem. She is WAY too happy now! It's frightening! I've never seen her this happy! It's unusual!

I intend to make sure she stays that way, so get used to it!

Mark glanced at his watch and grinned from ear to ear. Right about now, Fran's phone would be ringing at work. She would go out into the lobby to find a flower deliveryman, with a very specific bouquet—five roses with rhinestones in their centers. She would open the card, and it would say simply, "5!" Five months until their wedding day.

Mark kept an eye on his watch and counted it down. By now, he knew his girl. Five…four…three…two…one…

His phone rang. "Mark, these are amazing! These roses have rhinestones!"

"I know. They're special, just like you. But you shine brighter."

"Aww." He could hear the smile in her voice. "I guess I know what the card means."

"Five months until our wedding."

"It seems like forever. I can't wait to see you tonight."

"Oh, by the way, what would think about a change in venue? Instead of the Japanese restaurant, we go to RJ's Courtyard?"

"The place where we met?" she asked.

"Yeah. I think that might be nice for Valentine's."

"Sounds good to me. See you then. I love you."

"Love you more."

*　　*　　*

The butterflies in Fran's stomach were rising in swarms. Was this a Valentine's Day celebration, or was it something else? With Mark, you could never tell. She was afraid to hope.

He made sure they were seated at the same table where they'd met on Halloween. As they studied the menu, she noticed that the restaurant offered frog legs. She pointed it out to Mark. "I can't see those words without thinking about this poor little toad in high school."

"What happened?" Mark looked relaxed but a little on edge, as if he were dragging the evening out. Waiting for something, even. "Tell me about it."

"I was in tenth grade. I remember because we were dissecting frogs in biology class. So, I saw this little toad outside, and I thought, *I'll just practice on this toad. I'll give him a painless death and then practice on him.*"

He stared at her. "Painless death?"

"Yeah, I suspended him upside down inside a gas can, thinking the fumes would put him to sleep. Telling you this now, I can't believe I did it. I love animals. It seemed humane at the time."

"What happened?"

"The fumes put him to sleep, all right. I got him on a paper plate and did the incisions like we did in biology class. It was textbook."

"Only…"

"When I got to his heart, I was horrified to see that it was beating."

"So you were doing a surgery, not an autopsy. Big difference."

"I had no idea what to do at that point. I couldn't sew him up. He'd be in too much pain and probably wouldn't live anyway."

As he pictured the situation, Mark tried to control his sympathetic laughter at the horror Fran must have felt in that moment. "What did you do?"

"I slid the whole paper plate into a Ziploc bag and put it in my mother's freezer at the bottom, where she never looks. I figured the poor little fellow would freeze to death and wouldn't have to wake up in pain."

"Did your mother ever find him?"

"Not as far as I know."

The server brought their meals and they dug in. "I have my own frog story," Mark said.

"I bared my soul, now you have to bare yours."

He cut into his steak. "Well, there was a pond near our house in Athens, and there were tadpoles. I was about ten or eleven years old. I collected maybe twenty of them and took them home to raise."

"Tadpoles are cool. I remember seeing them in our neighborhood swimming pool before it opened up for the summer."

"Yeah, they're cool. I took care of them and fed them and watched them while they grew their little legs and started to be able to walk, then hop. I loved those little frogs."

She took a bite of chicken, then a drink of her Pepsi. "What happened?"

"The big day came, the day the frogs were big enough that I could let them go. That was the plan all along. There was this big stump in the front yard, and I did like a little ceremony. My whole family was there. It was frog release day." He stopped and grimaced.

"Why do I get the feeling this story isn't going to end well?"

He shook his head. "I said my little speech and put my precious little frogs down on that stump, then stood back and waited for them to hop away. But there was tar on that stump, and it was sizzling hot. My frogs fried and died right there before my eyes."

Fran could see the scene as he described it. "That's terrible!"

"So I'll never say a single bad word to you about your frog story," he said. "Mine is worse."

"You're the first person I've ever told that to, and I'm sure you'll be the last."

"Patrick will know before he goes to bed tonight." He toasted her. "It's too good to keep."

They had chatted and consumed their meal, and Mark glanced at his watch. Fran looked at hers, too. It was eight-twenty, the exact time they'd met in the parking lot on Halloween. He took a deep breath, smiled softly, and met her eyes.

"Okay, so I have two questions for you. You have to get the first question right before you get the second one. Are you ready?"

"I'm ready." She looked uncertain.

"What's the square root of 2704?"

She stared at him, flummoxed, then smacked him on the shoulder. "You know I don't do math. That's why I'm a writer."

"You'll figure it out," he said, unmoved.

"Am I allowed to use the calculator on my phone?"

"Sure, go ahead."

Of course, her phone's calculator did not have a square foot function. Neither did her iPhone. She was panicking, about to Google it or ask people at the table next to her, when Mark spoke up again, laughter in his eyes and voice.

"Need a hint?"

"Please, yes."

"If I live this many MORE years, I want to spend the rest of them with you, babe."

Knowing him as she now did, she suddenly connected the dots. The answer was his current age. "Fifty-two," she said.

"Now you get your second question." He went down on one knee and took her hand. "Fran, will you marry me?"

"Yes." The tears poured. "Yes, yes, yes." She cried as he slid the exquisite diamond on her finger. People at neighboring table were watching, mouths open. The waitress took photos. The manager came over and loved hearing the story about how they'd met.

Through it all, Fran glowed. She couldn't take her eyes off her ring. It caught the soft light and exploded with color. But it was no brighter than the love in Mark's eyes.

When they finally paid the bill and left, Mark said, "This is not over. We haven't even celebrated Valentine's Day yet."

"We haven't?"

"That was the engagement part of the evening. The rest is waiting at home."

"I'm not sure I can stand any more."

Standing in the parking lot, they texted everyone who needed to know what had just happened, then turned their phones to silent and headed to Mark's house.

*   *   *

They pulled into the driveway, got out of the car, and held hands as they slowly approached the front door, which was unusual in itself because Mark usually entered the house through the garage.

"Where's Patrick?" she asked.

"He'll be home soon."

He unlocked and opened the door and held it for her. She slowly walked in, eyes getting bigger as she took it all in. Candles were lit everywhere, and a trail of rose petals led through the foyer and into the kitchen, where she found a single long-stemmed rose with a Valentine's card and a candy box.

More rose petals led to the living room, where a wine holder held a small bottle of sparkling cider—Mark knew Fran hated the taste of alcohol—and a whole bouquet of roses.

She stood there, tears in her eyes, overwhelmed. He uncorked the cider and poured them each a glass. "To the future Mrs. Smith," he said. "May these stars always stay in your eyes."

They clinked glasses and sipped, and the tears now poured

down Fran's cheeks. "You know me, and you love me anyway," she whispered, still unable to believe it. She'd always hidden part of herself away, feeling that anyone who really knew her would run in the opposite direction. Mark saw her heart and knew her for who she really was, and yet here he was, looking at her with naked love in his eyes.

"No," he said. "You've got it backward. I love you *because* I know you."

He reached down to the coffee table and picked up a new music player. "I found this today. We can both listen to it at the same time. I made us a playlist."

He'd chosen the songs carefully, all selected because the lyrics could have been specifically written for the two of them. He'd chosen Lady Antebellum's "Just a Kiss," Christina Perri's "A Thousand Years," Brad Paisley's "Then," Lonestar's "Amazed," Jo Dee Messina's "Because You Love Me," and Shania Twain's "From This Moment." The last song, of course, was their first. Rascal Flatts' "Nothing Like This."

He slid two headsets into the player and gently fitted the earbuds into her ears, then his, He gathered her in his arms as the music came on, then slowly, carefully, danced her around the room. Eyes closed, lost in each other, neither of them noticed when Patrick came in quietly, took in the scene, and went up the stairs smiling.

Mark opened his eyes and cocked his head to the side when he heard the bedroom door close upstairs. "I guess Patrick's home," he said softly into her hair.

"Mmmm." She opened her eyes and tipped her head back. "He was very quiet."

"He knew what was going to happen today. All of them did."

"All of them?"

"Yep."

His gaze went to her lips, and his hands slid into her hair. She knew what was coming. She ached for it, like her next breath. The kiss went instantly deep and passionate, but it was somehow even better this time. Just as electric, just as consuming, but now there was more. They were together before, but now they were committed. The ring on her finger said so. The wonderful man in her arms was going to be her husband.

It was a good thing that Patrick was upstairs, because she had no idea how they were going to wait for five months.

76

The time flew. Five months is not long to plan a wedding and a honeymoon, completely renovate a house, and combine two large households—plus hold down full-time jobs and parent five children.

Mark and Fran still had date nights faithfully every Wednesday. Other days, they prowled Lowe's and Home Depot picking out fixtures, floors, countertops, tile, and paint for their new home. Mark contacted contractors and work began. Most days after work, Fran went straight to Maryville to check out the progress. When Veronica didn't have homework or cheerleading, she came along.

Date nights were always unpredictable. When March came, the redbuds bloomed, and Mark announced it was time to fish. "Crappie are spawning now," he explained. "We need to catch them on the beds."

The first time he took her out, she'd never seen or heard of a trolling motor. Her family had owned a speed boat. Mark backed the boat into the water, and she sat in it while he parked the truck. It started to ease away from the dock, and she grabbed frantically before it could get too far away.

"Whew," she said when he joined her. "I was about to have to find an oar."

"Why?"

"Because the boat almost drifted away. You would have had to swim for it."

He stared at her, then started laughing out loud. "I really love you," he said. "You make everything fun."

"What's so funny?"

"I'll show you."

He revved the boat, and they flew across the water to one of his favorite fishing spots. He cut the motor, then climbed up on the front of the boat, sat in the chair, and eased something down into the water. Silently, smoothly, he used a foot pedal to expertly maneuver the boat close to a tree in the water.

She stared. "What's that thing?"

"It's a trolling motor. It helps us get close to fish, real quiet-like."

She'd fished as a child, and quickly remembered how she loved it. They caught a cooler full of keeper crappie that day, although Mark pronounced it "croppie," which Fran found hilarious because that's not the way it is spelled and not the way it is pronounced in South Carolina. Over the next few months, they haunted the lake. By necessity, Fran learned to drive the boat and back the trailer, and could soon put it on a dime in the dark at night.

Another fishing day, Fran unexpectedly hooked a big small-mouth bass with a bad attitude. Mark managed the trolling motor, got all the other gear out of the way, and watched, amused. Fran squealed and fought the fish as it tried to run under the boat several times. She tried repeatedly to hand the rod off to him, but he just shook his head and laughed. Finally, breathless and triumphant, she got the fish in the boat.

Another date night, Mark brought the boat and picked Fran up at work, and they went to Watts Bar Lake. They weren't planning to fish, just speed around the lake and picnic. They spotted a bench at the edge of the water, where they ate their dinner and watched the sunset.

Another time, Fran had to go pick up her wedding dress from the alternations lady. Mark said he'd go with her, and they'd figure out what to do from there. They ended up on U.S. Highway 129, also known to motorcyclists and sports car enthusiasts as the Tail of the Dragon. It's bordered by the Great Smoky Mountains and the Cherokee National Forest, with no intersecting roads or driveways. The Tail of the Dragon has more than three hundred turns in eleven miles. They ate fantastic burgers at Deals Gap Motorcycle Resort, then headed back, chasing sunsets all along the way.

Another bright spring day, Mark got Fran out on the golf course. She gave him a doubtful look, remembering how poorly it had gone the last time she'd held a real golf club. "You don't know what you're asking," she said darkly.

"Come on," he said. "It's a beautiful day. It'll be fun."

"Okay, you asked for it." He'd find out soon enough, she thought. It was a good thing she already had a ring on her finger.

He pulled out Lisa's old golf clubs—which she'd never used—and got Fran suited up.

He lit up the course. She loved watching him, and she didn't embarrass herself too badly—except for a whiff here and there. She did have fun, though, and this was something else they could enjoy doing together.

Date night by spectacular date night, their close relationship grew.

* * *

A gall bladder attack sidelined Mark at the end of March. He spent one night in the hospital, Fran at his side, to have it removed.

"I hate surgery," he muttered. "I've had enough surgery. My back, my hernia, and now this."

He bounced back quickly, and the next day he was up on a ladder ripping down the old wallpaper in the kitchen so renovations could proceed on schedule. He pushed himself hard, day after day, to renovate the Maryville house and get the Oak Ridge house ready to go back on the market. His back was hurting him badly, but he said he was just overdoing a little and would rest later.

Matt and Patty Monroe remained a big part of their grandsons' lives, but they found themselves unable to participate in Mark's happiness. Their grief was still too raw. Mark missed them greatly—Matt had been one of his best friends, and Patty was like a second mother—but he understood.

Contractors came and went. Mark worked as hard as they did. He and Fran designed their new two-person, four-headed custom shower with a bench, meticulously arranging the tiles by hand for the contractor to put into place. A custom window was being made. They chose every piece of the new basement, which would include a living area, a recreation area, a kitchenette, a bedroom, and a bathroom. The kitchen would be brand-new, with the old blue Formica giving way to new granite countertops. Veronica picked the paint for her room—lime green with a chalkboard wall. Patrick didn't care about his, so they picked it for him. Furiously, they worked. At night Fran rubbed Mark's back to ease the aches.

"It doesn't all have to be done before the wedding," she told him. "We can finish when we get back from our honeymoon."

"I want it to be finished when you walk in this door as my wife," he said stubbornly. "By the time you're Mrs. Smith, this will be your house."

*　*　*

Near the end of March was a family day. Julia, Cecil, Chris and her boyfriend, Duane Brayton, came to down to take some furniture back with them and have Chris pick out her bridesmaid dress. Mellie and Olivia were also coming in from Virginia, and Lisa and her two daughters were going to join the group at David's Bridal.

Chris's husband, Jesse, had died unexpectedly in 2001, and she and Duane had been a couple for a while now. They loved each other, but she had no interest in getting married, at least not yet. Fran was ecstatic to have so much of her family here this weekend. It was nice to be able to show them the house where she would be living after July and all the renovations taking place.

"I understand why you chose this house over your other one," Chris told her after taking the tour.

The bridesmaids all picked different dresses in the same color purple. Veronica, Fran's maid of honor, already had her dress. Chris, Lisa, and Mellie would be bridesmaids, and Olivia would be flower girl. Scott would be Mark's best man, with Rick, Patrick, and Doug serving as groomsmen. Brody would do the music, and Fran's friend Peg Jarrett would sing. Andy would escort his grandmother, who was now eighty-five. Cecil would give Fran away.

They ordered, addressed, and mailed over a hundred invitations. The colors were orange, purple, and white—which coincidentally are Clemson's colors, but that wasn't why Fran chose them. She was marrying a man who—miraculously—loved her for who and what she was. These colors were a symbol of that.

The honeymoon was taking shape as well. Using their wedding date of July 14 and the Tour de France conclusion on July 22 as anchor points, they'd come up with a schedule that had them staying in Atlanta their wedding night, then flying into Geneva, Switzerland, the next day. They'd spend the next week driving around Switzerland—Mark made reservations for them to ride the train to the top of the Jungfrau in Interlochen—and then take a train to Paris on July 20. They'd end their trip by driving south to Nice, then taking the train back to Geneva.

It was a trip beyond Fran's wildest dreams, something that would check off several items on both of their bucket lists.

*   *   *

The time continued to fly. Veronica had several cheerleading competitions, and Mark learned how to be a cheer dad. He was there for the one in Knoxville when her team won the title. Veronica was a flyer, so she was at or near the top of every stunt. While Mark shot video, nervous for his new daughter, Fran alternately explained everything to him and squealed at each successful trick.

When it was over, he looked at Fran, drained. "I had no idea how dangerous cheerleading is."

"It is very dangerous. Girls get hurt if they don't know what they're doing."

"Well, I always wanted a daughter. Now God's given me a fifteen-year-old."

"Fun, isn't it?" she grinned at him. "Let's go congratulate her."

The next competition was in Nashville. They made a weekend of it, going to the zoo in between competitive rounds. At the mall, Mark surprised everyone and made Veronica giggle when he sent a paper airplane from the balcony and then ducked out of sight when it tapped a walker on the ear down below.

The season finished in Destin, Florida. By that time, school was nearly out. Veronica planned to spend most of the summer in Aiken, coming back for the wedding in July. She still had a decision to make about where she wanted to live beginning next year, and school would begin early in Maryville. She would decide before the wedding, she said.

Fran, Mark, and Veronica traveled to Columbia, South Carolina, to watch Andy lead his tennis team in the state championship match, which the team lost in a heartbreaker. Soon after, he graduated from Aiken High School magna cum laude and committed to play his college tennis at Limestone College in Gaffney, South Carolina.

77

As Fran and Mark rode back to Maryville from church one Sunday with their two youngest children, she was pensive. They'd been going to Sevier Heights Baptist Church every week. Every week, Hollie Miller's invitation at the end of the service was three-fold. People were invited to get saved, get baptized, or join the church.

She was already saved. At some point, she knew, she would officially join Sevier Heights, transferring her membership from South Aiken Presbyterian Church. They were scheduled for premarital counseling in June.

But what about being baptized?

Having been a Presbyterian all her life, it had simply never occurred to her. She'd been sprinkled as an infant in the Methodist church, then grown up Presbyterian. Presbyterian babies have water sprinkled on their heads as a sign of the covenant. Hebrew infants were circumcised to show they were a part of the covenant family, and Presbyterians viewed infant baptism in the same light. All three of Fran's children had received infant baptism.

Later in life, people come to salvation in their own way, as Fran had when she was eight years old, and Mark had when he was ten.

The last few months, though, hearing Brother Hollie preach about it and reading the Word for herself, she felt God calling to her. She was a different person spiritually now than she'd been when she met Mark, and she wanted to show the change outwardly. Her only hesitation was doing it in the baptistry at church. It seemed so impersonal and sterile. She wanted it to be more heartfelt.

She glanced at the man beside her, and it hit her.

"Babe, you're an ordained minister, right?"

"Yes, why?"

"Is there any reason you couldn't baptize me?"

They pulled up at a traffic light, and he gave her his full attention. "No, absolutely no reason. I've baptized lots of people. What brought this on?"

"I've been thinking about it a lot. I think I need to get baptized, but I don't want to do it at church."

"It's a public profession of faith," he said thoughtfully. "Where would we do it?"

"What about your sister's lake house? We could invite all our family and friends. I'd like to be baptized in the lake."

He took her hand and kissed it. "I love you so much," he said. "I'd be honored. We'll check with Lisa, but I'm sure she'd love it."

A couple of phone calls later, and the baptism was set for the Saturday of Memorial Day weekend, just days before Veronica would go to South Carolina and Patrick would be leaving to spend six weeks as a counselor at Boy Scout camp. Everyone in Mark's family except his mother was there—including George, Mellie's husband. It would be the first time Fran had met George.

After a wonderful, relaxing day of swimming, boating, and tubing, the extended family and a few friends grilled hamburgers and hot dogs. When sundown neared, Mellie read some Scripture that Mark had chosen, and Mark read some remarks that he had prepared about baptism—and this particular baptism. Lisa and Mellie stood on the dock, crying, as sundown approached.

As the sun's last rays cast rainbow beams across the cove, Fran descended from the back of the boat and slid into the water. She and Mark both wore white. She waded to him in waist-deep water, her eyes never leaving his.

Eyes shining, he raised one hand for her to take it. She held her nose with one hand and gripped his hand with the other.

"I baptize you, Fran, in the name of the Father, the Son, and the Holy Spirit."

He swiftly and gently dunked her in the chilly water of Watts Bar Lake and brought her back to the surface. She waded back to the bank, where Veronica waited with a towel.

Mark stayed where he was. "Would anyone else like to be baptized today?"

"I would," Patrick said and eased into the water. "I feel like I was really saved after I was baptized the first time, and I'd like to do it again."

So Mark baptized his son, and then George baptized Olivia.

Everyone got into dry clothes and sat around the living room, recapping the wonderful day. Before Mark and his family left, Lisa pulled out a large wrapped package. "This is an early wedding present from the kids and me," she said. "Welcome to the family, Fran."

*   *   *

Mark's back worsened, but he continued to push hard. He said there would be plenty of time after the honeymoon to slow down and rest.

He continued to create unforgettable date nights, and in early June he outdid himself. Every year, people flock from all over the world to a tiny spot in the Great Smoky Mountains—Elkmont. Throughout its history, Elkmont had been an Appalachian community, a logging town, and a resort area. Now, the once quaint cottages and big hotel that once served wealthy tourists were in ruins, and their future was uncertain. Mark and Fran had wandered in once before, just exploring.

Every year in late May and early June, Elkmont is home to a natural light show. Many fireflies—at least nineteen species—live in the Great Smoky Mountains National Park, but only one can synchronize their flashing light patterns, and they only do it for a few days a year as part of their mating ritual. There are only two places on earth that this happens—the other is in Southeast Asia—and only one place in America.

People enter a lottery to be allowed to park at the Elkmont campground and see the fireflies. Less than two thousand free passes are issued each year. Mark knew his fiancée loved fireflies, and he wanted her to see the show.

They arrived at the Elkmont campground well before the sun went down and were turned away. "Maybe you should plan better next year," the guard told them condescendingly.

"We'll do that," Mark said pleasantly, then drove on down the road and found a place to pull off near the Laurel Falls trailhead. He cut the engine and grinned at her. "Ready for a walk?" he asked.

"What are we doing?" Fran asked.

"Grab your fanny pack. You'll see."

He led the way through the woods and down a trail that really wasn't a trail. Before long, they emerged on the edge of Elkmont Campground.

"You're a genius," she said.

"Now, we just blend in and wait for the show."

They prowled around Elkmont and picked a spot near the Little River, behind what used to be a grand hotel. When full dark came, the fireflies came out. Their lights weren't perfectly synchronized at first, but just like a fireworks show, they built in urgency and speed and reached a crescendo, just like a symphony. The show lasted for nearly an hour. Fran watched, dazzled.

When the show was over, they made their way hand in hand back through the pitch-dark forest, along the trail that really wasn't one, and found Mark's truck. They unloaded their fanny packs into the back seat and collapsed into their seats.

"Well," Mark said, "I guess we should plan better next year, like the man said."

"That was the most amazing thing I've ever seen," she said, wonder still in her voice. "I wouldn't change one single thing. Thank you for making this happen."

"I just want to make you happy. That's all."

78

The last major milestone before Mark moved on to his new life was June 14—the anniversary of Lisa's death.

All her pictures were already taken down and packed away to give to the boys one day. He'd already told Fran everything that needed to be said. She knew what he'd been through, and she knew what this anniversary would mean. This was the day he would let it all go. He gave himself permission to go back and remember one more time. It was probably selfish of him, but he didn't want to face it alone. For the first and only time, he watched the thirty-minute tribute video that he had made for Lisa's funeral. Fran watched with him, holding him tight and crying with him.

The pictures on the screen showed the transformation Lisa had made from young bride, to radiant mother, to cancer patient. She went from healthy and beautiful to pale and emaciated. And still, for her family, she'd fought what she knew would almost certainly be a losing fight. She'd inspired countless numbers of people with her courage.

Silently, Mark thanked God for using the horrible situation for His glory, and then hand-delivering such a wonderful woman to go with him into old age. What had he ever done to deserve such grace? Nothing.

The video finished and flickered off. Mark shifted his gaze down to his fiancée, who was staring up at him with tear-drenched eyes. He framed her face and softly kissed her lips. "Thank you," he said, "for understanding that I had to do that."

She hugged him tighter. "Of course," she said.

"Let's put our new closet together, what do you say?"

*   *   *

The last days before the wedding flew. Andy spent two weeks at Wimbledon with Jamie Spruill, his best friend and doubles partner—Fran's high school graduation present to him. Mark and Fran completed their pre-marital counseling, had engagement pictures taken, and locked in final plans for the wedding and honeymoon. The house was finished, and moving day was scheduled for Monday, July 8. The Oak Ridge house would be completely furnished with items they intended to sell, so it would still be habitable.

Finally, July 13 was here. Friday the 13th, but they weren't superstitious people and didn't care. They were fully aware that their union was God's will, and there was something God would want them to do as a couple for Him, although they didn't know yet what it was. The devil would do whatever he could to derail that. But here, now, their trust was in God Almighty.

It was a beautiful night for the rehearsal dinner. Bill Cabage, Mark's assistant Scoutmaster, brought his bluegrass band to play. The whole family from both sides had come in from Virginia, Tennessee, and South Carolina, and friends had driven from as far as South Carolina and Texas to be there for this special day. The only person who was not there was Mark's mother. She had strong feelings about their wedding and could not be a part of it, she said. Sharon had shingles a few days ago, so that's what Mark and Fran told everyone. It wasn't a lie.

That night, back at Maryville house, Andy went looking for Mark, to have a man-to-man conversation. "I see how happy you make her," he said. "I see how happy you make each other. You have my blessing, man." And he hugged Mark tight. Fran watched, smiling. The blessing of her children meant everything.

79

The day of the wedding dawned clear and hot. Fran opened her eyes and went to find her family. Julia, Chris, and Veronica were going to go with her to get their hair styled that morning. Then they would head straight over to Heritage Park and supervise final preparations. Fran had asked Cynthia Spitler to be a runner, to pin boutonnieres on people, and do whatever other things needed to be done so that Mark wouldn't see his bride before the wedding. With one exception. Mark and Fran had to be different. The wedding was at three o'clock. They were going to clear everyone out of the bridal chamber at two o'clock so that they could see each other in all their finery. They wanted the chance to look into each other's eyes one more time before they became husband and wife.

Fran was ready in her wedding dress, sitting at the vanity and finishing her makeup, when Mark came in. She watched him in the mirror as he approached. Even in the low light, she could see the amazement on his face.

He took her hands and helped her stand, then turned her around so he could see her from all sides. Her strapless white lace dress fitted her perfectly, hugging her figure and then flaring out and flowing just below her knees. She had no veil, just baby's breath tucked into her blonde curls.

"Baby," he said. "Wow."

She looked him over from head to toe. He wore a dark, sleek suit with a white shirt and a white tie. His short hair and mustache were perfectly trimmed, and his shoes were like mirrors. But the best part was his eyes. There was a light there, in the deep blue depths, that spoke every word Mark was feeling about his love for his bride.

"I will not cry," Fran sniffled. "I have something for you." She turned and found Mark's boutonniere of an orange rose and a small purple flower. She'd wanted to do this one herself. She carefully pinned it onto Mark's lapel, her hands coming to rest on his shoulders. "Now," she said. "You're perfect."

"I'm yours."

"Thank God."

They hugged and kissed lightly. He stroked her cheek, still in awe. "I'll see you out there," he said.

They parted, and Fran's wedding director, Rhonda, reentered. "It's almost time," she said. "There's a lot of people out there."

Fran wasn't surprised. A few people had made the drive from South Carolina and Oak Ridge for her, but the vast majority were there for Mark, because he'd made such a profound impact on their lives and they loved him.

Rhonda led them down the path toward the large covered porch on top of the mountain where the wedding would take place. Fran could hear her friend singing "From This Moment." Then Brody began to play the processional music, and the bridesmaids made their way slowly down the aisle. Mellie, Lisa, Chris, Veronica, and Olivia. Mark, Scott, and the groomsmen were already standing at the front with Brother Hollie. The music shifted to the Bridal March, and Fran knew it was her turn. She looked up at Cecil with soft, tear-filled eyes, and he hugged her. "I love you, Fran. I'm so happy to be able to be here for you like this today."

"I love you, Cecil." She smiled. "I will not cry!"

Brother Hollie spoke about the marriage sacrament, then led them in the old, timeless vows. Then, also, they'd written their own. Fran went first, reading so she wouldn't forget.

"Mark, our journey to this point has been magical and incredible. If I hadn't lived it, I would have said it was unbelievable. A year ago, we didn't even know each other. Now, you're as essential to me as breath and air. Every day, I thank God for leading me here and getting us together.

"You have taught me what real love is. You've shown me how it

346

feels to love and be loved, completely and unconditionally. In you, I've found my other half, the one person who completes me. We make each other better. I'm so happy to share life with you and grow old with you. And on this special day, I make these vows to you in before God and our family and friends.

"I pledge to you my whole heart, body, and mind, everything I have, and everything I am.

"You have my complete loyalty, now and always. I will always be on your side, no matter who is on the other side.

"I will be your partner in life, meeting the ups and downs head on together, hand in hand.

"Your children are my children. I will do my best to be what they need me to be to them.

"I will always be trustworthy. I will do my best to never let you down.

"I will always love you completely and totally.

"I will treat you as what you are—the lifelong mate chosen for me by God Himself. I commit to grow with you and learn from you spiritually, as we discover God's purpose for our union."

Mark listened to her, staring into her eyes, the joy in his own eyes radiant. Then it was his turn.

"Fran, my dearest one. I commit to love you all the remaining days of our lives.

"If sickness, poverty, or sadness come, we will face them together, no matter what.

"I commit to stand beside you to comfort and encourage you, care for your physical, emotional, and spiritual needs. I will dry your tears and shout with you for joy. I will make you laugh, and I hope not to make you cry.

"I plan never to relinquish the role that I have taken from your family as your number one fan. Your family is my family now. Your teenagers are my teenagers. Until they are on their own, may the good Lord help us both!

"I will take responsibility for my spiritual role in our home. I will guard, cherish, and protect you, wherever God chooses to place us."

"I will be true to you, and you only, for the rest of our days.

"I promise these things to you, Fran, before these witnesses, and—most of all—before the true and living God, our Savior and Lord, Jesus Christ.

"This is my pledge to you this day, July 14, 2012, now and forever."

With that, they placed the rings on each other's fingers, and Brother Hollie declared them husband and wife.

They exited to the music of the "Darth Vader Theme" from *Star Wars*. People looked around, eyes wide. Was that a mistake? No, it was not. Fran and Mark watched everyone's reactions and grinned. It was just one more way they were different from any other couple, ever. God was going to do something amazing through this union. They just didn't yet know what.

80

Their honeymoon was more perfect than anything Fran Smith could have imagined. She stared the gold band on Mark's hand and thought to herself, "That man is actually mine." She hugged herself, barely able to stand the giddy feeling she had inside whenever she thought about that.

Being his in every way, being able to do whatever they wanted, whenever they wanted, had been even beyond her expectations—and she'd expected a lot. She'd expected fireworks and chemistry—but there was something more when Mark touched her. There was a softness, an intimacy, a deep love from his heart, all of which transmitted to her through his fingers and lips. She was a happy bride.

They floated through Switzerland for a week. They rode the train to the top of the Jungfrau and played in the ice caves. They drove the Swiss countryside, gasping at one dazzling mountain vista after another, unable to imagine that the next one could be even more beautiful—and then it was.

They did the touristy things in Paris, amazed at Notre Dame, the Louvre and the Arc de Triomphe before flopping in the park in the shadows of the Eiffel Tower and eating lunch. They strolled along the Seine, eating fresh crepes and watching people play games on the river bank. And then they checked off a big item on Mark's bucket list when he watched Bradley Wiggins race across the Tour de France finish line on July 22, the day Fran turned fifty-one years old.

Two days later, Fran checked an item on her bucket list when they drove to Nice and parasailed over the Mediterranean. She'd never seen a view as beautiful as the one from their hotel balcony.

They could sit there and see all the way down the Nice shoreline, across the incredible blue-green of the Mediterranean. They break-fasted on the balcony and fought the pigeons.

During their trip, taking a break from the beach, Fran sat in her swimsuit and checked her email. She found a message from Veronica. *I hope you're having a great honeymoon! I've decided to live in Maryville with you and Mark. See you soon. I love you both.*

Fran gasped in joy and relief. "Babe!" she said. "Come here quick."

He came, towel flung around his neck, and read the email over her shoulder. "Oh, that's so good!" he said. "I'm so glad. I really, truly do have a daughter."

She reached back and hugged him upside down, gasping a little as his hands came to her midsection. It never got old. "This calls for a celebration," she said.

"What did you have in mind?"

"Oh, I think we can think of something."

*   *   *

Life continued, just as golden and full of promise. On the first weekend in August, to celebrate Mark's fifty-third birthday, they made it a family weekend.

Saturday was a bike ride through Cades Cove. Fran and Veronica were a little scared—both of them could ride bikes, but neither was very good at it. Veronica wasn't a klutz like Fran, but she was very inexperienced.

It was supposed to be a big scout group, but it was raining and cold, and everyone else bailed out. Only the four of them hit the road for the eleven-mile scenic loop around the historic spot. It was a nice family outing until they were about four miles in. Fran and Veronica were at the back of the pack, chattering away. They had to walk up the hills, anyway, so why hurry? Fran got a little distracted and did not see the sign warning bikers to walk their bikes because of a steep grade and sharp turns ahead.

She knew she was in trouble when her front tire slipped off the edge of the pavement. The bike bounced along the ground for what seemed like forever, and then she went over the handlebars head first and skidded along on her bare hands and knees in the rough gravel at the side of the road.

Veronica stopped. A park volunteer stopped. Veronica screamed for Mark to stop, but he and Patrick were having a short race, and he was out of earshot. She got on her bike to chase him down. He was on his way back anyway, having finished his race with Patrick. Finding no one behind him, he was headed back to see what was going on. When Veronica told him Fran wrecked, it scared him to death, and he flew the rest of the way to get to her.

Meanwhile, Fran was sitting in the ditch, resisting treatment for her shredded knee and arm because she didn't want to move until Mark said it was safe. Other than being shaken up and scared, she was okay and able to get back on the bike and continue.

They finished the scenic loop and ate some of the lunch they'd packed, then Fran and the kids piled in the truck and Mark got back on his bike. He wanted to ride part of the way back. They gave him a short head start, then set out after him.

At first, Fran thought she'd leap-frogged him because it took so long to catch him. But then she caught sight of him, far ahead, flying down the mountain road. She caught up to him at the juncture of a couple of mountain streams. Mark, hot and sweaty, stripped down to his base cycle outfit and, shouting, did a watermelon into the water.

They all watched him, open-mouthed, and then Veronica took off her shoes and followed him. Fran watched her daughter, unable to believe what she'd just seen. Veronica was a fun-loving girl, but this? This was completely out of character for her. When Veronica emerged from the water, she immediately called back to her mother, gasping. "Don't do it, Mom! It's freezing!"

Fran didn't see that she had much choice. She took off her shoes, put the truck key into her shoe, and leaped into that freezing mountain stream. It was so cold it took her breath away. She'd waded in streams before, when she was much younger, but had never swum in one before. She literally couldn't breathe at first. Then, as she got used to it, it became invigorating.

Patrick at first stood forlornly on the rocks in his Scout uniform, then seemed to realize that if there were chicks in the water, he had to jump in too or lose man points.

They spent the next little while skipping stones, basking in the sun, and looking at some of the magic of the river. Mark showed them how some rocks have colors when you scrape at them, and he and Veronica painted their faces. They looked at some of the wildlife, like small freshwater clams, leeches, and tiny organisms that live on the rocks. Then they rode the rapids with their bodies to get back to the truck.

The second day of the birthday weekend began at Pancake Palace in Gatlinburg. They rode roller coasters at Dollywood and water rides at Splash Country, then fit in a game of miniature golf at the end of the day. Mark and Veronica teamed up against Patrick and Fran.

Fran expected to lose, but not like this. She and Patrick completely missed the concept of team golf. Whenever one of them crashed and burned, the other followed suit. Meanwhile, Mark made some uncharacteristic bad shots, and Veronica came through and bailed them out. Mark scored a three on the last hole. If Veronica could score a one or a two, she would win for her team. She made a conservative first shot, then calmly and carefully sank a clutch putt for her team.

Fran watched her daughter with pride. As far as she knew, this was the first time in Veronica's life when she had played putt putt with someone who looked at her as a valued contributor rather than a liability.

"What a competitor! How smart!" Mark raved. "You brought it home for us. Way to go, Lil Bit!"

Veronica beamed, and Fran was so proud of her. She was tackling her new life with courage. Maryville High was the third school she'd attended in the past three years. She'd enrolled in Maryville Singers and had become hooked on theatre, which Fran understood because she'd done drama in college and in Aiken and had loved it.

Watching her now, Fran had hope and confidence that her daughter would be just fine.

*   *   *

Just weeks later, Mark and Fran made their first major purchase as a couple. He came to Oak Ridge to help with the house, and they met after work and had supper. On a whim, they stopped in at Oak Ridge Nissan. They were on the lookout for a fun car, something that they could take on their little adventures.

A beautiful, barely used, plum-colored Infiniti hardtop convertible had just come in. It hadn't even been cleaned up yet, but the salesman drove it out for them to look at.

Mark had always wanted a convertible, and this one was dazzling. It looked sleek, like a crouching panther. The purr of its engine promised power.

They test drove it back to Maryville for the night to show it to the kids, but Veronica was the only one at home. They whisked her away and zipped to the top of Look Rock. Sun on their faces and wind in their hair, they all laughed in delight.

The next day, they traded in Mark's Mazda SUV, along with a little cash. They named the car Kylie.

81

Fran's resume now included hiking, biking, fishing, and golfing, but Mark had one more thing in mind. He wanted to take her on a real hike—an overnight, backpacking trip, where they would sleep in a tent and cook out on a campfire. He wanted her to have the experience and know she could do it.

The middle of October came, and he had an idea—White Rocks. Exactly one year ago, he and Susan Bryant Roberts had sat on that very rock, and he had briefly contemplated sliding off it into the emptiness below. Susan had talked him into being patient and seeing what the Lord had in store, and doing what he could to serve the kingdom while he waited.

Two weeks later, he'd met Fran. Mark shook his head, smiling. God indeed did have a sense of humor to go along with His limitless love and compassion for His children.

He broke the idea to his wife when she got home from work that day.

"I've got an idea for this weekend," he told her.

"Do tell," she said as she put her briefcase down and looped her arms around her husband's neck. "I always like your ideas."

"White Rocks."

"Where's that?"

"It's a beautiful national park in Cumberland Gap, up where Tennessee and Virginia and Kentucky meet. It's an historical area where there are some cool things to see and do. I've taken my Scouts there before."

"Sounds good." She eyed him and waited for the other shoe to drop.

"It's a good hike, over three miles to White Rocks and another half-mile to the campsite."

"Campsite?"

"We'll backpack in and spend the night."

"Babe, I'm not too sure about that. It's not that I don't want to. I've loved the hikes we've done. I'm just not sure if I can backpack. I'm not very strong."

"You can do it. I promise you."

She trusted him and agreed to the adventure, so they spent the rest of the day packing for the trip and testing the tent. Mark found a backpack that one of his boys had used and managed to pack it, so it weighed only twenty-six pounds. They packed sleeping bags, a two-man tent, food, clothes, and various other camping essentials that Fran had never even heard of. They had to carry water. Lots of water. But Mark said it would be essential because no water would be available until they got to the top of the mountain.

They set out on Saturday morning for the two-hour drive to the Cumberland Gap area. After looking around the quaint historical area, they hit the trail about three o'clock.

Mark settled the pack on Fran's back, and her knees buckled a little. "Oh, my goodness," she said.

"You can do it," he assured her.

They took it slow and easy, and rested often. Once, Mark went ahead of Fran and dropped his pack, then came back and carried hers up a rough slope for her. Two other times, he got behind her and pushed and shoved her up steep slopes.

"Nobody likes this part," he told her as they sat, panting, and drank water. "But it's what you have to do to get to the part that's fun and beautiful."

They dropped their packs at the campsite at the top of the trail and split off to go the Rocks. Standing there, looking out over the breathtaking vista, Fran understood. White Rocks is actually a series of large, flat rocks at the top of the ridge. The day was clear, and they could see four states. The long day and hard climb were so worth it.

They sat, resting, soaking in the grandeur, and Mark told her the history of this spot.

"One year ago," he said, "I sat on this very rock—right here in this spot—in despair. I was afraid I was destined to be alone. A dear friend gave me some good advice that day, then two weeks later God brought me you."

"He's got a reason, you know," Fran said. "There has to be some reason aside from the fact that we're meant to be together. There's something He wants us to do."

"I know. I pray every day for Him to reveal that to us."

Fran looked out at the vista and was silent. "I think it has to do with you," she said.

"Me?"

"Everything you've done, the people you've touched. When you tell me the stories about Alaska, I can feel it. It's a story that needs to be told."

"I'm not sure about that. Who'd want to read about me?"

"I think you'd be surprised. Look at the things God has done through you."

"Hmmm." He thought about it. "Maybe. If anyone could write it, it would be you."

"I've always known that one day, God would want me to use my gift for Him. Maybe this is what He had in mind all along."

By the time they got their backpacks and made their way down to the campsite, two other small groups were already there and had claimed the best camping spots. Mark and Fran found one with a good cooking area and a nearly level sleeping area. They put the tent together, blew up the sleeping mats, zipped the sleeping bags together, and put everything away. Then they gathered firewood, and Mark started their campfire.

They heated some of their water on a little camp stove to cook ramen noodles and a pasta pouch, and shared a good supper. Then they took a night hike back up to White Rocks and sat looking at the stars for a long time. When they got back to the campground, the other two groups were already in bed. They stirred up the fire and sat beside it for a long time, talking, giving each other shoulder rubs, and soaking in the warmth. Then they crawled, shivering, into their combined sleeping bag and snuggled up tight, keeping warm by sharing their body heat.

The next morning they heated the last of their water and made coffee and hot chocolate, and ate granola bars. They took down the tent and turned the sleeping bags inside out, and set them all out to air. Then they set out for Sand Cave. Having no backpack, Fran discovered, made an enormous difference. Sand Cave is a cavernous opening carved out under a limestone shelf with sand worthy of any beach thick on the ground. There's a waterfall right in front of it. They stayed there for a while and just drank in the silence and each other.

"Time to restock our water," Mark said.

"What? How?"

"I'll show you."

He pulled out some empty bottles from his backpack and got water from the stream, then pumped it through a portable purifier. Fran watched, fascinated, while he did the whole bottle.

"Here, you do one," he said and handed her one.

She quickly discovered that it took some muscle, but she did exactly what he'd done and produced a second bottle of clean water.

"That's so cool," she said.

"It beats carrying that much water in our backpacks."

They headed back toward the campsite and made a final trip to White Rocks, where they sat on the rocks, made tuna salad, and had their lunch.

Fran was wandering around the rocks when she noticed some shallow pools of water. Looking closer, she saw some tadpoles swimming around in the pools and called Mark over.

"Want to atone for the past?" she asked him with a smile. "These guys won't be alive when this pool evaporates, anyway."

"The way the sun is coming down, that will be today."

"Let's take them home and raise them and set them free like you tried to do before."

They collected some of the tadpoles from the pool and added some of the moss that the little creatures seemed to be feeding on. The tadpoles rode safely down the mountain, carefully sealed in a water bottle, with holes punched in the top.

As they drove home, Mark asked Fran what she'd thought of the trip. "It was fun," she said. "I loved White Rocks and Sand Cave, and I even enjoyed sleeping in the tent and cooking by the fire."

"But?"

"I wish there was a way to do all of that without having to carry a heavy backpack up a mountain. That part was not fun. It's the hardest thing I've ever done in my life. I wouldn't have made it up there without your help."

"Nobody thinks that part is easy," he said, "but now you know you can do it. Sometimes, it's the only way to get where you want to go. But there is an alternative, a way to get the camping and hiking experience without backpacking. We'll try that next."

They rode in silence for a while, holding hands. She was driving because the day had been rough on his back. Then Mark said, "You're a river rock girl."

"Is that good?"

"It's a rare treasure," he told her, then related a story from his years in the lumber business.

Real old-timers, he explained, seldom praise their spouses in public. One day, Mark and Vernon Harris, the moonshiner-turned-gospel-singer, were sitting companionably in rockers on Vernon's front porch. Vernon's wife brought them some tea. Mark said something complimentary about the woman.

"Yep, she's a river rock girl," Vernon said.

Mark had no idea what that meant, so he just kept his mouth shut and raised his eyebrows.

Vernon reached down and picked up a large, perfectly smooth rock that was holding the screen open. He handed it to Mark. "This," he said, "is a river rock. The rocks in a river get tossed around by years of storms and strong currents. Bumps, scrapes, and turmoil work on them for years until all the rough edges are worn down. In time, choice rocks find their comfortable place in the river. Then the storms and currents don't dislodge them but only make them smoother with the passage of time. They're a true mountain treasure."

"What an amazing analogy!" Fran said.

Mark reached into the backpack at his feet and pulled out a large rock, perfectly smooth, perfectly proportioned. He placed it in her hands. "I found this at Sand Cave this morning. This is you, babe. You're my river rock girl. You're my treasure."

82

A month later, they loaded up the truck and the little Ford Focus and headed for the Elkmont campground. Mark and Patrick were in the truck, and Rick would be joining them later. Veronica, Fran, and Veronica's friend, Monroe, were in the Focus. Veronica now had her learner's permit, and the Focus was her car while Fran drove the truck to work every day. Both vehicles were loaded down with camping gear. This, evidently, was what Mark had been talking about that day on White Rocks when he said there was an alternative to backpacking.

They set up three tents at the campground. During the setup process, Veronica noticed a bunch of granddaddy longlegs on the camping pad where Mark and Fran would have their tent. Although she was nearly as afraid of them as her mother, she picked them off and threw them far away before they could terrify her mom.

Fran didn't see this, or she would have been in the car headed back home. But Mark saw it.

"Thank you, Lil Bit," he whispered to her. "That would not have been good."

"Have you actually ever seen her when she comes into contact with one?"

"Not close up, no."

"You don't want to. I've known her go into a public restroom and refuse to touch the door to come back out because there was one of those things on it. She wouldn't get near enough to the door to open it. She just waited, paralyzed-like, until someone else came in, then ran out shuddering. We couldn't figure out what was taking her so long."

"You're kidding."

"I am not. It's serious. We just protect her."

"I've told her that our house will be a dll-free zone, so we don't even have to say its name."

"Kind of like Voldemort," Veronica said. "He who shall not be named. I like that."

"Who's Voldemort?" Mark asked.

"From Harry Potter?"

He looked at her blankly.

"Never mind," she said.

The group set up camp, cooked supper over the fire, and snoozed snug in their tents until dawn. They were up early the next morning to cook breakfast and head out to hike Charlie's Bunion with a detour to the Jump Off.

Fran watched Veronica all day and silently saluted her. Veronica was very much like her mother in some ways—she'd never done any of this before, any more than Fran had. But she was jumping in, willing to adapt and try new things and give this new life and stepdad a chance. She slithered through cracks and scrambled up rocks and hauled herself to the top of steep trails, then stood at the summit with the rest of them, gazing out at the mountains.

Fran had always loved her daughter, but now she had a special respect and admiration for the steel-spined, smart person at her core. Veronica was truly Julia's granddaughter, which was the ultimate compliment.

They spent one more night on the campground, then packed up and went home the next day.

*   *   *

In November, during one of their walks, Fran and Mark found a terrified kitten. She was tiny, fluffy, mostly white with cute black spots on her face and body. They took her home and presented her to Veronica, who fell in love with her and named her Cookie.

Thanksgiving followed, then Christmas, and then their first New Year's together as a family. Mark found a great deal for a last-minute cruise to the Bahamas, and he booked it as a surprise for his wife. They stayed at Donald Trump's Doral resort near Miami overnight and caught the ship the next day for a weekend of relaxation in the Bahamas. They were intent on enjoying every minute together and checking off bucket list items wherever they could.

Rick decided that he hated college and was wasting money, so he moved back home and into the basement bedroom until he figured out what he wanted to do. His part-time job at Vitamin World became full-time.

Veronica went back to Aiken for a few days while they were gone but was back in time to celebrate her sixteenth birthday on January 7. By now she was well ensconced in life at Maryville High and excited at the spring musical the Maryville Singers were putting on. Theatre had become her greatest joy.

Life seemed golden and good. No one had any idea that these were the only normal, good months they would ever have together. Darkness was coming on stealthy feet, completely unseen and unanticipated. The *someday* that Mark's doctor had warned him about fifteen years ago was about to arrive. And it would be devastating.

83

March 16, 2013 dawned like any other day. Fran had recently had minor surgery to remove some arthritic spurs from the joint in her right big toe, and she was still wearing a boot on her foot. She was feeling better and going stir crazy, so she and Mark had planned a short hike.

It was a beautiful day, so they took the top down on the Infiniti and drove up to the Abrams Falls trailhead in Cades Cove. Where they could have turned left to walk toward the falls, they turned right and made the easy, half-mile walk to the historic Elijah Oliver homestead. They took their time, taking in the main cabin and all the outbuildings made of hewn logs, dating back to 1865. Mark was particularly fascinated with the fact that part of the cabin was built over a trickling spring, which provided refrigeration for eggs, butter, milk, and other perishables.

There was a chicken coop, a smokehouse, a corn crib, and a springhouse—providing the Oliver family everything they needed to survive in these mountains. Mark could appreciate this after his time in Alaska.

They had decided that Fran would write a book about Mark's year in Alaska. It would be called *Cleft of the Rock*. She had already started writing it while recovering from her surgery but had little spare time with a two-hour commute to work every day, a full-time job, and a husband and three kids at home. With their income tax refund this year, Mark and Fran were planning a trip to Alaska in the summer so Fran could see everything for herself. When she was writing about something, it helped her if she'd actually seen it.

The reservations had already been made. They would leave at

the end of June and be gone for two and a half weeks. Veronica would be in Aiken and Patrick at Scout camp. They would fly into Anchorage and spend a day at Brooks Lodge on Katmai Peninsula, watching the bears feast on salmon. Then they would fly to Nome and see all the sites of Mark's ministry. Coming back, they would see Fairbanks, Talkeetna, and Denali. Then they'd catch a Charles Stanley cruise from Vancouver through the Inside Passage, where they would see Juneau, Skagway, and Ketchikan.

Perhaps more than anything else, Mark was looking forward to being able to hear Dr. Stanley in person again. This was the man who'd lit a fire under him spiritually when he was a freshman in college. He would love to let Dr. Stanley know what a significant role the man had played in his life. Whatever fruit Mark had borne for God was because of Dr. Stanley's influence.

Now, at the Oliver homestead, they sat down on tree stumps to eat their lunch. Fran stiffly put her foot out in front of her. It hurt, but she was happy to be out in the fresh air.

"I can't wait until Alaska," she said as she put their tuna salad kits together. She was more adept at these things than Mark was. He said his fingers were too fat. Manly, she always said. They were manly, not fat.

"I've always wanted to go to Alaska. Talk about bucket lists!"

Chattering away, Fran suddenly noticed that her husband was very quiet. When she glanced up at him, he looked back at her vacantly. She'd never seen this look in his eyes before, almost like a child's. He looked helpless and scared.

"Babe?" she said. "Are you okay?"

"No," he said slowly. "I'm not, and you're going to have to get us down this mountain."

She stared at him in terror. "What's wrong?"

He was obviously formulating his words with great difficulty. "I can't think," he said. "It's like I'm in a thick fog. My ears are ringing, and the sunlight feels like arrows in my eyes. I can't even see. Please, get me home."

Somehow, one step at a time, she got Mark down the mountain

and to the car. He leaned the seat all the way back and closed his eyes for the entire trip home. Her thoughts raced.

What in the world was she going to do? Obviously, they had to get to the bottom of this. Mark didn't even really have a doctor, just Dr. Cochran, who did his Scout physicals once a year and prescribed his Ambien. Mark had not really seen a doctor, other than Dr. Colquitt for his two surgeries since Fran had known him. Should she take him directly to the emergency room? Or somehow get through until Monday and call Dr. Cochran? She really needed Mark to tell her what he wanted.

God, what do I do? Helplessly, with no direction and no better idea, she steered the car to the Blount Memorial Hospital emergency room. Mark cracked his eyes open when they turned in. "What are you doing?" he asked. "No hospital. I just want to go home and rest."

"Babe, you need help."

"Not here," he managed. "Not now. Just get me home. Don't let the kids see."

She drove the short distance to their house and pulled Kylie into the garage. Neither Veronica's car nor Rick's was in the driveway, which likely meant Patrick wasn't here, either. It was a beautiful Saturday afternoon, so of course they weren't at home.

She helped her husband out of the car and up the stairs to their bedroom, where he collapsed on the bed. "Would you close the blinds, babe? The light hurts. And rub my neck a little? I've got to relax."

Fran rubbed his neck and shoulders silently until he dozed lightly. The instant she stopped rubbing, he roused and moaned. Downstairs she heard the door open and close, and voices in the kitchen. The kids were home. What in the world would she tell them, if Mark didn't want them to know what had happened?

"Just tell them I've got a headache and I'm resting. That's the truth," he told her faintly, moaning with the effort it took to speak. "Please come right back. I need you."

Somehow, she went down the stairs and faced Mark's sons

without letting them see her fear. They accepted her story without questioning and disappeared downstairs. Veronica wasn't as easy to fool because she knew her mother too well. Fran looked into her daughter's eyes, and tears spilled over.

"Mom? What's wrong?"

"Mark's just not feeling good, honey. I'm a little worried about him. That's all."

"What's the matter with him?"

"A bad headache. I'm trying to help him feel better."

"Can I do anything?"

Fran racked her brain. It would be nice not to have to worry about dinner. "You can call for pizza for yourself and the boys. That would help."

"Got it. Don't worry about us."

84

Mark had never had this happen before, but somehow he knew that if he could sleep, really sleep, it would be like pushing a reset button, and he'd feel better. While Fran was downstairs with the kids, he stumbled to the bathroom and dug out his bottle of Ambien.

Fuzzily he tried to count the pills. Ambien was a controlled substance, so these had to last him until the next refill. If he ran out, there would be no sleep at all until he got more. He squinted to read the date on the bottle, but it hurt too much.

It did not matter, He could not bear this pain. Sleep was essential now. Right now. He shook three tablets out of the bottle and crunched them in his mouth, then staggered back to bed.

*   *   *

Fran eased the door open quietly and took her place at Mark's side. He seemed to be resting now. She curled up behind him, covering them both with a blanket and snuggling her body against his. She rubbed his neck and shoulders gently, soothingly, and soon felt his breathing level out. He was solidly asleep. That had to be a good thing.

She prayed fervently that the morning would be better. Watching Mark today had been torture. She could face anything with him by her side, but today she'd been entirely alone, responsible for them both in an unfamiliar environment. It had been terrifying.

Suddenly she realized that this was how her mother had felt, all those years ago. Pete had taken care of Julia from the time she was seventeen years old, and Julia had found herself alone and responsible for not only her sick husband but also a tiny daughter. How she had done it, Fran couldn't begin to imagine.

Julia would be the one who would understand now, but Fran couldn't call her. She would hear her mother's voice and break down. She snuggled closer to Mark, closed her troubled eyes, and finally drifted to sleep with him.

* * *

Mark opened his eyes warily Sunday morning. He squinted at the bright sunlight, relieved that it didn't cause stabbing pains in his head. The ringing in his ears was gone, and he could think clearly. He carefully rotated his neck. It popped softly—not a good pop. The pain started to come back. He deliberately relaxed, and it subsided.

He looked down at his sweet wife, sleeping soundly on his chest. He knew he'd scared her, and he also knew it wasn't over. His doctor's words in 1997 came back to him now, echoing in his heart and mind:

> Every single one of your discs is at risk for future problems. You might go for months or years with minimal pain, but one by one, your discs will get to the point where they no longer serve as cushions. You'll be bone on bone, and your nerves will become exposed. You'll have to deal with those problem areas one at a time, as they give you significant trouble.

His doctor had told him clearly that fusing L5 and S1 would fix the immediate problem, but it wouldn't fix him permanently. Because of a degenerative disc disease, there would be further trouble. He hadn't helped the problem by doing the strenuous things he'd done the past two years. He had kicked the can down the road, and now someday was here. *Bone on bone*, the doctor had said. *Bone on bone.*

Mark felt sick. He only hoped there was something they could do. Until then, he would have to cope as best he could.

85

Mark's orthopedic surgeon from 1997 and 2003 had retired, and this wasn't an orthopedic problem now anyway. Dr. Cochran wouldn't listen, so Fran found her husband a new doctor, a general practitioner who might refer him to a specialist. It was hard to get a new patient appointment with a good doctor—they were booked months in advance.

They finally got in to see a doctor at a medical center in Alcoa. Dr. Rankin was a good, thorough doctor, but he wanted to address Mark's symptoms one at a time. Ringing in his ears? Light sensitivity? Debilitating migraines? Mental fogs? Blurred vision? It didn't add up. Round and round they went. March turned into April, and April into May. Sitting in examining rooms was torture. Mark was unable to express himself, and Fran had to speak for him. No one understood.

Mark adamantly refused to cancel the Alaska trip. Fran could take care of him, he said. And if he were unable to go out and do things, he would stay in the hotel room. God wanted her to write the book, and to do so she had to go to Alaska. Go, they would.

And so they coped. The days began to have a routine. Mornings were best. The pain came back in the afternoons, and Mark was confined to a dark room. Ambien was precious, so he began using alcohol to get through the evenings until it was time for bed. It helped him relax, he said.

But it made Fran's life a nightmare. She now understood what Lisa Smith had undoubtedly known, the reason she'd banned alcohol from her home. Mark was a different person when he drank, even just a little. The loving, caring man she'd fallen in love with disappeared. He became mean, saying and doing things he would never have done otherwise. Even if Fran didn't know he'd had a drink, she could tell. She began to eye her husband warily as evening approached, never knowing when he would say or do something that would break her heart. If she got too close, he would grab her and hurt her without meaning to, so she kept her distance. If he grabbed her robe, she slithered out of it and hid until he went to sleep.

Most nights, she had to hide the car keys. When alcohol and Ambien mixed, Mark didn't know what he was doing and could easily get behind the wheel. He crashed around the house and shouted Fran's name and demanded the keys, and she hid and prayed and wondered if she should call for help. She never did. Veronica got a job at Mr. Gatti's pizza, and on bad nights Fran would text her and tell her to go to her room and hide her keys when she got home.

Thankfully, somehow, all three kids stayed in their rooms. Sometimes Mark became determined to talk to them, and Fran had to forcibly keep him away from their rooms, knowing he'd be horrified when he came back to himself. They had to know something was wrong, but they never asked. They just became more and more distant. Veronica's eyes took on a wounded look.

Eventually, Mark would go to sleep. In the morning, he would have no memory of anything that had happened. He would wake and be back to the man she loved, and everything would be okay. And Fran knew that if she told him what he'd said and done, it would break his heart.

He was still adamant that no one could know, not until they had a definitive diagnosis and a path forward. Pain was a sign of weakness, and this was intolerable for a manly man. Fran became the cushion that insulated him from the people who loved him. When his mother and sisters called, she answered his phone and shielded him. Eventually, they stopped calling. Fran became distant from her family, knowing she was hurting them but unable to tell them the truth.

Her relationship with God deepened as her anguish grew. She cried out to Him for help and mercy and wisdom. He helped her through it, one step at a time.

Finally, mercifully, school was out, and Veronica went to Aiken for several weeks while Patrick went to Scout camp. Rick was never home. The Alaska trip came and went.

Then came the night in July that changed everything.

86

Mark and Fran had been home from Alaska for only one week. The trip had been tough but wonderful at the same time. Fran had managed to carefully schedule their activities so that Mark could rest in the afternoons. Alcohol was severely limited by necessity because they were on the road, and Fran carefully doled out the Ambien. In Talkeetna, she even found a hostel that would rent a room for two hours. She explored Talkeetna while Mark slept. Then they took a small plane to a glacier near Denali and raced up the river on a speedboat.

At Brooks Lodge on Katmai Peninsula, they were awed at the enormous size of the bears, which were everywhere. People knew that this was bear territory, and they'd better watch out. On the trails, in the camp, on the riverbanks—bears had the right-of-way, and people had to wait.

In Fairbanks, they met the legendary musher Mary Shields and even got to see and play with some sled dog puppies.

Nome was amazing. Fran got everything she went for—eyewitness looks at the places she'd heard so much about. Anvil Rock, the church, the Bering Sea, the jail—she saw all of that and more, and she knew that she could now write compellingly about those places.

Dr. Stanley's cruise was the capstone on their trip. Fran understood how the man had lit a spiritual fire under Mark, and she felt privileged to have been able to hear him herself.

When they woke up the morning they were to come home, Mark snuggled his wife and kissed her. "I know it was tough for you to arrange all of this around my condition. I want you to know I appreciate what you did. It meant we could both enjoy the trip."

Now they were home, trying to get back into the swing of life. Veronica was in Oak Ridge visiting some friends. She went to the pool with them and planned to spend the night. Rick was working late, and Patrick was with friends, making the most of these last days before school started back. Veronica and Patrick would be juniors this year.

Alcohol was back in the picture. Mark went out while Fran was at work and bought wine and whiskey by the case. Tonight, as far as she knew, he hadn't drunk anything except for one glass of wine at dinner, but he seemed upset about something. About what, Fran had no idea. He would sometimes get crazy ideas in his head, things she could do nothing about. Sometimes an old memory came back to him about something she'd said or done months ago, and he got mad at her all over again.

That seemed to be the case tonight. Fran knew better than to ask. Mark shuffled around the house, muttering to himself. Fran held her breath, stayed out of his way, and hoped the night would be over soon. It was late, and they were both dressed for bed, but she did not dare make the suggestion. She'd seen him taking his Ambien already. Surely he'd go to sleep soon.

She was in the kitchen when she heard a sound that froze her blood. It was the purr of Kylie's engine. She would know that Infiniti rumble anywhere. No one was home but her and Mark, so that meant...

She raced out into the garage just as the sleek car pulled out, Mark at the wheel. The top was down, so Fran hurled herself into the back seat and belted in. Maybe she could stop him, or calm him down, or get him to let her drive. Something. Anything.

Her presence only infuriated Mark more, and he floored it. He squealed through their neighborhood and out onto Montvale Road, where they raced through the night down the narrow road. Montvale had no shoulders, no room for error. He weaved from side to side, deliberately trying to scare her. She prayed nonstop for God to deliver them from this.

"You think I can't drive?" he screamed. "Watch this! I can drive just fine!" He swung the car into a spinning turn in a church parking lot. For a moment, the car sat still. Fran stared at him, eyes dark with terror.

"I can see that," she said.

That made him mad again, and he jammed the accelerator to the floor. He flew back down Montvale toward home, again weaving from side to side, Fran crying and praying as they went. Finally, as they prepared to take a turn, Mark's luck ran out. His right wheel clipped an uneven spot in the road shoulder. He overcorrected and went left, careening across oncoming traffic, and went off the road. The Infiniti crashed through trees, sideswiped a telephone pole, went airborne, and smashed through a homeowner's fence. Finally, they came to a sudden, jolting stop.

Prayers and Infiniti safety systems worked. Mark and Fran both climbed out of the car, unhurt, to the amazement of all the people who came running. They said they were okay—they had gone for an evening drive without their cell phones and were now going to walk the short distance to their home and call a tow truck. Once, Fran turned around and looked back at their poor, brave car. Kylie had deployed all of her safety systems to save them, and now there she sat, broken. For some reason, that broke Fran as nothing else had. Probably, she was in shock, and this was the last straw.

The night wasn't over, though. The police found them quickly as they walked toward home. They loaded them into two separate squad cars and took them back to the scene of the accident. Both were interviewed. Fran had no idea what Mark told the officers, but she told the truth as she knew it. He'd had a small amount of wine with dinner several hours ago, and a sleeping pill not long before they left the house. They'd gone for a drive and had an argument, and he'd lost control of the car. Mark was subjected to a field sobriety test, which he failed. He was charged with DUI and sent to jail for the night. The police took Fran home and said she could post bail first thing in the morning but not before.

She walked the floors all night, crying and praying for this to be what it took for God to get Mark's attention. *Please, God, let this be the eye-opener for him. Let him see that he can't keep doing this. Please, God. Let this be what it takes for him to be himself again.*

At eight o'clock in the morning, she showed up at the jail with cash. Breathlessly, heart in her throat, she waited for them to bring her husband out. Surely he would have had a change of heart after this. They'd go home and be themselves again, and they'd find a doctor who would help him.

After what seemed like hours, the door opened, and Mark emerged. He was sober now, undoubtedly. But he looked at her with anger, not remorse. "Why," he said, "did you tell them I took a sleeping pill?"

"Because you did," she said. "I told the truth. The blood test will show it."

He shook his head and stared at her coldly. "You cost me a night in the drunk tank. My back is killing me. Now I have to fight a DUI charge. Do you understand what you've done?"

*   *   *

The dominos continued to fall. It was no big surprise when Veronica decided to move back to Aiken to finish her last two years of high school. It made sense, she said, to establish residency because her college tuition would be paid by the South Carolina Tuition Prepayment Program, and she needed to be a South Carolina resident. She felt it was better to go now than to wait until she was a senior.

She told her mother all of these things while looking at her with wounded, knowing eyes. Fran could not argue. She didn't blame Veronica. This had turned into a nightmare house, and she'd leave too if she could. With a shattered, bleeding heart, she hugged her daughter tight and watched her drive away early one morning. *You've got our baby now, Jeremy,* she thought. *I know you'll take good care of her. I'm so sorry.*

In agony, Fran went to work that day and closed the door. She spent most of the day curled up in a ball behind her desk on the floor. She felt as if her heart had been physically ripped from her chest. She looked down and wondered why there was no bloody hole there; that was how badly it hurt. She lay on the floor and wailed and keened like a mortally wounded animal. Her boss came in and wanted to know if she was up to going to a meeting that afternoon.

"I don't think so," she said, unable to even hold a coherent conversation. "I'll make sure it's covered."

"Are you okay?" he asked.

"No," she said. "No, I'm not. I need to be alone for a while."

When she dragged herself home that afternoon, Mark did not understand why she was so upset. "She made a sensible decision," he said. "We'll still see her. She'll come visit."

But Fran knew in her heart that Veronica would not come visit, and she didn't blame her.

* * *

With the insurance payout from the Infiniti, Fran and Mark completely swapped out cars. They bought a Volvo C70 hardtop convertible and traded the truck for a Volkswagen Touareg SUV, which was the most comfortable car for Mark's worsening back.

They hired a good lawyer and were fighting the DUI. The evidence showed Mark's blood alcohol level was just above the legal limit. They watched his field sobriety test on a television in the lawyer's office, and they both cringed. He was obviously impaired. The only hope, the lawyer said, was to keep getting continuances and hope that after a while the prosecutors would lose interest. "In the meantime," he said, "keep your nose clean."

The next domino fell, and this one struck Mark down. Rick announced he was moving out. Where, he did not know. He would live in his car until he found a place to live, but he had to get out.

Rick left on a Sunday night. The next day, Fran was on her way home from work when she noticed a white SUV in the bushes at the entrance to their subdivision. She slowed and looked. Horror dawned on her for it was, indeed, a Volkswagen Touareg. The front driver's side was crumpled, and the car was empty.

"Mark, what have you done?" she muttered to herself in disbelief and zoomed for home.

She flew into the house and called for her husband. There was no answer. She found him in bed, sleeping peacefully. With no time to waste, she leaped back into the Volvo and headed back to the VW. The police were already there.

"Is this your car, ma'am?" one officer asked politely, gesturing to the Touareg in the bushes.

"Yes, it is."

"Were you driving it?"

Fran made a snap decision. She was not a liar. Telling the truth was the right thing, and it was far easier and safer; that way you didn't have to remember your lies. But this time, knowing her husband was asleep at home and was already fighting a DUI, she lied.

"Yes, I was," she said.

"Can you tell me what happened?"

Fran had no idea, so she made it as simple as she could. "I was headed out of the neighborhood, and I just got distracted for a second. The next thing I knew I was in the bushes. I walked home to get my AAA card so I could call for help."

"What about the mailboxes that are down?"

"Mailboxes?"

"Yes, two mailboxes are down, right there." He pointed.

"I guess I must have clipped them. I didn't even realize."

"Have you had anything to drink?"

"Not a drop," she said truthfully.

He looked at her doubtfully and put her through the story again. She stuck to it. Finally, a tow truck came and took the VW away. Fran went home and woke Mark up. He blinked blearily at her.

"What happened?" he asked.

"You don't remember?"

"Not much. I was sad about Rick, so I had a glass of wine and a pill."

"You crashed the car. I found it in the bushes. I told the police I did it."

He stared at her in relief. "Thank you. That would have been bad."

"I know. That's why I did it."

"Is the car badly damaged?"

"It looked bad to me. We've got to find our way out of this, babe. We can't keep doing this."

"When the doctors can figure out how to help me, things will get better," he said.

87

In September, Fran's management at work told her she'd been there for two years, and it was time to move to a new project. That was, after all, what was expected in senior leadership positions. Keep moving, keep growing.

"Move?" she said.

"Yes. We'll move you temporarily and put you on a bid team."

"I can't move. Not now."

"Your job here is going away at the end of the month. You have to. The alternative is to take a layoff."

She and Mark talked it over, and he said to take the layoff. She was needed at home anyway. This would give her time to write the book, and him time to get treatment and recover. "We'll be okay for a while, babe," he told her. "You've always wanted to write. Do it."

In October, the Oak Ridge house sold. In November, Dr. Rankin referred them to a neurologist, Dr. Stanton, who ordered a complete MRI of Mark's neck and back. The results were conclusive. Every vertebra, up and down Mark's back, was compromised, but by far the worst area was in his neck, in C5 and C6. His hand and thumb were now tingling and hurting, and the doctor said that was reasonable. It also explained his other symptoms.

"I'm sending you to Dr. William Reid in Knoxville," Dr. Stanton said. "He's the best neurosurgeon around here. He's going to recommend that you fuse C5 and C6."

"I know him," Mark said. "I saw him back in 1980 when I first got hurt. I wasn't in bad enough shape then for him to be able to help me."

"Now you are. I'll prescribe your Ambien and some pain meds

to get you through until your surgery. After you complete your treatment with Dr. Reid, I'll help you manage whatever comes next."

"Exactly what is that?" Fran asked. She almost didn't want to know, but she had to.

"This surgery should buy you some time," Dr. Stanton said, "but you can expect more things like this as your discs continue to decay. We can handle some of it with injections and ablations and medications, and there's an excellent pain management doctor in this building who can help with that. We'll treat the symptoms and help you manage the pain."

They left with an appointment to see Dr. Reid, who confirmed Dr. Stanton's diagnosis and scheduled surgery in December. He would perform a discectomy and fusion, going in through Mark's throat and completely removing the herniated C5 and C6 discs along with any arthritic spurs. He would use a cadaver bone graft to help speed the fusion process.

Dr. Reid explained that as with any spinal surgery, there was always a danger of paralysis. "But I've done hundreds of these procedures, and I've never paralyzed anyone," he said. "I think this will help you."

*   *   *

With a definitive diagnosis and plan, they told both families about Mark's upcoming surgery. No one knew the whole truth.

On the day of the surgery, Hollie Miller arrived early to pray with them before Mark went into the operating room. Sharon Smith came early as well and sat in the surgery waiting room with Fran, praying with her and holding her hand.

"I was wrong not to support you earlier," she told Fran over and over. "I see now how much you and Mark love each other and that you're a good wife for my son. I hope we can get to know each other now."

Fran accepted the support and sat numbly, praying over and over for the surgery to work. She wanted her husband back, and Mark could not go on like this. Julia and their sisters and children were waiting for news.

It didn't take long, only about an hour, for Dr. Reid to call them into a family room with news. The surgery had been a success. Mark would have normal surgical discomfort but should feel instant relief from the herniated discs being removed. Dr. Reid prescribed some pain medication to help with the discomfort for now.

They'd just bought some time.

88

The year 2014 dawned with more hope. *Cleft of the Rock* was published, to all five-star reviews. Mark and Fran spoke to churches and groups about his Alaska experience, only praying that his story would somehow touch people. Their prayers were answered as person after person came up to talk to them after their presentations. Fran began to work on her second book, also based on Mark's testimony. It would be called *Thorn in the Flesh*.

Mark fully intended to make the most of every new moment he'd been given. Fran wanted to learn how to study the Scriptures and get closer to God, and he would show her and teach her. All those years, Lisa had wanted to learn, but Mark had never taken any action to help her. Only in the last year of her life, as she was dying of cancer, did she draw closer to Jesus and become an example of faith for others.

Mark made a new mental bucket list. He knew what the end was going to look like, but he would delay it as long as he could, take good care of himself, and make every moment count. He and Fran would make some wonderful memories together, and he would teach her everything he knew.

In January, they made a last-minute trip to Puerto Rico to take in the 90-degree, sunny weather. They played in the surf, explored the island, and took a deep-sea fishing trip on which Mark hauled in a seven-foot-long hatchet marlin. It was an unusual species, and word spread by the time the boat returned to the dock. People swarmed for a good look at it and the man who had caught it.

In August, when Mark turned fifty-five, Fran presented him the gift of driving a real race car at Charlotte International Speedway.

The sight of him roaring around the famous track in a real NASCAR vehicle made her grin from ear to ear. He wiggled out of the car's window at the end and shouted, "That was the best thing ever!"

Patrick had only one more year of high school now, and the big house in Maryville was already much too big. Patrick lived in the basement bedroom, and Mark and Fran lived upstairs. The three of them rattled around like pebbles in paint cans. Mark and Fran discussed it and realized that this wasn't their forever house. Now, with Mark's condition, he was going to have to have a bedroom on the main floor, and fewer steps to climb. They were going to have to move.

Just as school was starting in Patrick's senior year, they listed the house for sale. In the meantime, they began unofficially looking for houses that would be good for them down the road.

By now Mark had handed over all of his Ambien to Fran, trusting her to dole it out so there would be no more disasters. She found online sources where she could buy supplementary sleep aids from overseas for him. It wasn't the good quality Ambien that was made in the United States, but it would help. It was cheaper by the bulk, so she bought it by the hundreds and locked it away in her personal safe.

She banned hard alcohol from the house—nothing stronger than wine. He kept assuring her that all he wanted was a glass of wine after dinner, and he could handle that as long as he kept the alcohol at the beginning of the evening and the Ambien at the end. As long as serious, prolonged pain wasn't with him all the time, he said, he could handle it. With trepidation, she reluctantly agreed.

They went to the Gaither Homecoming Event in Gatlinburg in May and the National Quartet Convention in Louisville in the fall. Fran soaked in the beautiful music and teaching.

The next January, they knocked off more bucket list items when they went to Arizona for the Phoenix Waste Management Open golf tournament. Mark watched his favorite golfers, Bubba Watson and Dustin Johnson, and they spent time at the most famous hole on tour—the raucous No. 16 stadium hole. They rented a spiffy yellow convertible and drove up to Sedona. They went hot-air ballooning, surprising livestock, poodles, and one agitated Great Dane as they flew low over neighborhoods and landed in a pasture.

Another blow hit in March when Mark was diagnosed with prostate cancer. They learned that all men, if they lived long enough, will get prostate cancer. Many choose not to have treatment at all because the disease moves so slowly. In Mark's case, since he was relatively young at fifty-five, they opted to knock the cancer out with seed pellet implants. It wasn't life-threatening, but it was uncomfortable and one more ordeal to get through.

In May, Veronica graduated from South Aiken High and Patrick from Maryville High. Veronica planned to attend the University of South Carolina Aiken ("I'm a Pacer, Mom, not a Gamecock," she said), and Patrick planned to go to the University of Tennessee.

In July, Mark went to see a chiropractor, one recommended by an orthopedist, for a specific problem. The chiropractor, Dr. Holtz, did his assessment and knew immediately that Mark had a displaced rib. He popped it back in place, and Mark had instant relief. The problem, Dr. Holtz said, was that all of Mark's vertebrae were now unstable and unable to hold his ribs in place. This was going to continue to happen and would get worse. Mark's golfing days, Dr. Holtz said, were over. The twisting motion required to swing a golf club was entirely out of the question. Based on the worsening condition of his spine, Dr. Holtz recommended that Mark consider filing for disability.

In August, Mark and Fran found the house they wanted. It was less than half the size of the big house in Maryville, a beautiful little gem tucked into the countryside on Rocky Branch Road, just outside town. It had two bedrooms on the main floor, with an additional bedroom and a large loft upstairs. It had a big back yard, a screened porch, and a workshop. For now, the loft would be Mark's office, and one of the small downstairs bedrooms would be Fran's office. The point was that this house had bedrooms on the main floor, which would be important down the road.

They bought the house and moved in September, and immediately listed their big house for rent. By December, they'd found good tenants on Craigslist.

After a full year of being out of the workforce, Fran realized she had to do something to supplement their income. Mark could not work at all, and their savings were dwindling. She continued to write, but it didn't bring in much money.

She followed in Lisa Smith's footsteps by hiring on at Extended Family Services as a personal living assistant, thinking that perhaps she could be a bright light for a lonely old person. Actually, as it turned out, they ministered to her more than she took care of them. She met amazing people who blessed her life.

She also, on a whim, applied at Cracker Barrel Old Country Store. She'd always loved eating and shopping at Cracker Barrel, and it seemed to be a stable company. She was hired immediately in retail sales and discovered that she was actually a pretty good salesperson. Her boss, Sue Davidson, tucked Fran under her wing and began to train her to be a retail manager someday.

In early November 2015, Fran surprised Mark with tickets to the Denver-Green Bay football game in Denver. Peyton Manning vs. Aaron Rodgers in a battle of undefeated teams. Mark had never seen his beloved Peyton Manning play—another item for the bucket list. Fran had always wanted to see the Rocky Mountains. Off to Denver, they went. They stayed in Golden, climbed mesas, and were almost blown off the mountain by the gusts of wind at Loveland Pass. They watched the Broncos beat the Packers, Mark showing his allegiance to Peyton by wearing a Tennessee hat. Everyone knew what that hat meant.

Later in November, Mark got a lawyer and filed for disability.

89

The first answer came back quickly from the Social Security Administration. Mark's disability claim had been denied. The lawyer said that was expected and told Mark to continually refile with more details as his disability worsened.

In late 2015 and early 2016, all of Fran's energy was devoted to giving her mother an enormous party for her eighty-ninth birthday in January. She and Chris chose to do it this year instead of next year because Julia's sister was in poor health, and they wanted her to be there. They held it in the fellowship hall in the church where Fran grew up—Friendship Presbyterian Church in Hickory Tavern. Nearly one hundred people showed up, from Julia's working years, the community, and both sides of the family. Julia said it was a day she would never forget.

In the spring, Fran finished her second book, *Thorn in the Flesh,* about the two years following Mark's Alaska ministry. Much of it was set at Pleasant Grove Baptist Church, which was only ten minutes from where they were living now. Fran wanted to meet the characters she'd written about, the people who lived in Mark's memory. She hadn't sent the book to the publisher yet, so there was time to make changes, and they wanted to get permission to use as many real names as possible.

In April, they visited Pleasant Grove for the first time. Mark hadn't been there since he had left thirty-four years earlier.

"It looks just exactly the same," he told his wife as they pulled into the parking lot.

The first person he saw when they stepped inside the church was Martha Galyon. Her expressive eyes flew open, her eyebrows shot up, and she raced across the room and grabbed him in a bear hug. "Mark Smith!" she shrieked. "Robert! Come quick! Look who's home!"

Her husband, Robert, folded Mark in a welcome-home hug. "You've stayed away for far too long, brother," Robert said to him.

The Galyons were older than Mark but not old enough to be his parents—they were more like a big brother and big sister. Being with them now, Mark couldn't remember why he'd stayed away so long. These were the people with whom he'd guided that youth group for two years. Through them, God had made dramatic impacts on many lives.

Mark saw more familiar faces as he and Fran walked down the hallway toward the Sunday school rooms. These were people whose sons and daughters had been in his youth group. They swarmed around him, hugged him, and welcomed him home. Beside him, Fran was getting the same treatment. They'd never seen her before, but they were welcoming her like family. Mark's heart swelled with emotion.

On the list for the Board of Deacons, he saw Jimmy Long's name. That was Jimmy, from Mark's youth group, without a doubt, the same Jimmy who'd gone into the Air Force after high school and was now a deputy sheriff with the Blount County Sheriff's Department. Down the hall, he saw a blonde head that could only be Angie Galyon from his youth group—except he'd heard that she was now Angie Galyon Kirby, a local real estate agent.

Mark checked the bulletin and saw that Greg Wilson was still the music minister. They'd hired in on the same day in 1980. Greg had gotten married not long after Mark left, to a beautiful young flight attendant named DiAnne, who was now a Sunday school teacher here. And who was the pastor now? His eyes landed on the name. Greg Long. That had to be the Greg Long who had been just ahead of him at Maryville High. Big Greg Long, the athlete whose picture Mark had taken for the yearbook dozens of times. They hadn't exactly run in the same circles of friends, but look at Greg now—he was a pastor, a shepherd.

Mark and Fran were herded into the Happy Helpers Sunday school class where DiAnne Wilson served coffee and doughnuts and Chris Fowler, the president, conducted business and did prayer requests. As she finished, she led a heartfelt prayer that brought tears to everyone's eyes. The teacher, David Carter, did an excellent job on the lesson, bringing it to life in new, interesting ways.

When the class was over, a lady who'd been sitting on the front row came up to Mark and Fran. "I'm Charlsie Owens," she said. "Welcome to Happy Helpers!"

"Thanks," Fran said. "We thoroughly enjoyed ourselves today. Thanks for the hospitality."

"Well, we hope you come back. Mark, I know who you are, and we'd love to have you teach us some time, maybe even be part of the teaching rotation. We use several different teachers, so you only have to teach every few weeks."

Word spread, and over the next few weeks, different classes at Pleasant Grove asked Mark and Fran to come speak to them about *Thorn in the Flesh* and their ministry. In a nutshell, their message was that God uses ordinary people to accomplish extraordinary things—if you just get out of His way and let Him work. The incredible events of Mark's life were prime examples. The people of Pleasant Grove drank it in appreciatively.

In May, Andy got his bachelor's degree from Limestone College and accepted a job as assistant tennis coach at Coker College, where he would have the opportunity to earn his Master of Science in Collegiate Athletic Administration in less than two years—for free. Days later, Brody earned his bachelor's degree from Clemson. It had been seven long years, but he'd made it.

The Smiths knew they'd found a new church home. At the Mother's Day service, they walked forward and presented themselves for membership.

90

Mark was getting by, but it wasn't easy. Everything he did, he did for Fran. She was his reason for living, his purpose for getting out of bed in the morning. He didn't want his pain to mar her life any more than it had to.

Dr. Harris, the pain management doctor in Alcoa, was helping. He used injections to control the inflammation and pain in the trouble spots along Mark's spine. Prescriptions for Ambien, hydrocodone, and now Lyrica helped take the edge off. A glass of wine, controlled carefully, helped even more. Ultimately, thankfully, the DUI charge had been dropped, just like his lawyer had hoped. Mark never wanted to go there again. When he drank, he told himself, he would stay at home.

He still took his wife on short hikes, and they still fished together. His neck was better, but bright sunlight hurt his eyes and brought on migraines. When they went fishing, they very deliberately found places with shade nearby, so they could tie up in the heat of the day and let Mark rest. If he overdid it—which he almost always did—he would be flat on his back the next day.

His disability still hadn't come through, and the road ahead looked long and cloudy. There were so many people out there who were filing for disability just because they didn't want to work. Probably, he was going to have to go to specialists, expensive doctors whose analysis the judge would trust. It would take time for his case to float up to the top and a judge to realize that he was truly disabled and not just lazy.

It was difficult for Mark to watch Fran work while he sat at home. She worked hard every day, either at Cracker Barrel or with her clients at Extended Family. By the time she got home, usually late at night, she was exhausted. And between those jobs, the rent from Heritage Square, and her pension from the Savannah River Site, they were still not making ends meet. Maintaining two houses was expensive. The taxes alone on Heritage Square Court were six thousand dollars a year.

He put on a good face for his sons. Rick, now twenty-three, rarely came to the Rocky Branch Road House. When he did, Mark gathered all his strength, determined not to show weakness in front of his oldest child. They sat on the screened porch and talked and did light household projects together.

Fran watched with a little sadness because Rick had never let her into his heart. He was bright, funny, and quick-witted, just like his dad. She would have liked to be his friend, if not his mother. But she could understand—Rick had been nineteen when she and he had met. His relationship with his mother had been strained, and he had no need for another female in his life.

After one year at the University of Tennessee, Patrick decided it wasn't for him, and he wanted to pursue culinary arts at Pellissippi State Community College. He'd worked at Chick-Fil-A and Arby's in high school, and now he settled in at The Soup Kitchen, a soup-and-sandwich restaurant in Maryville. He moved into the house Rick was renting, and they shared expenses. Before long, he dropped out of school entirely because he didn't want to rack up debt.

Veronica was thriving in Aiken, performing at USC Aiken and at Aiken Community Theatre. She was majoring in sociology, but theater was her passion. The girl could sing like an angel.

Sharon Smith was also having health issues, and she was diagnosed with cervical cancer at the age of eighty. Mark and Fran were there for her as she fought it and ultimately won, but that involved her living with them for several weeks while she recovered from surgery. She had apologized repeatedly for not being there for them in the beginning and reiterated how much she loved Fran now.

Mark had accepted the Happy Helpers' invitation to be in their teaching rotation. While he had his mental faculties, he poured himself into Sunday school preparations. Fran watched, fascinated, while Mark pored over the Bible, spectacles on his nose, hopping around in Scripture as the Spirit led him. He used his books from seminary to track down the roots of words back to the Hebrew and compared different aspects of Jesus' life as presented in the four gospels. He listened to the Spirit, and he knew how to use his resources. His preparation was fascinating, and his lessons were riveting. He had records of every lesson he'd ever taught, every sermon he'd ever given, and these lessons joined his files.

Fran admired him but knew she would never be able to do such a thing and told him so.

"I don't teach anything that the Spirit doesn't give me," he told her. She listened but didn't really understand what that meant—until one week he was scheduled to teach and went into one of his mental fogs. Friday came, and he was still confined to the dark bedroom.

"Babe, you're going to have to sit in for me and teach this lesson," he told her.

"I can't!" She was horrified. "I can't do what you do!"

"You'll do it your way. Get into the Scriptures and the lesson and watch what God does. It's your time now, babe."

Without any real choice, she agreed. The Scripture, Isaiah 9:6, was a familiar one.

For a child will be born to us, a son will be given to us; and the government will rest on His shoulders; and His name will be called Wonderful Counselor, Mighty God, Eternal Father, Prince of Peace.

How many thousands of times had this Scripture been taught? What on earth could she say that would be illuminating? Fran was terrified, but she calmed herself. This couldn't be about her. It had to be about God through her. *Open my mind and heart, Father,* she prayed. *Tell me what You want me to say.*

She gathered different versions of the Bible along with various commentaries that Mark said he trusted and holed up in her office for two days. She read and made notes late into the night, and the light dawned in her heart, just as Mark had said it would. She knew this message wasn't from her—it could never be from her. It was from God Himself. Knowing that, she had the courage to stand up before the class on Sunday morning and deliver the lesson.

After class, Charlsie Owens approached her and asked if she would join the teaching rotation. Before she even thought about it, Fran said, "That's not my gift."

Charlsie eyed her. "I respectfully disagree."

"Teaching has never been my gift. Writing is my gift."

"I just watched you teach. God gives us different gifts at different times for His purposes."

Fran opened her mouth and closed it again. She was remembering something that Mark Lowry of the Gaither Vocal Band had said on stage at the National Quartet Convention in Pigeon Forge.

"The pot doesn't get to tell the Potter what the pot is worth," Lowry had told the huge audience. "The Potter tells the pot what the pot is worth. The pot doesn't get a vote. It's in our best interest to agree with God. It's very rude not to."

Then she remembered that God had indeed given her the message she'd just taught. It had most definitely not come from her. If He was going to give her lessons, who was she to tell Him she couldn't teach them? That would be rude, just as Mark Lowry said. She would not be a rude pot.

"You're right," she told Charlsie. "You can put me in the teaching rotation."

91

In the spring of 2017, things in the Smith household got as bad as they had ever been. And then they got worse.

If Mark had taken his prescription medications properly, and not combined them with alcohol, things might have been fine. But that was not what happened.

He drank wine to relax, he said. One glass became two, and two became three. Before the night was over, he'd consumed a whole bottle. Hydrocodone and Lyrica were now always in his system. Later in the evening, Ambien joined the mix.

Fran would usually take refuge in her office downstairs, listening as Mark walked heavily around upstairs. When he called her name, she kept her door shut and pretended she didn't hear him. One night he got out his gun and shot two holes in the house, one through the floor and one through the wall. Another night, he shot a round off the back porch.

Several times, he fell down the steps, hitting the wall at the bottom of the stairs so hard he punched a hole through it. Twice, Fran had to take him to the emergency room. She began sleeping on the bedroom floor between the bed and the door, so she could catch him and keep him from getting on the steps. One night, that backfired because Mark tripped and fell on her and broke two of her ribs.

One particularly horrible night, Mark ripped everything off the walls in his office upstairs and threw the precious pieces over the banister to the floor below. When he was finished with the pictures and diplomas, he started on the furniture. The prayer bench he'd used with his boys hit the floor and shattered. A one-of-a-kind painting by his grandmother, destroyed. His Boy Scout memorabilia, which had been painstakingly gathered and arranged in beautiful shadowboxes, gone.

When the noise faded and Fran dared to emerge, horrified, from her office, she found her living room looking like a battlefield, a foot deep in broken glass. Mark stood on the steps, weaving. "I was just trying to get your attention," he slurred.

One night he called the police because he was convinced Fran was abusing him, and that's what he told the policemen. The officers walked around and listened to him and watched her, and they clearly knew the real story. They took her out on the front porch and asked her if she was okay. She said she was, and everything would be fine when Mark went to sleep.

Another night Fran caught Mark as he was heading for the handgun in his top dresser drawer. She physically wrestled it away from him and hid it, then quickly found the other handguns in the house and hid them too. He screamed at her to give him back the guns, but of course she refused. He sat on the top step and stared down at her, to where she stood at the bottom. "Give me the guns!"

"You're forcing me to call for help," Fran said. "Is that what you want?"

"Yes."

She stared at him. "You're telling me to call for help."

"Yes."

When the police came that night, they found Mark sitting on the floor beside the bed, all the rifles and shotguns and ammunition spread out around him. They talked to him for a long time, but he was making no sense. They spoke with Fran and asked her what she wanted them to do. "You can sign the papers, and we can take him away and get him into detox," they said. "He's obviously not able to make that decision for himself."

Fran thought about that, about Mark and his poor back, trying to go through something like that. She couldn't do it. "Let's get the guns out of the house and get him to sleep," she said. "He'll be okay if he can go to sleep."

"Are you afraid of him? Do you feel like you're in danger?"

"Not when he's himself, no. He just needs to get to sleep."

So the police sat with her in the house that night until Mark went to sleep.

As the violence in her home continued to escalate, Fran began to break. She'd never told anyone the whole truth about what was going on. The situation had stayed between her and Mark and God.

She knew she could never tell any of her family. They would just want to come get her and kill Mark. But she began to confide in Lisa and Mellie, and Scott and Doug—the people other than his mother and sons who loved him most. Mellie, who was a trained and experienced counselor, explained to Fran that she was an abused woman, whether Mark had ever laid a hand on her or not. Lisa and Doug told Fran that she had to get out for her own safety because while God wanted her to honor and be true to her husband, He did not want His daughter to be in danger.

"Mark would never hurt me," she protested.

"Fran, he shot a gun through the house," Doug pointed out. "That bullet went through two walls. He could easily have shot you."

"I'm afraid that if you stay, there will be a murder-suicide," Lisa said.

Scott offered the little cottage behind his house as a refuge whenever she needed it. All of them told her that she had to tell their pastor, Greg Long. Greg, who was a police chaplain and had seen all sides of domestic violence, wholly agreed with what Fran's friends and sisters-in-law were telling her.

"You need to get out, and we need to do an intervention."

Fran was terrified of what would happen if she left. "I'm afraid he'll kill himself," she said. "I really think he might."

"That's how he's holding you hostage," Greg said. "I hope he doesn't do that, but it's not your fault if he does. You need to get out, and we need to get him some help."

Fran prayed that God would make it abundantly clear when she was supposed to get out. In May 2017, He did.

When she walked in from work that night, she could tell it was going to be bad. Mark's eyes were dilated, which meant he'd been drinking. Her heart sank. Alcohol was the kindling that started it all. Without alcohol, he remained himself. With it, he was a different person. Tonight, he was mad at her from the time she walked in the door. He trailed behind her wherever she went and screamed profanity at her. Mark only ever used profanity when he was drunk.

Fran had always hated profanity before, but now she couldn't tolerate it at all. And tonight, she was finished backing down. She screamed right back at him. The situation escalated. A rack hung over the kitchen island, holding all their pots and pans. Mark ripped it right out of the ceiling and slammed it across the room.

Then he picked up an old pizza-sized baking stone, which Fran had had for twenty-five years. Mark slammed it down on the tiled kitchen counter and shattered it, then hurled the shards at her.

The voice shouted in her heart. This was the clear guidance she'd been praying for. Sobbing, terrified, she grabbed her phone and purse and ran out the door.

*   *   *

Scott Spitler wasn't home that night, but his wife knew what was going on. She took Fran's hysterical call and had a bedroom ready for her. Word spread quickly among the small group that had come together to support her. Greg, Doug, Lisa, and Mellie knew and were relieved she was safe. They were praying for her. Doug was planning to lead the intervention, as soon as he could make it to town.

"You can't talk to him," Lisa told her sternly. "Don't answer the phone or respond to text messages. He has to hit rock bottom before he can find his way out."

"I can't even answer a text message?"

"No, and he knows where you work, so stay alert. He could follow you home, and we don't want him to know where you are."

Sitting on that bed in the Spitler house, shaking, Fran made one more call that night.

"911, what is your emergency?"

"I just need you to please send someone and make sure my husband is okay." Fran's teeth chattered in shock.

"What is the situation?"

"He scared me, and I got out, but I'm afraid for his safety."

"You're safe?"

"Yes, I'm safe."

"What is the address?"

Fran gave it to the operator. She'd done all she could do.

*　　*　　*

The next morning, Greg Long sent a police escort to help Fran get her clothes. Mark sat on the porch, surprised when three cruisers pulled up in the yard.

"What's this all about?" he asked her. "I cleaned up the house for you."

"You need to get some help," she told him.

"When will you be home?"

"When I feel safe."

Without further words, tears streaming down her cheeks, she gathered the few things she needed and left. She really, really hoped it would not be for long. She just wanted her husband back, without alcohol. They could handle anything if he would quit drinking.

*　　*　　*

It did not take long nor did it take an intervention. Mark could not live without his wife, and she was dying inside without him. Within days, Mark willingly called Don Wilson at Sevier Heights and arranged counseling. They sat together in Don's office and told him the whole story.

Don pulled no punches. "You almost destroyed your wife and your marriage," he told Mark sternly.

"I know." Tears streamed down his face.

"You can't mix alcohol and pills."

"I know."

"You can never, never take another drink again. Ever."

Mark sat silently. Fran waited.

"I understand, but I have such anger," he finally said.

"What are you mad at?"

"Everybody. My mother, my wife, my children. God. I hate being like this, and I hate that Fran has to work so hard, and I hate what it's doing to us, and I hate that disability hasn't come through."

"And all of that anger comes out when you drink."

"Yes," Fran answered. "It does. He only has a temper when he drinks."

Don gave Mark a homework assignment.

"I want you to write down everything that makes you mad. Let it all out. Then when you get it on paper, take a good hard look at it. That's what we'll talk about next time."

The exercise showed Mark that none of the things that made him so angry were in his control. He had to consciously and deliberately let each of them go and give them back to God.

After just a few sessions, Don was satisfied. He suggested to Fran that she very intentionally find some close, godly female friends, so she would have a healthy outlet if she had issues in the future.

He released them, and Fran went back home to her husband. He did not drink. He was her Mark again.

92

Mark and Fran were invited to speak to churches, civic clubs, college classes, and even on local television and radio shows about their second book. One lady at Virginia College came up to Mark after their presentation and told him that her life had been changed that night.

A lady at East Maryville Baptist Church said that she'd sent *Cleft of the Rock* to her sister, who shared it with her husband, who was in prison in Alabama. The man got saved and was now doing Bible studies in prison—thanks to *Cleft of the Rock*, she said.

They applied for a booth at the National Quartet Convention but were told that the 2017 convention was full. They would be placed on a waiting list for next year.

Darell Coppenger, the head of Sunday school at Pleasant Grove, contacted Mark and asked if he would be interested in taking over as teacher of the Wisdom Seekers Sunday school class. The current teachers, Clyde and Peggy Dockery, had been teaching for ten years straight and needed a break.

Mark leveled with Darell about his health and told him there might be times when he would be unable to teach.

"Do you have a backup?" Darell asked him.

"Do I ever," Mark said.

"Then we should be fine."

In September, Mark took over as teacher of the Wisdom Seekers. The first six weeks were about dark forces and how they are real and pervasive in everyday life. He knew that all too well and spoke compellingly on the topic.

Every month after that series was over, Fran looked at the topics coming up and chose one that she wanted to teach. She'd grown to love digging into the Word and hearing God speak to her. Teaching, she'd discovered, makes a person get into Scriptures in a different and powerful way. The Bible clearly says that teachers are held to a higher standard, and she understood why. To be a teacher, you had to take it seriously. You couldn't just open up the lesson book and lead a discussion. It had to be Spirit-inspired.

Fran started a small women's group, inviting a half-dozen women to join her once a month for prayer and fellowship. That group consisted of Martha Galyon, DiAnne Wilson, Angie Galyon Kirby, and three others Fran had become close to at church. One was Mary Gene Roberts, the ninety-two-year-old wife of Charlie Roberts, who, as it turned out, was on the search committee when Mark was hired at Pleasant Grove back in 1980. Being with godly women and praying with them helped.

Fran was so proud of Mark. Alcohol was now out of the picture, so he was handling himself the right way now. When she came home from work, she didn't have to worry about what she would find. It was always and only her wonderful, clear-eyed husband. They laughed and talked and studied and watched movies together. She knew he was hurting and could see it in his eyes. She spent hours every evening working on his shoulders and back to try to give him some relief. He continued to get periodic injections and chiropractic treatments. They coped and made their life the best they could.

Finally, in the fall of 2017 came the news they'd been waiting for. Mark had been granted a disability hearing. His lawyer said now was the time to go to the specialists, the ones whose opinions the judge would respect. It would be expensive, but it would be worth it. They made torturous trips to Greeneville, Tennessee, to meet with those doctors. The hearing was scheduled for February.

In December, they were notified that they had a booth at the 2018 National Quartet Convention, which would be in Pigeon Forge in September.

93

Because of everything that had been going on, Fran and Mark hadn't been on a vacation in two years. They had a timeshare, and they decided they wanted to go somewhere warm and just relax, somewhere they could drive to and take their boat. They could lie beside the pool, fish, sightsee, and be lazy. No schedules, no commitments. It sounded like heaven.

In January 2018, they hooked up the boat and headed for Weston, Florida, just south of the Everglades, near the southern tip of Florida. It was a twelve-hour drive, so they took it slow and easy and let Mark stretch and rest whenever he needed to.

His mother paid for them to hire a fishing guide one day. "Peacock bass," the guide told them. "That's what you want to go for. They're fighters." The guide took them into canals in neighborhoods and instructed them on the proper bait and technique for catching peacock bass. Huge iguanas basked on the banks of the canal. They caught quite a few fish, and Mark could clearly see what kind of habitat was good for peacock bass. Now he knew where to go and what to do when they took the boat out on their own.

Fran had always wanted to see the Florida Keys. One day they hopped into the car to go to Key Largo, which is the first key in the chain. One key led to the next, and by the end of the day, they were watching the sunset at Key West.

She'd always wanted to see the Everglades too. She got her wish when they eased their bass boat into the water in the canal beside Alligator Alley—the same canal where Mark had hooked the big gator nearly thirty years ago.

They cruised up and down the canal and watched as the big gators lazed in the sun, slitting their eyes at the boat as it passed. Sometimes they slid into the water. Fran respected the huge reptiles, but she was unafraid. After years at the Savannah River Site, she understood their behavior. She knew if she and Mark didn't do something stupid—like deliberately try to hook one—they had nothing to worry about.

They floated up to the very end of the canal, where buoys held a mesh barrier in place from the surface down to the bottom. A mid-sized gator lazed in the good-sized pool beyond the buoys. Fran and Mark put on shiners and cast into the water. They got some strikes, but the barrier provided a place for the fish to run and they always got away.

Fran made another cast—and wham! Her rod jerked almost out of her hand. "Mark!" she gasped.

"I see it, I see it. Keep it steady, that's it. Don't give him any slack. Keep him away from the barrier. That's good."

"Do you want to bring him in?"

"No, I want you to do it."

The fish tried to run to the barrier, but Fran gritted her teeth and forced him away. The gator watched the proceedings without in-terest. After fighting the fish for a good fifteen minutes, Fran finally dragged him close enough to the boat for Mark to scoop him up with the net. He was the biggest fish either of them had caught during the whole trip. They took pictures with the fish and then turned him loose.

She looked at her husband with glowing eyes. "That was so much fun!" she said.

"I loved seeing you do that." He was genuinely proud of her. He always was.

The next morning, they packed up, relaxed and tanned and happy, and set out for the long trip back to Maryville.

94

In February, Mark had his disability hearing. After two years and three months of fighting, this was the end of the line. Either he would be approved for disability now, or he would be denied permanently. If the judge ruled in their favor, she would set a date of disability, which was also important to their future.

Fran and Mark were just hoping and praying for a favorable decision. Anything more than that would be amazing. Fran wasn't allowed in the room. Mark and his lawyer, Chip, went in alone. She sat in the waiting area, praying. She felt like Moses at the edge of the Red Sea, the Egyptians closing in, out of options.

For the first time in her life, she felt guided to a specific Scripture. She had no idea where it was and had to find it. She tapped in some key words on her Bible app, and up it popped. It was in 2 Chronicles, the story of Jehoshaphat calling to the Lord for help as Israel was about to go to battle against an invincible enemy.

Thus says the Lord to you, "Do not fear or be dismayed because of this great multitude, for the battle is not yours but God's."

She scanned further down. The story continued.

"You need not fight in this battle; station yourselves, stand and see the salvation of the Lord on your behalf, O Judah and Jerusalem. Do not fear or be dismayed; tomorrow go out to face them, for the Lord is with you."

The next day, during the battle, the Israelites watched and sang praises while their enemy destroyed themselves.

This battle is Mine. Fran could hear the voice in her heart.

Watch and see the victory I will give you.

She read this passage over and over again, no longer frightened but confident. When Mark and his lawyer came out, their faces were carefully blank, but she knew.

"Let's get out of here," the lawyer murmured to her. They went out, away from the earshot of the other people and the security guards.

When they were alone, Chip said, "I've never seen anything like it."

"What happened?"

"Well, first, there was an occupational specialist on the phone that was a witness for the government. The best you can hope for is that this person doesn't hurt your case too badly. I was ready to counteract anything he said, but he testified on Mark's behalf.

"Second, judges never tell you on the spot what their decision is. They get all the facts, and then they write a decision, and you hear about it weeks later. This judge told us just now that she was ruling favorably."

Fran gasped, tears springing to her eyes.

"She actually apologized to me, babe," Mark said. "She apologized that it all took so long. She said she didn't want to put me through any more of this. I'm approved."

"God fought this battle for us," Fran said.

"He absolutely did," Chip said. "There's more. She gave us reason to believe that the decision will be retroactive. How far back, we don't know, but you stand to get a lump sum retroactive payment."

Fran collapsed on the bench, sobbing in relief. All of their debts could be paid off. Mark would get a payment every month for the rest of his life, and he'd have Medicare. It was more than she could take in. *Thank You, Lord. Thank You.*

95

In May, they traded in their old bass boat for a more comfortable one, so Mark could enjoy being on the water without bending and straining his back so much.

In June, Veronica was cast in the lead role as Wednesday Addams in *The Addams Family, The Musical,* at Aiken Community Theatre.

In July, Mark's pain level skyrocketed, with muscle spasms in his neck and shoulders and the return of the migraines. A knot had now been identified in his thoracic area. The pain management doctor looked at them regretfully and said he'd done everything he could. Surgery was the only option, and he didn't even know what that would look like.

Bone on bone, Mark thought, the words of that long-ago doctor coming back to him again and again as he writhed in agony. *Bone on bone.* That day was here.

He tried to talk to his wife about the reality.

"One day," he told her, "the pain will get too bad." She couldn't hear that, wouldn't understand what he was trying to say. They'd talked numerous times about what they wanted, and she knew where to find insurance documents and financial information. He didn't need to go over all of that again. She didn't want to hear it.

As it always did when Mark was in pain, alcohol tried to creep back in. One night Fran came home and found him drunk and confrontational. She refused to talk to him in that condition, so he called 911. When they arrived, he told them that his wife wouldn't speak to him.

"I'll talk to him after he sobers up," she told the officer, who'd been to the house before. He completely understood. After making sure Fran was safe, he and his partner left.

Mark finally went to sleep. The next morning, she confronted him. "Mark, this is non-negotiable. If you choose alcohol, you don't choose me. It almost destroyed us before, and I can't do it."

Time after time it tried to creep back in, and time after time Fran put her foot down.

She came home one day to discover that Mark had decided he was going to cut the grass and had gotten the mower stuck between the two trees in the front yard. He'd then gotten the bright idea to use the Volkswagen to pull the mower out, and done several thousand dollars' worth of damage to the car, the fence, the mower, and the house.

He was unable to teach Sunday school through the summer months. Fran set up a schedule of guest teachers and told Darell Coppenger that they would be unable to continue teaching after this year.

Dr. Holtz, the chiropractor, said he'd done all he could do, but that there was one neurosurgeon who might be able to help. He made the call for them and discovered that there was a cancellation. They snapped it up. The surgeon's name was Dr. Strong.

The Smiths spent an agonizing two hours at Dr. Strong's office. He and his assistant looked carefully at Mark's MRIs and focused on one shadowy area that could be causing his latest agony.

"Look at this," he pointed at the area. Fran could see nothing, but Mark painfully nodded his head. "This is it. This is pressing on the nerve and causing the spasms. If we fix this, I think you'll get some relief."

"It will stop the spasms and the headaches?" Fran asked.

"I think so, yes."

"What about mobility?" Mark asked.

"We'll be fusing C3 and C4. You shouldn't notice much difference in mobility."

"Let's do it," he said. It was his last hope.

The surgery was scheduled for the middle of August, which

should give him plenty of time to recover before their big week at the National Quartet Convention in September. He was worried about being able to function at such a big event, but Fran assured him that he didn't need to put pressure on himself. It would be great if he could be there, but she could handle it. They'd already paid the fees and ordered supplies. There was no going back.

The day of the surgery dawned. Friday, August 17. Everyone knew how important it was. Mark and Fran arrived very early at Parkwest Medical Center in Knoxville. Greg Long came, along with several people from the Wisdom Seekers Sunday school class. Sharon Smith was there, and Lisa Lambert had driven in from Nashville, where she'd recently moved to be near her daughters and new grandchildren.

Fran sat in the waiting room, praying. The word came that the surgery was finished, and the doctor would meet them in the family room. Greg went with Fran and sat by her side as Dr. Strong explained that he'd removed and replaced the two diseased discs and also found arthritic spurs that were pressuring Mark's nerves.

"When he wakes up, he's going to be in considerable pain," the doctor said. "His neck will think it's broken, and it will react accordingly, but when we get him through that initial stage, he's going to feel better."

Fran sagged in relief. "Thank you, Dr. Strong."

"I'm just glad I was able to help."

The crowd dispersed. Lisa took Sharon back to Maryville, and Greg left for other hospital visits. When they called her, Fran went to the recovery room to be with Mark. He was wild-eyed with pain and couldn't swallow or talk as a result of surgery and the tube they'd put in his throat. She took one look at him and knew.

"He needs something for pain," she told the nurse. "He has a very high drug tolerance."

"I'll have to call his doctor," she said.

They gave him more and more, but it did not touch the pain. When they moved him to a hospital room, he still looked terrified and panicked. He could talk a little now, and if he sat up, he could swallow. He wanted only Fran. No one else was allowed to see him like this. He would not let her out of his sight, even for a minute.

"I've never had this kind of pain in my life," he whispered. Fran had to lean close to be able to hear him.

"The doctor said your neck thinks it's broken, and it's defending itself. That's why it hurts so much."

"It would have been nice if someone had warned me about that."

Minute by minute, they got him through the night. Fran rubbed him and comforted him and helped him sit up and lie back down. The next morning, the drainage tube was removed from his neck, and he was sent home.

Mark's recovery began. The symptoms he'd had before were better now, but the muscle spasms were markedly worse and would not go away. He went for his follow-up appointment and was told that muscle relaxers would be his best friends. Under new, stricter opioid laws, the surgeon was restricted as to the strength of painkillers he could prescribe. Dr. Stanton, his neurologist in Alcoa, also regretfully refused. Legally, the new laws had tied their hands.

"I can't be your pain doctor anymore," Dr. Stanton said.

Mark sat in the examining room and sobbed like a small boy.

96

The weeks leading up to the National Quartet Convention crawled by. This was by far the biggest opportunity they'd ever had with their books. Thousands upon thousands of people would be there throughout the week from around the world.

Their favorite artists would perform, including the Talleys, the Isaacs, the Gaither Vocal Band, the Kingdom Heirs, and the Mark Trammell Quartet.

Fran arranged for volunteers from church to help at their booth, but she was the author and would have to be there from start to finish every day. Mark so badly wanted to be there that Fran found a hotel room across the street from the venue for the week. This way, he wouldn't have to make the forty-five minute trip to Pigeon Forge. He could rest in the hotel room when he wanted, or be at the convention when he felt up to it. Patrick agreed to come to the house every day, collect the mail, and take care of the cat.

On Sunday, the day the convention began, Rick and Patrick helped them unload and get set up. They wandered around and got their bearings, learning the timing of the event and when people would be wandering around the booths. They heard some gospel music, talked to some people, and sold some books.

Monday, Mark got up and made a quick trip to Knoxville. He had an appointment with the nurse practitioner in Dr. Holtz's office. She was going to give him some trigger point injections and a prescription for steroids, hoping that might help him get through this big, stressful week. He arrived back in Pigeon Forge Monday afternoon, and he and Fran stayed at the event together through the evening. The highlight of the day was meeting Lauren and Debra Talley.

They went back to the hotel together after ten o'clock. As they passed the desk, Mark noticed a small bottle of wine in the cooler. He picked it up and looked at it. "What do you think?" he asked his wife. She studied it dubiously, as if it had fangs. The bottle said it contained two servings.

"It's supposed to be two servings. If you could discipline yourself to have half tonight and half tomorrow night, it should be okay."

"I need to relax," he said and bought one little bottle of wine.

They went upstairs, showered, flopped onto the bed, and tried to unwind. Fran had to be back at the venue first thing in the morning, so she needed to get some sleep. Mark would come over whenever he felt up to it.

He tried to be quiet and let her doze off. He took his Ambien but knew sleep would be far away this night. He could still feel the shots in his neck and shoulders from this morning, and the steroids were powering through his system. It felt like he had ants under his skin. Neither the injections nor the steroids had done anything to address his pain. It was just there, always there, gnawing at his surgical spot like a greedy rat. Spasming in his muscles. He was so tired of pain.

He drank one serving from the bottle of wine, then downed the rest of it.

At home, he would be able to go out on the back porch and sit. He could look at the stars and listen to the wildlife scurrying through the trees. He knew who they were now, the raccoon that thought he was being sly, the family of skunks that went along the edge of the property at the same time every day, the squirrels that jumped from tree to tree. Sometimes there was even a bear. And always the birds. The same families of birds had raised their babies in the eaves of the house since he and Fran had lived there.

The clock turned over to two o'clock in the morning, and Mark could stand no more. He got up and started getting dressed.

Fran stirred. "What's going on, baby?"

"I have to go home," he said. The way he said it, she could tell it wasn't a good idea. She glanced at the bottle of wine and saw it was empty and knew by deduction that he'd also had his sleeping pills.

"Now?" she asked.

"Yes, now. Right now. I don't feel good."

"You're not driving anywhere," she said.

"I have to go home," he reiterated.

She sighed. "Then I guess I'll take you."

The drive home was silent. Fran was furious. Once again, Mark hadn't been able to restrain himself with alcohol. He was his drunk self now, and she had no interest in talking to him.

Finally, he broke the silence. "You don't like me very much, do you?"

"Babe, I love you. But I don't like what you're doing."

They got home about three o'clock in the morning, and Fran sprawled on the bed in the downstairs bedroom so she wouldn't wake Mark when she got up. She would have to be up and out very early. She had helpers coming to their booth at nine o'clock, and she had to show them the ropes.

Tuesday morning, she crept upstairs and kissed her sleeping husband lightly on the cheek. He did not stir.

They talked and texted throughout the day, and Mark sounded like his old self. He just did not feel very good. His stomach was upset, he said. Maybe it was the new prescription.

"I'm calling Patrick and telling him I'm here, so he doesn't need to take care of the cat today," Mark told his wife. "There's plenty of food here that I can heat up. You just keep on doing what we went there to do. Steer this ship. I'm okay."

"Faye and Cecil are bringing you your car on their way back today," Fran said. Faye and Cecil Levi were members of their Sunday school class who had volunteered to help with the booth this morning.

"That's sweet of them."

"This way, you can come back whenever you feel up to it. Definitely by Thursday. That's the Gaither Vocal Band."

"You know I want to be there for that."

"Feel better. I love you."

Faye and Cecil did take Mark his car on Tuesday afternoon. Mark came onto the porch in his pajama shorts, and Cecil had prayer with him.

Mark and Fran stayed in continuous contact throughout the day and the evening until Mark knew his wife was safely secured in their hotel room.

Wednesday dawned to more of the same. Fran woke to several texts from Mark, suggesting ways to get people's attention and get them to come to their booth. He still did not feel well, he said, and thought it best to stay home today. He had a few errands to run in town, but other than that, he was staying put.

For years, Mark and Fran had used an app called Glympse to track each other on the road. It made them both feel better, and it saved the necessity of texting or calling. She watched on her phone as he went to the post office and the grocery store, then back home.

As Wednesday evening wore on, the tone of Mark's texts changed. He went from encouraging and uplifting to melancholy and sad.

Kind of sad eating your mama's chicken stew without you, he wrote about eight o'clock.

I never knew being at a convention was such hard work, she wrote.

You need me, he said.

I absolutely need you. You'll be back tomorrow to see the Gaither Vocal Band.

About the time the convention was ending for the night, the tone of his texts changed again. He became confrontational and mean. She looked at the texts in dawning dread and made her decision.

I'm coming home for the night, she texted him.

What, so you can take a Tylenol PM and knock out? You're not sincere.

She tried to call him. He didn't answer the phone. She texted him. *Answer the phone.*

I can't.

Why not?

No answer.

She stepped on the accelerator as hard as she could and raced for home.

*   *   *

At midnight, Fran barreled into her driveway and sprayed gravel as she slammed on the brakes. Maybe Mark was just feeling lonely. Maybe that was it. She'd spend some time with him tonight and sleep in their bed, and then they'd go back to Pigeon Forge together tomorrow. It was the big day—the Gaither Vocal Band.

She eased in the front door, locking it and chaining it behind her. The cat ribboned around her feet. "Babe?" she called. She could hear the television in the office on the second floor. She walked lightly up the stairs, deliberately putting a smile in her voice. "Where are you?"

She found Mark on the sofa in his office, the telltale dilated look in his eyes. But she sank to her knees on the floor in front of him and wrapped her arms around him. "Hi, babe," she said softly.

Mark did not hug her back. He looked into her eyes and muttered a profanity, then grabbed her arm so hard it hurt.

She tried to yank away, but his hands were too strong. No. This could not be happening again. Not after everything they'd been through. She couldn't take it.

"I'm going to take a shower," she said faintly and wrestled her arm away.

More screaming. Fran could hear crashes through the roar of the water as she took her shower.

God, please. She begged through tears. *Show me very clearly what to do. Maybe he could just go to sleep? That would be good. If not, show me. Don't leave it to doubt. Make it so, so clear.*

She turned off the water and listened. Silence at the moment. Warily she dried herself and stepped out of the shower. Knowing what she would find, she checked the closet shelf. A box of wine sat there, half empty. She went into Mark's office and couldn't believe her eyes. His massive desk, weighing hundreds of pounds, was shifted several feet. The stool where he always propped his feet was across the room, awry against the wall. Debris littered the room.

She heard sounds coming from their bedroom and found him sitting on the floor in the closet, punching out sleeping pills from a blister pack. Every night, he took astronomical amounts of sleeping pills because his system had become so resistant to them. He stuffed about twenty pills into his mouth and crawled across the floor to the bed.

Maybe he'd go to sleep now, and they could start over in the morning. She went to sit on the bed with him and rub him, as usual.

He grabbed her arms in a vise grip, and his eyes glittered with alcohol ice. He looked straight into her terrified eyes, uttered another profanity, and then clearly said, "Stop being yourself."

Tears poured from her eyes, from both the physical and emotional pain. "What?" *God, please...*

"Stop. Being. Yourself."

He released her arms and grabbed the lamp off the nightstand. He physically ripped it apart and hurled it across the room, then reached for her again.

Run. Get out. The voice in her heart had never been so clear. *Now.*

Fran scrambled out of his grasp, sides heaving with sobs, eyes never leaving Mark's. From a safe distance, she told him, "I'm going back to Pigeon Forge, and it's your fault."

Get out!

He lunged for her again, and she ran down the steps and out into the night. She hurled herself into her car and raced away.

Somehow she made the forty-five minute drive back to the hotel. She was still in shock, unable to believe what had just happened. She'd been very clear—if he chose alcohol, he didn't choose her. He'd made his choice, and now she had to make hers.

She had no wish to divorce him, now or ever. She only wanted to be safe and for him to get help. Maybe that meant being apart from him for now. God's direction at the moment had been very clear.

She got to her hotel room at one-thirty in the morning. She'd seen Mark take a large dose of sleeping pills. Surely he was asleep now, but she sent him a text saying she'd arrived safely back in Pigeon Forge. She got no answer and had expected none.

Then she made two calls. With Martha Galyon, she shared her heart and her anguish. With Sue Davidson, her boss at Cracker Barrel, she asked about transferring to a different store for a while. "We'll talk about it when you get back next week," Sue told her.

She did not sleep that night.

97

Fran checked her phone before she got out of bed on Thursday morning. No text from Mark. He was probably looking around at the damage and trying to decide what to say to her. It was just as well—she was still too angry and hurt to talk to him now. How could he buy alcohol, after everything they'd been through? She could not understand it.

She called Lisa Lambert and told her what had happened. Lisa said what Fran had expected her to. "This is it, Fran. You need to get out of here."

"What do you mean, get out of here?"

"Move back to South Carolina for a while, until he gets straightened out. Get out of the picture. You can always transfer back to Tennessee."

"What do I do when the convention is over? Transfers don't happen instantly."

"Find a short-term place to live. God will provide. He always does."

Fran hung up the phone, and it buzzed with an incoming text message from Angie Galyon Kirby. *Hey, what's going on with your rental house? Do the renters want to buy when their lease is up?*

Fran quickly shifted mental gears. This was clearly out of the blue because Angie had no idea what had happened last night. *I don't think so. Why do you ask?*

I have a buyer who wants a house in that neighborhood, in that price range. They rode by yours, and they like it.

What price range? Fran wrote back. *It's not even on the market.*

I told them what it was listed at before. Check with the renters and let me know.

Will do.

Fran quickly texted her renters and discovered that they were financially unable to buy the house. Fran shared that information with Angie and gave her the green light to show the buyers the house—a small bit of encouraging news in this otherwise dreadful day.

As Fran got ready for the day, she pondered. Clearly, she couldn't check on Mark herself, but she wanted someone to. She texted Patrick.

Hey, your dad's not feeling so hot today, and I'm stuck in Pigeon Forge. Would you take him some food later?

Sure. Patrick's reply was almost instant. *I'll take him some soup when I get off work.*

Thank you, honey. He'll enjoy that.

Fran went to the convention and got through the day. It was, as expected, huge. She almost expected to see Mark come in the door to see his beloved Gaither Vocal Band perform, but he did not. About four o'clock, a text from Patrick came in.

Couldn't get Dad on the phone and he didn't answer the door, so I went in and left the food on the kitchen counter. Heard him snoring upstairs and didn't want to startle him.

Another spark of anger went through Fran at that. Was he still drinking? Sleeping it off? He must be out hard to sleep through all of that and snore loud enough for Patrick to hear him from downstairs. Well, at least he was okay. Knowing that, she was able to put it out of her mind and do what she'd gone there to do.

*   *   *

By Friday morning, when Fran had heard nothing from Mark, she was starting to worry a little. She called Greg Long and asked for his advice. "I have someone coming to help with my booth this morning, so I have a window to go check on Mark," she said. "Should I?"

"You stay put," Greg said. "God's got Mark, and He loves Mark even more than you do."

Fran got through Friday and then Saturday. She tried to call her husband but got no answer. Since they'd met on Halloween 2011, they hadn't gone more than a few hours without communicating. She was still angry, but now she began to feel sick. As she broke down the display and lugged everything to the car by herself, she knew that Mark would not have left her to do this alone.

By Sunday morning, something in her knew. She called Lisa. "Lisa, I'm worried about what I'll find when I walk in that house."

"I'm worried, too," she said. "Don't go alone. Take someone with you."

Fran went from Pigeon Forge straight to church that Sunday morning. She talked to Martha and Greg. They both had commitments right after church. As she walked slowly down the church steps toward her car, she felt like her shoes were encased in concrete. She looked up at Greg. "Do you think it's dangerous?"

"I don't know. Call me."

She drove the short distance from the church to her home and pulled up in the driveway. Everything looked fine from the outside. It was a beautiful fall day in East Tennessee. *God, please be with me. Hold my hand when I walk in that house and help me deal with whatever I find. Please, God.*

I am with you, came the holy whisper. *Be strong and courageous. I will never leave you.*

She unlocked the front door, but the chain was on. The cat was meowing frantically. She walked around the house and went in the back door. The cat met her, a panicked look on her furry face. She leaped into Fran's arms.

The first thing Fran noticed was the food Patrick had left on Thursday. It was still on the kitchen counter, with the note Patrick had left for his dad. It all looked untouched. The kitchen was a cluttered mess, but that was Mark.

Fran listened to the house. She heard no creaks, no footsteps, not even any birdsong from outside—just the soft murmur of the upstairs TV.

She slowly made her way up the steps and stopped at their bedroom door. She didn't have to go one more step, because there he was. Lying on the bedroom floor, his head in a pool of blood. Eyes half open, skin gray. Not breathing. A gun at his feet. Fran registered all these things in seconds. Thanks to some power beyond her, she did not go into the room, but the picture that seared itself into her memory would stay with her forever.

*   *   *

In shock, she stumbled down the steps and tried to call Greg, but the WiFi was down and she could not get a call out. She ran back to her car and out onto the main road. When she finally got a signal, he picked up on the first ring.

"Greg, he's gone," she sobbed, shaking all over with the shock. "There's a gun."

"Where are you?"

"I had to come back to the main road to get a signal."

"Listen to me." His voice was calm, and she latched onto it like the one solid thing in an angry sea. "We have to call the police. I'll call them, and you go back home. Sit in your driveway until help comes. I'm on my way."

Thirty seconds after she pulled into her driveway, a police van pulled in behind her. Fran started to get out of her car, but the officer warned her to stay put.

"Should there be anyone in the house other than your husband?" the officer asked as he got a firearm out of the back of the van.

"Just the cat." Fran sat in the driver's seat and trembled. "Is it okay if I unlock the front door for you?"

"Yes. Then go back to your car."

It did not take long. The officer came back to her car and squatted beside her, eyes grim, writing on his clipboard. Fran broke the silence. "He's gone, isn't he?"

"Yes, ma'am, I'm sorry, he's deceased."

"When?" Suddenly it was essential for her to know that.

"I don't know, but it looks like it's been quite a while. The medical examiner will be able to tell for sure."

More tears spilled. Fran had not known she had so many in her.

419

The officer began to ask her details on both her and Mark—names, dates of birth, social security numbers, places of birth. Fran woodenly rattled off the information from memory.

Greg Long pulled up, followed shortly by Jimmy Long and three more cruisers. Jimmy, one of the top deputy sheriffs in Blount County, one of Mark's youth, was weeping. He went into the house with his men. Greg stayed on the porch with Fran.

"We need to call his family," Fran said numbly.

"I'll do it," Greg said. "Do you have their numbers?"

Greg started with Lisa because he'd known her since high school. He stepped to the end of the porch, and Fran could not hear the conversation. After Lisa, Greg called Rick and Patrick. Lisa said she would call her sister. Together, they would come to Maryville and tell their mother.

Lisa would later say that when she saw Greg's number pop up on her phone, she knew. When Mellie heard Lisa's voice, she knew. And when they arrived at their mother's house, she knew before they said anything.

Thankfully, because Fran and Mark had talked about it, she knew that he wanted to be cremated and have his ashes spread at their favorite fishing spot. He did not want a gravestone. Greg knew whom to call and swiftly put the wheels in motion.

Fran called her mother and sister, and left messages for her children asking them to call. There was no easy way to tell them since no one had known how bad things were. Mark had put on such a good front to everyone, showing his true self only to his wife. The shock was horrendous. Julia, now ninety-one years old, immediately hit the road with Cecil. They would be there in four hours. Chris rounded up Jason and his wife, Jennifer, and they were on their way as well.

Police came and went. Investigators asked Fran questions. Greg sat beside her and helped her provide coherent answers. It dawned on Fran that she might logically be a suspect. She had, after all, been here late Wednesday night. But the police only treated her with kindness and respect. She realized later that there was a history here. Because the police had been here so many times, they knew the situation.

"It will take a while for your family to get here. You need someone with you," Greg said. "Who do you want?"

"I want Martha and DiAnne," she said. "Call Peggy Dockery too, and Faye Levi. They'll want to know."

DiAnne Wilson was there within minutes, Martha and Robert Galyon hard on her heels. The women sat and held Fran and rocked her and cried with her, and took her onto the back porch so she wouldn't see when the police took Mark away. Jimmy Long told her that the police had cut a large hole in the carpet in the master bedroom because the blood had saturated the carpet down to the wood. Martha cleaned the kitchen and sobbed.

Pleasant Grove Baptist Church swiftly showed the love of Christ. People swarmed into the house with food, hugs, and tears, clearly intent on making sure Fran was not alone for one second until her family arrived. Peggy and Clyde Dockery quickly showed up, stunned. They were closely followed by Alfred and Jackie Bumgarner, Bob and Fran England, Jim and Gisela Hill, Cecil and Faye Levi, Martin and Mary Mueller, and Vernon and Marty Stephens. All of them came and did whatever was necessary. The Happy Helpers class and the Boy Scout troop brought food. No one had to be asked. Shocked and sober, they just showed up.

Fran's children called her back, first Brody, then Andy, then Veronica. Horrified and stunned, their only concern was for their mother.

Brody, now working toward his graduate degree in music education, told her sternly, "Don't do anything stupid."

Andy, now the head tennis coach at a small college in South Carolina, was driving his team back from an away match when he got her message. Stunned, he had no words. He just told his mom he loved her.

Veronica, in her third year at USC Aiken, had been there for some of the horror, and she had developed a unique gift for helping people who were hurting. She talked to Fran for forty-five minutes, and her advice was simple. "Don't feel guilty for feeling relieved," she said. "You're not there yet, but you will be."

Word came that Julia and Cecil were lost. The men from Wisdom Seekers went out and found them, and led them to the house. Chris, Jason, and Jennifer were right behind them. Fran's church family hugged her and left.

Haggard, horrified, and more than a little angry, Fran's family gathered around her and loved on her. For the next two hours, they just talked. Fran gave her family details they hadn't had before, clues into what had been going on in Tennessee and why she'd been so strange and distant, and completely and totally focused on Mark.

Chris stared at her. "You've been through hell."

"Yeah."

"When will you see Mark's family?"

"Tomorrow morning. They're all coming over to plan the service." That still did not seem real. How could they be planning Mark's service? He was going to be walking through the door any moment. He wouldn't do this to her. He would have left her a note or something. He would not have just shot himself, knowing she would be the one to find him. And he most definitely wouldn't have left her alone to face the rest of her life without him.

Her thoughts skittered around like a hamster in a ball. She was mad because Mark had gone to buy alcohol, after all they'd been through. Then she was sad because she knew Mark had been outside his mind when he pulled that trigger. Then she thought there was some mistake, and he wasn't dead after all. Wherever he was, he would wake up and come home. She couldn't imagine life without him. The center had been jerked out of her world. Mark was her center, and she had no idea how to put herself back together.

She fell asleep from complete exhaustion, in the room she and Mark had shared, with the big oval cut out of the carpet.

98

Somehow, Fran kept putting one foot in front of the other. The big picture was too big to even contemplate, so she just did the next thing, then the next, then the next. Mark's family came over Monday morning to plan Mark's service. All of their faces were white with shock, and their eyes were red. Patrick and Rick, now twenty-one and twenty-five, silently and constantly wept.

As Fran went through the next few days, she knew very well that God was carrying her. She didn't have the strength to write Mark's obituary, but she did. She couldn't read it to his family, so Rick did it.

When Greg Long met her and Sharon at the funeral home to see Mark one more time, Fran's knees buckled, but she held onto her Father and looked on Mark's dear face for the last time. They'd done an amazing job, but she could see the damage. "I can't leave him, Greg," she said. "Not when I know I'll never see him again."

Greg kept it real. "You have to, Fran. He won't be suitable to be viewed for very much longer. He's decaying as we look at him."

Greg and Sharon left her alone with her husband. She kissed his forehead and was amazed at how cold he was.

Sharon went back one more time and said, "I saw him into this world, and I'll see him out."

Someone had to go through pictures and put together a tribute slide show for his funeral. Fran didn't have the strength, but somehow she did it. She had tons of pictures, and Scott and Doug sent her more.

How could she call his friends, like Tom Taylor, and break the news? Strong men were reduced to weeping in seconds when they heard the news, because of the sheer shock of it.

She couldn't do any of these things, but she did it all in God's strength. Certainly not in hers. She could feel Him holding her hand and even physically carrying her when she could not go another step.

The service was all arranged. Doug Taylor, Hollie Miller, and Greg Long would speak. Jimmy Long would sing, as would Greg and DiAnne Wilson. The Talleys' song "Applause" would play. And the congregation would sing "When We All Get to Heaven." Boy Scout Troop 87 would present the colors and lead the pledge. Fran had no idea who was coming. Kevin Kilpatrick was handling that.

Doug called Fran Tuesday and asked what she thought about tackling the issue of suicide in his comments. She asked Greg about it. "I don't want to tarnish his witness," she said.

"He's already done that. I think we have to address it."

She finally agreed, trusting them to do it tastefully and respectfully. She would have liked this to be a celebration of his life, but the circumstances were too raw and terrible and tragic. People were hurting too badly. Questions were being asked, especially from the young men Mark had helped lead in scouting. Those questions had to be answered, and some level of comfort had to be given.

Too quickly, Thursday came. Doug came to Fran's house early, to visit with her and get his thoughts in order. Scott Spitler arrived soon after. Fran wanted some time with these two important men in Mark's life. They both looked stunned, heartbroken, and angry.

It haunted Fran that the last words she and Mark had said to each other on this earth were unkind, and that the one person who was supposed to love her the most had told her—twice—to stop being herself. She could not get past that and did not think she ever would. All her life, until Mark, she'd felt unlovable, like no one who truly knew her could possibly love her. Now she felt that way again. Mark's words had proved the point. There was nothing anyone could say to make her feel better. No one could undo what had happened. She just had to deal with it, and somehow go on.

The family was due at the church at noon for a family meal.

Mark's entire family was there, plus Doug Taylor and Matt Monroe, who had been a widower for a year and a half. The Wisdom Seekers provided the food.

At two o'clock, the family went to the sanctuary to begin receiving friends. The line quickly grew down the aisle, across the foyer, and out into the parking lot. Dozens of Boy Scouts appeared, in uniform and out. One young man, one of Mark's first Eagle Scouts, flew in from California. People came from Mark's church in Athens, from when he was a small boy, and his dad was the pastor. People came from Sevier Heights and East Maryville, and of course from Pleasant Grove. The sheer number of people Mark had touched in his life was staggering. Their shock was palpable.

Here at Pleasant Grove, it had come full circle. Greg Wilson, who was hired the same day Mark was in 1980, played the piano, sang, and directed the music. His wife, DiAnne, was now one of Fran's best friends, and the first to arrive at her side that horrible day. Jimmy Long, one of the members of Mark's youth group in 1980, was one of the first police responders on Sunday and now would sing for Mark's service. Martha and Robert Galyon, hearts crushed, were as much a part of their lives now as they had been nearly forty years ago. Angie, who'd played Miss Piggy in that long-ago Muppet group, was now one of Fran's closest allies. They did not know it then, but God would use Angie to help Fran go home to her family.

Fran's Cracker Barrel family came. Her boss, Sue Davidson, came up to her and just hugged her hard. She was followed by Fran's two best friends from Cracker Barrel—Wendy Coppedge and Kris Beltz. In their embrace, Fran broke.

Jean Smith, one of Fran's long-time clients from Extended Family Services came, with her two sisters and her daughter. They were old and had their walkers, but they came. They sat in the pew directly behind Julia.

Don Wilson, who'd done their counseling at Sevier Heights, came through the line and enveloped her in a bear hug as she sobbed on his shoulder. "You're going to need some help," he told her frankly.

"Will you help me?" she asked.

"Of course."

The last person through the line was a red-eyed Tom Taylor, the mayor of Maryville, the man who'd given Mark the chance to be a Scoutmaster in 2003.

Jimmy sang a beautiful, emotional rendition of "I Pledge Allegiance to the Lamb," then Doug took the podium. He told stories about him and Mark growing up together and learning from each other. "Iron sharpens iron," he said. "That was Mark and me."

Then he got serious.

"Some of you know this, but maybe some of you don't," he said. "For thirty-eight years, Mark has struggled with intense pain. It's been a constant effort to manage the pain and the surgeries and the medications and the side effects of the medications. Sleep deprivation was huge. That's what people do when they torture you— they deprive you of sleep.

"Eventually, with all these struggles, this ordinary man who we love so much gave in to that. We might experience all kinds of feelings about that. You may be angry at Mark or angry at God. You may be angry at yourself, thinking you might have been able to do more. I'm there myself. All of that is the life we live, and we have to surrender all of that to God.

"It's a joy to know that Mark is face to face with Jesus. If Mark were here today, he'd tell us to trust God and follow God."

After the Talleys' song played, Hollie Miller stepped up. After talking about knowing Mark and having the privilege of performing their wedding in 2012, he tackled the elephant in the room head-on.

"There's so much confusion about the sensitive subject of taking one's own life. I've heard it, and you have too—if a person takes his own life, he doesn't go to heaven. When you hear that, understand that the person who's saying this doesn't know the gospel."

Brother Hollie looked up from his notes and looked people around the room in the eyes, one by one. "Here is the gospel. Jesus

Christ paid for our sins on the cross. He was buried, He rose again, and He said. 'It is finished.' All of our sins are paid for, past, present, and future. When you give your life to Jesus, as Mark did, a miracle happens in the throne room of heaven. God takes the righteousness of Jesus and applies it to you. And He takes all of the guilt and sin and condemnation and applies it to Jesus by His death on the cross.

"Paul said, 'There is now therefore no condemnation for those who are in Christ.' Do you know what that means? God never condemns His children. Does that mean there are no consequences for sin in our lives? Of course not. Every time you sin, there are consequences.

"And what a tragic decision it is to take one's life. How could that happen to a child of God? Children of God make good decisions and bad decisions. Right decisions and sinful decisions. Normally, a tragic decision like this begins with bad, sinful ones. Our sinful choices can sometimes affect us emotionally, so we're not thinking straight. And then you add in the chronic physical pain to the emotional instability."

Fran sobbed. Hollie was talking specifically about Mark, obviously. He looked at her for a long moment, compassion in his eyes.

"There will be disappointment when I stand before the judgment seat of Christ because of my failures. But there will not be condemnation. Mark is in heaven now because he loved Jesus and committed his life to Him."

Greg Long talked about the vast numbers of Boy Scouts in the room, both in and out of uniform. "This is an example of investments made and lives touched," he said. "Mark Smith led thirty-nine young men to Eagle rank but think about how many others he touched. He made a difference, and now those young men are going to go on to make a difference."

He paused and continued. "A lot of you are going to be asking why. That's Satan, and don't let him do it. Change that question— change it from why to what, and follow it with God. Because even in the midst of tragedy, even in the midst of bad decisions, God is

427

going to do something amazing.

"You might ask, how can God make something good out of this? Just watch and see. God is a great, wonderful, all-powerful God. He's reigning, ruling, and will one day return. Nothing is impossible for Him. Stay surrendered, invest in the lives of others, and watch the God of all creation work and move and minister, not only in you but around you."

The Scouts closed the ceremony. One of Mark's Eagles stood and explained what they were about to do.

"Scouting has many traditions and symbols," he said. "Trail symbols are used to mark a path and guide the way for others to follow. There is a special symbol used by Native Americans and other cultures to mark the end of the trail. This symbol, which means 'Gone Home,' is a dot surrounded by a large circle. This symbol marks the tomb of Scouting's founder, and we'll render it here today as we offer one final salute."

Two scouts unrolled a scroll with the symbol on it. Every Scout in the room, in uniform or in regular clothes, young or old, stood and gave the Scout salute, one more time, for Mark Smith.

The service was over, and now it was time—somehow—to begin living again.

99

The Monday after the funeral, Rick and Patrick wanted to go ahead and scatter Mark's ashes. It was another of those things that Fran did not have the strength to do, but God carried her.

On Monday, October 8, on a beautiful fall day, they launched the boat at Notchy Creek, near Vonore, and sped across the water to the cove she and Mark had loved. There was a tree at the bottom, where crappie lurked year-round.

"We need to fish," Patrick said. "Dad would want us to fish."

Fran, knowing exactly where to drop her hook because Mark had taught her so well, caught the only keeper of the day. They said a prayer and took turns scattering the ashes. As they puttered out of the cove, a bald eagle, Mark's favorite creature on earth, flew over the spot.

Rick and Patrick came and went through the house, taking anything they wanted and everything that Fran knew Mark wanted them to have. She could not stand to look at his clothes. They took what they wanted, while she selected a few precious items, packed them away tenderly, and donated the rest. His gun collection, his tools, his fishing gear, his camping and hiking gear—all went to his sons. Fran knew she would not want to go with anyone else and would never go alone.

She began to feel an urgency to go home, back to her family, to finish her third book and lavish love on her mother and sister and sons and daughter. A Cracker Barrel in Anderson, South Carolina, was eager to have her join their retail team and complete her training to manage her own retail store someday. Fran gave notice to Sue Davidson effective March 5—thinking it would take her that long to tie everything up.

Angie Kirby asked Fran what she could do to help, and Fran said, simply, "Sell my houses."

Heritage Square Court had been on the market for years without a nibble. It had been rented for two years and now wasn't even listed for sale, and yet God brought a buyer the day Mark died, before anyone even knew he was gone. Fran replaced the carpet at Rocky Branch Road and patched and painted the walls. Angie listed it for sale, and two days later she received an offer for the full listing price, from a family with four adopted special needs children. They took one look at the open Bible on the desk and knew they were home. Both houses were scheduled to close on January 7.

In a laborious, painful process, Fran went through everything in the house and made decisions. Their trailer sold. Her little Volkswagen CC sold, leaving her with only the Touareg she and Mark had bought together back in 2013. The lawn mower sold. The boat sold. She began the probate process, knowing it would be essential when the closing date came for Heritage Square Court, because both people listed on the deed were dead, and she was the executor of Mark's estate.

Day by day, miracles happened and pointed the way to get Fran home quickly. She and Angie both consciously, deliberately kept their hands off the wheel and watched God work. Both were amazed and humbled at His providence. Scott Spitler offered her his cottage for the two months between her house closings and her move to South Carolina. The cottage had no television and internet—a perfect place to finish *Lamp to My Feet*. She quickly found a temporary place to live in Anderson and scheduled movers.

People were not surprised when Fran said she intended to finish the trilogy. This book would complete Mark's story; but with God's help, it would tell the story in a way that would help people who'd been through pain and suffering and abuse and heartbreak. Fran would have to rip the book out of her heart and soul, but it was worth it if it helped somebody.

Details began to emerge of Mark's death. Fran now knew for sure what she'd known in her heart—Mark had shot himself while she was on the road back to Pigeon Forge that night. No one could have helped him; it was too late. Toxicology reports were shocking but not surprising—he'd had an alarming amount of alcohol and sleeping medication in his body when he reached for the gun. As always, the combination made him do things he would not normally have done.

When Patrick came with food the next day, it was only by the grace of God that he didn't climb the steps and find his father himself. Something—some sound that must have been the television—had turned him around on the steps.

Fran knew clearly that God had told her to get out. Those who knew the whole story affirmed her conviction that if she hadn't fled, she'd be dead too. Don Wilson helped her through the anger and the sadness. When things got too bad, and panic attacks threatened to steal her very breath, Veronica was there for her, coaching her through it.

A welcome diversion, a spark of joy, came in January, just before the houses closed. Andy called on Thursday, January 3, when the moving crews were packing up her house. Clemson had blasted Notre Dame and punched its ticket to play Alabama for the national championship. The game would be played on Monday in Santa Clara, California, at the home of the San Francisco 49ers. Fran's houses would close at four o'clock, and she'd already asked for the evening off to watch the game.

"So," Andy said in his rapid-fire, excited way, "ticket prices have dropped because fans can't afford to travel that far, and I know you said we're going to the championship game next year, but what if something happens and Clemson doesn't get there? I think I've talked myself into going this year."

"That's great, honey!" Fran said enthusiastically. "If I didn't have a house closing Monday afternoon, I'd go with you."

"That's kind of why I was calling. To see if you wanted to go."

Within thirty minutes Fran had juggled everything so that Cecil, Chris, and Jennifer would meet the movers at the Anderson condo the next day, and the title company would allow her to sign the papers at noon on Friday.

She called Andy back. "Book it," she said. "We're going to California!"

That trip, and being with her precious son to watch their Tigers trounce Alabama by four touchdowns, gave Fran the joy and the spark she needed to finish everything she had to do.

*   *   *

In March 2019, she packed everything she had left in a U-Haul, put her cat in a crate, and left Tennessee behind. As she drove across the bridge, over the lake into South Carolina, a beautiful sunset beckoned. She smiled through tears. She and Mark had always loved sunsets. The light created miniature rainbows in the facets of the diamond still on her left hand—the diamond that, as far as Fran knew, would stay there until the day she died.

Fran allowed herself to look back at the combined devastation and joy of the past seven years. How would God use this? She did not know, but she knew clearly that He would. It was her job to follow where He led, listen for His voice, keep her eyes on Him, and let Him work through her.

She now knew how to do that because of Mark. He'd left a roadmap on her heart.

She rolled down her windows and breathed in the sweet air of home. She murmured soothingly to the meowing cat in the back seat. It was time to look ahead and do whatever it was that God had for her. She'd spend time with her family, maybe even go into the mission field herself. A new life awaited, terrifying but exciting.

She had no idea what was in store, but she knew that God would lead. Day by day, as He had promised in His Word, He would be the lamp to her feet.

And now listen carefully to the good news!

God goes ahead of you to be your guide
God is beside you to be your friend
God is behind you to encourage you
God is above and below you to sustain you

So whoever you are
And whatever you do in God's good creation
And whatever happens of good or of ill
Remember that Jesus Christ is Lord and Savior

Amen.

AFTERWORD

Mark Smith was a wonderful man who loved the Lord more than anything. He touched countless people in his life, teaching the Word and reaching out to children and elders. He was at his best with the very old and the very young. His story lives on through *Cleft of the Rock, Thorn in the Flesh,* and now *Lamp to My Feet.* I am blessed and privileged to have known him and been his wife.

Mark was in pain, and when people are in pain, they do and say things they would not do and say otherwise, especially to the people who love them most. When a person is in long-term, chronic pain, the issues are multiplied. Now you have the possibility of addiction, depression, and worse. People just want to feel better, to feel normal, to live life.

I am aware that there are issues in our society with opioid abuse. I am aware of how serious those issues are. But I have been made aware of life on the other side. Stiff laws have been enacted to keep opioids out of the hands of abusers, and that's all well and good, but what about the people who really, honestly need the medication? The ones who aren't addicted or misusing it? The ones who are sincerely in terrible pain? Doctors shouldn't have their hands tied from responsibly prescribing pain medication to those people.

When Mark had his neck fusion surgery in 2013, he was on pain medication for ninety days. That was long enough to help him recover. When he had a similar surgery in 2018, they started weaning him down after one week. I watched him weep like a child when he was denied medication that might have helped him tolerate his surgery pain. I watched him lose hope. I watched him turn to destructive pain management techniques, because it was all he had. Ultimately, it cost him his life.

I'm not saying my husband would still be alive today if he'd had sufficient medication to help him get over his surgery and cope with the pain, but he might. He might. Right now we might be out on our boat, enjoying the spring sunshine and pulling in a cooler full of fish or ticking off the next item on our bucket list. I might still be able to feel his warm embrace and see the love in his eyes. But the best I can do is the wedding picture that's sitting on my desk, and the ring on my finger. That last horrible mental snapshot from September 2018 will always be with me.

I am also painfully aware of the role of the caregiver. I would like to reach out specifically to spouses of people who are hurting. The stories on this topic in this book are painfully true, and I didn't even tell all of them. For years, I lived a secret life, not telling anyone how bad things were because my husband didn't want anyone to know. It was embarrassing to him. He would get up in the morning and patch the holes in the walls from the night before, where he punched a hole or fell down the stairs. Our house always looked like a war zone.

He didn't hit me, so I rationalized that he wasn't abusing me. I told myself that he just didn't realize his own strength when he squeezed my arms and hands. I now know that's all untrue. When your spouse makes you afraid, and you live in dread of coming home, there's something wrong. God doesn't want us to live like that. He wants us to use all the means at our disposal—prayer, fellowship, counseling, treatment, etc.—to save our marriages and love our spouses and glorify Him for all of our lives. But that doesn't mean staying in a place in danger.

Find support. Find help. Reach out. People do care—I found that out in the most amazing way through the love of Christ shown to me by my family, my friends, and my church.

If you don't know anyone and you feel lost, like you're at the end of your rope, please reach out to me at fran@cleftoftherock.org. If you're dealing with pain and uncertainty related to suicide, try watching Mark's funeral service on the Pleasant Grove Baptist Church website, pgbctn.org. It's under the Videos link. Scroll back to October 4, 2018.

Just know you're not alone. There are people who have walked where you are, who are walking that path now, and they want to take your hand and help you through.

ABOUT THE AUTHOR

FRANCES SMITH is a thirty-year veteran of journalism, public affairs, and communications. She is the author of three books, all based on true stories surrounding her and her husband's spiritual journey. She has learned that God does, indeed, use ordinary people to accomplish extraordinary things.

She holds a Bachelor of Arts degree in English from Columbia College and a Master of Arts degree in English education. She enjoys reading, Clemson football, and spending time with her family. She loves to speak to groups and share her and Mark's testimony.

She has four sons, a daughter, and a cat, and lives in the foothills of South Carolina.

To contact the author:

Call or text her at (865) 567-0516

email her at fran@cleftoftherock.org

or visit her website at francessmith.com.